The Weekend Dad

ALISON WALSH

HACHETTE
BOOKS
IRELAND

First published in Ireland in 2018 by HACHETTE BOOKS IRELAND
First published in paperback in 2018

3

Cataloguing in Publication Data is available from the British Library

ISBN 9781473660748

Typeset in ArnoPro by Bookends Publishing Services

Printed and bound in Great Britain by Clays Ltd, Elcograf S.p.A.

Hachette Books Ireland policy is to use papers that are natural, renewable
and recyclable products and made from wood grown in sustainable forests.
The logging and manufacturing processes are expected to conform to the
environmental regulations of the country of origin.

Hachette Books Ireland
8 Castlecourt Centre
Castleknock
Dublin 15, Ireland

A division of Hachette UK Ltd
Carmelite House, 50 Victoria Embankment, EC4Y 0DZ

www.hachettebooksireland.ie

To Eoin, Niamh and Cian, who changed things forever

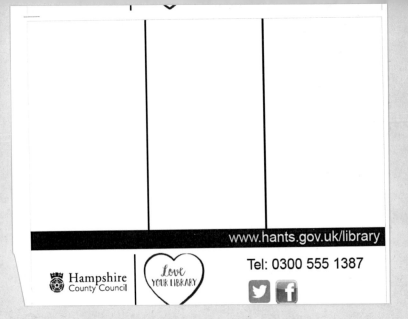

Alison Walsh has worked in publishing and literary journalism for a number of years. She wrote a popular and humorous column on family life for the *Irish Independent* for some years, and this was followed by a memoir on motherhood, *In My Mother's Shoes*, which became a number-one Irish bestseller in 2010. She is a regular contributor to the *Sunday Independent* books pages.

The Weekend Dad is her third novel.

Alison lives in Dublin with her husband and three children.

Follow her on Twitter at @authoralison or visit her website at www.alisonwalsh.net.

ALSO BY ALISON WALSH

All That I Leave Behind
The House on Seaview Road

Daisy

Wexford, Easter 1975

It's dusty under the bed and it smells like the back of Nana's wardrobe. There are little balls of dust, like mini moons, across the carpet and there's a broken flip-flop, too. The bit that goes in between your toes is sticking up in the air. I know that flip-flop, because it has a big, red flower on it and I've seen it before. I don't know what it's doing in here though.

We are lying on the floor, side by side, and my nose feels itchy. I'm trying not to sneeze and I screw up my face with the effort. You start to laugh and I feel it then, a giggle rising in my tummy and bubbling up and out through my mouth. I press my hand over it, but a little bit of it escapes. Now you are laughing, really hard, and your face is squeezed up and bright red and I am finding it very hard not to copy you, to laugh and sneeze at the same time. We do that a lot – we laugh and read and play cards under the bed. It's our hiding place in the house, like the den is our hiding place on the beach.

Then your face goes really still and you poke me in the side with your elbow. 'Ow—' I begin, but you put your finger to your lips.

You are lying in front of me and over your head, I see the bedroom door open. A pair of legs appears in the doorway, red and hairy, attached to brown leather sandals and green socks, which have been pulled halfway up, to the calf muscle. The legs come closer, followed now by another pair of legs, these hidden in a big yellow maxi dress. The feet are bare and brown, the toenails painted red. It's only April, too early in the year for bare feet and I feel a shiver as I think of it. The sandals come closer as we lie under the bed. I can feel you tense, holding your breath. I stop breathing too. Then there's a squeak as someone sits down on the bed, a big bump appearing in the wire mesh of the bed base. The bump is just above your head and you lift your eyes to it, before glancing over at me. I want to laugh, but I think it's a scared laugh, not a real one.

Then the red-painted toes come close and there's another squeak, and another bump appears, this one just above my head, the wires of the base almost touching my hair. I want to itch and scratch and push it away, but I don't dare.

There's a long silence then, followed by a squeak, and the bump above my head moves closer to the bump above yours. There's a kind of silence then, but it feels full, as if something is happening, and I can hear a kind of squelching sound, then a small 'pop', like the sound you make when you put your finger into your cheek and pull hard. You look at me and make a face. I feel it again, that bubble of laughter rising inside of me. I know that I have to keep it down, but the effort is making me want to laugh even more. I think I might wet my pants. Then I see your face, as we both hear a low moan. You look as if you're going to be sick.

'Stop,' a voice says from above our heads, a woman's voice, low and husky. A smoker's voice. 'Someone could come in at any minute.'

'That makes it all the more exciting,' a man's voice replies. 'Don't you like it, the thought that we could be caught. Doesn't that make you all hot and bothered? C'mere and let me get my hands on you ...'

There's more squelching and moaning and then a rustling sound. 'I mean it. Stop.'

'I can't help myself. You're driving me wild, Bridget. I've never felt like this before. Nuala doesn't ...'

'Shush. No names. I told you that.'

I want to grab your hand and jump out from under the bed, to run screaming out of the room, but I can't move. I don't even want to turn my head to look at you because I don't want to see your face.

'What are we going to do?' the man says.

'What do you mean, what are we going to do? We are going to do nothing. There's nothing to do.'

'Some day we'll be together,' he says hopefully.

The woman just laughs, that tinkling laugh she makes when she finds something funny, even if it's not. 'I don't think that's going to happen, now, is it?' The red-painted toenails wiggle in front of my eyes. 'I mean, this is just a thing, a holiday fling, if you like. It doesn't mean anything.'

There's a long silence then, and then the hairy legs move, very slightly. 'A holiday fling? Is that all I am to you?'

'Francis, don't be silly—'

'I thought what we had was real. I thought that you felt about me the way I feel about you.'

'I do, Francis. Look, I think you're really sweet, but you know that this can't go any further.'

'What? You mean because of Michael and Nuala?'

I reach out and take your hand and squeeze it as hard as I can. You screw up your face in pain, but then I feel you move closer to me, so that I can feel the denim of your brand new jeans against my leg. You turn your head to me then, even though it's really awkward in the small space and you smile at me and I can see that you are trying to make me feel better, to focus on your face, so that we don't really hear my mother and your father talking above our heads.

'You should have thought about them before you got into bed with me,' the woman's voice says then.

There's another silence, then the word 'Bitch'. The word is like a gunshot in the room, big and loud and ugly. The bump disappears suddenly from above your head, and the hairy legs move towards the door, which opens quietly. The sound of laughter and chat echoes down the corridor, then fades as the door is closed quietly again.

'For God's sake,' my mother's voice says tiredly. The bump above my head moves slightly on the bed and then we can smell cigarette smoke, can hear the slight swish as she inhales and exhales, the 'hiss' as the cigarette is put out in the ashtray beside the bed. My mother always puts cigarettes out really well, crushing them and pressing them really hard into the ashtray, because she's terrified of dying in a fire. Then she, too, gets up. She goes to the door and, when she opens it, you make a small sound. I put my hand over your mouth and your breath is warm on my palm. She hesitates for a second. We both hold our breath, and then she is gone.

Later that day, we play on the beach under the tarpaulin that Dad gave us, its navy blue stretched above us as we lie on the cold, damp sand. I wonder if I should talk to you about what we heard – if it would make any difference. And then I think that maybe I didn't hear it at all – maybe there was something about Mum and Francis that I didn't understand properly.

I look at you and you are staring into the darkness of the tarpaulin, at the tiny pinpricks of light that shine through the material. I'm about to say something when you turn to me and say, 'Do you know that the Milky Way is made up of between a hundred and four hundred billion stars?'

'Oh, really?' I try not to say anything else, because I'd only encourage you to go on and on about the Milky Way when we have other things to be talking about. 'Emmett?'

You are silent for a moment before saying, 'Yes?'

'Will we always be friends, do you think?' I think about adding 'after tonight', but I know that you will understand anyway.

You are quiet for a very long time, but I know that you're just thinking. 'I hope so,' you say eventually. So I know that you do understand.

The previous summer, we'd lain under the same tarpaulin and said that we'd be friends for ever and ever, as long as there were stars in the sky, even though you'd started on again about how many stars in the galaxy were disappearing 'due to supernovae'. 'But it's OK,' you'd said, 'because there are new stars being made every year.' Now, I wonder if we'll ever lie here again. I don't really think so. That makes where we are now, right this minute, seem all the more important. I want time to stretch, the way you say it can in black holes, to keep expanding on and on into outer space, light years away. Maybe if I concentrate hard enough, I can make it happen. I can make time stand still.

We hear the voices then, over the crashing of the waves. At first, they are faint, as if they are being carried off on the wind, but then they grow louder. I know that time isn't going to stretch after all – it's going to speed towards us, like a really fast car, so I sit up and take your hand in mine. 'Promise me that we'll always be together, even just in our thoughts.'

You give me that look, the one that says you feel sorry for me. 'But that's not possible, Daisy. Unless you believe in psychic communication—'

'For God's sake, Emmett, now is not the time to be a clever clogs.' I'm yelling at you and I know that's wrong, but I also know that time is nearly up. Tomorrow, I'll be gone and I'm not sure if I'll ever be coming back.

You look hurt. 'Sorry. Excuse me if I don't want to be ignorant for my whole life …'

'It's not that,' I say more quietly. 'It's just … I want you always to think about me. Even if you never see me again. And I'll always think about you. And then one day …'

'Yes?' You look hopeful, as the voices grow closer now.

'Then one day we'll be together. All we have to do is wait.'

'How long?'

'I don't know. A long time. But you have to wait and so do I.'

You nod then and offer me your hand. 'We'll shake on it.'

But I don't take your hand. I lean forward and I kiss you instead, on your cheek, which smells of Fruit Salad chews and something else, like the smell of under the bed. You go bright red, but I know that you're pleased. 'As long as it takes,' you say.

'As long as it takes.'

Then the tarpaulin is lifted and a bright light shines in. We have to cover our eyes. A hand reaches in and takes mine. 'There you are, Daisy. Mum's been looking for you everywhere. She's frantic.'

I get up and let Dad lift me out of the den and into the evening air, *telling me that I really shouldn't worry Mum like that, but I don't care. I look behind me then, because I think it might be the last time I see you, but you're not there. I turn back to look up the beach towards the house, but the sand is completely empty. You have already gone.*

Emmett
1.

London, winter 1995–1996

I'm not a grown-up, I think miserably to myself as I sit hunched over the kitchen table of a tiny flat in north London. I'm really not. I don't have a job, or a bank account, or savings, or a pension. I don't have a wife, or a dog, a car, or a house. But I do have a daughter. And because I have a daughter, I have leapfrogged every one of the staging posts along the way to adulthood to become a fully fledged grown-up overnight, and it's terrifying.

And because it's terrifying, I'm doing what comes naturally – hiding.

I'm due to meet my new daughter in an hour, as I do every Sunday for a few hours, and I'm trying to write her a poem to tell her how I feel. I'm a poet, so it's not exactly a huge deal. Before, it would only have taken a bit of looking out the window of my office in the Department of Fisheries onto the rainy pavements of Molesworth Street or walking around Merrion Square pretending to be Patrick Kavanagh, but, of course, I'm not in Molesworth Street any more, with the view of a tiny corner of the verdant playing fields in Trinity College. I'm in London, in my brother's flat in a grubby street off the Holloway Road, with a water heater hissing noisily in the corner and the rumble of the Tube in the distance.

'Misty,' I begin, 'with your nut-brown hair ...'

Oh, Christ. I cross that out. 'Misty ...' I stop, pen poised over the page, because I can't think what might come next. I want to say something profound to her, something dad-like, something about how every time I look at her I understand the meaning of fatherhood, but I can't, because I don't. Fatherhood is alien to me and, even though I might say otherwise, I know in my heart that I would really like to keep it that way.

I close my eyes and I see her, her dark-brown hair pulled into bunches on either side of her head, tied up with red bobbins, her little bee backpack on her back, looking at me, with eyes the same hazel as my own. She's taking me in, this new arrival in her life, and she's wondering what on earth to make of me, this person she's told is her dad, whom she'd never heard of until a few weeks ago.

'Hello, Emmett.' Those were her first words to me when we met in front of the penguin enclosure at London Zoo four days after Christmas. I'd never thought my name could sound so sad. Amanda thought it was better to meet somewhere 'neutral', as if we were dogs that might attack each other instead of father and daughter. Then, my first thought was: not 'Dad', just 'Emmett', and I tried to suppress that mixture of relief and disappointment that bubbled up inside me. Relief, because I wouldn't have known what to do if she had called me 'Dad', and disappointment, because she hadn't.

I wonder if this makes me more like my own dad.

My aunty Maeve used to call me a chip off the old block and it used to make me seethe. The last person on earth I wanted to be was *him*, I thought. A liar. A cheat. Mum knew, of course, because she'd lean over to Aunty Maeve and say, 'Do you know, Maeve, I think he's more like my side of the family.' And she'd put an arm around my shoulders and squeeze.

Mum. She was always on my side. Which is why it hurt so much to see the look on her face when I told her, that time I came home to Galway from Dublin to visit, three days after I got the letter that began, 'Dear Emmett, I suppose you thought you'd never hear from me again. Well, this may come as a surprise to you …'

Mum had been sitting in her favourite spot: in the Parker Knoll armchair that was a wedding gift from her mother, beside the range, the winter sun streaming in through the living-room window. She had her feet up on the ancient red leather pouffe and Joanna Trollope's latest novel on her knee, scanning the words eagerly. When she saw me, she beamed and showed me the cover. 'I've finally got my hands on it. That madam Mary O'Brien had it out of the library for six weeks on account of her dyslexia, she says, the fibber, and she was about to get it out again only for Jacinta, who put it under the counter for me.' She gave a fist-in-the-air gesture of triumph, but, seeing my expression, her face fell. 'What is it? It's not your brother, is it? I told him not to go to London—'

'It's not Tom,' I said. 'It's me. Mum, I need to tell you something.'

I try to put the memory of her expression out of my mind as I sit here, pen in hand. Her face was rigid with shock and then I could see it change as tears filled her eyes and she tried to hide her disappointment. Then she rallied. 'Nothing could make me think any less of you, son,' she said, which quite naturally made it worse. 'Do you hear me?' she'd said, clutching me to her cushiony bosom and patting my head. 'Nothing. We're all human, love, and we all make mistakes. It's what we do about them that counts.' At this, we exchanged a meaningful look, before she said, 'You know what to do, love – don't you?'

I'd nodded silently, all the while wanting to wail, 'But I don't want to do it!'

'Good man,' she'd said, patting me on the shoulder.

She told Dad for me, murmured voices in the kitchen when I was upstairs in the bathroom, brushing my teeth. Of course, he didn't say anything to me – how could he? He was hardly in any position to lecture. Instead, he and Mum sat silently in the car in front of me as we drove to the travel agent's in Galway city to buy my ferry ticket, then sitting beside me, nodding, as I requested an open return.

'Planning a long holiday?' The girl behind the counter smiled.

'He's going for good,' Dad replied shortly. The girl had looked from him to me to Mum, then nodded and continued filling out the carbon sheets of the ticket.

'He's got a job offer,' Mum added. The fact that she said it out loud made the lie more obvious.

'Isn't that great,' the girl said faintly, stamping one of the sheets with the company logo.

We said our goodbyes at the front door, Mum and me, because Mum can't drive, so 'Muggins', as she calls Dad, was to drive me to the ferry in Dún Laoghaire. Mum was in her candlewick dressing gown that she'd had for twenty years, and she'd squeezed me as tightly as she could, before holding me at arm's length. 'Oh, son,' she said sadly. 'It's not the life you'd planned, but you're doing the right thing by Amanda, I know you are.'

Mum had liked Amanda the moment she'd met her, on that one visit she'd paid to Galway, years before. Every so often, she'd ask me about her and I'd tell her that I hadn't spoken to her since and she'd look faintly disappointed.

'I don't want to do the right thing,' I'd blurted.

'No, but you will. And' – shooting a sharp glare at Dad, who was busy defrosting the windscreen with a kettle of boiling water and a plastic scraper – 'you're to stop in Hayden's in Ballinasloe, do you hear? There's no need to be rushing all the way to Dublin as if you were being pursued by the hounds of hell.'

'For God's sake, Mary, he's not a child who needs a toilet break,' Dad muttered as he scraped.

'I know that, Francis,' Mum barked. 'But it might be good to be civilised for once.' She smiled at me slyly. 'Keep him on his toes.'

I know that she loves him, in spite of everything, even though, as she told me once, 'he needs to know that he's not off the hook – I learned that the hard way.'

Of course, we didn't stop in Ballinasloe but drove straight through the rainy streets, past the chipper and the town hall, until we were back out on the Dublin road, doing the remaining trudge through the quiet midwinter towns of middle Ireland in complete silence. Finally, without a word, he stopped at a petrol station in Kinnegad, as the cattle trucks and buses whizzed by, taking a cigarette from the packet he always kept in the breast pocket of his jacket and lighting it, letting it hang from his bottom lip while he filled the car up with petrol, cupping it in his hand as he went into the shop to pay, then coming out with a sandwich tray with two white-bread ham sandwiches in it and a bottle of Lucozade. He offered me one sandwich and chomped the other himself, feeding bits of white bread and ham into his mouth 'like an animal', as Mum would have said, washing it down with a swig of the fizzy drink.

Then he put the key back into the ignition, started the car and drove on. He said not another word to me, nor I to him, until we were standing at the ferryport in Dún Laoghaire, buffeted by the winter wind.

'Not a bad day for a sailing,' he said finally.

'No, it isn't,' I agreed stupidly.

He pulled the packet of Rothmans out of his pocket, removing a cigarette with a swift gesture, lighting it then going to the boot and taking out my duffel bag. He handed it to me, cigarette clamped between his lips, eyes squinting against the cigarette smoke, like a cowboy in one of the Westerns he loved so much.

I nearly didn't hear what he said because I was saying thanks, so his words stumbled out over mine. 'I'm disappointed, son.'

'I know,' I replied.

'You need to be a man now, do you hear?'

'What, like you?'

I'd heard him say it a million times before and had managed to ignore the obvious hypocrisy, but now, the retort came out before I could stop it. The expression on his face changed just a fraction. A crease appeared between his eyes and his mouth pursed slightly. When he reached out, I wondered for a minute if he was going to hit me but, instead, he just placed a hand on my shoulder and gave it a little squeeze, nodding softly to himself. 'Time to put the dreams away,' he added. 'It comes to us all.' With that crushing statement, he gave me a little shove in the direction of the ferry terminal, the way he used to give me a shove onto the soccer pitch on rainy Sunday afternoons. I stumbled forward, then righted myself and walked up the steps to the terminal door. I didn't even turn around, but just pushed through the doors and joined the queue of others off on the boat to England.

'Be a man.' I used to think that meant throwing a ball further up the rugby pitch, drinking more pints than anyone else in the college bar or finding the most interesting way to smoke weed, but it's not. It turns out that it's a lot more complicated than that.

Which is why I'm here at half-past seven on a Sunday morning, sitting at a kitchen table, taking up more space than I should in Tom's flat, the rumble of the Tube outside my window, the clang and rustle of the market stalls being assembled on the little laneway outside. Tom's out at work – some extra job he does on a Sunday to add to the money he gets on the building site at Canada Square. He's up every morning at five o'clock, and I wake from my perch on the sofa to see him standing in front of the fridge swigging from a carton of milk. His arms are huge from all the lugging and digging he does, and his hair is permanently covered in a fine coating of cement dust. He likes big fry-ups and outings to the Galtymore or the Swan in Stockwell to see Irish bands, and, as I look at him, scratching his arse with one hand as he sniffs a pack of bacon with another, I wonder how the two of us are brothers.

I stare at my notebook, a blanket draped over my shoulders. The two-bar heater doesn't do much more than warm a small space at the back of my legs. I'm trying to write that poem, but everything I write is just … bad. Of course, I don't want to write bad poetry – I'm not doing it deliberately – but the rubbish words just keep pouring out. You'd think that fatherhood would give me something to write about – profound poems that express universal truths about being a parent – but, instead, I find myself writing about the Tube or the Indian corner shop, with its display of phone cards and models of Ganesh, the shops on Holloway Road or the Turkish barbers on Greenlands Avenue, where I had a haircut last week. I write about my pilgrimage to the Coach and Horses pub and waiting for Jeffrey Bernard there one Sunday afternoon, lurking on the horrible red banquette in the hope of a glimpse of my hero, hoping for a *bon mot* and a bit of bad behaviour. But it's all trivia, really, when I'm avoiding the one subject that's in front of my very eyes. I can write about Jeffrey Bernard all I like, but it won't make any difference to the truth.

I sigh and chew my pen a bit more. 'Misty …' I try again, but the words won't come. I end up throwing my pen onto the ground in frustration and then put my head in my hands and contemplate having a little cry to myself. I tell myself to get a grip. I sigh and reach for the book that I found in a second-hand shop on Holloway Road one Saturday afternoon when I was just walking around. I do that a lot here, just walk around. I think that if I do, I might somehow get a grip on this vast place, begin to understand more about the jumble of streets and parks and libraries and bridges and football stadiums, the long red-brick terraces that seem to stretch for miles, the shops that sell everything from wigs to jars of olive oil, the greasy-spoon cafés next to the curry houses. It just seems to go on and on for ever, until you reach that grim bit of motorway at the end, the great big slab of concrete that heads north.

The bookshop advertised itself as a 'Fantasy Emporium', which I took to mean a certain kind of fantasy, until I noticed the big stack of *Lord of the Rings* inside the doorway. In the shop was a large model dragon made out of plastic, resting on top of a big novel by Raymond E. Feist and, beside it, on a narrow shelf, a few tatty paperbacks. 'Men's Interest' read the little sign, in biro, taped to the shelf. I flicked through *The Crisis of Masculinity* – God, no – then *Iron John*, which I opened and read for a bit, wondering if I needed to dig deep into my psyche and find my inner Wild Man. Maybe that's the problem, I told myself – I don't have a Wild Man inside me. I'm one of those Soft Men that the author talks about, in touch with my feminine side, unable to reach the hairy man that lurks within because a half-century of pampering has ensured that I no longer know where he is.

I closed the book and sighed. I didn't need to find my inner hairy man – I just needed a few pointers on how to be a dad in a book that didn't feature a smiling man in a pair of dungarees.

I picked up another book with a stern man on the front, arms folded, clad in army fatigues – *SAS Dad: The Military Approach to Parenting*. I looked at him for a long time, wondering if I could ever see myself in combats, urging Misty to polish her shoes and put knife-edge creases in her bedsheets. God, I thought, is it any wonder masculinity is in crisis. I turned to a book on parenting that had one whole chapter for dads, which told me that I needed to tune in to my baby's needs and balance playful activity with nurturing. That sounds a bit more like it, I thought, reading that I needed to send 'Mum' out of the house so that I could be Dad for the day and carry my daughter around in a sling to bond with her. A picture of Misty's legs dangling out of an oversized sling popped into my head, which almost made me smile, before I slammed the book shut. For God's sake, why weren't there any instructions on what to do when you've missed the first seven years of your child's life? I don't suppose it's been written, I thought gloomily, ignoring the guy with the beard behind the till, who was ostentatiously clearing his throat.

'We're closing,' he said eventually.

In a panic, I picked up the smallest and therefore least intimidating book on the shelf, brought it to the till and proffered the requested 20p. I didn't even look at it until I got outside. It was one of those American paperbacks, with red block lettering – *Be a Dad: How to Ignore the Advice and Trust Your Instincts*. That sounded about right, I thought, looking at the smiling man on the front, with his bald, egg-shaped head – Dr Jasper Johnsson. He looked warmly sensible and kind and not too intimidating. In the absence of anyone else, he would have to do.

I begin to read, now, from chapter two – 'You Are Good Enough!' Yes, I am Good Enough! I think, turning the pages. Apparently, I have to keep repeating the mantra to myself, but I find that I can't because I don't feel it's true. How can I be good enough if I haven't even done anything? My eyes are burning and my head feels heavy because of the extra pint I drank in front of *Match of the Day* last night, feeling sorry for myself. I don't even like *Match of the Day*, but the north-London derby was on and I thought it would bring me closer to my new home. I'd opened the window earlier to hear the match live, the roar of the crowd at the Highbury ground a half-mile away as their team scored another goal. Then I woke up this morning at half-past five, my mind filled with random and unhelpful thoughts.

I decide that I'll rest for a second, just so I'm fresh for Misty later. I lie my head on my arms and feel my eyelids grow heavy.

2.

When I wake, the sounds from outside are different. The market traders' shouts are louder now, as if they are in full swing, selling their hairdryers and magic weighing scales, and there's a general air of daytime busyness about the place. I jump to my feet, the blanket dropping to the floor, and glance at the clock above the kitchen window. Half-past eight. Better get a move on, I think, but then I squint at it again. 'Jesus fucking Christ, it's ten o'clock!' My voice sounds shrill in the silence of the kitchen. Fuck, fuck, fuck, I think, as I spin around in the room. Amanda will fucking kill me.

'Right, don't panic,' I say unnecessarily, bolting into Tom's bedroom, where I keep my stuff, and yanking on a pair of jeans. I haven't changed my underpants since yesterday, but there's no time. I half-run, half-scuttle into the bathroom, pulling my jeans up around my waist, attempting to grab my toothbrush at the same time and put a smear of toothpaste on it. I wonder if there's any really quick way to brush your teeth, as I jab the brush around in my mouth, spit and then rinse. It turns out that there isn't – you have to do all three in sequence – and then I run into the bedroom again and hunt under the thin duvet with the horrible maroon cover for a pair of socks. I only have three pairs, and the other two are on the line over the bath in the bathroom. I fumble around, cursing and swearing, before finding one. Where the hell is the other? I think, looking under the bed. Too fucking late. I'll just have to wear one sock then, I think, as I pull my shoes out from under the bed.

My bare foot protests as I shove it into my shoe, but I lace it up anyway, and then the other and I grab my bag, shove my notebook and pen into it and run, whipping my coat off the hook on the back of the kitchen door and bolting down the stairs. I get to the bottom and remember that I've forgotten my glasses and that I can only half-see without them, but there's no fucking time. I think vaguely about what it will be like to spend an entire day peering into a kind of fuzzy fog, but it's too late now.

I spend the Tube journey to King's Cross inventing excuses in my head, while trying to conceal my one bare ankle from the curious gaze of the elderly woman opposite me. Maybe I can say that the Tube was struck by a meteorite or that a group of mad nuns hijacked it and held us all hostage. My thoughts grow increasingly hysterical as the Tube rattles along through the dark, and when it finally stops, I bound out of the carriage and up the escalators, charging through the ticket barrier, cursing and swearing in my head as I get stuck behind the crowds milling around the ticket hall. They look like sheep, shuffling along with vacant Sunday-morning expressions on their faces, and I find myself only barely resisting the urge to yell at them to get out of my way. Can't they see that I'm a man in a hurry? 'Excuse me!' I say, over and over again, elbowing and nudging past a man in a huge puffer jacket and bucket hat, baggy jeans hanging around his backside. 'Easy mate,' he protests.

'Sorry, it's my daughter! I'm late!' I say as I bolt for the steps and out into the winter sunlight. 'My daughter.' What a grown-up thing to say, I think as I stand there for a second, trying to get my bearings. I know that it's up Pentonville Road and then left … or is that right. Oh, Christ. And I've no *A–Z*. I flap my arms for a bit and feel the bitter winter wind whistle around my bare ankle and the panic begins to rise in my chest, but then I remember that I'm Good Enough, even if I am a bit late. I summon my inner strength … Left, I suddenly think. It's left. And I turn left and run up Pentonville Road.

I'm almost at the top of the hill, my lungs burning with the effort, my ankle chafing in my shoe, when I see a small, furry object on the footpath. It looks like a cat and I hate cats, so I kind of do a little jump around it and keep going, legs heavy as I jog along. Then I look back and it's still sitting there, ears pricked. I haven't got the time, I tell myself – I'm already an hour and a half late – I cannot stop to examine some odd creature on the pavement. I turn again to start running, but then I swear under my breath. 'Fuck's sake,' and I turn around. I walk back to it, and it looks up at me with eyes bigger than its tiny furry body. It's a dog – at least, I think it is. It's the smallest dog I've ever seen, with a tuft of ginger fur on its head and sticky out bits on its ears, which look kind of crimped. It has a blaze of white on its chest and four tiny white paws. It regards me with an imploring look, its bug eyes fixing on mine.

'Hi,' I say.

It continues to stare at me, and then I notice that its tiny body is vibrating with the cold. I lean down and find myself picking it up, and it turns its little head away from me, a faraway look in its eyes, before turning back and giving me a brief lick on the chin.

'Where did you come from?' I say. 'Hmm?'

Naturally, he's not going to oblige me with an answer. He's not wearing a collar, so he could have walked from Southend for all I know. As he looks about six inches tall, it's unlikely, but still. I look around, as if his owner might spring from the bushes, but the road is empty.

'What am I going to do with you?' I say.

His answer is to turn his head again and repeat the brief lick to the chin before looking away, as if to say, 'You know the answer to that.'

'Fuck's sake,' I say, tucking him under my jacket and continuing my run up the hill.

'I'm sorry – there was a security alert on the Tube,' I blurt as soon as the door opens, and regret my stupidity instantly. It's not Amanda standing there but her boyfriend, Roland, and I find myself feeling as stupid as I always do around him, sweating gently on his doorstep, in one sock, a tiny dog tucked inside my jacket, as I peer myopically into the gloom behind him. I feel like a schoolboy giving the teacher an excuse.

'No worries, man!' Roland clamps a large hand on my shoulder and ushers me inside. 'I don't think Mist is ready anyway.'

He calls her 'Mist', which is even more stupid than Misty. I didn't have any say in the name, obviously. If I had, I would have chosen Siobhan or Mary, something plain and honest, but then, as Amanda had reminded me crisply when I'd asked how she'd come up with the name, I wasn't around to 'contribute'. I would have been, I thought, the first time we spoke, on a crackling phone line – you only had to ask.

'Thanks.' I step into the enormous hallway, hovering just inside the door, taking in the huge tapestry on the wall, the vivid blues and pale sandy colours of the Caribbean. Roland's mum had made it, apparently, and had shipped it over to her son to remind him of his home in Jamaica. It's the only homely touch in this vast space, with the huge lampshade made out of tuning forks that Roland picked up at some art fair. It looks pretentious and a bit silly, like somebody's idea of good art, but it works in this slightly silly house.

Actually, it's not a house, according to Roland, it's a 'property'. He's in that line of business, so I suppose words like that come naturally to him, words like 'leverage' and 'overexposed', in spite of the laid-back way he behaves, as if he's strolling along a beach with the sand between his toes. He wears his success lightly, with his big, handsome frame in his expensive designer jeans and ancient-looking T-shirts designed by students at St Martin's and the brick-like mobile phone he keeps under the hall table, so as not to appear to be trying too hard. That makes it worse, I think as I stand there, sweating like a racehorse after the 3.30 at Kempton Park, the fact that it just seems to come so easily to him to be wealthy and successful and a nice guy at the same time.

I remember the dog then, quivering under my armpit and I reach into my jacket and pull him gently out. He still has the same dignified look on his face, surveying his surroundings.

'Nice dog, mate.' Roland's craggy face splits into a grin, revealing his magnificent teeth. Roland radiates good health.

I look at the tiny creature and understand that he is the least manly dog you could possibly imagine, and I blush to the roots of my hair. I glare at the dog, as if hoping he'll understand just how much of an eejit he's making me look, but he just gives me that imploring look again, followed by a damp sneeze. I contemplate explaining to Roland exactly how I found him and that he's a stray and that I'll be bringing him to the pound as soon as I can, but the dog turns his head then and licks my chin again.

'Thanks,' I find myself saying. 'He's called Bran.'

'Right,' Roland says doubtfully. 'Like the breakfast cereal?'

'No,' I reply. 'After Fionn Mac Cumhaill's dog, in Irish mythology.' Even as I give my explanation, it dawns on me just how pompous I sound.

'Of course.' Roland gives a patient smile. 'We have legends too where I'm from.'

Touché.

'Anyway, why don't you and Bran Flake come into the kitchen,' Roland says, strolling down the hall into an equally vast kitchen, a temple of gleaming granite worktops and white cupboards. He's barefoot, loping along, but my bare heel is beginning to chafe against the back of my shoe, so I have to kind of hop along after him.

'You OK, man?' He turns and gives me a puzzled look.

'Yeah, it's nothing,' I say, wincing as I press my foot into my shoe again. 'Just picked up an ankle injury playing five-a-side.'

'Right.' He gives a small smile and I want to cringe. I haven't played five-a-side since I was in college and, even then, I was always in goal, the safest place for someone whose foot wouldn't connect with the ball and whose arms were twice as long as anyone else's.

He goes to the enormous fridge in the corner of the kitchen, sticking his head inside then pulling out a large green bottle. 'Water? Amanda won't touch the stuff in the tap.'

I really want a double vodka, or even a nice, creamy pint of Guinness even at 11 o'clock in the morning, but I nod and accept the huge glass Roland is handing me. I spot a chair and go to sit down, Bran on my knee, but Roland looks alarmed for a second. 'Hang on, man, you're going to sit on my sound system.'

'Oh, sorry,' I say, 'I forgot.' I stand up again, putting the dog on the floor, where he stands for a moment, looking around, before going to inspect the long line of immaculate cupboards, sniffing under each one. When he gets to the last cupboard, beside the kitchen door, he lifts his leg and a surprisingly vigorous spurt of yellow shoots out and splashes against the cupboard.

'Oh, God, sorry,' I say, running over to him. 'Bran, bold,' I say, in what I hope is a stern voice, but he just gives me a blank look before continuing his investigation of the kitchen.

'Oh, no, man!' Roland says. 'I hope that dog urine doesn't stain.' He looks as disturbed as I have ever seen him as he approaches the cupboard with a J-Cloth and a large bottle of kitchen cleaner, his face screwing up in distaste as he dabs at the wee. 'Amanda will kill me,' he says as he wipes. 'She spent a fortune on these cupboards. They have some kind of special laminate to give an extra sheen … See?' he says, demonstrating proudly. 'They cost a packet too, so they must be good.'

'Right,' I say, as I lift Bran up, giving him what I hope he understands is a stern look. 'I'll find you a seat,' Roland says, after dabbing for a bit.

'Thanks,' I say, as he goes to one of the tall cupboards and opens it to reveal a stack of neatly folded chairs, pulling one out and offering it to me. I can't for the life of me understand why you wouldn't have actual chairs in a kitchen – or a table, come to think of it. 'It's minimalism,' Roland says, as if reading my mind. 'Mands and I saw this really cool article on it in one of those interiors magazines and we decided to go for it. I think it's great in this kind of space.'

'Mmm,' I nod, as I lower myself gingerly onto the chair, dog on my knee, wondering why it can't just be a kitchen. Why it has to be a 'space'.

I think of Mum's kitchen in Ireland, with the yellow Formica cupboards that Dad put up in 1973, the macramé pot-holders that Mum made in one of her evening classes. I think of her standing at the window in her pink dressing gown, mug of tea in hand, the view outside, the ditch with its row of bright orange montbretia swaying in the wind and, beyond it, the field of sheep that ends in the blue sea. Even though I haven't lived at home for ten years, I feel a sudden sense of the loss of it, a longing to be there, walking along the beach, picking up crabs' legs and bits of shell, looking out at the waves crashing against the lighthouse. How strange, I think, when all I used to want was to be down and out in London or Paris, with nothing but a pencil and notebook to sustain me. It hasn't quite turned out like that.

There's an excruciating silence for a few minutes, me sipping my water, Roland leaning against the stone counter top. I'm not very good at breaking silences, so I concentrate really hard on pretending to look relaxed, leaning back in the chair, crossing the ankle with the sock over the bare one, even though the dog wobbles and then tries to struggle off my lap. I grip him firmly and smile at Roland. He's a nice guy and he's taken the sudden appearance into his life of Misty's dad with more dignity than I'd muster in the same position, which makes our Sunday encounters all the more gruesome.

'So, written any poems lately?' Roland eventually asks, eyeing the dog suspiciously. I don't think he's a poetry lover, but I appreciate the effort.

'Oh, a few,' I say. 'London's a great source of inspiration.' I'm lying, of course. 'How's the property business?' I ask, hoping that the response will be brief.

'Ah, ticking along, mate,' Roland says. 'Got a new development just off the King's Road. Nice flats. You should have a look at one. It'd be right up your alley.'

'Great!' I find myself replying. For fuck's sake, I'm a poet, jobless, with a hundred quid left in the whole world, enough to pay for another week in this city, providing I don't want to eat and drink at the same time – I'm not exactly looking to jump on the property ladder. 'But I'd probably be looking for something a bit closer to Misty,' I find myself saying, as if I was actually contemplating his offer.

'Oh, sure, man,' Roland says, 'of course you would,' pushing himself off the counter top and clapping his hands decisively. 'Wonder what's keeping the girls?' A slight roll of the eyes and a conspiratorial wink – 'girls, they're all the same', the wink says. I play along, as if the two of us, me and my replacement as Misty's father, are best mates sharing a joke.

As if on cue, Amanda marches into the kitchen, her blonde

ponytail bobbing, a teddy bear under her arm. 'Mr Bear needs a wash, apparently,' she says to Roland, before spotting me in the corner in my chair. 'Oh, I didn't know you were here.' She seems to forget what she's doing with the bear for a moment, propping it on the empty kitchen counter, where it leans to one side before falling gently on its ear. We all look at it and the silence lengthens. Then Amanda catches my eye, and she quickly looks away. I wonder if she really wants me here. Maybe I'm embarrassing her, reminding her of a lapse in her usually good judgement, of the one time she didn't aim for a guy like Roland. But then, she asked me to come, she asked me to be a father to Misty – and here I am.

After she sent that letter, the one that changed my life completely, she rang me at home. I had given her my number all those years ago and had spent the following three months waiting for the call that never came, finally understanding that a summer fling on a grape-picking holiday in France followed by one stilted visit to Ireland didn't constitute a relationship. Until six weeks ago that is.

I stood in the hall, shivering – Mum never puts the heat on there, because 'it'd only get sucked out of the front door' – nodding and yessing, my head spinning, Mum in the background in her dressing gown, mouthing, 'Who is it?' When I told her later, she'd looked happy and sad at the same time.

Amanda didn't say much when I phoned the following day to tell her that I was on my way to London. I hadn't been expecting her to roll out the red carpet but, still, I allowed myself a moment's self-pity when she simply said that that was 'nice' and asked me to meet her in a café on the King's Road. She'd explain more when we met up. And so, I found my way from Euston Station at seven o'clock in the morning, eyes gritty from lack of sleep, my hair greasy, though I'd managed to brush my teeth at a sink in the station toilets, splashing my face with lukewarm water. I got on the Tube to Earl's Court, then a bus down the streets lined with lovely white houses, praying that I was going in the right direction. Like the country hick that I was, I'd asked the bus conductor to tell me where King's Road was, and a little old lady with a budgie in a cage on her knee said she'd be sure to let me know when to get off.

'Ooh, you're Irish,' she said. 'I do love the Irish. Here on a little holiday?'

'Well, I'm visiting … relatives,' I managed.

'That's good. You Irish do love your families, don't you? You all stick together like glue, not like us English … I haven't seen my sister Doreen in twenty-five years,' she said sadly. 'He's all I've got,' and she nodded in the direction of the budgie, who turned his head, as if he'd been listening all along.

'I'm sorry to hear that,' I said.

The little old lady's words rang in my ears as I trudged down the King's Road, past trendy shops with lovely clothes and fierce-looking shop assistants. I don't want Misty to end up with nobody but a budgie, I thought. It was silly, I know – I didn't know who she had in her life, but she had Amanda; she wasn't going to end up on a bus in Chelsea, her only friend in a cage on her knee. I wondered then if Misty ever felt lonely because she didn't have a dad, if she'd ever wondered who I was, but then I stopped myself. She mustn't have done if Amanda had only contacted me now, when she was seven years old.

It was the first question I asked Amanda, when she slid into the booth opposite me in the little café, all chintzy light fittings and floral wallpaper. I felt as if I were trapped in the soft furnishings section of a department store. I didn't mean to, but I lost my composure and just blurted it out, like an eejit. 'WhydidyounevertellmeaboutMistybeforenow?'

She gave me that look that I still remember, even though we'd spent only the best part of a week together almost eight years before, her clear blue eyes flicking over me, sussing me out and finding me just about acceptable – acceptable for a few nights under the stars, but clearly not for anything else.

'Sorry,' I blurted. 'I just—'

'It's fine,' she said, taking off her mac and placing it carefully over the back of the chair. I had a sudden flashback of her insisting on placing her T-shirt and shorts over the end of the bed before hopping in beside me. It had driven me mad. I felt myself going red, looking fixedly down at my coffee while she ordered a tea from the waitress. 'Earl Grey, please, no milk.' And then she turned to me. 'You look terrible.'

'Thanks. You look great,' I found myself saying. Because she did look great. She looked shiny and healthy, her ponytail a bright mane down her back, her cream T-shirt and grey slip dress elegant and trendy at the same time.

She shrugged, as if she was used to getting compliments, and she probably was. Amanda is terribly pretty, in a fine-boned English way, all cheekbones and narrow wrists. It was easy to see what I'd seen in her, as a sweaty twenty-one-year-old, straight out of an English and Philosophy degree, but what she'd seen in me was quite another matter. I don't think she actually had seen anything much more than a summer fling.

'What was it like?' I blurted now.

She stopped stirring the spoon in her teacup. 'What was what like?' She looked at me sharply, suspiciously.

'Finding out that you were pregnant with Misty.'

'Oh, God.' She relaxed and her features softened. 'It was a bit of a shock, to be honest. I was still in college and I remember sitting on the loo in the common-room toilets, four tests open in front of me. Every time I did one and it came up positive, I'd throw it into the bin and open another one. But I had to believe it in the end.'

She gave a small shrug and a half-smile, and I tried to imagine her perched on the loo, holding the test up in front of her. I felt a dart of jealousy then, that she had been the one to see it, to discover it, while I'd been hundreds of miles away in a dusty office, churning out fishing licences and hunting permits blissfully unaware of what I'd done – of how I'd changed Amanda's life for ever. It was a strange emotion because all I had felt to that point was numb shock, with a dash of panic for good measure.

'How did you manage by yourself?'

'Oh, I just did, I suppose. I had no choice,' she murmured. 'Well, I suppose I did.' There was a long pause. 'But I made the choice to keep her.' She started stirring her spoon in her tea again, over and over, until I wanted to snatch it out of her hand. She looked at me then. 'It was because of you, believe it or not.'

'Because of me what?'

'That I had Misty. I knew that I couldn't do it, you know … knowing that you were at home in Ireland and you weren't even aware—' She stopped. 'It didn't seem right.' For the first time, her composure slipped and her eyes filled with tears.

I reached out and patted her hand awkwardly, like an elderly uncle, and I immediately felt foolish, but she grabbed my hand and squeezed it, while reaching into her handbag for a tissue with the other. She blew her nose with a loud honk, which would have been amusing under any other circumstances. 'Thanks.'

'That's OK,' I said. We stayed like that for a few moments, and I remembered sitting across from her in a little café in St Paul de Vence, nursing an espresso, smoking a cigarette and feeling very French. The sun had burned down and the sky had been a livid blue, of a kind I'd never seen before. Everything had seemed brilliantly clear and intense, unlike the soft blurs of home, the muted greys and greens. Here, it was orange and yellow, bright, almost lurid colours that hurt my eyes. Amanda had been sitting opposite me, a diabolo fraise in front of her. She'd been wearing a huge sun hat, equally huge sunglasses and a little white sundress that had shown off her legs, which were long and slender. Sitting opposite her, my sallow skin burned brown by the sun, I'd felt like a movie star, not a graduate postponing life for a few months. Now, here we were, surrounded by acres of William Morris wallpaper, dingy lighting and wonky pale-green tables, her nose and eyes red, my face pale and hair lank. We sure weren't movie stars now. Now, we were new parents, or rather I was. Amanda had been a parent for seven years, but I was going to be a grown-up for the first time in my twenty-eight years.

'So,' I repeated.

A silence settled over us both, and I could hear the hum and clatter of the café around me as we sat there, digesting the enormity of it all.

Amanda spoke first. 'Would you like to see some pictures?'

I hesitated for a fraction too long and saw the look of hurt on her face. 'I'd love to,' I managed, pinning a smile on my face. After all, what father wouldn't want to see pictures of his daughter? A father who was scared, that's who.

Amanda reached into her handbag, took out a bulging Filofax and opened it, extracting a handful of photos. 'This is the day she was born, in Finchley Hospital.'

I looked at the soft pink bundle in the photo, at the tiny pointed face, bright red from the effort of being born, her mouth an 'o' in mid-yawn, her eyes scrunched up under her little pink hat. The expression on her mother's face was a mixture of exhaustion and elation, and as I looked at little Misty, I felt a sudden pain in my chest, as if someone had thumped me right over the heart, a feeling of being winded.

'She looks so tiny,' I croaked.

'She was.' Amanda's smile was soft. 'She was six pounds, and I used to torture myself wondering if I hadn't eaten enough in pregnancy or had taken the wrong vitamins, but the doctor said some babies are just small. He asked me if she took after her dad.' And she gave a brief smile, as I sat hunched over the too-small table. 'I said no, that her dad was a giant.' She laughed briefly, then, catching my expression, said, 'Well …'

We looked through the photos – Misty blowing out her candles on her first birthday cake, Misty sitting on a donkey on Brighton Beach, looking uneasy about it, Misty eating an ice-cream under a palm tree in the south of Spain, a handsome man on one side of her, Amanda on the other.

'Who's he?' I tried to keep the accusatory tone out of my voice.

'Oh, that's Roland. Misty's D—, I mean, my partner.'

'Oh. Right.' What was I expecting? I wondered – that she'd been waiting for me for all of this time? I looked again at the photo of a happy family. Where did I belong? I couldn't see where I'd fit in. I looked up at her, wondering if she expected more from me, that I'd 'ooh' and 'ah' over the photos, like a normal person, but she seemed to understand.

'I'm sorry,' she said.

'What do you mean?'

'I'm sorry I didn't tell you before now. I didn't mean to keep it from you and you have every right to be angry with me, I just … didn't think it was fair to involve you.'

'And what changed?' I said, more sharply than I'd intended.

'Misty keeps asking about her dad. When she got to six, she became obsessed with dads, asking me why everyone else in her class had one except her, and she kept looking at books about Ireland and asking me about it and where you came from. She even bought a map of the British Isles at the school fair, and she wanted me to tell her exactly where her dad lived and to explain exactly why he had never been able to be her dad.' She shrugged, then blew her nose again, her leg jigging up and down under the table.

'What did you tell her?'

She shook her head and the tears flowed again, but I didn't reach out to hold her hand this time. I just let her cry, because I didn't know what to do or say. I had been a clearly dispensable part of her life for seven years, until I suddenly wasn't any more, and I didn't know how I felt about that – angry or sad, or both.

She shook her head sadly from side to side. 'I told her I didn't know,' she whispered. 'But I promised her that I'd find out, so I did.

She needs you, Emmett. She wants you in her life and I want you in her life.'

I realised that, while I was listening, I'd been holding the photos in my hand, and they were now warm and sweaty, my hands clammy. I felt as if I was falling from a height, the wind rushing past my head as I descended, wondering when I'd hit the ground.

'Emmett?'

'I need to think,' I said, and I jumped up from the table, yanking my bag so hard onto my shoulder that the chair fell over onto the floor. I bolted for the door and out onto the street, where I gulped in huge lungfuls of cold air, resting my hands on my knees until my breathing began to steady.

I was examining the pattern on the pavement beneath my feet when I felt a warm hand on my back. 'Are you OK?'

I looked up to see Amanda above me, her face soft.

I nodded. 'Sorry, I was just … I didn't mean to run off like that. I mean, I'm not scared,' I said, realising as I said the words that that was exactly what I was. I was scared. Terrified of my own child. How terrible is that? I remembered the way Dad had looked at me when I'd told him, the intense disappointment on his face, but the guilt too, for the mistakes he'd made many years before. I could see it and I'd wanted to shout, 'You're just a hypocrite,' but I'd gone along with the charade that the shame was all mine. I'd only felt brave enough to say otherwise when I knew I wouldn't be seeing him for a while. A parting shot, because I didn't have the nerve for anything else.

I looked at Amanda and understood how disappointed she was in me too. How she'd been expecting me to be the big man, to step up, and all that I'd done was run from the scene, a look of panic on my face. 'It's too soon,' she said eventually, reproachfully.

'What, after seven years?' I said bitterly. 'I wouldn't call that too soon, Amanda.'

She nodded quietly. 'No, you're right, and I don't think I can ever explain to you why I didn't tell you or find you before now. It wasn't fair, I can see that, but—'

'But you didn't really want to speak to a guy you'd never expected to see again in your life.'

'That's probably true. But you're here now.'

'Yes, I am.'

'Will you come to see Misty? Please?'

'Of course I will,' I answered, almost before she'd finished asking. I said 'of course' because it was the right thing to do.

And so I did. We'd sat opposite each other in one of the cafés in London Zoo, and she'd held the stuffed emperor penguin I'd bought her on her lap. We'd looked at each other and we'd said hardly a word. I could see the weight of it on her little shoulders, the responsibility of finding the words to talk to her actual dad. And I could see that I probably wasn't the man she'd imagined in her dreams, as she'd pored over her map of the British Isles. I was her dad because she'd been told I was, but I was a stranger to her, this very tall man perched on a plastic chair in front of her, offering her chips from a soggy cardboard tray.

'Is that a *dog*?' Amanda glares at me now, her nose wrinkled in distaste. I know she's ambivalent about me because I haven't lived up to her expectations as a dad. I've complicated matters, muddied the waters and, what's more, I've turned out to be a bit of an idiot. I wonder if she's regretting her decision to tell me anything.

At the word 'dog', the little creature's ears prick up and he gives a bark, his ginger tail swishing. His bark is awful, a high-pitched squeak.

'Oh, God, it is,' Amanda says, backing away as if he were a bull mastiff and not some kind of minute toy breed.

For God's sake, I think. 'His name is Bran,' I say, 'and I thought Misty might like him.' I hadn't thought any such thing, and it'll make taking him to Battersea Dogs Home harder, but I'll cross that bridge, I think, when I come to it.

'Like the cereal?'

'No ...' I begin, before concluding that more pomposity is not needed. 'Not exactly.'

'Well, I hope you're not expecting us to look after him,' she says, giving him a wary look.

'Oh, no, he'll be staying with me,' I lie. He won't be staying with me because I can barely feed myself, never mind a dog, even one this size, but why make things worse?

And then Misty appears behind Amanda, her bee backpack on her back. Her dark-brown hair is neatly parted and plaited, a bright-red bow at the end of each plait. Underneath her blue duffel coat, she's wearing her favourite pink long-sleeved T-shirt and her jeans with the patchwork pockets. She stands half-behind her mother, as if I'm some ogre and not her dad. She puts her thumb in her mouth, then, remembering that her mum has told her she's too old for that, she whips it out again. She doesn't smile at me, just nods her little head and her brown eyes meet mine. My brown eyes. She gives me a look that tells me that she doesn't expect anything from me, a look that devastates me every time.

'Hello, Emmett,' she says.

'It's 'Daddy', love,' Amanda says. 'Emmett's your daddy.'

'I like calling him Emmett,' Misty replies. 'It's a nice name.'

'Fine.' Amanda says tiredly, tucking a strand of pale blonde hair behind her ear. For a second, she looks like the girl I met in France – shy and lovely, her face soft, but then she stiffens and looks anxious again. 'You'd better get going – we have a thing on later and Misty has to be back for her tea and bath.' She looks at me enquiringly.

'Right,' I say, attempting to be decisive, lifting Bran up so that I can pick my bag up off the floor, whereupon Misty shoots forward, an avid look on her face. She holds both her hands out and lifts Bran up gently, before holding him to her chest. He has the same dignified look on his face, his bug eyes looking imploringly at Misty, before giving her a lick on the chin. She has never once smiled when she's been with me but, now, she giggles and when he licks her again, she laughs even harder. 'Silly dog,' she says, tucking him under her arm.

Oh no, I think. How on earth am I going to get out of this? Amanda gives me a look that tells me that it's my mess to sort out, so I say, 'Right, Misty, let's go. We're going to the National Gallery.' I say this like a teacher announcing to her class of bored schoolchildren that an educational tour is in the offing. I'd really like to sit in a darkened corner of a pub, a fire roaring in the grate, the sound of the pinball machine in the background, downing a nice pint, but that's not exactly appropriate. Amanda expects me to 'educate and inspire' Misty, so I'm trying to rise to the occasion.

'With a dog?' Amanda says.

'He's small. I can probably fit him in my bag.'

'Right …' She looks at me sceptically.

'So, let's go, Misty,' I say, offering her my hand, which she accepts,

Bran still under her arm. 'See you, Roland,' I shout as we stand in the hall.

Roland has disappeared upstairs to his home office, which I saw once, and it looked like the command station of the Starship Enterprise, all chrome and black leather and those clacky balls that whack off each other, which must be a terrible distraction. I could never imagine myself sitting there, looking at a computer screen, examining long rows of numbers and balance sheets. Sometimes, I think it would be better if I could.

'Yeah, see you, mate. Bye, Mist, bye, Bran Flake,' his voice drifts down from above.

I don't bother correcting him, but just head for the door.

3.

I stand on the doorstep and take a deep breath, sucking the soot-filled air into my lungs, before looking down at Misty. 'All set?'

Misty isn't listening. She's nuzzling into Bran's gingery fur, as if he's some live cuddly toy, which he doesn't seem to mind, the same faraway look in his eyes, as if he's pondering life's great mysteries.

'Misty?' I repeat.

'Yes, Emmett?' She looks up and her face has lost that guarded expression that she usually wears with me.

'We'll have to put him in my bag,' I say, as we round the corner onto the main road and the number 38 trundles towards us. She clutches him to her more closely, but I hold the bag out to her and, reluctantly, she puts Bran inside. He looks perplexed for a minute, before sighing and settling down on a copy of Seamus Heaney's *The*

Haw Lantern. I like that collection, I think, as he shuffles his doggy bottom around on it. I fold the top of the bag over loosely, so he isn't smothered, and we hop on the bus together.

'Emmett?' Misty says, as we take our seats on the top deck at the front, where she always likes to sit. She shuffles her bottom happily into the seat, then holds out her arms for the bag, which she places carefully on her knee. She lifts the flap and looks adoringly inside, before closing it with a wistful sigh.

'Yeah?'

'Is Bran staying with me tonight? My friend Cindy got a Larbador—'

'Labrador,' I correct, cringing as I do. What's wrong with Larbador anyway?

'A Labrador, but he had to go away because he ate all of her dad's shoes. Will you send Bran away?'

'Well, it's early days yet,' I fudge.

'Can I keep him, Emmett?'

'We'll see.' As I speak, I remember that Mum used to say 'we'll see' to me when I nagged her about something. Does every parent take refuge in 'we'll see'? I wonder as the bus speeds towards town. Is it basically a lie, to cast doubt, when I have every intention of handing Bran over to a cheery lady in Battersea Dogs Home? To soften the blow of reality, I have hidden behind a parenting cliché. Maybe I should just be straight with Misty and tell her the harsh truth, but then the bag moves and she gives a little giggle and I decide that I can't possibly tell her now. Not when Misty is very slightly warming to me because of Bran.

The bus rounds the corner into Holborn and I catch a glimpse of Lincoln's Inn Fields, a sliver of green between the buildings.

I found my way there a few Sundays ago, I remember, walking all the way from Holloway Road, through the lovely streets of Barnsbury, looking into the posh shops with their handmade shoes and designer knitwear, then into Clerkenwell and the tree-lined Theobald's Road, past the red-and-white of the Italian church, with its lovely arches and the fresco of the Twelve Apostles, then a gastropub, the Eagle – with its hip-looking people sitting outside, quaffing white wine and eating giant plates of bangers and mash. I have seen four different Londons in an hour, I'd thought, as I caught a waft of frying sausage, deciding to sit down and spend some of my last few quid on a drink, remembering the toasted sandwiches in their red-plastic wrappers that constituted food at the Stag's Head in Dublin with a certain amount of nostalgia. I'd still be there, I thought, with Peadar from the office, listening to him going on about rising house prices, if it weren't for Amanda. And Misty, I reminded myself.

Now, I have an idea. 'We're getting off here,' I say.

'Are we not going to see the boring, pooey old paintings?' Misty asks.

'No, we are not,' I say, trying not to laugh. 'We are going to see something much more interesting,' I add, pressing the bell and offering her my hand so that she can hold it while climbing down the stairs. She gives a small shake of her head, so I let it drop to my side, feeling hurt.

'I'll take the bag,' I offer.

She shakes her head. 'No, Emmett. I am minding Bran by myself.'

'Misty, the bag's too big for you, and you might fall—' I begin, but she slings the strap over her shoulder and begins to totter down the stairs. I follow, putting out a hand when she wobbles, as if that will make any difference. She makes it down to the bottom and squares her shoulders in triumph, giving the bell another press for good measure.

We get off at the corner of Old Holborn and walk down towards the grand red-and-yellow brick gate, with its crenellated top and pretty stone turrets, that marks the entrance to Lincoln's Inn Fields. 'I wonder if you'll walk through this one day in a wig and gown,' I say to Misty.

'What's a wig and gown?'

'It's what a barrister wears when they are at work. A big black gown and a wig made of horsehair. And they go to court and make sure that the law is followed.' I make it as simple as I can, imagining Misty in fifteen years' time, that dark hair of hers flowing beneath her wig as she strides into chambers. 'My daughter's a barrister,' I will tell anyone who cares to listen.

'I think I would like to be a vet,' is Misty's response, as she puts the bag down on the ground and opens the flap to let Bran hop out.

'Of course. Well, that's a lovely idea,' I say.

She ignores me, quite rightly, and runs after Bran, who has taken off across the park, tail aloft, nose down. He snuffles around a couple huddled on a park bench, looking hopefully at them, then allows himself to be picked up and kissed by Misty, before giving a little bark. 'OK, then,' she says, 'off you go', and he races off to a tree, sniffing it appreciatively, then lifting his leg. He is clearly in doggie heaven.

When we get near the exit, I realise that I don't have a lead or collar for him, so I have to use the strap of my satchel, tying it loosely around his neck, before we walk out the gate and across the road to a pale-yellow building with arched windows, set into the terrace of chocolate-brown four-storey Georgian homes. 'Here we are,' I say, holding out the bag.

'Aww, Emmett, does he have to?'

'Yes, he does.'

We remove the satchel strap and she lifts him gently into the bag and he settles himself back down on top of Seamus.

'Do you know who Sir John Soane is?' I say.

She shakes her head, her thumb in her mouth.

'Well, he was a very famous architect. He designed the Bank of England and he collected lots of really interesting things for this museum. It even has a sarcophagus in it. Do you know what that is?'

The head shakes again and I think to myself that I'm being a pompous ass again. 'Let's go and see.' I insist on taking her hand as we climb the steps and walk through the entrance into an Aladdin's cave of books, sculpture, painting and murals, in a series of stuffy, brightly painted rooms, with lurid ceilings and frescos, all piled on top of each other. It's mad, I think, and beautiful at the same time, and I find myself wandering from room to room, peering at the marble statues, at the fragments of Westminster Cathedral, at the astronomical clock and the cast of a Michelangelo sculpture, the floorboards creaking under my feet.

Misty isn't looking at anything: she has her thumb shoved in her mouth and she's sucking on it loudly, walking in a zig-zag pattern across the parquet flooring.

'What are you doing?' My voice is sharper than it should be.

'I'm stepping over the lines in the floor. I have to get to every third bit, and if I step on a line on the way, I'm out,' she explains, having removed her thumb.

'Well, could you pay attention to the exhibits? That's why we're here.'

She shrugs, but her eyes cloud and I wonder what I said wrong.

'Let's go and see the dead body,' I say. We trundle down to the basement, where we admire what looks to me like a cattle trough on little pillars. 'Imagine, an ancient Egyptian king was buried in that.'

Misty isn't listening. She's humming to herself now, eyes cast downwards, feet crossing and uncrossing as she gives a series of little hops. For Christ's sake, I think.

'Let's sit down,' I say heavily. I spot a little bench that looks as if it can be sat on and I fold myself onto it. I'm in the middle of ancient dead people, but it feels peaceful. I sit there, Misty silent beside me, the bag between us shuffling every now and again, and I wonder what I can say to my daughter. 'So, how's school these days?' I try.

She looks at me reproachfully. 'Fine.'

'Oh. Good. How's ballet?' Misty hates ballet, and her forbidding teacher, Mrs Dostoevsky, a woman with a bun so tight it lifts her eyebrows practically up to her hairline and a thick Russian accent that I suspect is fake.

'I hate ballet. Emmett?'

'Yes.'

'Do dogs go to heaven?'

I have no idea how to answer that. Eventually, I decide on the truth. 'I don't know. I suppose it depends on whether or not you believe in heaven.'

'I do. My mum says that she does too and that you do because you're Irish and every Irish person believes in heaven.'

'They do?'

'I think that Granny won't go to heaven because she swears in the car and won't let me eat ice-cream cones.'

'What kind of person doesn't let you eat ice-cream cones?

'Granny's not nice,' Misty says sadly, reaching her hand under the lid of my bag and stroking Bran inside.

'I'm sorry to hear that,' I say. 'My mum's very nice. You'd like her.'

Misty continues stroking Bran inside the bag. 'Is she my granny too?' she finally says quietly, and I feel my stomach tighten. I want to reach out and squeeze Misty to me, but I've never done more than hold her hand crossing the road, so I don't think it would be appropriate.

'Yes, she is your granny.'

'Is she nicer than my granny in England?'

'I don't know. She's very nice, though. She's snuggly and she likes giving hugs. And she makes very nice apple tart.' I can say a lot more about my mother, but these are the essentials.

'What's apple tart?' Misty's nose wrinkles in confusion.

'Like apple pie, only much nicer. It has a secret ingredient in it,' I say. Now, she looks interested. I remember that kids love things like that – magic and secrets and things outside themselves and their little worlds – it's only when they get older that they understand that magic doesn't exist. I'm wondering what it might be like to believe in magic, right now, as a twenty-eight-year-old sitting in a museum with his daughter. To believe in ghosts and fairies and witches and in their power to make strange and wonderful things happen. If I still believed, what would I make happen?

Suddenly, I'm eight years old again, on a windy beach in Wexford, huddled under a tarpaulin. I'm trying to light a camp fire, but I'm not having much luck. 'Maybe I can use my magic powers,' Daisy says. 'Just watch.' She takes the match in her hand and says,

'Shalakazoom,' and she strikes it firmly along the side of the box. The match springs into life, the flame burning brightly as she turns the match downwards and flicks it onto the little pile of twigs. There's a curl of smoke and then the little flame grows bigger.

'How did you do that?' I ask.

'Magic.' She laughs, crossing and uncrossing her eyes.

Daisy.

I haven't thought about her in so long, but suddenly she's as real to me as Misty is. It must be magic, or something like that.

'Emmett?' Misty is looking at me, eyes round. She opens her mouth to say something, but I'm saved by the small bark that comes from inside the bag. It starts to shake. Uh-oh.

'C'mon, Misty, we'd better get out of here.'

I'm surprised when she takes my hand and skips out the door.

We lift Bran out of the bag when we're outside on the steps and his tail lifts as he sniffs the wind.

'I think Bran needs another walk,' Misty says.

'I think you're right,' I say. We put on his satchel-collar-and-lead and set off in search of the ice-cream I'd promised her, walking back up to the bus stop. I let her sit on top, near the front again, and she's almost chatty, pointing out a man in a big beige overcoat with a huge kidney-brown Weimaraner.

'He looks just like his dog,' I say and she giggles, and then she sees an elderly lady shuffling along with a Jack Russell. 'Look, Emmett, they look the same!'

The game of 'owners who look like their dogs' lasts us until we get to the top of Amanda's road, and we've found a Dalmatian, a pug and a poodle that bear distinct resemblances to their owners, Misty doubling up with laughter every time. I have a warm feeling inside, a sense that I've finally connected to this solemn little person, and when a lady smiles at us both, I smile back. 'See?' my smile says. 'I'm a parent. Look at how good I am at the job.'

I even give the woman a jaunty parental wave as we get out at the top of Amanda's road and walk down past the little row of shops – the post office, the Asian supermarket with the grumpy lady behind the counter, the little hairdresser's, picturesquely called Headcases. And then I see it. I stop, Misty and Bran beside me, the three of us looking at the window of the last shop, a bookshop. It doesn't look very promising, with its dusty grey facade, 'Farrell's' written above the door in gold paint, the last 'l' smudged with birdshit. The window is filthy, and there's an odd display behind the glass, a mixture of Frederick Forsyth novels, along with a signed photo of the man, and books on trout fishing, as if they are the only two subjects in which anyone could be interested. Written on a pink index card Sellotaped to the window is a notice: 'Wanted, bookseller. Must have intimate knowledge of Japanese history. Apply within.'

I hesitate. Do I have an intimate knowledge of Japanese history? No, probably not, I think as I turn away again. In fact, I don't know the first thing about Japanese history. Then I stop. Am I mad? Can I not just bluff it? God knows, I need a job. 'C'mon you two,' I say, picking Bran up and tucking him under my arm. 'Let's go in.'

I'm about to step inside the door when I see a woman come towards me, a baby in a sling on her front, so I hold the door open for her. She looks up at me to say thanks, and she sucks in a breath. What? I think. Do I have something in my nose? Then she mutters a thanks and moves under my outstretched arm, a smell of talcum powder and vanilla wafting past as she walks inside. I find myself distracted for a second as she disappears, as if my thoughts have stopped. I look towards her retreating back, at the bright-green winter coat that flaps open as she walks. A 'granny coat' as Mum would call it, but which looks oddly good on her. Her strides are long and as she lopes along I can see the baby's feet bouncing off her legs. It's strange … I feel … well, I'm not sure what I feel. Distracted, that's it.

The smell of vanilla stays with me for a bit, but then another smell overwhelms me. I think it's the whiff of mouldy carpet, warm and fetid at the same time. I want to gag and I wonder for a moment about turning around and going straight back out again. Could I honestly work with this smell, day in, day out? Then I look down at Misty and Bran, tucked under her arm. Two mouths to feed. Yes, I bloody well could.

4.

My nose is filled with the scent of vanilla all the way home – which is a good thing, because the alternative would be for it to be filled with the smell of rancid carpet. I let the nicer smell soothe me as I lean my head against the pole in the Tube carriage and think about the sheer strangeness of Farrell's Bookshop. It was like I'd disappeared down the rabbit hole, like Alice in Wonderland, to a place where everything was familiar, yet strangely distorted.

I can't possibly work there, I think now, as I let the rumble of the train soothe me – I'll go out of my mind. Even the thought of those tottering piles of dusty books, the empty shelves, the bizarre categories of subjects that no one could possibly be interested in, like 'Crafts – Victorian' and 'Real Tennis' – I can't imagine that there's an unquenchable thirst among the reading public for books about real tennis. And then there were the even stranger staff members, tweedy men who looked as if they went home and cooked meals for one on a single gas burner and that girl with the glasses and the large breasts, who introduced herself as the senior bookseller and who told me that the job was mine, because no-one else had applied, which was doubly worrying. I didn't even need to dredge up my minute knowledge of Japanese history. I blush as I think of her, pale flesh spilling over a too-tight cardigan, like Betty Boop. I hope I didn't stare – New Men don't stare. I'll have to find a point just left of her eyes and fix my gaze there tomorrow when I start. Tomorrow, in just twelve hours' time.

Oh, God, I think. What have I got myself into? I shake my head and try to focus on the fact that at least I'll have a job, with actual money, and Amanda seems to be pleased with me for the first time since I arrived. Even Misty seems to have thawed just a tiny bit, thanks to Bran.

When we'd got back after my 'interview', which had consisted of asking me my date of birth and what books I liked, while Misty wandered off to the children's section, Amanda was standing on the doorstep, the light from the silly tuning-fork chandelier spilling onto her hair and shoulders, burnishing the silver dress she was wearing with a yellow sheen.

'There you are, Misty,' she'd said. 'Monica's been here for half an hour – she's in the den, waiting.' And she looked at me and her face flushed slightly. 'We have a business thing … some group of developers. They want to build luxury huts in the Caribbean.' She said this half-apologetically, as if she thought that I, a mere poet, would be envious of her and Roland, two halves of a property empire. As if. It didn't stop me wondering what it might have been like to live here with Amanda, tying my bow tie in my study, admiring my designer furniture, my spacious home. Except, of course, we wouldn't have been living here at all, would we? Not on the fifty quid prize money from my one publication to date. A reminder, if I needed one, of why Amanda chose Roland, the successful, wealthy entrepreneur to be a full-time father to her daughter, instead of Emmett, the penniless poet.

'Right. Great,' I said. 'You look nice.' Then it was my turn to blush – is it inappropriate to compliment the mother of my child? I wondered.

'Thanks.' There was a moment's silence, and then Misty yelled, 'Emmett's got a job!' I cringed. I didn't want to tell her yet – I wanted to find a way to make it all sound a bit more important before telling her. That I was a manager in 'retail', not the humble bookseller behind the counter in Japanese history, being paid a fiver an hour. Amanda is a lawyer so, frankly, anything other than being a brain surgeon would probably not impress her, but still, I wanted to try. It felt suddenly important.

Amanda folded her arms, looking at me steadily. 'Oh, well, that's good news. Will you be working with Tom?'

'Why would I be working with Tom? Not every Irish person works on a building site, you know,' I bit back.

'I didn't mean it like that,' she said softly.

'He's not working on a building site, Mummy. He's working in the bookshop on the corner of our road! And it's smelly, but not smelly like his flat. A different kind of smelly. And there are books on everything. I read one about *Titanic* and it was brilliant!' Misty looked more excited than I'd ever seen her.

'What do you mean, smelly like my flat?' I said. 'It smells perfectly OK – nothing that a bit of air freshener won't fix.'

I'd brought Misty there the previous Sunday, when it was too wet to do anything, and she'd entertained herself by feeding the electricity meter with ten pence pieces and watching an omnibus edition of *Brookside*, which I wasn't sure was all that suitable, with its warring families and adult themes.

She giggled again. 'Tom leaves his dirty pants on the floor!'

'Yes, he does,' I agreed, eyeing Amanda, who was looking faintly appalled.

'I like it,' Misty suddenly said.

'The smelly pants on the floor?'

'No. The way that there's stuff all over the place and chairs at the table. You don't have to take them out every time you want to sit down. And I like all the books that you have on the shelf … Mummy and Daddy don't have a lot of books,' she said wistfully, before catching herself and looking up at me.

It's OK, I wanted to say to her. I don't mind that Roland is 'Daddy'. I don't mind at all. In fact, I like it. I can feel jealous of him, while being pleased that he's the one with the responsibility, not me.

'Well, good for Emmett,' Amanda said, looking at Misty. 'I'd say that would be right up his street, wouldn't you, Misty-boo?'

'What does "right up his street" mean?' Misty said, as she let herself be licked by Bran, whom she'd picked up from the doorstep and was now nuzzling enthusiastically.

'I mean, something that he'd enjoy and that he'd be really good at,' Amanda said, looking at me. 'And it's local – sounds good, Emmett.'

I felt mollified, even if only slightly. But I hadn't really thought that I'd be good at bookselling, that it could be something I'd enjoy, but then I suppose I would – I like books. And I like people. I find them interesting.

'Yes, he would be very good at it,' Misty said. 'And he says that he's going to get me books so that I can read more, too.'

'Well, that's fantastic,' Amanda said, putting an arm around Misty. 'Now, inside for tea. Go on, Roland's upstairs – you can help him to tie his bow tie.'

When Misty disappeared, Amanda hugged herself, wrapping her arms around herself against the February cold. 'So.'

'So.'

'You got a job.'

'Yeah.'

'That's great, Emmett.'

'Thanks.' She was being a bit patronising, but still.

'It looks like Misty had fun today.' She turned and looked into the hall, then back at me.

I shrugged, unsure whether the slight thawing in Misty amounted to 'fun'. Then I noticed that Amanda's bare shoulders and arms had a covering of goose pimples on them.

'Would you like my coat?' I offered.

'Hmm?' She looked confused for a moment. 'Why?'

'Because you look cold.'

She flushed. 'Oh, no thanks. I have a wrap thing in the kitchen.'

I cringed. 'Sure.'

'But thanks for offering.' Then, as if the conversation had strayed further than she'd have liked, she rescued us both. 'I'm glad that you're encouraging her to read more. We don't do enough of that.'

'Oh. Well. Good.' It had never occurred to me that I could add something to Misty's life – that I wasn't just a mystery presence, someone who had come to upend her existence, but I could make a difference. Maybe I might even start to write decent poems again, instead of the drivel that has been coming from my pen. Maybe.

Amanda looked anxiously behind her into the hall, then her face brightened as Roland came down the stairs, looking like James Bond in his dinner suit and shiny patent-leather shoes. 'There you are. Honestly,' she said, tapping him playfully on the shoulder. 'I thought women were supposed to take hours getting ready.'

'What, don't I look the part?' He smiled, placing a hand on Amanda's shoulder, his skin dark against her pale white, his strong, handsome face close to hers. She sighed and turned her head slightly towards him and he placed a tender kiss on her nose.

I need to leave, I thought, looking down at my scuffed shoes, at the paleness of my naked ankle, at my too-small corduroy jacket. 'Well,' I said, with mock cheer. 'Good luck!' I made a kind of 'go get it' gesture with my fist.

'Thanks, mate,' Roland said easily. Then he turned and called out, 'Mist, come and say goodbye to Emmett.'

A little voice came from the living room. 'I'm watching Casualty with Monica and there's a really big accident.'

'Don't be rude to your dad, Mist,' Roland began, but I interrupted.

'She's already said goodbye. And besides, I'm in a bit of a rush. I have a … thing on.'

'Sure,' Roland said. 'Have fun, mate.'

'You too.' I beamed, turning and walking down the steps, feeling about three feet tall, wondering if Amanda and Roland, these two totally perfect beings, were looking at me, feeling sorry for me. The unhappy thought accompanied me all the way home, a kind of existential gloom draping itself over my shoulders. And then, just as I rounded the windswept corner past the art deco bulk of the Odeon cinema, I stopped, the smell of vanilla filling my nostrils again. I turned around, expecting to see the woman in the green granny coat, but the street was empty. I shook my head and walked on. Get a grip, Emmett, I thought.

When I get back, Tom is in the kitchen, standing up in a pair of Superman Y-fronts, a cereal bowl to his lips, inhaling its contents. 'Ergh, urgh …' he says when he sees me.

I wave back and put Bran down, and he scurries off across the kitchen floor, hoovering up the bits of food that have fallen onto the ground. Tom puts the bowl down. 'What's with the dog?'

'Long story. He's off to the pound tomorrow if I can't find his owner.' As I say this, I think of Misty and how disappointed she'll be in me; how I'll be letting her down, further demonstrating my inadequacy as a dad – I'm the kind of parent who tempts his child with a cuddly animal and then dispatches the poor thing at the first opportunity. No New Man dungarees for me, I think, as I go to the cupboard and take out a tin of tuna, scraping the fish into a bowl and putting it on the ground. Bran bounds towards it and hoovers it up and, when he's finished, gives a little shimmy of pleasure, looking up at me with those awful bug eyes set in that little squinty face. I can't imagine that anyone else would want to look at that face, but maybe some little old lady is crying her eyes out right now, mourning the loss of her pooch.

'I think he likes you,' Tom says.

'Yeah, well, he can just forget it. I've enough on my plate right now,' I grumble. 'I'll track his owner down tomorrow.'

Tom leans back against the fridge, arms folded. He gives me a look that tells me that I am well and truly rumbled. 'How's Misty?'

'Oh, you know …' I say. 'She's good.' I shrug and pretend to be interested in filling the kettle and putting a teabag into a mug. 'Want one?'

'Don't change the subject.'

'I'm not changing the subject,' I mumble, stirring my teabag in the mug, before blurting, 'I can't decide whether she likes me or hates me. One minute, she's giggling away; the next, she's looking at me as if I have six heads when I ask her patronising and stupid questions about school and ballet, like an annoying uncle, which, I suppose, I am. What kind of things does a seven-year-old like anyway? What kind of language do they speak? I have no fucking idea and I also have no fucking idea what I'm doing here.' I thump my fist on the counter and Bran gives a little yelp, shooting underneath the table, a pair of bug eyes now looking at me from his shelter. 'Sorry,' I say to him, bending down and stroking his little lion's-mane head. He's vibrating with fear and I regret instantly my outburst.

Tom doesn't say anything for a few moments, pulling on a bright-green Italia '90 T-shirt, removing his underpants in the process and flinging them into a corner.

'Do you have to do that?' I say, as he stands in the kitchen, genitals taking the air.

'What?' he says, bending over to the clothes horse which is hanging off the radiator, giving me a glimpse of hairy backside as he does. 'I'm just changing my underpants. In case I score tonight. Don't want to let a pair of manky pants get in my way,' he says proudly, finding a bright-green pair and pulling them on. He looks like a giant leprechaun.

'They're mine,' I say.

He shrugs. 'What's yours is mine. Anyway, in answer to your question, you do know what you're doing here. You're being a dad.'

'A crap dad. A deadbeat dad,' I mutter. 'Does it sound rubbish to say that I don't want to be here? That I didn't ask for any of this?' I whine.

Tom gives a loud belch and rubs his stomach. 'No, it doesn't sound rubbish,' he says. 'But it does sound childish. You're the adult now, Em, so you have to grow up. You're a dad, whether you like it or not, so you have to get on with it. What is it Dad used to say? "Time to be a man." He'd say that every time he gave me a good shove onto the football pitch.'

'Me too,' I say, not adding that I used to think, You'd know all about that, wouldn't you?, when he'd urge me on, imagining the look of hurt on his face and my feeling of shame and triumph. Tom thinks that Dad is just an ordinary guy who spends his time at work, in the greenhouse or at Gaelic matches, slightly semi-detached from the rest of us for reasons he doesn't question.

Mind you, Tom's right, of course: I am being childish. But I suddenly long to be back in my office in the Department of Fisheries, where the only decent thing was the view, watching my colleague Maurice pick his nose or David refuse to fax a report over to the minister's office because it was 'outside mandated working hours'. I used to think I could die in the department, could have a heart attack or a stroke at my desk, and be found, months later, slumped across a book of rod permits with no one having noticed my demise. The Department of Fisheries was the end of the road, a place where good men went to die (there wasn't a single woman), and which I find myself suddenly, unaccountably longing for. For the comfort of it, the familiarity, the sense that nothing unexpected would ever occur within its walls. There was a safety in that. Now, everything is uncertain, the future I'd planned – to use all of that spare time to do good work, to be an up-and-coming poet, one to look out for, then to win a major prize and have everyone talking about me – has vanished.

'Look, come and get drunk with me tonight,' Tom says. 'A crowd of us are off to the Spinning Wheel. Forget about everything for a few hours, and then tomorrow get up and get on with it.'

'Ah, Christ, not the Spinning Wheel,' I say. 'That place is like the feckin' Ballroom of Romance, full of Bridies and Liams all longing for the Old Country.'

'You're just a snob.' Tom laughs. 'You think you're Byron.'

'Well, maybe that's not such a bad thing. At least Byron didn't hang around the Spinning Wheel looking for a shift,' I reply, more tartly than I'd intended.

'No, he didn't, he just hung around with that Shelley fella, contracting syphilis in the process,' Tom replies.

'And writing some of the greatest poetry of the time – in fact, any time,' I say rather pompously.

He doesn't answer for a moment, just opens the fridge door and examines the contents, pulling a carton of milk out, putting it to his lips and glugging it. Why do all builders have to glug milk like that? I think. It's barbaric, like they're apes, not men. And Tom, of all people. He was a tiny, scrawny boy with a 'weak chest', as Mum used to put it, and I used to fight his battles for him, standing in front of him in the schoolyard to protect him from that little shit

Tony Convery, but now he could wipe Tony Convery out and I'm the one who needs someone to stand in front of him, to fight his battles for him. The thought makes me feel ashamed. Tom is right, I am a child. Mum had made me promise to keep an eye on him when I'd set out for London: 'he's only twenty, Emmett, God knows what might happen to him'. If only she knew, even though Tom's only been here for a year, it's been the other way around.

Tom gives a massive belch, putting the milk carton down on the counter, making space for it in between the pile of unwashed dishes and the half-open tins of baked beans. 'Big brother, I'm pulling your leg. C'mon, I'll buy you the first pint, seeing as I feel sorry for you.'

He's not pulling my leg at all, but I decide to let it drop. 'Thanks, but you won't need to. I've found a job.'

'Yeah?'

'It's in a bookshop.'

He stands up, buttoning the top button on his Levi's, patting his backside then looking around for his wallet. I'm waiting for his response, as if I expect his approval. Eventually he sighs. 'For God's sake, Emmett.'

'For God's sake what?'

'Could you not be a bit practical for once? How are you going to raise a family on that? Bet the pay's crap.'

'It is, compared to you with your hod-carrying and brick-laying, but at least I won't have to kill myself day after day, Paddy Irishman. I won't end up with shot knees and a stoop at thirty-five.' I make it sound like a joke, but both of us know it's not funny. Tom has always found my ambitions silly. 'You're just a dreamer, Em,' he used to say, 'and dreamers don't get anywhere.' I'd thought at the time that it depended on what you'd define by 'anywhere'. Now, I'm beginning to wonder if he has a point.

He picks up his discarded Y-fronts and lobs them at me. 'When I have a big house overlooking Galway Bay, you won't be calling me Paddy Irishman, that's for sure,' he says.

A big house on Galway Bay is the last thing on earth that I want, I think, ducking as the pants come flying past me. I want something else. Something very different. In the meantime, I content myself with picking them up and lobbing them back at him. 'Fuck off.'

'Fuck off yourself. Now, let's go and get drunk.'

'Gladly, even if it is the bloody Spinning Wheel. Why can't we go to the Coach and Horses or somewhere interesting – we might see Francis Bacon or Nick Cave, someone worth seeing.'

'Is Francis Bacon going to drop his knickers for me after a few sherries and a kebab?' Tom says.

'For God's sake,' I say. And then, 'Quite possibly', and we both guffaw with laughter. Then I think for a moment and say, 'You know, I think you'll meet someone good tonight. I have a feeling about it. And I don't mean your usual,' I add.

'Fuck's sake, not the psychic routine again.' Tom snorts, punching me in the arm. 'I just want a ride, that's all. I'm not like you, brother. I don't believe in love.' He laughs, shoving his wallet into his back pocket and pulling on a jacket.

'Oh, you do,' I say. 'Just you wait and see. You used to be a bit of a dreamer yourself, little brother.'

His cheeks flush and for a moment, he's silent, before saying, 'Yeah, well, dreams don't get you anywhere. I learned that the hard way.'

The silence goes on for a bit too long, while I decide whether to ask him what he means, then, cravenly, decide not to press it. Not now, when order is almost restored between the two of us. Let's leave it for another day, I think. 'First round's on me, on account of my new high-flying job.'

'Now you're talking,' he says, thumping me on the shoulder.

I was right, of course. I always am, I think, much later that night, as I lie on the sofa in my sleeping bag, head pleasantly spinning from one too many pints with whiskey chasers – it's a blessing and a curse.

We had hardly sat down in the Spinning Wheel, the two of us hunched over our pints, when two girls made a beeline for us, sliding in beside us on the plush banquette seats. Two grand big girls from Roscommon, a nurse and a teacher, who seemed to want to take command of the situation, getting Tom to buy them both drinks and subjecting us to a barrage of questions. I felt like I was being assessed – and not even very subtly. They'd obviously decided which one of us each liked, because Dympna, the nurse, waylaid Tom in conversation while Tracey, the teacher, a big blonde girl with a scattering of freckles across her nose and round blue eyes, which made her look like one of those dolls that closes its eyes when you lay it down, subjected me to the full CV check. Thankfully, she quickly realised that she was wasting her time. 'A bookshop?' she said, when I told her where I was going to be working, wrinkling her nose as if there was suddenly a bad smell in the room. I was clearly not a marriage prospect. But when Tom looked over her head at me and made a face, I at least tried, asking her where she worked and weren't kids really interesting.

'God, not the little knackers I work with,' she guffawed. 'They've been dragged up, not brought up, let me tell you – honestly, the language out of some of them – all "facking" this and "facking" that. And some of the foreign ones – they come in the door without being able to speak a word of English, and all you can do with them is sit them somewhere where they don't get in the way too much because they hold all of the other kids back.'

'Oh, I like the mix of kids in classes here,' I heard myself say prissily. 'My daughter—' I began, but I didn't get the chance to get any further because at the mention of the word Tracey was up and off that seat like a greyhound out of a trap. I couldn't help myself – I gave a small smirk as she disappeared off to the bar, where she didn't have to wait long before a fine young man in a Mayo jersey slunk over to her. Five minutes later, they were snogging with a vigour I found impressive.

'What the hell did you say to her?' Tom said when Dympna went to the ladies', winking at Tom as she scuttled off.

'Nothing,' I protested. 'She was talking about the kids she teaches – like a fascist, I might add – and I just said that Misty liked school, that's all …'

'You mentioned Misty?'

'Eh, yeah.'

'For fuck's sake. What woman wants to know that the shift she's going to have is already a parent? It's not exactly conducive to getting your leg over, is it?'

'Ooh, "conducive". Aren't you the wordsmith?' I said, trying to deflect Tom's accusation, realising that I had used my daughter as a weapon – classy.

'Fuck off.'

'Anyway, when you take Dympna home, you won't be worried about things being conducive,' I began, thinking that Tom would find it hilarious – one-night stands being his thing, after all, but instead, he just looked at his pint.

'What did I tell you?' I said.

'What did I tell you what?'

'I told you you'd meet someone tonight. It was as fate decreed. '"Men, at some time, are masters of their fates. The fault, dear Brutus, is not in our stars …"'

'And he's off,' Tom said, but his cheeks flushed very slightly.

'Don't rush it,' I found myself saying. 'If it really matters.'

'Thanks for the advice.' He smiled, twirling a beermat, then flipping it down onto the table. 'But it's not what you think.'

'Right.' I said nothing further – I didn't need to – and when Dympna came back, a fresh layer of foundation and slick of lipstick on, I said that I needed an early night. I wondered if I'd be seeing Dympna a couple of hours later anyway, with, as Tom would put it, 'a few sherries' and a bag of curry chips inside her.

I didn't see her. And when I asked Tom as he stumbled around in the kitchen in the early hours, he muttered something about her living with her aunty. I knew better than to say more – Tom must really be taking her seriously if he hadn't just taken her home to bounce around on the bed.

I settle down in my sleeping bag again, Bran a midget-sized hot-water bottle on my feet, and I think blearily that maybe I'm beginning to come to terms with this new life of mine. I did the right thing by Amanda and Misty coming here, but I did it because it was the right thing, not because it was a next step in my life. Still, I suppose that was the manly thing to do: to shoulder the responsibility, to get on that football pitch of life and score, even if it meant 'putting the dreams away' as Dad said. Maybe this is adulthood, I think, as my eyes droop closed: putting to one side the day-dreaming, the looking out of the window and wondering, the hoping and wishing, the pouring out of your soul onto a blank sheet of A4, your future a great unknowable ahead of you. I lie there, listening to the Tube rattle in the distance, a fight between two drunks beneath my window, and I think about all of the days to come and wonder if they will all look the same, just as they did for my father in his time, the rituals of home, work, then home again, played out over and over again. As I think about it, my heartbeat quickens. That'd make a man panic. Maybe that's why – but then I stop myself. Why nothing. It was all his own fault. I told myself I would never be like him, and I won't be.

I think suddenly of the girl in the bookshop. The girl with the baby, disappearing into the gloom. I shake my head and close my eyes and try to find sleep again.

5.

God, that was a disaster, I think, as I let myself in the door to Tom's flat, throwing my satchel on the floor. After the longest two weeks of my entire life, I'm determined that I am never, ever going to work in that place again. Of course, I have no choice and will return to work in Hell the day after tomorrow, my solitary day off in a fortnight, but pretending I do gives me a psychological boost.

The only good thing about Farrell's Bookshop is the senior bookseller, Muriel, I think, as I slump onto the sofa, removing my shoes and lying back to close my eyes for a few blissful moments' peace. I allow an image of her in her black polo neck to form in my mind. Not the best choice for the ample-busted, I think, as I recall her jiggling across to her office – I read that in an article somewhere

– but fashion's loss is my gain, I think mistily, deciding that, for me, she will always be Betty Boop. Bran comes over to me, jumps on my chest and yaps repeatedly, before pressing his nose into my chin.

'All right,' I say grumpily, pushing myself up off the sofa. I shuffle into the kitchen and extract a bowl from the pile of unwashed crockery filling the sink, give it a quick rinse, then empty the little can of very posh dog food I'd bought for him at great expense into it. I'd found a pet shop at the bottom of Holloway Road on my way home at the end of my first week in Farrell's, having extracted Bran from his hiding place in my satchel and walked him through the rush-hour streets, gaining admiring glances from old ladies. 'Aww, inee cute,' one of them had said, stopping to admire him. You have him then, I'd thought miserably, as I'd nodded and lied about him being a handsome devil while he'd stood there, tail swishing, basking in the glow.

To get to the counter of the pet shop, we'd had to make our way through a narrow corridor piled high with glass tanks, each one containing a snake or unpleasant and lethal-looking arachnid. I thought about turning around but found that I couldn't in the too-tight space, so had no choice but to keep moving towards the whip-thin man behind the counter with a face like a fox to ask him what a minute dog like Bran would eat.

'Oh, you wouldn't want to give him just anything,' the man said, as I held him up. 'Aww, cute little fella, aren't you?' He chucked Bran under the chin. Bran is not cute – those bug eyes and that squinty little face are not cute. 'Did you get him from a breeder?'

'Why – what is he?'

'He's a cross, I'd say. Pom and long-haired Chihuahua, but bred that way. Fine specimen.'

What's a Pom? I wondered, thinking of one of those little round tufts that people wear on hats.

'Well, I found him on the street. He must have strayed. In fact,' I said, putting Bran down in the hope that he wouldn't hear me, 'I'm looking for his owner. I can't keep him because I work all day and, well, it's expensive to keep a dog.'

The man looked at me as if I'd said I was going to chop Bran up into little bits and feed him to the pigeons. 'He's only little,' he tried.

'I know, and he's nice ... but I can't.'

'Give me your number. If anyone asks, I'll ring you,' he said, lips pursed.

I left the shop with a collar and lead, three squeaky toys and a pack of tins of dog food with a picture of a tiny Yorkie on the front. 'Your dog deserves the best,' the slogan said on each tin.

That stuff cost me twenty quid, I think now, as Bran chases a squeaky chicken around the kitchen, grabbing it and making ear-splitting shrieks as he chews it. Now I only have eighty whole pounds left in the world, which, after paying Tom for my bed and board, amounts to about a tenner left for the rest of this week. Thank God Farrell's pays weekly – although I'll be lucky to last there much longer.

'What does the word 'bookshop' conjure in your mind?' I ask myself as I put a couple of rashers on the frying pan. Now, let me see, I think – a haven of warmth, light spilling out onto the street, a little welcome sign in the window? I'd look in and see a lovely table with books neatly arranged on it, a tantalising display calling me in. I'd push the door and a little bell would clang, and then I'd find myself inside, in the hush, like a church. I'd browse the lovely – clean – shelves filled with books, and discover all kinds of literary gems, and I'd pick one and flick through the pages, admiring the prose. 'Oh, you like that one,' the bookseller would say, having materialised beside my left shoulder. 'Have you tried … ?' and he or she would lead me to some undiscovered literary masterpiece. I would return home, a package under my arm, and spend the afternoon in glorious peace, just reading.

I sigh as I push the fantasy away. Instead, Farrell's reminds me of the summer job I'd had cleaning at the local mental hospital back home, pushing a mop back and forth across the tiles with a slick of Dettol, the strength of which had made me gag, as a succession of poor souls passed me by, moaning and muttering and yelling, or else completely silent, staring out of the window at the sheep in the fields. I'd always had the feeling that nobody wanted them, that they'd been cast out – it wasn't true, of course: I could see the love in the grey faces of the visitors in the waiting room on Sundays – but it felt as if those people were completely alone in the world. Farrell's feels the same way – as if it's full of people who have been rejected by life, washed up on the third floor to be told to eff off by Fabrice, my boss, a loathsome little Frenchman full of acid-tongued remarks and general misanthropy. I have no idea how I'm going to stand him for any length of time. And he has a complete obsession with stock-taking: the first '*travail*' he made me do was to do a complete count of origami books in a giant ledger he produced from under the counter. There were forty-three, and I had to fill in each name in my best, primary-school copperplate. When I returned it, feeling quite pleased with myself, he put a big line through it in green biro. '*Dommage*,' he said. 'You missed two. Do it again.'

I'm wondering about ways in which I might kill him, when the phone rings. It never really rings; Tom usually arranges his social life with a series of meetings on the Holloway Road, announcing to the person that he's bumped into that a crowd of them are heading to the Galtymore or the Swan on Saturday night, and somehow it gets transmitted through the Irish bush telegraph. The only other people who use the phone are Mum and Dad. I suck in a breath and pick up the phone, ready to hear my mother's voice, to put a positive spin on my new life. 'I've found a job!' I try, before picking up the receiver, to make sure I get the tone right.

'Hello!' I say breezily.

There's a long silence, followed by some rustling and muttering and then my mother bellows down the line, 'Hello, son!' For some reason 'trunk calls', as she calls them, make her shout, as if she has to cover the miles between home and here physically.

Of course, the minute I hear her voice, I can't help myself. 'Oh, Mum,' I say sadly, all notions of breeziness forgotten.

'Ah, what is it, son?' Mum roars – so loudly that I have to hold the phone away from my ear.

'It's nothing,' I say. 'It's just …' and then the tears come and I find myself blubbing away like a five-year-old.

There's a silence at the other end of the phone, then I hear her stage whisper. 'I don't *know* what's wrong with him, Francis – would you ever let me find out?'

'Fine,' I hear Dad say in the background. 'You'll get more sense out of him.'

'I will, now will you go and put on the kettle and leave me in peace.' She clears her throat then and says, a little more softly, 'Emmett, love, what is it?'

By this stage, my sobbing has subsided a bit because Bran, alarmed at the sounds coming from his master, has decided to sit on my foot and lick the leg of my jeans. Strangely, it makes me feel a tiny bit better, even if it does make my skin crawl. 'Will you stop it?' I say when the sensation becomes too unpleasant.

'Stop what?'

'Sorry, it's just the dog.'

'You have a dog? Do you not think you have enough on your plate, pet?'

Yes, I think miserably. I have quite enough, thank you, but then Bran looks up at me with his bug eyes and his little bottom quivers on my foot. 'He's fine. Anyway, I'm just looking after him while his owner is … away.' His owner is never coming back, I add to myself, as no-one has responded to the notices Misty and I put up in all of the local shops – but you never know. I might get lucky.

'Love, are you feeling all right. Are you sick?' There's more muttering. 'He's sick. Maybe he should go to the doctor – sure aren't they free over there? I'm not interfering, Francis, and, yes, I know he's a grown man but—' She returns to the phone. 'Is it Misty, love? Is that it?'

'No, well, yes, it's just …'

'Tell me, pet.'

I always could tell Mum everything, I think, feeling my heart lift a little for the first time this miserable day. I begin with the awfulness of my day in Farrell's. 'It's not the mess,' I tell her. 'It's the smell. The carpet must be a million years old and it's clearly infested with something and then there's microwave food at lunchtime. Honestly, it makes my stomach heave.'

'You always did have a delicate stomach, son,' Mum says helpfully, as I continue my litany of the awfulness of Farrell's. Hardly a single book on a shelf, like an old Soviet supermarket – dusty, empty shelves, under white plastic signs that hang on chains from the polystyrene ceiling. I had never seen so many books in my entire life, big tottering heaps of them on a bewildering array of subjects, from the obvious ones, like World Wars I and II, to the Crimea, Sebastopol, the Boer War. 'Dad would have loved it,' I say to Mum. 'Remember how he used to love *Zulu*?'

'Ah, he did, the old bore,' Mum says. 'Used to go on and on about Michael Caine and Stanley Baxter and being outdone by all those fellows with big spears, and, sure, weren't the Irish the same, able to outdo the Brits. Honest to God,' she says. 'Change the record.'

I smile to myself, thinking that saying things aloud makes them somehow less dismal. I wonder if it's because of what happened with Dad that I've always found it so easy to talk to Mum. It wouldn't take Freud to work that out, I think, as Mum tells me that it won't be that bad when I get used to it. 'Just give it time, son.'

She's filling me in on parish gossip then, about how Gay Hennessey, the farmer up the road, still lets his cattle roam everywhere and she found one of them staring in the kitchen window at her last week, but I'm not really listening. For some reason, I'm back at home, in the kitchen, on the morning Dad left. I can still remember it because he had to climb into the attic to get down the only suitcase we possessed, putting his socks, which Mum had folded, and his Y-fronts and his mesh vests into it, along with two pairs of slacks and four shirts. Mum was running around helping him, even though relations had been frosty for the previous month.

I was told that Dad was going on a business trip. The fact that Dad had never taken a business trip in his life – his job in the Roads Department of Galway County Council didn't require much foreign travel – was explained away. Dad had to go to the UK to look at roads, apparently. 'Near Birmingham,' Mum had explained helpfully. I was only eight, but I wasn't stupid. I knew why Dad was leaving and I also knew that it was all Daisy's fault. If she hadn't said anything, we could both have kept quiet about what we'd seen. We could both have just let it eat away at us – couldn't we? – instead of letting it all out, the way she had, over cornflakes and those little French rolls that Bridget used to love to put on the table, even though she believed eating them was a sin. I wonder what would have happened if Daisy hadn't looked around at the assembled adults and said, her mouth full of cornflakes: 'I saw Mum kissing Francis last night.' The silence that followed was deafening, and then … I close my eyes at the memory.

'So, how's Misty?' The question brings me back into the present, into Tom's living room and the rumble of a truck outside the window. Why on earth am I thinking about Daisy now? I wonder, when I've so successfully buried all memory of her. I can smell vanilla in my nostrils again and I wonder if I'm losing my marbles.

'Hmm?'

'Don't "hmm" your mother. Tell me how it's going. It can't be easy, son,' she says softly.

'It's not,' I reply honestly, because there's no point in lying to Mum. 'She's just very … well, one minute she's giggling and laughing away; the next minute, she's giving me the cold shoulder. I don't know what to do, really.'

'It'll just take time, son. She's known that fellow, Roland – is that his name? – her whole life. As far as she's concerned, he's her dad. I know that Misty wanted to meet her real dad, but she still has to work out where you fit in her life.'

And I need to work out where I fit in hers, I think. 'Thanks for the pep talk, Mum. I feel a bit better now. Sorry for blubbing at you.'

'Sure, what are mothers for?' There's a pause and then, 'Do you think I'd be able to meet my granddaughter soon?'

My stomach lurches. I've been fooling myself that this is somehow not a permanent arrangement, but if Mum comes over, well, then we'd really be family, and I'm not sure how I feel about that, deep down.

'Of course,' I find myself saying. 'When things have settled down.'

'Lovely,' Mum says, and I ignore the slightly hurt tone. She continues, more brightly, 'That bookshop will be grand – we all have to start somewhere, you know. You were only mouldering away in that civil service job,' she adds. 'It's no place for a young man who's going places, like yourself.'

'Going places.' I give a snort of laughter.

'Oh, you can laugh, but I know I'm right. When I'm standing behind you at that Booker Prize ceremony, you'll thank me for keeping the faith.'

'Thanks, Mum, I appreciate that,' I say, not pointing out to her that the Booker Prize is for novels. The T.S. Eliot would do me, but then I'd have to actually write poems to win it, I think morosely. I decide to change the subject. 'So, how's Dad?'

There's a brief pause. 'Ah, you know. Under my feet all the time. He was up on the roof yesterday checking that all of the tiles were in place. For God's sake, we only had it redone last year. It's the retirement. It's killing him. And it's killing me,' she mutters, then there's more rustling and she says, 'What? The milk is where I put it. In the fridge.' There's tutting and muttering and then she's back.

'Listen, love, the oul eejit couldn't find something if it was two inches in front of his face. I'll have to go.' She sighs heavily.

'Mum? Is everything OK?'

'It's grand,' she says firmly. 'I'll call your brother on Saturday. Will you tell him? And he's not to be in bed with one of his girlfriends the way he was the last time.'

'Right.' I quell the urge to laugh.

'Do not make fun of your mother. Your brother has some unhealthy habits. He might be eight years younger than you, but it's time he settled down and stopped gallivanting, but it's not off the stones he licked it,' she says darkly. 'Now, go, and look after yourself.'

The phone is put down with a heavy thud. Mum always did end phone conversations abruptly, slamming the receiver down as if it had given her an electric shock, and the memory makes me smile as I go back into the kitchen and put the heat on under the pan for my rashers and sausages. I'll treat myself to an egg, I think, because I deserve it. I'm feeling a bit better now and my stomach, which was heaving, is now emitting a hopeful grumble. Time to eat.

I have the egg in my hand and am about to crack it into the pan when the phone rings again. For God's sake, I just want to eat my dinner, I think, as I go to pick it up. 'Mum, could I call you back in a minute? I'm just about to eat.'

'Erm, hi. It's Amanda.'

'I know,' I say, unable to hide my surprise. What's Amanda doing, ringing me on a Monday night?

'So … how are you?' She sounds a bit breathless, as if she's been running up the stairs.

'I'm fine. What's the matter? Is it Misty?'

'No, well, yes … listen, I wonder could we talk?'

'We're talking,' I say, eyeing my fry-up on the pan and wondering how quickly I can scoff it.

'No, I mean … could you drop over?'

'What, now? I've just got home. I could have come after work if I'd known.'

'I'm sorry,' Amanda says mildly. 'Would it be very inconvenient? Maybe you could read Misty a bedtime story. You can even bring that dog if you still have it.' I can practically see her nose wrinkle in distaste.

'Well, I'm just about to eat,' I say.

'Please? It's important.'

'Oh, OK. Give me a half an hour.' I put the phone down and wonder what my mother would say if she could hear me, whether she'd tell me to 'get up the yard', with my selfish behaviour.

The thought puts me off my fry-up and I give Bran a sausage, even though the man in the pet shop warned me that small breeds have irritable bowels. He scoffs it, of course, and then sits on the floor, an avid look on his face. 'That's all,' I say. He looks disappointed and scuffles off, while I scrape the rest into the bin and wearily put my shoes and coat on. 'C'mon,' I say to him, attaching the new silver lead that I'd bought in the pet shop to his collar. I leave a note for Tom: 'Gone to Misty's. Back later,' and head out into the night.

I could get the bus, I think – after all, I walked the mile and a half home, but it's a crisp, dry night, so 'what harm?', as Dad would say. We walk past the Odeon cinema, where I'd gone to see *The Usual Suspects* but had had to leave halfway through because of the noise levels and the smell of Chinese food wafting from the seat in front of me. I'd seen the man climbing the steep steps, plastic bag in hand, but had thought it was simply popcorn or chocolate until I'd seen the cardboard containers appear, watching him carefully undo the foil lid, a smell of chicken chow mein filling my nostrils.

Then we pass the bakery, which makes the most deliciously artificial macaroons, full of almond essence and jam, and Marks & Spencer, where a woman had regaled me with unwelcome details of her salmonella infection while we'd queued at the deli counter.

We walk past the post office and then the casino, which always has a nervous-looking man huddled outside, smoking, then down past the Nag's Head shopping centre. It feels like a uniquely north London establishment, down at heel, grubby, with no aspirations to be anything very much. At home, a new shopping centre would be called something out of a fairy story, shiny and glittering, full of promise; here, it's merely a place to shop, women with pull-along trolleys shuffling in and out of the dingy shops, although Misty loves the shoe shop in the corner, where nothing is made out of actual leather. She made me buy her a pair of pink plastic shoes, which Amanda told me that she wore to bed that night, before asking me not to buy her anything else without discussing it first. The Admiral Nelson is our last stop before turning the corner onto the green space of Highbury Fields. It's a huge cavern of a place, karaoke blasting out the doors. Tom tells me that it's a favourite IRA haunt, middle-aged men hunched over the bar, discussing bombing campaigns. I see plenty of Irishmen around here – faces that I'd see walking up the Main Street towards me at home, cheeks red, noses a mass of broken blood vessels, a little sway as they pass. They look respectable from a distance, in their Donegal tweed jackets and slacks, but when you get closer, you notice that the hem of the slacks is frayed and the tweed jacket, probably given to them as a present when they left home thirty years before, is grubby and stained. They are lost souls, wandering up and down the Holloway Road.

When I get off the Tube at the end of Amanda's street, the air seems cleaner, the shops brighter. There are no dingy places here, nobody is talking to themselves on street corners, there are no IRA pubs. Instead, there's a lovely neighbourhood feel about the place, flowers in the gardens, bins neatly stacked inside the front gates, medium-sized cars parked on the kerb. There's a little block of flats, with a cluster of cherry trees outside it, and beside it a row of those garages that they love here and a little park, with a fountain in the middle and a duck pond and a little farm in the corner, where Misty likes to go sometimes. I walk up the row of lovely Victorian houses, the only sound a cat meowing, at which Bran gives a little bark. 'Quiet,' I command, walking up to Amanda's front door, congratulating myself on how he seems to understand me. We have a symbiotic relationship, this little ratty dog and me.

When Amanda answers the door this time, she seems nervous. 'Thanks so much for coming,' she gushes. She doesn't normally gush, and when I put Bran down on the floor, she doesn't even wince but instead bends down and gives him a nervous pat. 'Hello, little doggy,' she says. We stand in the hall, the two of us, for a moment, her clutching her expensive cardigan around her. I know it's expensive because I saw the woman who makes them featured in one of the Sunday newspapers – she puts a velvet border on perfectly ordinary cardigans and charges two hundred quid for them.

I remember to remove my shoes in honour of the thick cream carpet and then say, 'I'll go and say goodnight to Misty.'

'Sure, of course,' she says nervously. 'I'll be in the kitchen when you come down.'

'Great.'

'Right. Good,' she says, disappearing down the hall, under the tuning-fork chandelier and into the kitchen. I hover for a moment before saying, 'C'mon, Bran, let's go and see Misty.'

I stand at the top of the stairs trying to remember which room is Misty's. I was only invited to see it once, Misty solemnly leading the way into a shrine to all things pink, a pink canopy over the bed and a fluffy pink duvet cover, and now that I see a faint pink light spilling out onto the landing, I remember. I hesitate for a moment before knocking. 'Misty ... there's a visitor to see you.' I mean Bran, not me.

Misty is sitting up in her pink bed, in the marshmallow glow of her bedside lamp, and she gives me a careful look, but when she sees Bran, she squeals, lifting him up onto her bed and hugging him, pressing her face into his fur. 'Oh, Bran, I missed you,' she says softly, and he licks her chin, that faraway look in his eyes. He missed her too, it's clear. They were made for each other.

'Misty,' I begin. 'You know that I found Bran ...' I have to have this conversation sooner or later, I think – the longer it goes on, the harder it'll be to say goodbye to him.

'Yes, aren't you so lucky, Emmett, and when Mummy and Daddy go to Jamaica, he'll be able to come here and live with me!' She jumps up in the bed with excitement, in her Barbie pyjamas.

'Right ...' I say, thinking that Amanda and Roland must be going on holidays. 'That's nice. We'll have to ask them, OK? Now, I brought a book for us to read,' I say, lifting my bag up on the bed and pulling the book of Irish myths and legends out of it.

It was supposed to be a Christmas present, but when Amanda had rung me, I'd shoved it in my bag. I needed the comfort of it, whatever about Misty. To remember my own mother reading the same stories to me, years before, from a big green hardback, which, when she'd opened it, emitted a smell of dust and damp, rust-coloured dots of mould scattered over the line drawings of huge men with swords and women with long, flowing hair. Mum had told me once that she read stories to me because she wanted me to be better than her. 'I never got the chance to go to college or to read books – they weren't part of my life, but I want them to be part of yours,' she'd said. And I now want them to be part of Misty's, I think, as I look around her bedroom, with its scatter cushions and fluffy nightlight, and complete absence of reading material.

'Right, you choose,' I say, opening the contents page and helping her to pronounce the names, 'Diarmuid agus Gráinne', 'Niamh agus Oisín', 'Tír na nÓg'. She repeats them after me and then giggles. 'Geermid ahgus Grawnya', and she falls around laughing.

'Don't mock your inheritance,' I say.

'What does that mean?' The look on her face is eager, and although I know she's only half-understood what I said, the idea feels strange to me – that I am her inheritance, and my parents and theirs, and on and on. The line that stretches back and connects me to my past connects her too. Because she's mine.

It's obvious, of course, but overwhelming and, for a moment, I'm silent, till I slap my knees in jaunty-uncle fashion and announce, 'I know, let's read the Children of Lir, you'll like that one.' And I open the page and begin to read the story. Misty finds Bodb Dearg hilarious, and every time his name is mentioned she collapses, but as the story goes on, and the children are turned into swans and have to live on the water for nine hundred years, her face grows still and she puts a thumb in her mouth, stroking Bran's fur gently with the other hand. Finally, when the priest turns them back into humans, who can't live because they are so old, she takes in a little short breath, before letting it out again slowly.

'It's a bit sad,' I say. 'Sorry about that.'

She's silent for a long time, thinking. 'If I had a brother or sister, would I stay with them for ever so they wouldn't have to be alone?'

'I'd say you would.'

'Yes, I would. But I don't have a brother or sister, so I'd stay with Bran for ever instead, and we'd fly over London and look down at all the people,' she says wistfully. 'I think it wouldn't be sad at all. I think we'd be happy that we'd be together,' she says as she reaches out and pulls him gently to her.

Oh, God. There is no way on earth that I can get rid of that dog now, I think. Not unless I'm planning to lose my daughter into the bargain. Why the hell didn't I just step over him and keep on walking?

'Or maybe you might take a friend?' I say.

She shakes her head. 'Sophie was my friend, but she isn't any more, so I denif— denif—'

'Definitely.'

'Definitely won't take her flying.'

'Oh, that's a pity. What happened?'

'She wanted to be friends with Hannah instead,' she says sadly. 'When I was in Miss Hedge's class, we sat together all the time and I'd give her my hummus, because it's disgusting, and she'd give me her cheese sandwiches, but when I went into Miss Grace's class,

Sophie sat with Hannah and now they share their lunches. And I don't have anyone any more.' She looks at me with her big, round eyes and I put an arm around her and give her a little squeeze. To my surprise, she leans into me, lifting a hand up to suck her thumb.

'You do have someone,' I say. 'You have Bran. And you have me. That's two people.'

'Bran isn't a person, silly.' She giggles, and then she adds, 'and anyway, you can't be my friend because you're my father.'

'Oh. Why not? Is there a rule against it?'

She says nothing for a bit, eventually shaking her head. I can guess what she's thinking: that I can't be her friend because she doesn't really know me – maybe I'll be like Sophie and decide to have my lunch with someone else.

'I could probably learn to play Barbies,' I say, attempting to change the subject. 'I'm very good at brushing their hair. Watch.' I reach over to the elaborate Barbie dressing table beside the bed and extract one of the row of dolls from her perch, along with a tiny blue hairbrush. She's wearing a red-and-yellow striped ski suit, a pair of white goggles with blue plastic lenses and two bright white ski boots. I proceed to stroke the yellow nylon hair, pulling the brush downwards, as the little bristles catch in the tangles. Eventually, the brush gets stuck and I have to tug at it, tangling the brush further in her hair. Who knew that brushing Barbie hair could be so difficult? I give it a yank, but the brush just gets embedded further in the hair. I stifle the desire to swear.

'Not like that!' Misty says, snatching the doll from me. 'Emmett, you are rubbish at this.'

'Well, you show me.'

She sighs and puts Barbie down on the bed, gently removing the strands of hair from the brush, then lifting it out. 'That's better.' And then she pulls the brush gently through Barbie's hair.

'I don't think I'm very good at that. I'm sorry.'

'That's OK. Maybe you're good at other things … you tell good stories.'

'I do.' I nod. Then there's a little pause while Misty sucks her thumb. She looks tired and I persuade her to snuggle down in the bed, promising her that Bran can stay until I leave. As I pull the duvet around her, I say, 'You'll make a new friend soon, I know you will. You're a lovely girl and it won't take long before someone else sees that.' As pep talks go, it's not amazing, but it's the best I can do. I haven't had much experience.

'Did you have any friends, Emmett?'

'In school?'

'No, anywhere.'

I know what she's getting at – that somewhere out there, there might be a new friend for her. That those little madams aren't her only option. But still, the question blindsides me. 'Erm, yes. Yes, I did.'

'What was he like?' She sits up in bed now, ready to hear my story.

'Oh, it wasn't a he. It was a she.'

'Was she your girlfriend?'

'Oh, no. We were only eight. But she was my best friend in the world.'

'And did she go off with someone else?'

'No, it wasn't like that,' I say.

'So, what was it like?'

Oh, God. I really don't want to answer, but I say, 'Well, we used to go on our holidays together, my mum and dad and me and her mum and dad and her. We used to play on the beach all day and build sandcastles and eat banana sandwiches and we used to have a den in the spare room, where we'd read comics and eat sweets …'

Misty is looking at me, eyes round with astonishment. 'Mummy doesn't let me eat sweets.'

'Well, we used to eat sweets until our tummies ached and read the *Beano* and war comics and pretend to be the Germans in their planes.' We used to make machine-gun noises and dive bomb each other, me swooping down from the bed onto the floor. '*Achtung*!' I'd shout. She loved the war games, mounting attacks in her Spitfire, spraying me with a hail of bullets. She wasn't a girly girl – no pink for her, I think, looking around Misty's bedroom.

'I'd like a friend to play with me every day,' Misty says sadly. 'But I have to go to classes. Mummy says I'll be pleased when I'm a famous ballerina one day, but I hate it.'

I pat the duvet gently, glad of the change of subject. 'Well, I'll ask Mummy if you can have a friend over some time, OK?'

'Thanks, Emmett,' Misty says sleepily.

'Now, time for bed,' I say, as Misty snuggles down beneath the duvet.

'Night night.'

'Night, Misty.'

Amanda isn't in the vast empty kitchen when I come downstairs, but the French doors are open to the garden, a chilly breeze blowing the gauzy curtains into the room. When I go outside to investigate, Amanda is sitting at the outdoor table, smoking. She's thrown a blanket over her, but her legs are jigging up and down with the cold.

'Misty's nearly asleep,' I say, pulling out a chair and sitting down. 'It's freezing out here.'

'Sorry. I don't like to smoke in the house.'

'I didn't know you smoked.'

'Only when I'm nervous,' she says, taking a deep pull and blowing smoke out into the air.

'What have you got to be nervous about?' I ask warily.

She takes another drag, fiddling with the cigarette packet with her other hand, turning it round and round on the table. I have to suppress the urge to put a hand out to stop her.

'How is work going?' she asks.

'Fine. Terrible.'

'Oh – why?'

I tell her about the curious clientele of Farrell's and having to smuggle Bran into work in my bag and pray that he wouldn't bark and the awful Fabrice, with his three-piece-suit country-gent look and mania for stocktaking – he'd made me do another inventory of the entire bonsai section, which was no joke because Farrell's has no fewer than a hundred books on the little wizened trees. I don't mention Betty, in case I let my ungentlemanly little fantasy out of the bag, but I let rip about the rest of the place and I'm expecting a nod of sympathy, but I'm a bit put out when she just roars with laughter. 'Oh, that's so funny, Emmett!'

'It's a fucking nightmare, is what it is,' I protest. 'In what way does it sound funny?'

'It's the way you tell stories,' she says. 'You always were hilarious,' she adds, more quietly. 'That's why I liked you so much – I'd never met anyone with a sense of humour like yours before.'

I don't know what Amanda's getting at. I don't want a trip down memory lane – it's too painful and so much time has passed and, anyway, Roland is a terrific guy, even if he seems to speak a foreign language sometimes.

Amanda sees my look of confusion and shrugs.

'What is it, Amanda? I'm sure you didn't call me because you wanted to talk about my sense of humour,' I say. 'I mean, I'm flattered and everything, but ...'

'Sorry. No. No, I didn't,' she replies, fiddling with the cigarette packet again. I shoot out a hand and place it over hers. It's freezing, a tiny collection of bones under the pale skin, like a bird. I give it a little squeeze, then take my hand away. 'So.'

'So ... I'll just come out with it then. Roland is going to Jamaica to develop these luxury beach huts. You know, the ones I was telling you about.'

I have no memory of luxury beach huts but say, 'Great, good for him.'

'Try to sound less sarcastic.'

'Sorry.'

'Anyway, he's asked me to go with him.'

'You should go. I'm sure the weather's lovely at this time of year – all that sea, and sun, and ... palm trees,' I finish.

'You've never been to Jamaica.' She smiles.

'Are you telling me that there's no sea or sun or palm trees?'

'There are all of those things,' she agrees.

'Well, what's the problem? Misty will love it. It'll be a great experience for her. I mean, I'll miss her, of course, because I'm only just getting to know her …'

I try not to sound too relieved, my mind spinning with possibilities. Would it be too late to go back to the Department of Fisheries – David said they'd keep my seat warm for me – but then, they have to, because it's the law, but can I seriously see myself sitting back at that desk? Or maybe I could get another job, I think, or even a grant for one of those writer's retreats …

'The thing is, I don't want to take Misty.'

I don't hear her at first because I'm not listening, my mind is somewhere far away from grim Holloway Road and here and Farrell's, and the life I've ended up in but didn't ask for – and then the words filter into my brain. 'You don't want to take Misty?'

'Erm, no.'

'Why not?'

Amanda sighs heavily. 'I don't want to disrupt her schooling and her routine.' The words sound reasonable enough, but something tells me that Amanda is hiding behind them.

'But she'll get used to it – don't they have schools in Jamaica? And besides, it's a fantastic opportunity for a child.'

She gives me a wry look. 'It isn't that simple.' She sighs heavily and opens the packet of cigarettes, taking one out and lighting it, puffing smoke into the icy night air. 'When I met Roland, I wasn't living here,' she says. 'I actually lived in a grotty little flat in Crouch End. I'd picked it in *Loot* because it was a nice neighbourhood and I thought it would be good for Misty, but the flat was awful – damp and cold – and I hardly had any money. When I'd run out, I'd just eat cornflakes – Misty always ate, of course … I had this terrible job' – she smiles – 'working in a school canteen, would you believe, and all the kids would come up and say nasty things and complain about the food and tell me to fuck off and I used to feel so guilty because I'd given up on my dreams. After Misty came along, none of it seemed important. You know the way it is.'

I nod, even though I don't.

'And then Misty got a bit older and I knew that I couldn't live like that any more. That I had to get my shit together and set a good example.' She's shivering, and I take off my coat and put it around her shoulders because it's the chivalrous thing to do, even though I'm bloody freezing. She looks at me for a moment, her eyes large and grey and clear – she always had lovely eyes – and says, 'Thanks.'

'Go on.'

'So I studied at night and I got a Master's degree in business, but then I realised that it was kind of useless because I didn't have any contacts – and it's all about contacts,' she says knowingly. 'Anyway, I did a law conversion course – not because I actually like it, but I thought it would give me some kind of direction. I mean, who ever wants to be a lawyer?' She rolls her eyes to heaven and smiles. 'That's where I met Roland. He was lecturing on contracts and … well … he's been great.' She blushes. 'Most of the time.'

I know, I think miserably. I have witnessed his greatness on more than one occasion and 'most of the time' looks pretty good from where I'm standing.

'And Misty loves him,' Amanda adds helpfully.

I'm silent, thoughts spinning around my head. Why did she never get in touch when things were so hard? Why did she try to manage on her own, in a dingy flat in Crouch End for all of those years? She could have made contact, I could have helped, I could have done something – could have stepped up, taken responsibility for my child and her mother. That's what men do, I thought – that's what my father did his whole life … But then my mind stops. My father didn't actually do that for his whole life – he fled from that responsibility too. Just once, but it was enough. Maybe the apple doesn't fall far from the tree, I think sadly.

'You didn't trust me,' I say finally. 'That's why you never got in touch.'

'Well, we were both so young,' she says kindly. 'And you were going to have this great literary career and I would only have held you back …'

'That's not true. I made a perfectly good job of holding myself back,' I say. 'I had all of this time and space, but I had nothing to write about. I found that I had all of that freedom, but it didn't matter because I had fuck all to say. I'd have been better off here, with you and Misty. I could at least have helped you.'

I'm not sure I really mean it and I also know that she picked Roland for a reason – a perfectly sensible reason – but she doesn't seem to be listening, staring out over the garden, over the dark shapes of the manicured rose bushes that a little man comes to tend every second Tuesday.

Then she turns to me. 'Emmett. You can help me now. I need you to look after Misty for me for a little while.'

I'm silent for a moment too long, so she fills in the space.

'Roland and I … well …' she looks as if she's about to say one thing, but then she decides on another. 'I want to make a go of it – just the two of us. I owe it to him. He's only ever known me and Misty and I feel that he deserves just to have me – just for a bit. And this development. It's huge for him – for us. There's a lot riding on it and, well, he needs me there, and I want to be there … and …'

'How long?'

Amanda's been fiddling with the cigarette lighter, but her head shoots up and her eyes widen at my tone. 'Two months. Maybe three.'

'Well, is it two or will it be nearer three because I need to know? I'll have to sort things with work and stuff.'

I'm well aware that I don't sound like a man who has been handed a golden opportunity to spend precious time with his newly found daughter, but someone who feels put upon, as if they've been given a burden they didn't ask for. 'Shame on you, son.' I can hear my mother's voice in my head. 'Shame on you.'

Amanda's all business now, standing up and pushing the chair in under the table. 'I understand. If it's too inconvenient, I'll just have to ask my mother, I suppose …'

I can see the hurt in the tight set of her chin, the muscle working in her jaw. I can see it in the way she holds herself bolt upright, attempting dignity in the face of insult and I wonder how she feels, knowing that her daughter's father is failing the test she set him. Already.

'Do it,' I say, more pleasantly this time. 'Go. It'll be good for you and Misty will be fine with me. I promise. You can trust me.'

She looks at me searchingly, her eyes locked on mine. She's asking a question that I'm not sure I can answer, so I take hold of the cigarette packet, tip the lid open and take out a cigarette, putting it to my lips. I accept the light she offers and I inhale so deeply that I start to cough and she has to bang me on the back.

'Emmett, are you all right?'

I nod, between gasps and coughs.

'Will you be all right?'

I nod. 'Of course I will – we will. Go. Have a wonderful time, be there for Roland and when you get back, we'll be waiting.'

6.

Roland has insisted that I drive his car while he's away. It's a bloody huge Mercedes and I haven't told him that I only have a learner's licence. When he made me sit in it the week before they went and 'give her a whirl', I had to pretend to be really interested, the way men are supposed to be, flicking the button to turn on the heated seats, feeling an uncomfortable sensation of warmth spreading under my rear end. Mum always told me I'd get piles if I sat on a heat source, I thought, as I turned the key and started the engine with a loud rumble. 'Bit less throttle, mate.' Roland grinned, peering in through the half-open window. What's 'less throttle'? I wondered.

I chugged off up the street in a series of jerky bunny-hops, reminding me of Dad's attempts to teach me to drive in the car park near the beach, hands gripping the seat, repeating 'find the biting point' over and over again, while I lifted my foot too quickly off the pedal and the car cut out. My efforts were all the more disappointing because Dad loved driving and, in spite of his fairly lowly position in Galway County Council, bought a new car every three years, courtesy of Tim Myler on the Dublin Road, and Mum and much later, Tom, would wait by the gate to see him driving up the road towards us in the latest model. As he came closer, he'd rev the engine and give a bip on the horn and Mum and I would clap our hands with excitement. 'Sacred Heart, Francis,' Mum would say, no matter what kind of car it was, 'would you not have bought something a bit less showy? You'd swear it was a Rolls-Royce!' But she'd laugh and her hair, which she wore long in those days, would swing around her face as she leaned in through the window to examine the upholstery.

'Time for a spin,' Dad would announce and we'd hop in. He always made sure to set off with a big roar of the engine and we'd all laugh and then the ditches and trees would fly by in a curtain of green as we zipped along the country roads, me sitting in the back – quite naturally without a seatbelt – watching the back of their heads as they sang along to a song on the radio, 'Song, Sung Blue' – Neil Diamond was a big favourite of Mum's and she'd always turn the volume up, her voice strong as she sang along. And then she'd look at Dad fondly and he'd look back at her and they'd exchange a smile.

I sure don't take after Dad, I thought as I ground the gears again, but Misty seemed to find it highly entertaining, sitting behind me, safely belted in, Bran on her lap, while I screeched to a halt at the corner, looking left and right and left again, just in case. After I'd done a slow circuit of the block, I returned in triumph to see

Roland standing on the footpath, waiting, trying to conceal the anxious look on his face.

'Make sure you give her a regular spin, will you, mate? Stops the battery going flat.'

I will never set foot in that car again, I thought when I got out, bum singed, sweat trickling down my back. It's just one more thing that I don't seem to be ready for, I thought later, another thing that makes you an adult – sweeping along the road in your manly car, indicating, cornering, reverse parking, without giving it a second thought. Because you're a grown-up, and that's what grown-ups do. Why do I find it all so hard? I wondered bleakly to myself the night before I moved in to Amanda and Roland's for my extended babysitting job.

Tom helped me to move my stuff from Holloway Road, piling it all into the back of a black cab, the contents of my life pushed into two bin liners, old socks and Y-fronts spilling out of the top. I packed my books into a suitcase, lining up the rows of John Montague and Stevie Smith, Ted Hughes and Seamus, of course. As I put each book in, it seemed to reproach me. 'Call yourself a poet?' Stevie declared from the front of her *Collected Poems*. I know, Stevie, I thought sadly. I'll do better when I get settled in – I promise. It's not easy to be a poet and a parent, I thought miserably. Stevie gave me the look I deserved , so I turned her over.

Tom and I squeezed in beside the bin bags, allowing Dympna, who was now Tom's girlfriend, to sit on the pull-down seat opposite us. It turned out that I'd been right – the two of them have been inseparable since that night at the Spinning Wheel. I never saw my 'date' again, but Dympna turned up the next day at the front door, fresh from a game of camogie for the London Lionesses, a big herd of girls who whack balls around a field in Camden on a Sunday morning. She came in to the flat, sniffed, made a face, then got to work. An hour later, the second of two washes was running in the machine, all traces of dirty underpants had been removed, a fresh pot of tea had been brewed and Tom and I found ourselves sitting in front of two plates of bacon, sausage and pudding.

'Told you,' I said, after Dympna had gone home later that day, having sat on the couch with Tom for the afternoon watching the *EastEnders* omnibus.

Tom said nothing, leaning back on the sofa, scratching himself.

'Well?' I said, trying to provoke him. He was normally all too easy to rouse, but this time, he just blinked fixedly at the TV, even though all that was on now was *Songs of Praise*. What's got into you? I thought. Maybe it's love.

'Ah, you know,' he said eventually, over the din of 'Jerusalem'. 'Time to do the respectable thing. Jesus, is there nothing else on?' He grabbed the remote and pointed it at the TV.

You sure aren't behaving like a man in love, I thought.

Still, Dympna turned up again the next night, and the two of them headed off to the Odeon with a bag of Chinese, confirming my prejudices about that place, and next thing she was sitting on the sofa or stirring a pot every time I came in from Farrell's.

'Tom, will you sort out the pipe under Mary's sink later?' she said while we were in the taxi, reaching into her handbag and pulling a Filofax almost as overstuffed as Amanda's. 'Then we've got Sean and Kate's engagement do to fit in before we head over to the concert.'

'The concert' was *Riverdance* at the Hammersmith Apollo, which Dympna reliably informed me she'd been waiting to see for a year and which my brother swore he'd have to be drugged and kidnapped to be forced to see. I couldn't understand why he didn't just make an excuse – maybe he liked being bossed about. That could be it: he liked someone clucking away in the background, the way Mum used to in her dressing gown, for ever at the cooker, stirring. It wasn't exactly modern, but I suppose Tom was only conforming to what was expected of him, even if, when Dympna wasn't looking, I saw a vague look of panic flit across his face.

'*Riverdance*?' I mouthed.

'Fuck off,' he mouthed back.

Of course, Misty loved Tom, who within five minutes of meeting her had swung her up onto his back and carried her off up the stairs, Bran yapping at his heels. 'I have to see this fairy grotto for myself,' he could be heard to say. 'Legend has it that a beautiful princess lives there, but I've never seen her … have you?'

'No!' Misty squealed back, giving a little guffaw of pleasure. I felt a dart of jealousy as I stood at the bottom of the stairs, bin bags beside me, wondering why I couldn't be like that with Misty. Couldn't be a big bear of a dad who threw her up on my shoulder and made her laugh. Dympna, meanwhile, made all the right noises about the house, admiring the minimalist kitchen – 'Sure, my mother would love to hide away all the kitchen stuff like this: it's so clever!' – and oohing and ahhing over the tuning-fork chandelier. 'Oh, it's magnificent,' she sighed. 'Amanda, you have such amazing taste.'

Amanda and Roland stood there and beamed, shooting me the odd glance, clearly wondering where I'd been hiding my much-better relatives all of this time. Eventually, Amanda eyed my plastic bags and said, 'So, would you like me to show you your room?'

'Your room.' It sounded as if I was a guest in a posh hotel, but I allowed myself to be led up the cream-carpeted stairs to a room on the other side of the landing to Misty's, with a neat double bed, an ornate French wardrobe and a flowery Victorian washstand, which was at odds with the modernist tone of the rest of the house. 'I decorated it for Mum,' Amanda explained, when she saw my expression. 'She likes that kind of thing and it made it easier for when she visited.' She shifted from one foot to another and bit her lip.

'Does she not visit any more?'

'She doesn't like Roland.'

How can you not like Roland? I thought. Roland is perfection – rich, handsome, successful, easy-going, a great dad. Wonder what she'd make of me.

'She's basically a racist,' Amanda added helpfully.

'Oh.'

She gave me a small, bleak smile and I wondered how hard it would have been for Amanda to ask her mother to mind Misty. Not that it mattered now that I'd done the right thing.

I looked out the large window onto the row of garages and, to the right of them, the long, narrow back gardens of the houses behind Amanda and Roland's. I caught a glimpse of a swing set and a deflated paddling pool, an aviary, small shadows of birds flitting around behind wire-mesh screens. A little boy was waving a stick four gardens down, lifting it higher and higher, and I could imagine his little dog jumping in the air. I wondered if Misty knew him, but then she didn't seem to have many friends in the neighbourhood – no wandering around all day the way Tom and I did when we were children.

All those gardens and all those lives that can't be seen from the street, I thought as I stood there awkwardly beside Amanda at the window. At home, I could look at every house I passed in the car and know pretty much what was going on inside. I knew Mr O'Malley and his ancient collie, Shep, and I could see them both snoozing beside the fire, Mr O'Malley's swollen arthritic hands placed gently on Shep's head. Then there were the two Misses Riordan, who were always beetling around in their Nissan Micra, two heads, side by side, and John Behan, whom I used to help out with the lambing, his wife, Majella, hovering over the range, a pan of rashers and sausages sizzling away for our breakfast after our night's work. I knew all of those people almost as well as I knew myself. Of course, you can never really know anyone, not really – God knows, I understand that – but our lives intersected every hour of every day. Not like here, where people's lives seemed to go in parallel, never meeting. I didn't know whether that was a good thing or not.

'I can't believe how much of a he-man Tom is,' Amanda giggled. 'Those muscles! The last time I saw him he was just a skinny little boy.'

'He was. He had a massive crush on you,' I replied. 'He kept writing you notes and leaving them under your pillow, do you remember?'

'I remember,' Amanda said softly, her cheeks flushing. The silence went on for a tad too long, then she said, 'Thanks again for doing this, Emmett.'

I turned to see her standing beside me, her hands in the back pockets of her jeans.

'Of course,' I said. 'You'll have the time of your lives,' I added, pinning a smile to my face.

She gave a small shrug and her face fell. 'I hope so,' she said in a small voice. I put an arm around her tiny shoulders and gave her what I hoped was a brotherly squeeze. She surprised me by turning in to me, laying her head against my shoulder and wrapping her arms around me, hugging me tightly and for just a little bit too long.

Oh, no, I thought, gently pushing her away from me and holding her at arm's length. 'C'mon, Amanda, it'll be great. Roland's beach huts will be … amazing, or whatever, and you'll have the time and space you need, the two of you.'

Amanda gave a little shrug. 'Of course.' And she gave a faint smile.

'You're not having second thoughts, are you?' I said, trying to keep the note of hope out of my voice.

She sighed and shook her head. 'No, it's just …' She shrugged. 'Last-minute nerves, I suppose.'

'Of course,' I said ably, 'it's perfectly normal.'

She sighed, ' I feel like it's a test, and we have to pass it, you know?'

'We?'

'Roland and me.'

'Right,' I said cautiously. I wondered if I should try to hug her again, but she might get ideas. Instead, I opted for a brotherly pat on the back. 'But it's also an opportunity and you'd kick yourself if you didn't take it. I know you.'

She turned to me and her smile was brighter this time. 'Oh, you do, do you? Well, Emmett, I might just surprise you.'

'Good,' I said, ignoring any subtext that there might be. 'And Misty will be fine with me. I promise.'

She looked doubtful for a minute – as doubtful as I felt. I wasn't sure that Misty would be 'fine' – well, she would be 'fine' in the strictest sense of the word, but in the looser sense, I didn't know. I hadn't tested that yet. So I tried what I hoped was a reassuring grin, but Amanda didn't look terribly convinced. 'Emmett?'

'Yes, Amanda?'

'If anything happens to Misty while I'm away …'

'It won't,' I say. 'I promise.'

'Good, because I will kill you,' she said. 'Am I clear?'

'Yes, Amanda.' I felt like a five-year-old, not the man to whom she's entrusted her daughter's care. Our daughter's care.

'There's nobody else,' she whispered then. 'Only you.'

'I know. And I won't let you down.'

'Good.' Her gaze held mine for an uncomfortably long time, then she was all business. 'Now, all of the instructions are in the ring binder on the hall table: school times, outings, payments, classes. She goes to Madame Dostoevsky for ballet on Tuesdays and Thursdays after homework club, so you have to pick her up immediately and run to the Tube. It's only one stop, but you'll need to make sure you have Misty's snack ready so that she doesn't get indigestion. I normally give her hummus and carrot sticks after school, but she uses the multigrain flapjacks for ballet – there's a supply in a tub in the larder and a recipe on the back of the larder door. And there's artistic expression on Saturday mornings with Sasha – that's in Crouch End, so you'll need something more substantial then. There's a wholefood café that we normally go to afterwards. She can have a raisin bar there – the rest is all just sugar and she's not to have any.' She sucked in a deep breath. 'Sorry. Am I fussing?' She gave me her searching look again, the one that said, 'Can I trust you?'

I knew what she wanted to hear. 'You are fussing and it will be fine. Promise.'

It's not fine, of course. It's 7.45 a.m. and Roland and Amanda have been gone one whole day, but who's counting, I think, as I hunt for an iron in the kitchen, opening and closing every one of their secret cupboards to reveal an array of expensive kitchen gadgets, but no

iron. We should have left the house by now because I have to drop
Misty off to school and get to work for nine o'clock, to face another
long day in Farrell's. I found it hard enough when I was in Holloway,
trying to get myself out the door – locating matching socks and
clean underpants, once having to remove a pair from my brother's
sleeping backside because I couldn't find any anywhere. I think
Dympna must have taken them home for a special clean – if only
she knew. Now ... well, I didn't know that children took so much
organising. Earlier, Misty had sat in the early-morning gloom of her
bedroom and spent an hour parting her hair exactly in the middle
so that she could do her plaits, howling in frustration every time
there was a hair out of place. Honestly, I thought, while I pulled
them into shape, why can't she just do a nice pony tail and make
it easy? But then, I thought, her mum and dad – her real mum and
dad – have just gone away for what must seem like years to a child
and she's been left with a near-stranger. Who can blame her if she
throws a fit?

'You are quite good at plaits, Emmett,' she'd said to me, slightly
mollified, while I rummaged in the dish on her dressing table for a
bobbin.

'Thanks. I've had a bit of practice, now that I remember,' I'd said,
twisting her chocolate-coloured hair into the cherry-red bobbin.

'Was that with your friend?'

'What friend?'

'The one who liked the war comics and the sweets under the
bed.'

'Yes, it was. Well remembered.'

She sighed then and put her little chin on her hands, looking like
a wise old woman. 'Do you know something, Emmett?'

'No. Tell me.'

'I think you might have been in love with your friend.'

I stopped tidying for a moment, my heart thumping in my chest, the blood swishing in my ears. 'Oh, really? What makes you say that?'

'Because when you talk about her, you get a kind of wafty look on your face.'

'Wafty?'

'Yes, like something lovely has wafted by your nose and you are smelling it.' Misty giggled.

'I see,' I said, before changing the subject. 'Do you have anyone that makes you feel wafty?'

She snorted with laughter. 'Of course not, Emmett! I'm only little.'

'Bet you do.'

'Well …' She blushed bright red and began to fiddle with the little china things on her bedside table. 'Maybe.'

I didn't say anything, just patted her on the shoulder and told her to come down for breakfast when she was ready. I knew better than to make light of her feelings because I had had them myself when I was her age. Once upon a time, somebody had made me feel wafty and I've never forgotten it.

'Emmett?' Misty turned to me, plaits swinging, in her little pink dressing gown.

'Yeah?'

'What was your friend's name?'

'Oh, I can't remember. It was a long time ago, Misty.'

'You are lying, Emmett.'

'Yes, I am,' I admitted.

'What was her name?'

'Daisy. Her name was Daisy.'

Misty thought about this for a long time, then nodded to herself, satisfied.

I feel that I've bonded with Misty over the plaiting and am congratulating myself on that, trying not to think of the fluttering feeling that I have in my stomach, the vague sense of irritation that I want to bat away, as I shove half a slice of toast in my mouth while trying to iron Misty's school shirt, having located the iron in the pantry, wondering why she didn't tell me before now that it needed to be pressed. It's an awful nylon thing and the iron keeps sticking to it, and I swear under my breath. Misty has come down to the kitchen and spent ten minutes already ferreting around looking for the ingredients for her morning porridge, but I'm too busy to tell her to get a move on.

Then I hear a long wail and I turn around. Misty is standing beside the kitchen cupboard, an empty jar in her hand.

'What is it?'

'There are no apricots!'

'Right ….' Pity about you and your apricots, I can hear my mother say.

'And I always have them in my porridge and now I can't have any!'

Jesus. I pause in my ironing for a few moments then say, 'I know.' I rummage in the massive floor-to-ceiling larder, among the bags of dried pulses and the tins of expensive fish, until I find the contraband – a packet of dark-chocolate buttons, neatly tied shut with a bit of

Sellotape. I think that they're actually cacao nibs, because chocolate is quite naturally poison, but I know that Amanda uses them in the organic flapjacks, so I sprinkle some in Misty's porridge, putting it in the microwave so that they melt.

I put the bowl down in front of her. 'Eat up.'

Misty looks both alarmed and excited at the prospect of chocolate for breakfast. She lifts her spoon and takes a tentative bite. 'Mmm, nice, Emmett,' she says. 'I think I'll do this every day.' Then she beams. 'But don't tell Mummy!'

'It'll be our secret.' I smile, relieved that another disaster has been averted. I turn back to the ironing board. 'Oh, FUCK!' the words are out of my mouth before I can stop them. I left the iron down on the shirt and a little plume of smoke is now spiralling up from it. As I lift the iron, the shirt comes with it and there's a terrible smell. I peel the shirt off gently and look at the brown stain on the back.

'Emmett, that is such a bad word,' Misty is saying as she appears beside me, cereal bowl in hand. She doesn't say anything for a few moments, just looks at the singed mess in my hand, then her eyes fill with tears and she flings the bowl down on the ground and runs out of the room. I stand there, holding the shirt in one hand, looking down at the porridgey, chocolatey mess on the floor and think hard about not crying. Bran comes over and starts sniffing and licking at the bits of food and broken china and I give him a small kick with my foot to nudge him out of the way. He whimpers and looks at me with those bug eyes.

'Don't you start,' I say.

I am never going to survive this day, I think, as I go upstairs to find Misty face down on her bed in her pink room. The fluffy clock on her bedside table reads 8.10 and I begin to wonder how I can sneak in late to Farrell's – Petrus, the owner, has a thing about timekeeping, along with his many other 'things'. At least, so Betty tells me, because I have yet to actually set eyes on Petrus J. Farrell.

'C'mon, Mist, I'm sorry. We'll get another shirt out of the cupboard and put it on.'

She doesn't lift her head, her voice muffled in the duvet. 'Don't call me "Mist". Only Roland calls me that.'

'Sorry. Misty. Look,' I say, going to the chest in the corner of the room, opening it and extracting a new, clean shirt. It's not ironed, but it'll have to do. 'Here's a new one. Will you put it on please?'

She shakes her head, the plaits I managed to tie for her this morning now a mess of hair and tangles. Then she lifts herself up on the bed and looks at me. 'I don't think I like you at all, Emmett.'

'I know,' I say, thinking, I'm not sure I like you much either right now, 'but you have to go to school and I have to go to work, so we'll talk about it later. Please? Just put it on, Misty. Otherwise, I'll be late for work and I'll get the sack.'

'Whats "the sack"?' She suddenly looks interested.

'I won't have a job any more.' I feel bad now, because I shouldn't be guilt-tripping a child, but I'm desperate.

Slowly, she gets up off the bed and, without making eye contact, sticks a hand out and accepts the shirt.

'Great. I'll be downstairs. Will you brush your teeth and put on your socks and shoes?' I say, running back down to the kitchen, which now smells of singed nylon. I remember to unplug the iron, congratulating myself as I do so, then hunt in the larder for the bloody organic sunflower bars or whatever they are, smearing two pieces of brown bread with butter and jam and sandwiching them together, shoving the whole lot into the little lunch bag that hangs at the side of Misty's schoolbag. Amanda won't let Misty eat the school dinners, so this will have to do instead. I'm feeling that I have things a bit more under control now and half-wonder if I might risk a cup of coffee, but a yell from upstairs, coinciding with the sharp ring of the doorbell, tells me otherwise.

'Misty, you nearly ready?' I shout as I run down the hall to the door, opening it to reveal a very small, very old lady in a housecoat, a cigarette hanging from her lip. Her skin is the colour of walnut – a kind of yellowy-brown – and her face is a mass of wrinkles. 'Oo are you?' she says, peering around me into the hall. 'Where's Mandy?'

Mandy? Amanda has never been called 'Mandy' in her life. 'I'm Emmett, Misty's father, and Amanda's … overseas at the moment.'

The wizened walnut gives me a sharp look. 'Oh, you're 'im, then.'

'I suppose I must be.'

'Well,' she sighs and reaches into her housecoat, producing a bottle of Toilet Duck from the depths of her baggy pockets. 'Be a love and open this for me, would you?'

Why now? I think, taking it from her and twisting. It turns out that opening Toilet Duck is harder than you might think because the bloody thing won't give. 'Safety,' Walnut says, taking a drag from her cigarette and, without asking my permission, sidling in through the half-open door to the hall. 'Misty, love, you in?'

'Yes, Queenie, I'm upstairs.' Misty's voice wafts down the stairs, and she appears a few moments later, with half-tidy hair and her socks and shoes on. She gives Queenie a small smile and disappears into the kitchen.

'You'd better follow me,' I say. 'I'll need to find something to open it with.'

'All right, love,' Queenie says, passing me out and walking

ahead into the kitchen. Don't mind me, I think, as she shuffles ahead, a small trail of ash dropping behind her onto the expensive floor.

Bran, normally silent, begins a frantic barking when he sees her, jumping back and giving a little growl, then hopping from side to side squeaking. 'Sling your 'ook,' Queenie shouts, and he retreats to the back of the room, growling. 'Mandy doesn't like mutts,' she adds helpfully.

I know, I think. 'Now, let me see what I have to open your … product,' I say, putting the Toilet Duck on the counter and rummaging through Amanda's kitchen drawers, revealing a host of expensive corkscrews and other kitchen implements that don't look very helpful. Eventually, I find a pincer-like garlic crusher that looks as if it could do the job, placing it around the pink nozzle and twisting as hard as I can. Thankfully, it comes away with a little crack and I hand it back to her. 'There you go.'

Queenie doesn't say thank you, just taps her cigarette ash out onto the ground and says, 'Bit of a mess in 'ere, ain't it?' surveying the mess of broken crockery and breakfast on the floor. 'Mandy wouldn't like that. She wouldn't like it one little bit,' and she shakes her head regretfully from side to side.

For Christ's sake. It's now 8.30 and any hope I had of getting myself or Misty to school or work on time has now evaporated. I wrestle with the thought of asking Queenie if she'd like to sit down and have a nice cuppa, seeing as she has so successfully derailed my day, but tell myself that my mother always insisted that I be polite to the elderly. Then it occurs to me: she might well be a spy. Maybe Amanda asked her to keep a careful eye on her untested new babysitter. God knows what Queenie will have to say when she reports back.

'Well,' I say, 'it was a pleasure meeting you, Mrs ...'

'Queenie to you, love,' she says, taking the Toilet Duck and shuffling back out the door. 'You'd want to tidy a bit, duck, otherwise it all gets on top of you. Dust every day, clean the cooker, a quick squirt of this little helper and Bob's your uncle,' she says.

'Well, thank you for that,' I say, walking close behind her into the hall in the hope that she might get the hint and go quickly out of the front door. Instead, she skulks in the hall, reaching into the pocket of her housecoat and extracting a packet of Woodbines, taking one out and putting it into her mouth. Then she begins to talk, the cigarette wobbling between her clamped-together lips. 'I said to Mandy that it wasn't right, to leave a man alone in charge, looking after a child 'n' all. My Sidney was a proper mess every time I went down the bingo. I'd come home and he'd have had his cronies around drinking my good whiskey and littering my nice clean kitchen.' She makes a face. 'Better off without 'im, I say.'

I'm not sure if Sidney is dead or has simply gone somewhere – slung 'is 'ook, to use the vernacular – and I don't like to ask, so I just say, 'Well, I promise that I'm not Sidney. No friends around to play cards, no littering, I promise.'

She gives me a doubtful look and I wonder, not for the first time, why I keep getting them. Is there something about me that makes people doubtful? My mother always said that you could tell if a man could be trusted by the slant of his shoulders. A good straight line meant that a man could be relied upon completely. Anything else inspired doubt and mistrust. My shoulders are somewhere in the middle – not the straight line of the old-fashioned Hollywood hero and not the diagonal of the dodgy criminal, more of a slight slope – neither one thing nor the other.

'You mind that little girl, d'you 'ear?'

'I hear.'

'I hope you're not one of them deadbeat dads I read about in the paper. Dads who just spawn them and then leave.' She fixes me with a glare, cigarette wobbling on her bottom lip, Clint-Eastwood-style.

'I'm not a deadbeat dad,' I say wearily.

'Or – 'oo's that miserable sod in the ad on the telly, taking his son out for footy and a burger on a Saturday morning because him and the missus are divorced? The 'weekend dad'.' Her lip curls in distaste. 'Did you ever?'

'Never.' I shake my head.

'Fathers knew how to be fathers in my day, none of this once-a-week parenting nonsense.'

'I'm not a weekend dad either, honestly,' I lie, because, until this very day, that's exactly what I have been.

'You'd better not be,' she says grimly. With that, she is gone in a puff of smoke, shuffling down the steps and around the corner to the basement of the house next door. I take in a deep breath and let it out again, slowly.

'Who *is* Queenie?' I ask Misty when we eventually make it out onto the footpath, having scooped the porridge/china mess into the bin, she in her school uniform, with her bag and lunch, me in my cleaner-of-two-pairs of jeans and shirt, with my satchel over my shoulder. I've left Bran in the kitchen, thinking that he can't really get up to too much in a space with nothing in it, but now I can't remember whether or not I shut the door to the rest of the house. Oh, God, I think, I'll have to go back. I stop dead, hand pressed to my head, but then, I think, I can always pop back at lunchtime. I'll do that, I decide, marching on again.

Misty gives me a funny look before saying, 'Oh, she lives next door, but Mum says that she's never to come in because she smells funny and she drinks.'

'Right. You might have told me that before I let her in.'

'And she has these friends – they all sit around and they drink gin and talk and they laugh like this …' She gives an imitation of a smoker's cackle, clearing her throat and making a loud 'hah-hah' noise. Mum says that they are deger—'

'Degenerates,' I offer.

'I was about to say that, Emmett. I know the word, you know,' Misty says impatiently. 'Miss Grace says that I'm a really clever girl and that I'll go far.'

'Miss Grace is a very good judge of character,' I say, in the hope of redeeming myself. Misty doesn't reply. She just shrugs and we walk along in silence, and I look at the set of her tiny shoulders and the way she shuffles along, toes scuffing the ground, and understand again how difficult it is for her – the only person she has now is me. I don't think I could leave my child, I think to myself, and head off to the wide blue yonder, but then I realise that I kind of already did and it makes me feel sad, all of a sudden.

Misty leaves me at the school gate, walking into the yard filled with kids running, jumping, playing skipping games, her bag heavy on her back. 'Bye, Misty!' I yell, but she doesn't turn around. She's almost at the door when she's joined by a little boy with a red jacket and a head of tightly cropped hair. He leans towards her and says something and she laughs, and the two of them disappear inside.

I stand there for a few moments, feeling that I'm merely imitating all the other parents in the yard, looking fondly at my child as he or she disappears through the doors into the school. I look around at the huddle of mums lurking at the gate and realise that I'm the only dad. I try to catch the eye of one of them and smile, but she looks at me as if I'm some kind of pervert. I have no choice but to slink off up the road to Farrell's, like a beaten dog.

I spend the rest of the day on the third floor of Farrell's in my little dungeon, sorting a series of books on Japanese torture techniques of the sixteenth century – who knew that they had so many – into the correct order and fending off Patrice: not an easy task, because he seems to have taken his job as my boss to heart.

I've made it my project to tidy one shelf of Japanese history a day – to give me something to do, apart from anything else – but every time I wield my duster or line a book up on the shelf, he appears before me. '*Qu'est ce que tu fait?*'

'I'm sorry?' I had no idea that French was a requirement for this place, apart from an 'intimate knowledge of Japanese history', which seemed to have been entirely forgotten about. Betty says he's only trying to put me off and not to let him get to me. 'He's just a bit of an old queen, really,' she told me earlier. 'Take no notice of him.'

It's hard, I think now, when he's looming over me, a look of Gallic distaste on his face. 'You do what you are told, not *cette merde*,' he says, snatching the duster from my hand and handing me the bloody ledger again to jot down more nonsense in the margins. I busy myself with my pen, pretending to write then chewing the top of the biro and looking thoughtful, while Patrice puts a till roll into the cash register. He's got it the wrong way round, but if I tell him, he's bound to say something rude to me in French, so I leave him alone – and besides, it gives me a moment to study him. In no way does he look like someone who works in a bookshop, with his collection of expensive-looking three-piece suits and ties with little motifs on them and his silvery hair combed into a kind of quiff at the front – he looks like the head of a Paris fashion house, as if Yves St Laurent had crash landed in north London. It's mystifying, really, particularly as he doesn't seem to like working here. I'm treated to a constant stream of catty remarks and nasty observations on the few customers who made it up the dusty stairs. '*Putain, c'est horrible!*' he remarked of one woman with a brightly coloured shell top earlier – he had a point, but to tell her that that kind of fashion was for '*les drogués*', was probably unnecessary. Thankfully, she didn't look as if she understood.

'Hi, Patrice – are you putting the till roll in the wrong way again? Let me show you.' To my relief, Betty appears at the top of the stairs. Her cheeks are flushed and she's breathing rapidly. 'Whew, those stairs! No wonder you don't get many customers up here.' She smiles. 'Lucky you, having a bit of peace and quiet.' As she comes towards us, I notice that she's got a copy of Ted Hughes's *The Iron Wolf* in her hand. My heart flutters in my chest.

Patrice shrugs his shoulders and makes a face, but he hands Betty the till roll without complaint. Deftly, she turns it over and feeds it into the slot, pressing a button that sets the till whirring, and when a tongue of white roll appears, she tears it off. 'There's, that's better.'

'*Merci,*' Patrice mutters insincerely.

'You're welcome, Patrice!' Betty says cheerfully. So that's the way to handle him, I think as I watch. As if he's not a miserable, mean-spirited little Frenchman at all. Then I realise that she isn't wearing her usual tight-sweater/pencil-skirt uniform and I have to confess that I'm a bit disappointed. Today, she is wearing a check shirt and a pair of pale-blue denims and her fair curly hair is tied into two bunches, one either side of her head. It looks cute, I think – actually nicer than her pneumatic look – but if you were to ask me to choose …

'Hi. How's everything going?' She smiles at me when she notices me.

'Oh, fine!' I attempt to look enthusiastic, unfurling myself from my crouched position over a pile of books, then, conscious that I am towering over her, I lean against one of the shelves, affecting a kind of nonchalance that I think is pretty effective, until the shelf begins to slide slowly backwards. I hadn't realised that it was on wheels, but now I attempt to pull it back towards me, using only my elbow, while I make polite conversation.

'I see you like Ted Hughes,' I manage, the point of my elbow now providing me with an interesting searing pain up my arm, which I disguise by placing my hand firmly on top of my head, so that I look thoughtful rather than in agony.

'What? Oh, yes. It's for my poetry evening class. Everyone says that he was awful to Sylvia Plath, but I just can't help loving his poetry. Isn't that a bit wrong?' She grins and her nose wrinkles cutely. Unable to bear the pain any more, I decide to stand upright and own all of my six feet six inches, pretending not to notice as the bookshelf sails across the floor behind me. In fairness to Betty, it doesn't seem to bother her. I suppose she's used to the place.

'I know what you mean,' I say. 'Is it acceptable to love the art even if the artist is flawed?'

'That's it exactly! I mean, look at Woody Allen. I love his films, but I feel a bit guilty about it because of his personal life. It's like saying it's OK – you know? Anyway,' she sighs, 'unfortunately, I didn't come up to discuss artists we shouldn't like but do. I have a few tax forms to fill out with you – do you think you could look at them and sign them and pop them back to me?'

'Sure,' I say, taking the forms from her. 'Listen, you don't know of any good poetry readings in the area, do you? I was just wondering where I might find some. You see, I write poetry and I'm looking for inspiration.' I blush when I say this, wondering just how pretentious I sound, but Betty seems impressed. 'Wow, you're a poet – that's really something—' she begins, but then there's the sound of clicking fingers and Patrice is beside me.

'*Alors*, Muriel, you can see that Emmett is busy with inventory. Please come back later.' Lips pressed together, he marches over to me, takes my arm and steers me back towards my lair.

I turn around, expecting Betty to be annoyed, but instead, she has a hand on her hip and she's smiling broadly. '*Au revoir*, Patrice,' she says, giving me a wink, then turning on her heel and giving a little wave over her shoulder, before turning and wiggling away down the stairs. Her wiggle looks even better in jeans.

'She has a boyfriend.' Patrice's acid tones cut through my pleasant little daydream.

'I know that,' I say, attempting to pull myself together. I didn't, actually, but he's a lucky guy.

Patrice gives me a mirthless smile. Little git.

I say nothing further, just make loud ticks in the boxes in Petrus' stupid ledger, ticks that signal my resentment and rage.

I'm almost at the bottom of the ledger, and I'm hoping fervently that when I look up next the clock will have moved forward, even just a few minutes. The last time I looked, it said twelve o'clock for the third time in a row. That's another thing about hell – time seems to slow to a crawl the minute I step through the door.

'*Hi!*' I nearly jump out of my skin, dropping the ledger so that it lands on the floor with a thump. 'Oh, sorry, did I disturb you?'

I bend down to pick it up, then stand up to see a woman with red cheeks and mid-brown hair, dressed in a woolly jumper, flowery leggings and a bright-red hat, looking up at me, a big smile on her happy, open face. She has the flushed, slightly harassed look of some of the mums at the school gate.

'You must be Misty's dad! I saw you at the school this morning and went to say hello, but you'd sped off!'

'Yes, that's right!' I offer her my hand, wondering slightly at the excited tone in which we're both suddenly speaking. 'I'm Emmett.'

She accepts, pumping it vigorously. 'Diamanda,' she replies and, seeing the look on my face, giggles. 'I know, it's ridiculous, but my mother thought that if she gave me a memorable name, I might live up to it.' She gives a little shrug. 'She was wrong!'

'Oh, I'm sure that's not true,' I say. 'You look like a Diamanda. Sparkly.' I cringe inside in case she thinks I'm flirting with her, but instead she just laughs.

'Try telling my husband that – I haven't sparkled since the twins were born, but, hey, that's the mother's lot! They don't tell you, do they, that it's downhill all the way – that one day you'll wake up with no pelvic floor to speak of, no money, no time and you'll feel as if you've been run over by a truck! But I wouldn't be without them!'

The picture she paints is gothic, to say the least, but she delivers it with such cheery gusto that I'm not sure quite what the message is – that motherhood is awful or great – and what she wants me to say in response. She must be a mind-reader, though, because she swiftly adds, 'But I'm oversharing. David – that's my husband – always says that. "Diamanda, you would talk to a blank wall", but sometimes a blank wall is the only thing I speak to all day, at least until the twins come home at 3.30 …' Her voice trails off, and she looks sad for a moment, before remembering that she's supposed to be perky and she pins a smile to her face. 'But I just love being a mum!'

'I'd say you're very good at it. The twins are very lucky,' I add, hoping that that might cheer her up. I have no idea if the twins are lucky or not, but this poor creature needs something. 'Anyway …' I begin, indicating the ledger, 'how can I help you? Need something on hara-kiri?' I joke.

'What? Oh, no thanks. I don't really like it. Those horrible little trees.' She makes a face.

'Right.'

'Anyway, I'm here on a mission! You see, we're having a fundraiser for the community centre and I was hoping you might be able to put some posters up in the window.' With a beam, she unfurls one to reveal a child's drawing of the rather ugly red-brick community centre on Leopold's Road with what looks like a herd of zebras filing out the front door. 'My little Jamie did it – he's very creative,' she exclaims. 'He's the younger of the twins, but only by five minutes, but he didn't get the same nourishment in the womb, so he's a bit … well … he's got a real talent for art!'

'I can see that,' I say, as we both admire the effort. 'But you'll need to ask Petrus, I suppose, or Betty. She's the manager. I mean Muriel,' I correct myself, remembering that the Betty persona is for my fevered imagination only.

At this Diamanda blanches. 'Oh, I don't think I could ask Mr

Farrell. He can be a bit … unpredictable. The last time I asked him, he said yes, but then he added some … embellishments.'

'Oh.'

'Yes, he made a laughing stock out of poor Jamie,' she says.

'Well, tell you what,' I offer. 'I'll bring it downstairs and ask Muriel, OK?' It'll give me an excuse to admire her again, I think cheerfully to myself.

'Oh, you are so good, Emmett! The girls on the committee will be thrilled!' And then she pauses, as if she's just thought of something. 'Maybe you could even help!'

'Maybe,' I say dubiously, a vision of myself in an apron standing behind rows of wonky apple tarts and Rice Krispie buns coming into my head. Absolutely not, I think.

'I know, you'd be just brilliant at the therapy desk!'

'The therapy desk,' I repeat. What on earth is she talking about? 'I thought it was a cake sale.'

'Oh, no, it's a major event. We have all kinds of stalls – bric-a-brac, tombola, guess the number of jellybeans – but the therapy desk is a real favourite. People queue up and they give you a pound and ask you a question about something that's bothering them, a life problem, and you give them some advice. I'd say you'd be really good at that – you're such a good listener. I can see that by the way you listen so carefully to all my wittering!'

Christ almighty, I think. It sounds like a recipe for disaster. 'Oh, I don't think so, Diamanda. What if I give them bad advice and they act on it? It'll be all my fault then. I don't think I'd want the responsibility,' I say.

'Oh, that's disappointing,' Diamanda says softly. 'I thought it was such a good idea.'

Oh, God. 'Tell you what – why don't I read people a poem to help them with whatever problem it is. Like poetry therapy.'

Diamanda thinks about this for a while, a confused look on her face. 'Do you know a lot about poems?'

'A fair amount,' I say. 'I'm a poet, actually. Well, I work here, but I also write poems. And I've read a lot. There's a poem for every problem!' Exclamation marks might be more persuasive, I decide, and get me out of amateur psychoanalysis.

'A poem for every problem,' she repeats softly. 'That sounds good … yes!' She eventually concludes. 'That would be fantastic! Thank you, Emmett!'

'You're welcome,' I say. 'Anything to help!'

Diamanda goes off, delighted with herself, leaving me with a half-dozen zebra posters and a worry about what I might be going to do at the poetry therapy desk. What if someone has something really serious to discuss – running away from their partner or getting rid of the dog? Maybe they have only a month to live – what'll I say then? You'll just pick a poem that's vaguely about that subject and recite it, I think. It couldn't be simpler. And no advice need change hands.

Then it's lunchtime, thank God, and I take refuge in the illustrated books corner, enjoying the blessed peace, glad that Patrice has gone out to lunch with Nolan, a tweed-jacketed American who works in the American Novel department, appropriately enough. He's weedy and silent and shabby and I can't think what he has in common with Patrice, who is voluble and immaculately turned out at all times. They have lunch together every day and I wonder if they are more than just friends. Patrice did invite me, which was astonishing, as he doesn't seem to like me much, but I said that I wanted to read. I sounded a bit prissy, but *tant pis*, as Patrice would say. I need time to think and I haven't had much of it lately.

I sit on one of the stools that we use to reach up to high shelves and suck in a deep breath before letting it out again slowly. In and out and in and out. I close my eyes and try to let the first line of a poem fill my head, but instead I picture Misty, bent over a desk in school, tongue sticking out the way it does when she's concentrating or sitting with her lunchbox in front of her. I wonder if she's talking to her friend again or if the little madam is still giving Misty the cold shoulder. I remember what it's like, the feeling that my happiness depended on whether someone had decided to be nice to me, the feeling of joy as they bestowed a look or invited me to play football, even though I hated the game.

I wonder if she's looking out of the window, I think, the way I used to when I was her age, gazing out into the fields, watching the lambs springing about in springtime, the cattle that would graze there in summer and autumn, and the empty brown sludge in winter. I expect she doesn't get a clip on the ear or her head knocked into her neighbour's for not paying attention, though. 'Always a dreamer, Emmett O'Donoghue,' Brother Patrick would hiss. 'Dreaming never got anyone anywhere.' I wonder if Misty dreams, like me.

The thought makes me suddenly restless, and I get up to browse a pile of books on Japanese art. I flick through a lovely, glossy book on the paintings of Hokusai, with their precise detail, the slight variations in the many shades of blue, and I begin to relax again, leaning back against the end of one of the shelves and closing my eyes for a moment.

Then I hear her. Or rather smell her, because that scent of vanilla is what hits me first. I open my eyes and there she is, the girl with the sling. She's leaning down to examine a large book on Japanese flower arranging, and her curls keep falling into her eyes, so she's tucking them behind her ear while cradling the sling in her other hand. It all looks a bit awkward, and then the baby begins to cry. She looks up to see if anyone is around and makes a shushing sound, jigging around and patting the baby's back. 'Shh … shh …' she says, over and over, but the baby's wails become louder. You need to pat him a bit harder, I think, a rhythmic pat, pat on his bottom – it helps to soothe them. I remember doing it to Tom. Mum used to say that I had a knack with babies.

I get up off my stool to see if I can help, when I hear a voice. 'Where are you? These stairs are killing me. Would they not have a lift, for God's sake.' The accent is Irish, and the woman looks like Elizabeth Taylor, with a huge pink turban kind of thing on her head and a fur coat, the collar tucked up around her face. She's also wearing a pair of enormous sunglasses with huge round rims, of the kind Jackie Kennedy used to wear when she'd become Jackie Onassis. My stomach lurches.

'Mum, keep your voice down,' the girl says, standing up and continuing her dance, jumping up and down on the balls of her feet. She looks suddenly terribly tired, her face falling, her complexion, in the horrible strip lighting, is a pale grey.

'For God's sake, how can I?' the woman bites back. 'I can hardly hear myself think with the noise out of your man.'

The girl doesn't say anything, just stares off into space, still tapping and patting and shushing, her jaw set.

'Give him to me, for God's sake,' Liz Taylor says, holding out her arms. When the younger woman hesitates, Liz makes a flapping motion with her hands and the girl lifts the wailing baby out of the sling and hands him to her. 'There, there,' the woman says, rubbing his head and murmuring, 'Let's go and have a look at the lovely books, will we?' The baby's cries subside to a series of hiccups as Liz takes him over to a stack on Japanese gardening. 'Oh, look here, some lovely maples and a water feature, just like the one granny wants for her garden. What do you think? How about this pretty pagoda, hmm?'

The baby's cries and hiccups become a sudden giggle, as if there's nothing more amusing in the world than Japanese gardening. The girl stands there, hands down by her side, sling empty. Then she looks around, as if wondering what to do without the baby, as if she's a bit lost. Then her mother says, 'This one will do. It's got something about bonsai trees in it.'

'Right,' the girl says vaguely, turning her head to see if there's any sign of a bookseller. I know that I should appear to serve the customers, to see if I can help them, but I don't. Instead, I melt into the background, heart thumping in my chest.

I wait a full twenty minutes behind the counter, until a voice says, 'I think it's safe to come out.' I look up and it's Patrice. Oh, shit. But for once, he doesn't look irritated and when I get up, banging my head against the edge of the cash register, he looks at me calmly, handing me an immaculate handkerchief to place on the bump on my head.

'It's OK, it's not bleeding,' I say but accept it anyway, unfolding it, catching sight of the embroidered initials in the corner. It looks like everything else Patrice owns – expensive. I press it to my head for a few minutes, while Patrice continues to regard me as if I'm a specimen in a jar.

'You look as if you have seen a ghost,' he says, adding, 'as you English put it', giving me a mirthless smile.

'I have. I think,' I say, still holding the hankie in my hand, ignoring the dig. It's crumpled now and it does actually have a spot of blood on it. 'Sorry,' I say, handing it to him.

With a wrinkled nose, he accepts it, reaching in under the counter and pulling out one of the little plastic coin bags for the bank and pushing the hankie into it before placing it into his briefcase. Jesus, I think, I don't have the plague.

'You know what Flaubert says?' Patrice asks suddenly.

I shake my head.

'He says that only three things are ... infinite. "The sky in its stars, the sea in its drops of water, the heart in its tears."'

'Right.' I have no idea what he's talking about, but the words make me feel better. They sound wistfully romantic.

'*Allez, vas-t'en*. Go 'ome,' he says, making a flapping motion with his hands. 'Come back tomorrow and it will be as if nothing ever happened.'

'OK. Well, thanks,' I say, fetching my satchel. 'I appreciate it, Patrice.'

He tuts and rolls his eyes to heaven.

Was that who I think it was, I wonder as I trudge down the three flights of stairs to the bottom. And if it was – or is – what am I going to do about it?

'Nothing, you eejit,' I tell myself sternly. 'You are going to do absolutely nothing.'

7.

The community centre begins to fill up with people and I feel a trickle of sweat on my top lip as I sit sideways at my folding table, legs sticking out at an awkward angle because they're too long to fit underneath. The handmade sign that Misty made says, 'Poetry Therapy – A Poem to Soothe Your Every Worry.'

I'm waiting for my first customer, watching the hall fill up with locals. I'm beginning to recognise a few of them now. There's the Scut, a little whippet of a man who lives across the road and who shouts at his wife and children from morning to night, slamming the front door behind him, red-faced, and jumping into his Ford Capri with the furry dice hanging from the rear-view mirror. He's a little shit and everyone on the road has rung the police about him, but his wife refuses to kick him out. I see him lurking by the hamburger stand and send him evil vibes, feeling guilty that I can't do more. Then I see the Two Johns, two men who live in the house next door, who go out on Saturday mornings to Star Trek gatherings, John One dressed as Mr Spock, complete with pointy ears, and John Two dressed as Captain Kirk – a match made in heaven. I know that Diamanda wanted them to dress up for the fundraiser, but they wouldn't hear of it. John One had said that it was 'thoroughly undignified' at the fundraiser meeting a couple of weeks ago, which I thought was a bit rich, considering their Saturday dress code. Now the two of them are wearing identical jeans and cashmere sweaters, eyeing the Victoria sponges that Diamanda has made in the spare ten minutes when she wasn't organising the fundraiser, bringing her boys to endless 'rugger' games and driving that huge van thing of hers around the streets, full to the rafters with children and dogs. She's minding Misty for me while I do the poetry therapy and I spot my daughter's head of dark shiny hair, bobbing as she arranges fairy cakes on a plate.

Diamanda is standing behind a tea urn, the two bright-red patches on her face making her look like a doll, wearing her big, stoic smile, pushing a lock of hair back under her Alice band and asking a little boy how many Rice Krispie buns he'd like. I used to look down on people like Diamanda, with their relentless cheer and insane good will towards all, but now it strikes me as being very brave – to put other people first, to just be plain nice to everyone, no matter what. I must pick out a poem for her, I think.

I crane my neck for a better view of the entrance to the centre, to see if there's any sign of Tom and Dympna. He's promised me that they'll make an appearance after Dympna's camogie match against the Celtic Titans from Clapham. I can imagine Dympna as a camogie player, those fine thighs of hers striding up the pitch, those arms wielding a hurl like an ancient Celtic warrior. She's kind of scary, Dympna, even though she has Tom well managed, with their weekly trips to the Irish clubs and Sunday nights in front of the video of the previous week's *Late, Late Show* that her mother has sent over from Ireland. It's not a life I'd like to have, I think, as I open the *Penguin Book of English Verse* to remind myself of poems that might be useful, but if Tom looks a bit … unnerved every now and again, he seems happy to let Dympna have the run of him. Maybe he finds it easier.

I close my eyes for a second to focus, letting the noise and clatter fade away a bit. I'm nervous and it's everything I can do to stop my leg doing that involuntary jigging that used to drive Mum mad. I'm afraid that if I zone out too much, I might fall asleep. I haven't slept that well in the past week. Not since the girl in the green granny coat appeared in Farrell's. Ever since that morning, it seems like I've seen her everywhere: that coat disappearing up the road as I walk Misty to school, vanishing into a doorway as I make a furtive visit after work to Waterstone's on the green, with its much, much nicer selection of books and friendly staff. Sometimes, I wonder if I'm hallucinating – in the grip of some kind of mental illness because of a lack of sleep and the stress of being a working dad.

But then I begin to wonder where she lives, and what she's doing at any given moment, and before I know it, I'm back in Wexford again, the two of us in our lair under the bed. We have a box of After Eights and it's half-empty, a mess of balled-up wrappers on the carpet between us. Our parents are playing 21, the way they used to when they were young and living in Dublin, 'having the time of our lives,' as Mum would put it, before Dad got the job in Galway and he and Mum moved away. Daisy and I are playing Twenty Questions and the winner gets an After Eight, but Daisy's cheating, using more than simple 'yes' or 'no' answers.

'Daisy, will you stop? What's the point in playing if you guess it immediately – then it's just Five Questions or Four Questions, not Twenty Questions,' I say indignantly.

Daisy grins. 'That means I get an After Eight every four questions – I don't have to wait until the whole boring game is over.' And she shrugs, and I marvel at how much cleverer she is than me. Then the door opens and I see a pair of white patent-leather shoes appearing. They are about six inches from my nose and I find myself involuntarily holding my breath.

'Daisy?' The voice is shrill. 'Where are those chocolates? Do not let me look under there and find you stuffing your face like a pig with them. You know chocolate is fattening and yet still you do it. It's as if you're deliberately defying me.'

I look left and I see her, eyes squeezed shut, repeating a mantra to herself. 'Mummy is a silly cow,' over and over. I think she's brave and really bold at the same time. If I even thought of my mother in those terms, she'd know somehow, and she'd kill me. Besides, I think, I love Mum.

Daisy grabs my hand in hers and holds it so tightly that it's all I can do to contain the yelp of pain and laughter that's bubbling up inside of me.

'If I find out, there'll be hell to pay,' Bridget's voice slices through me. 'Do you hear me, Daisy?' Then the door is pushed open and a pair of brown Hush Puppies appears beside the white shoes. 'Bridget, Bill and Maureen have only been here fifteen minutes and he's on his second gin and tonic already, will you ever—' Then there's an abrupt silence, followed by a pause.

'Emmett, are you under there?'

'Yes, Mr Delaney.'

'Is Daisy there too?'

'Erm, I'm not sure.'

Bridget shrieks. 'Don't you lie to me, Emmett O'Donoghue, that little bitch …'

'Bridget, go and make yourself another drink, will you? It's only a few old sweets. I'll go out in a minute and buy another box.'

There's the sound of air being sucked in, then expelled in an angry gush. 'You'd better punish her this time, Mike. No more "Daddy's little girl", do you hear me?'

'Oh, I hear you, Bridget. No, go and do your hostess routine – you're good at that.'

There's another silence, followed by a hissed, 'Why do you always take her side?' The door is closed with a bang and then the two legs in their slacks are still, before a large dent appears in the mattress above us and a pair of cream socks and mid-brown shoes appear in front of us. There's a deep sigh, followed by, 'Give me one – no, two.'

Daisy's hand shoots out over mine, two After Eights, in their dark-brown wrappers, in her hand. Her father's big red paw grabs them, then there's a rustle and a murmur of pleasure. 'You can't beat an After Eight.'

Daisy gives a little giggle, as there's another rustle and the sound of Mike chewing. Then the voice says, 'Now, listen to me the two of you. This party is a big deal for Bridget and it means a lot to her, so no bad behaviour, do you hear me?'

'Yes, Mr Delaney,' I say solemnly, aware that I have got away with murder. I look at Daisy and she's crossing her eyes – I try hard not to laugh.

'Daisy, that goes for you as well. For once in your life, don't torment your mother. This is her chance to get in with the crowd down here and it's not fair to wreck that on her. It wasn't her idea to spend the summer here, it was mine and Mary's, so if this makes it halfway bearable for all of us, let her at it. Don't make it even bloody harder for me. Do you hear me?' Mike has a gravelly bass voice and it reverberates around the room, vibrating through the mattress.

Daisy tuts. 'Yes, Daddy.'

'Good. Now, the two of you get dressed and come into the lounge. You can make yourselves useful handing around the food. Not that lumps of cheese on a stick are any substitute for a good dinner,' he mutters. The Hush Puppies move towards the door and then it closes.

My eyes flick open, and it takes me a few seconds to realise that I'm back in a school hall in north London. I feel dazed and I wonder if I'll faint. A small crowd has gathered underneath the wheel of fortune, which is being run by Diamanda's husband, a florid chartered surveyor with slicked-back hair, and it spins rapidly around, a whir of different colours, before slowing to a stop, the ticking of the little metal stoppers rat-tatting as it slows. 'It's pink … no, green … no, red. Red 31!' he announces, holding up a bottle of wine. 'Well done, sir. Don't drink it all at once …'

Then I become aware of a presence beside me and look up from my book to see Queenie. She has swapped her housecoat for an outdoor one, a brown astrakhan that looks surprisingly smart, and she's sporting a pink hat that looks like a pincushion, with a kind of stalk sticking out of the top. She's not smoking, for once, and she looks a bit odd without the ever-present Pall Mall stuck to her bottom lip and without the variety of bottles that she requests that I open every morning, just when I'm leaving for work, everything from HP Sauce to Beefeater pre-mixed Gin and Tonic.

'You do poems,' she says.

I sit up, my mind clearing a bit. 'Oh, erm, yes, that's right,' I agree. 'They're supposed to be a kind of therapy. You tell me what the matter is and I pick a poem to help.'

She curls her lip, as if the idea is faintly ridiculous, but sits down opposite me, her huge black handbag on her knee. 'I need one for my back passage.'

'Your back passage?' I repeat, unnecessarily loudly, and she shushes me with a look.

'It hasn't been the same since Sid moved out. He used to do all the cooking. Now, all I can manage is a tin of Frey Bentos and it's got me all bunged up, like someone's put a cork in me.'

God almighty. 'Right, well, let me see. I'm sure we have a poem for that,' I say, flicking through my various collections, before finding Marge Piercy's 'My Mother's Body'. 'It's not specifically about … back passages,' I say, 'but here we go.' I read out the lines, and as I do, I realise how deeply sad they are, with the poet mourning her mother's decay and death, the erosion of the woman she had once been. It's a poem about dying and loss, not about back passages, and my cheeks colour as I read the pain and grief in the lines.

I am not off to a good start here, I think, and when I'm finished,

I look up at her, expecting a protest at how neatly I have described her own ageing, her own decay, but instead she nods in satisfaction. 'That's a good one. I feel better already.'

'You do?'

'Well, we're all going to go, ain't we? Sooner or later. Might as well say it as we see it.'

'I suppose so.' We both sit there, taking it all in, before she says, 'I hope someone misses me that much.'

'Oh, I'm sure they will.' I'm patronising her, I know, and she rewards me with a rueful look, shaking her head sadly from side to side. 'It's all right, duck, I've made my piece with it. We all die alone anyway, don't we? It's a fact of life, innit?' She sighs. 'It's when you get to my age that you start thinking, don't you? About life and such. About all the regrets you 'ave. If only I'd been a bit braver with my Sid, we might still be together.' She shifts slightly in her chair, a mournful look on her face.

'What do you mean?' For some reason, her distress reminds me of Bridget Delaney. Maybe that's all she was trying to do with the Liz Taylor get-up – just to stave off ageing and death. It's a depressing thought, and I try to focus instead on Queenie.

'Oh, he was all for adventures. He wanted to try everything – hang gliding, parachuting – he even signed up for those diving lessons at the Cally swimming pool.'

'Diving lessons?' I'd seen a picture of Sid – a large man with a red nose and cheeks and a thatch of ginger hair – in Queenie's flat when I'd gone to fix a blocked pipe under the sink. I couldn't picture him in a pair of budgie-smugglers jumping up and down on a diving board.

'Yes, you know, with the suits and the masks.'

'Oh. Scuba diving.'

'Yes, like that ... whatsisname ... Jacques Cousteau. He loved watching him on the telly. It was him who gave Sid the idea – he thought he'd go to Mauritius and swim with the fishes. For all I know, he's there now.'

'And what about you? Don't you ever feel like having an adventure?'

'No, love,' she says sadly, shaking her head. 'The only adventures I ever had were dodging bombs during the Blitz – I never really yearned for that kind of thing. Never saw myself jumping out of a plane. I like a quiet life. Bit of pie and mash of a Friday, *EastEnders* on the telly and I'm a happy woman.'

'Maybe you need someone who's on your wavelength,' I suggest, wondering what kind of adventure I'd have if I had the choice, but then, I think, I'm having an adventure right now, whether I like it or not.

'It's good of you to say, love, but who'd be interested in a dried-up old bat like me?' she says sadly.

I feel guilty then, because that's exactly what I'd thought about Queenie – that she was an old bat who had nothing better to do than squirt liberal amounts of Toilet Duck down the loo and smoke endless cigarettes, when she wasn't coming over to my house for a good nose around. I never, to my shame, thought of her as an actual woman.

She stares into space for a few moments, then seems to snap back to herself, shifting her handbag on her knee and saying, 'How's Mandy? You 'eard anything?'

I must have touched a nerve, I think. 'Oh, she's fine. She seems to be having a great time in Jamaica. And Roland's business venture seems to be going well.' I'm not really sure that it is, because when Amanda rang for her twice-weekly chat with Misty, she didn't exactly sound like someone stranded in paradise, but when I asked her, she said it was all 'fine, fine'. Then there was a slightly-too-long pause. 'Well … just a few things that need ironing out with the contracts. Nothing I can't manage.'

'I'd say that Roland would lead her a merry dance.' Queenie is sitting there, nodding her head, satisfied with her pronouncement. 'He's a nice fellow, don't get me wrong, but those business ideas – always thinks 'e's onto the next big thing. Bit of a roller coaster, I'd say.'

So that's why Amanda was nervous, I think. It wasn't just at leaving Misty in my semi-capable hands. Roland looks pretty successful from where I'm standing. Or sitting, but maybe that's not the whole story. 'Have you tried orange juice?' I say, desperate to veer away from this subject. 'Freshly squeezed is very good for, erm, bowels.'

'I'll remember that,' she says. 'I'll let you know if I'm regular from now on,' and she gives a little chuckle. She gets up because a queue is beginning to form behind her, and then she says, 'You can leave Misty with me, love, any time you want. You don't want to take her to that Farrell's Bookshop. That horrible little frog is so rude.'

Patrice. Who else.

'I went in one day to see if he had the new Sidney Sheldon and he told me he didn't sell that tat and then he said some French word and that I should be ashamed of myself if I read it. I don't see anything wrong with Sidney Sheldon. And 'im with a whole section of pornos.' When she sees my face, she looks triumphant. 'Ooh, yes. Naked men all over the shop – in leather, with lots of chains. Like

Freddie Mercury,' she adds helpfully. 'And those frogs never wash themselves, you know. I said I'd never darken the door of the place again. It's no place for children.' And she wags a finger at me.

'You're probably right,' I say, silently adding that it's preferable to Misty being marinated in cigarette smoke all the same. 'I might take you up on that some time,' I lie.

'You do, love,' she says, getting up from her seat. 'Thanks, duck. I feel a lot better after that.' She turns and walks towards the cake stall and, as she does, bumps into a figure in a tweed jacket, giving a little wobble. 'Easy does it,' a rich baritone declares, as the man reaches out a hand to steady her. He's tall, handsome, immaculate in pressed brown slacks, tweed jacket and blue v-neck sweater, a red tie neatly knotted at the neck of his shirt. Queenie looks at his hand on her arm, then right at him and her cheeks flush. 'Thanks, love.'

'You are most welcome.' The man beams, a bright beam splitting his face, his dark skin a mass of lines as he smiles.

'Yes, well,' Queenie says, turning to nod at me before shuffling out of the hall. Well, well, I think to myself, as I watch the man half-scuttle, half-dance across the hall to the sweet stall, his legs bowed by arthritis. 'Well, have you guessed how many?' he says to a little boy in a bright-red jacket, who is standing in front of a jar full of jelly beans. 'I've calculated it, Grandad,' the little boy says, 'and I've done a sum to work it out. Misty helped me.' Then I notice that Misty is beside him, their two heads close together as they examine the beans.

'Ah, of course,' the man says. 'Because Misty is a very clever girl.' He puts one hand on her shoulder and another on the little boy's, and the two of them lean into him, as if he's an oak tree and they are resting against him. Who is he? I wonder. Who's the little boy? Amanda would have demanded the child's CV at this stage, I think to myself, and asked where his parents had gone to university. Bad Dad here hasn't a clue, I think. I'd better get on it later.

I watch the boy and Misty writing something on a piece of paper before handing it to the lady manning the guess-the-number-of-jellybeans stall. I realise suddenly that I've seen him before, in the schoolyard. So, that's who he is, I think. Something about their closeness, about the way they do things in tandem, reminds me of Daisy and me, and my chest tightens. For God's sake, I think, I need to concentrate, reaching into my satchel for my collection of Irish twentieth-century poetry to see if there might be anything soothing in it.

'Can I have a poem please?'

It's the voice I recognise first. I make a great show of retrieving my notebook from my satchel, lifting it onto my knee, as if so engrossed in my art that I don't hear her, but my hands are shaking so badly that the notebook flies out of my hand and lands at her feet. I scramble up out of my chair and grab hold of it.

'Whoops.' I look up, as if I've only just become aware of her presence, but the pretence is useless. Even though I'm willing myself to stay calm, my palms begin to sweat and my heartbeat is galloping like a runaway horse.

She is wearing the green coat as usual, but she's done something different with her hair: she's tidied the mad curls into a little bun, but already one is escaping, springing up at her cheek, and she pats it down under a clip that's pinning the rest of her hair in place. It springs out again and she pats it down again, until she gives up, with a rueful smile, trying to sit down on the chair and balance the sling on her knee at the same time, the baby's two little feet poking out of the bottom, a blue bootee on either foot.

'Hello.'

'Hi,' I reply. There's a long silence while she studies my face with her big grey eyes, with their dark lashes the same colour as her hair, which is a really brown brown, the colour of dark chocolate. She used to have lots of freckles on her nose, but they seem to have faded, and her nose, which was small and neat, is now longer and stronger. She has Mike's nose. As she lifts her head slightly, I see that she still has the same tiny scar on her chin, just visible, and I recall that I gave it to her, hitting her accidentally with a tennis racket during a particularly vigorous game of Swingball.

I'm staring, but so is she and, for a moment, I think she knows who I am and my heart stops, but then she says, 'I know you from the bookshop!' Her face lights up. 'I was trying to remember. You work in the Japanese department, don't you?'

'That's right,' I say, 'You have a good memory.' But not as good as mine, I silently add.

'Oh, God, I don't think so. Ever since I had the baby I've a brain like a sieve. They say it's called "nappy brain", which I always thought was a bit sexist, but I have to admit it exists.' She gives a little smile, accompanied by a cute rolling of her eyes to heaven.

I know that I should do chit-chat, should reply to her comment with one of my own to the effect that there's nothing wrong with her brain, but I find that I can't. I say nothing, just sit there like a lemon and, even though my thoughts are racing, wondering how on earth Daisy came to be standing here in a community hall in north London, my brain refuses to offer me one sensible sentence to say out loud, so I settle for a kind of strangled 'aargh', which I hope she'll accept as a reply.

'Are you all right?' she says, looking at me curiously.

'I'm grand,' I reply, trying to regain my composure.

'You're Irish,' she says, in that slightly embarrassed way we acknowledge each other in this country, as if we're members of a secret society.

'Eh, yeah.'

'Where are you from?'

'Erm, Mayo,' I lie.

'I'm from Dublin, but I've been here for six years now, so I feel that it's home. What about you? What school does your daughter go to?'

'My daughter?' I sit back in my chair. How does she know about Misty? I look at her sharply, but her face is open and she's smiling politely and I realise that I'm being paranoid.

'Yes, I've seen you both around. She's really cute. What's her name?'

'You have? Erm, it's Misty.' This is officially the most excruciating conversation I've ever had and the effort of pretending is killing me. Why don't I just tell her it's me, Emmett, after all these years? What's the big secret? We can be old friends chewing the fat, reminiscing about things that we can hardly remember. She'll remember one version of events and I'll argue that it happened completely differently, and then we'll laugh fondly at our younger selves. We might even go for coffee for old times' sake and we'll share a scone and talk about the Old Country and … Oh, for God's sake. We won't do any of that because we'll both remember the truth about each other, and that, for me at least, the memories are as strong and raw as if it all happened yesterday. What if she doesn't feel the same way? If it doesn't mean as much to her as it does to me? And, besides, I let her down when she needed me. I should have stood up for her and I didn't. I should have opened my mouth at the breakfast table that day and said, 'I saw Dad kissing Bridget, too.' No, far better to pretend that I'm just the guy in the bookshop. That way, I can forget everything that happened.

'So,' I say briskly, 'what's the problem?'

'What do you mean?' She sits back suddenly in the chair, a look of alarm on her face, and I realise that I might have been a bit forceful.

'Well, you tell me your problem and I find a poem that helps.' I point to the sign. I pin a big smile on my face to make it seem like such fun.

'Oh, I thought you just read poems out,' she says. 'I was hoping for a bit of T.S. Eliot.'

'No. I offer psychotherapy too, even though I'm completely unqualified to do so.' It's meant to be a joke, but instead of laughing, she bites her lip.

'Have you got any poems about hating your mother?'

'I'd say there are enough of those to fill ten anthologies.' I smile. 'But let me see what I can find.'

I leaf through my collections, the much-thumbed Seamus Heaney, now with a coating of dog hairs, through W.H. Auden and T.S. Eliot. I find it quite easily, Schiller's poem about friendship, because I think that friendship is a more hopeful topic than matricide, and begin to read it aloud. It begins innocently enough with talk of easy contentment in friendship and I think it's going well, but as the lines go on, it becomes more and more purple –

'Did not the same strong mainspring urge and guide / Our hearts to meet in love's eternal bond?' – but I can't stop reading it or she'll suspect something, so I keep going, the words tumbling out as if I'm powerless to stop them, until I screech to a halt.

There's a moment's silence. 'Well, that was intense,' she says. 'I thought it was meant to be about my mother.'

'It's an allegory,' I improvise.

There's a sudden, long silence while she looks at me and I look back at her. She shakes her head then and says, 'I'm just wondering … have we … ?'

I open my mouth to tell her that no, we've never met, but then a soft wailing emerges from the sling and she springs back up again and begins to jog up and down. 'Sorry, it's just if I don't keep moving, he gets very cranky.' She's trying to be cheerful, but the look of exhaustion on her face tells another story.

'Why don't I take him for a moment,' I find myself saying.

'Sorry?'

'I'll take him,' I repeat. 'I have a knack with babies.' I do have a knack with babies. Even though I was only eight, I had the knack with Tom. I used to put him on my knee, lying him face down, and I'd rub his back in circles until he'd fall asleep, giving a little snore. Mum used to give him to me every night when he was a tiny baby and beginning his nightly crying session, legs drawn up to his chest with wind – 'It's my penance,' she'd say sadly as she'd hand him to me and I'd place him on my knees. At first, he was like a board, stiff with pain, but after a little rhythmic patting and stroking, his tummy gurgling against my knee while I watched *The Generation Game*, he'd give a giant burp and his head and legs would droop softly. Five minutes after that, I'd hear a little snore. When Dad would come in, after work or his Saturday game of golf, there Tom would be, draped over my knee, fast asleep. Dad would give me a careful look before going into the kitchen to Mum. He was always wary of my bond with Tom, as if it was somehow a threat to the peace that had broken out in the house after he'd come back from Birmingham. Wary, but not to the point of doing anything about it, like picking Tom up and dangling him on his knee or changing his nappy – that wasn't for unreconstructed men like Dad.

She looks at me doubtfully, but as the wailing is growing louder, she loosens the straps on the sling and pulls him out. He's huge, a big, red-faced bruiser with inky blue eyes and a tiny shock of blond hair on his forehead, like Tintin – only twice the size and the colour of a lobster. He's no looker, I think, but immediately I feel guilty – they say that all babies are beautiful in the eyes of their parents and I'm sure this one's no exception. I wonder what I would have thought of Misty if I'd seen her when she was a baby, as I take him in both arms and sit him gently on my knee. He gives me a wary look. 'Hello,' I say softly. 'What's your name?'

'Brian,' Daisy replies.

Brian? Who on earth calls a baby Brian in this day and age? I think, bouncing him gently on my knee.

'After his Dad,' Daisy adds helpfully, adding, 'not that he's around anymore', in a voice so quiet I'm not sure if she intended me to hear it. But I do, and my heart makes a little leap in my chest. I can't help myself. 'Oh?' I ask, feigning mild interest.

'No, he's scarpered,' she blurts, before catching herself. 'God, would you look at me – too much information!' She laughs softly. 'I'm sorry, I don't know what's come over me.'

'It's OK,' I begin, but then the baby reaches out a meaty hand

and grabs hold of the chain I always wear around my neck. To my embarrassment, he hauls out the Miraculous Medal that Mum gave me for my Holy Communion. It's a gold one, and even though I ceased to believe in the Virgin Mary about twenty years ago, I always wear it. Maybe it's superstition, or maybe, somewhere deep down, my faith is intact, ready to be dug up when I need it. 'I have one of those too,' she says, nodding at the Miraculous Medal.

I know, I think. My mum gave it to you when you made your Holy Communion. I don't reply, though, instead pretending that I didn't hear her, turning Brian to face me and holding his hands, jigging my legs gently up and down and singing, 'Horsey, horsey, don't you stop, just let your feet go clippity-clop. Your tail goes swish and the wheels go round. Hurry up, we're homeward bound.' On 'bound', I part my legs slightly so that he half falls, then bounce him back up again. His eyes widen with surprise, but then he lets out a guffaw of laughter. He bounces up and down, pulling on my hands. 'Again?' I say, and repeat the song. He throws his head back and roars with laughter once more.

'He never laughs,' she says wonderingly. 'I used to think there was something wrong with him,' she adds quietly. 'He always seems so … angry. When he was really small, I thought he didn't like me.'

'Babies aren't capable of disliking people. They just cry because they're hungry or tired or have a wet nappy – there's nothing else to it. We just pick up on it because we feel guilty that we can't make it go away.'

'You sound like a real expert,' she says. 'But, of course, you must be with your daughter.'

'Yeah,' I say, 'Seen it all!' as Brian tugs on my hands again for another go. I know that I should add that I haven't been Misty's dad from day one – that I'm actually a new recruit and a very green, useless one at that, but I don't. I just let her think that I'm some kind of parenting guru. I don't really know why, or why I want to impress her so much. It seems perverse, somehow, as if I want to present a newer, better me to the new Daisy. To reinvent myself, so that I'm as far away as possible from the boy she once knew.

We play the horsey game for another few goes, until Brian begins to grizzle. Then I put him over my knee and begin my patting and rubbing. At first, he lifts his head up and protests, but after a few minutes, he's snoring away.

'Wow. You're the Baby Whisperer,' she laughs.

'I wish,' I reply.

She opens her mouth to say something, but a voice declares, 'There's a queue here, you know!'

'Sorry.' Daisy turns to the angry woman in a purple fleece, with a giant plastic bag in her hands, stuffed full of paper. 'I'm just going,' she whispers, putting out her arms to me to take Brian. I lift him up as gently as I can, but the movement wakes him and he roars in surprise. There's much awwing and poor-babying as she takes him from me and kisses the top of his head. 'I'd better take him home. He's due a feed.'

'Oh,' I shout over the din. 'Do you live locally?' I can't help myself. Just one question, Emmett, I think to myself, even though you want to ask a million others. If you ask anything else, she might rumble you.

'At the end of Albion Road – number 34a – that's why I'm always in the bookshop. It's a real haven. Anyway, Thanks for the poem,' she half-shouts over his crying.

'My pleasure,' I shout back, giving a wave that I hope conveys a certain vagueness and a general air of benign but impersonal friendliness. 'See you around!' I don't feel vague, though. I feel quite the opposite. I feel precise, as if all my feelings have come to the surface and are hovering just inside my mouth, ready to burst out. I have to press my lips together to stop them, to keep them in.

Daisy looks at me again, her eyes scanning my face. She gives a small smile. 'What's your name?'

'Erm, John,' I improvise. For God's sake, I think, could I not have thought of something better than bloody John?

'Well, goodbye, John,' she says, the small smile appearing once more, and then she's gone, Brian's cries becoming fainter as she heads in the direction of the book stall, where I see the unmistakable figure of her mother, peering at a large, glossy book with *Vogue* on the cover. The turban has been replaced by some kind of hunting hat, or at least that's what it looks like: grey felt with a jaunty peacock's feather in it.

Oh, shit. I definitely don't want Bridget to see me. My hands trembling, I write 'Gone for tea. Back in ten minutes' on a piece of paper and place it on the desk, telling the lady in the purple fleece that I have low blood sugar and need a snack. She tuts, 'I'll be back in fifteen minutes. You'd better be good', and strides off in the direction of the cake stall.

I don't realise that I'm holding my breath until I see Bridget and Daisy head out of the door of the centre.

I drink my tea with shaking hands, scanning the crowds for any sign of Misty and her friend. I need to gather myself before I find them, I think. I feel as if I've fallen apart and I need to pull myself back together. My legs are like jelly and I can hear the roar of blood in my ears. I wonder if I might faint, so I take another swig of the sugary tea, and when Diamanda swoops down on me, I accept her proffered chocolate digestive. 'You look as if you've seen a ghost!' She giggles.

I have, I think.

I spend the rest of the afternoon dispensing advice and poetry to the people of north London, my mind whirring as I read. The lady in the purple fleece declares herself satisfied with my choice of poem about her dog, Buster, a flatulent boxer who has taken up a position beside her, ears pricked, and I remember to read Diamanda a poem about mothers – a nice one – and pretend to enjoy her obvious delight and her promise to keep me any leftover fruit cake. She doesn't know that I'm not the same man who turned up at half-past one, satchel laden with poetry books, a poem of his own beginning to form in his head. Now all thoughts of poetry have vanished, instead being replaced by flitting thoughts and memories of sand and wind and sun.

And then it's time to fold up my desk and chair and put my books away, and I dread the feeling of going home, being alone with my busy thoughts, so, when Misty runs over with the little boy and tells me that his name is Clive and he has to – 'absolutely has to, Emmett' – come for a sleepover, I go through the motions of saying that I'll have to talk to his grandad, even though I'd have any suitable-looking child over for the night if it would distract her and therefore me. A sleepover is just what I need.

I'm dragged across the hall and presented to Clive's grandad, the handsome man in the v-neck sweater, whom I'm told is Maurice.

He takes my hand and shakes it firmly, his dark skin wrinkling again as he beams. 'At last, we meet,' he says, in the musical singsong of the West Indies. 'Misty and Monica have told me such a lot about you.'

Monica takes Misty on Thursday and Friday afternoons when I'm working late, and Misty loves her because she wears belly tops and has multicoloured nails. I feel a dart of jealousy as I picture them both in Maurice's back garden having fun, while I'm slaving away in hell and I wonder what Misty's little life is like on those afternoons. A whole world that I don't know about.

Maurice and I agree that Clive can come for a sleepover and we exchange the usual parental bits of information and admonitions to behave and to remember our manners and to go to sleep at a reasonable hour.

'I know,' Misty says happily to Clive as they make plans, 'we can camp in the garden!'

My heart plummets and I have a sudden image of the makeshift tent that Daisy and I used to have on the beach. It was an old blue tarpaulin that her dad, Mike, had used to cover the boat he'd parked in the back garden. It was a big old yacht and he'd had grand ideas about restoring it and 'taking her for a spin around the bay', but Mike wasn't a 'taking a spin' kind of a guy. That would have meant not working and Mike lived to work. He loved standing in the hallway of Eagle's Nest, yelling into the phone, expletives flying as he ordered some site foreman around. Daisy and I used to listen, doubled over with laughter, to the stream of invective, repeating the words to each other later. 'Ya bollix, ya' and his favourite, 'arseholes'. The yacht never did get restored but was sold to a man from Wexford Town the following year and Daisy and I got the tarpaulin, for some reason. We spent a whole summer on the beach under it, lugging a cooler box with a bottle of red lemonade, jam sandwiches and a packet of Club Milks down the walkway from the house and onto the sand. We'd dig holes in the sand, elaborate channels that carried water down to the sea, that, in turn, were filled with the rising tide; we'd fish for shrimp with our yellow nets and—

Enough of the nostalgia, I think abruptly. I know what we used to do and it won't make any difference now. It'll only remind me of things that are painful, and I don't need that. Not with the life I have now. Things are complicated enough.

'It's a bit cold to camp in the garden,' I say. 'But you can pitch a tent in the living room if you like. Do we have one, Misty?'

'Oh, yes,' Misty says. 'Mummy bought a three-man tent for Roland and me and her to go camping in Greece last year. It was horrible because it was so hot and it got full of flies and then this kitten came in and I thought he was really cute, but he did a smelly wee all over Roland's new jeans.' She guffaws and Clive guffaws too.

'Well, there won't be any flies and we'll tell Bran not to wee on Clive's jeans,' I say, at which they guffaw again.

I spend the rest of the evening trying to erect a stupidly elaborate three-man tent in the living room, imagining Roland smoothly erecting it on a sunny beach in Greece. It isn't the usual frame, with the pole across the top, but a series of hoops, through which the tent must be threaded – if you thread the wrong bit, it all goes back to front. I try for two hours before giving up and suggesting that two bedspreads would make a splendid tent and that Misty and Clive could pretend that they are Berber traders in the Sahara. 'I know about Berbers,' Clive says solemnly. 'They are nomads who have roamed the desert for thousands of years, trading in camels.' He looks earnest as he says it, his brown eyes round, his hands by his side, and I bet that's what he does when he stands up in class to answer a question. I wonder if he gets teased about it, the way I used to.

'We don't have any camels, Clive,' Misty hoots.

'Maybe you could trade in Chihuahas,' I say, lifting Bran up and giving him a little hug. He gives me that bug-eyed stare before scrabbling to get down and join Misty and Clive in the Berber tent. Bran is Misty's dog now, and even though I'm pleased about that, I still feel an irrational sense of hurt that he doesn't actually like me – his rescuer from God knows what.

I go into the kitchen to make popcorn for the Berbers and get some fizzy water for them, so they won't get a sugar rush, and then I go back into the living room and see them lying there in their sleeping bags, Clive's tight curls beside Misty's long brown hair, their two heads close together on the pillows. Clive whispers something in Misty's ear and she splutters with laughter. I feel that my heart might break.

'Now,' I say, feigning cheerfulness, 'time for the Berber feast.'

The two sit bolt upright as I place the bowl of popcorn on the bedspread between them. 'Thanks, Emmett,' Misty says happily, helping herself to a handful, then continuing to speak, spraying popcorn all over the bedspread. 'Emmett, Can we say our prayers even if Clive is here?' Prayers are a new part of our night-time routine, and even though I have no idea what Amanda would make of this innovation, it comforts me. It also reminds me of Mum, who wouldn't let me into the bed without saying my prayers, 'In case the Good Lord takes you overnight,' she'd say ominously. I'm not religious, but I want to pass the tradition on to my daughter – that's what parents do, isn't it, without even thinking of it?

'Do you think you could ask with your mouth closed, Misty?'

'Sorry, Emmett,' Misty says, rolling her eyes up to heaven. 'Clive, do you say your prayers every night with Maurice?'

Clive nods solemnly.

'Well then,' I say, 'we can all say them together.' I turn down the main light as Misty wriggles out of her sleeping bag, taking up her position by the 'bed' of sleeping bags, hands joined in prayer, eyes closed. 'Come on, Clive,' she says. 'You have to do the same.'

Eagerly, Clive jumps out and kneels down beside her. Misty begins, 'Holy God, please bless Mummy and Daddy in Jamaica and Emmett and Bran and Queenie. Please help Queenie to stop smoking because it's very, very bad for her and please bless Clive and Maurice too. Oh, and don't forget Miss Grace, God, because she is having her wisdom teeth out on Thursday. Amen!' She roars this last bit, as if God might be deaf, and then it's Clive's turn.

He closes his eyes and says, 'Our Lord and Saviour, lest thou smite me down in my lowly place on earth, know that I have tried not to offend thee this day. I'm nothing but a poor sinner begging forgiveness and to you, Oh Lord, I pledge my faith until the day I die, whether it be in the burning fires of hell or in the angels' trumpet blast at heaven's gate ...'

Crikey. 'That's lovely, Clive, thank you,' I say, trying not to catch Misty's eye and answer the inevitable question I know is forming in her mind. 'I'm sure God will be happy with the lovely prayers,' I add firmly, nudging them both into their sleeping bags and thanking my own God that I can just have a moment to be alone. To think.

I close the living-room door and lean against the wall for a few moments, then climb the stairs and get into bed in my bedroom with the horrible floral wallpaper. I read the newspaper, scanning an article about whether I might be a Blur or Oasis fan and who would win the battle of the bands. Give me Oasis any day, I think. No weedy little songs about living in the country. When I'm finished, I distract myself by trying to remember the first lines of every song on *(What's the Story) Morning Glory?*, which Misty has on repeat on her CD player, in spite of my misgivings about cocaine and champagne references, humming 'Wonderwall' away to myself until I can feel my eyelids droop. Oh, good, I think. I'm going to go to sleep, in spite of everything.

Only when I am halfway through the song do I allow myself to think about Daisy, about her sitting opposite me in a crowded hall, the smell of sugar and mouldy books filling my nostrils, about what it felt like to see her again, about who we had been then and who we are now, after all these years. And then my eyes snap open and I'm wide awake.

8.

The staff meeting. It's the first thing I think about when I open my eyes. Oh, fuck. I can't go, I think. I'll just have to ring in sick, but then I remember that Betty said the staff meetings were 'mandatory', so I don't want to get into any trouble.

Apparently Petrus doesn't think that valuable selling time should be interrupted, so they are always held at 11 a.m. on Sunday mornings, so I have to get the kids up and into Queenie's, of all people, because Maurice has Sunday service to go to. They're both cranky from lack of sleep – I could hear sniggering and whispering and the odd thump as I lay awake last night – but I shove them into Queenie's with a wave and make my way around the corner of Albion Road, my eyes raw, my head muzzy from lack of sleep.

I walk up the road briskly because I know that I must walk really fast past Daisy's place, as if I barely know it exists. To think, all of those days that I walked up Albion Road on my way to work or brought Misty to school, I was just a few yards from her. From Daisy. The thought makes me feel as if I'm spinning in a washing machine, round and round, but I know that I must concentrate, keep walking until I get to Farrell's.

But, of course, I stop outside number 34a. I lurk, hovering behind the dustbin, waiting. It's a basement flat, a bright-yellow door down a steep flight of steps. How does she get the buggy down there, I find myself thinking, before chiding myself. I have met the love of my childhood and I'm wondering about pram logistics. Then the door opens and I scuttle off, the dustbin lid catching in my coat so that it clatters to the ground. Fuck, I think, flinging it back and marching swiftly up the road before whoever it is can see me. Pathetic, I think to myself. You're pathetic, Emmett O'Donoghue. Do you know that?

I am pathetic, I agree with myself as I push the door of Farrell's open and close it firmly behind me – Petrus has a fear of customers getting in on a Sunday morning, as if they are wild beasts that need to be kept at bay. As I walk in, Betty comes down the stairs in a vintage spotted dress and brown suede pumps. There's a fair amount of cleavage showing and normally that would cheer me up enormously, but I haven't got the energy. But even though I'm distracted, I can see that she is glowing. Her cheeks are pink and she looks softer, happier, her eyes bright behind her glasses.

'You look lovely,' I say. I hope that Betty knows that I'm not saying it in a predatory way, I think, but her happy face tells me that she sees it simply as a statement of fact: she does look lovely.

She blushes and I wonder if it's the same guy whom the jeans-and-plaid-shirt combo was for.

'What's his name?'

'Dave. He's into rockabilly.'

'Well, it suits you, obviously,' I say, as we walk up the stairs, wondering if I would say the same thing to Betty soon – 'Oh, my girlfriend Daisy's into ...' into what? I suddenly realise that I have no idea what Daisy's into now. I have no idea who she is, not as an adult anyway. The thought makes me stop dead for a moment. 'My girlfriend.' What am I thinking – even if there is no Mr Brian on the scene, it would still be plain wrong, wouldn't it? But really, it's because the words seem too normal, too casual, for the way I feel.

'Are you OK?' Betty looks concerned. 'You look a bit peaky.'

'I'm fine, thanks,' I lie as we climb the flight to the fourth floor. Apparently, Petrus likes to have meetings in his office. 'It's a power play,' Betty informs me. 'But don't worry about that.'

'Should I be worried?' I ask.

Betty shakes her head. 'I don't think so,' she says doubtfully. 'But you never know with Petrus. Anyway, what about you?'

'What about me what?'

'Is there anyone in your life?'

'Just Misty, I'm afraid.' It's the truth – there is just Misty. As I say it, I suddenly feel intensely lonely. I'd kind of forgotten, with everything that's been going on lately, that I haven't actually been out with anyone. I've turned into some kind of asexual monk over the past few months. I read an article once that said that men think about sex once every seven seconds. It made me feel kind of sad because I haven't thought about sex once in about six months. An image of Daisy in her green granny coat flits into my mind and I shut it down.

'I can't believe you haven't been snapped up,' Betty says. 'You are lovely – so tall and handsome. If I wasn't attached, I might go for you myself.' She blushes and gives a little giggle.

'Thanks,' I say.

'But I have a feeling that there's a Mrs Emmett out there somewhere. You just have that look about you, as if you're not … available.'

'That's just distraction, I can tell you,' I say.

She gives me a look that tells me that she doesn't believe me. She goes to say something, but we've arrived on the top floor now, and it's as ramshackle as the rest, big, dusty piles of books on the floor underneath a few plastic signs hanging on chains from the polystyrene ceiling, a huge set of those horrible white plastic shelves with a big crack down the middle and a yellowing poster of Neil Kinnock, for some reason, on an otherwise-bare wall. The putrid carpet is a bit less putrid here – a swirly patterned Axminster instead of a dirty puce – but it still has the look of an institution about it. Then I spot Petrus' office in the corner. The door is open and through it I see a wall of glass windows with spectacular views of the City, all the way down to St Paul's Cathedral, a jostle of silver and pale stone roofs, weathervanes and church spires, the giant green dome of the cathedral in the distance.

'Wow.'

'I know, it's amazing, isn't it?' Betty says. 'Typical of him to keep the best for himself,' she whispers, because a sudden hush has fallen over the assembled booksellers as Petrus appears. I can see Patrice's silver mane at the front, Nolan slouching against the wall beside

Petrus' office door, as if he could hardly be bothered to be here –
Nolan's default setting is the bored, rich American just in it for the
amusement value, like a character from an F. Scott Fitzgerald novel.
I feel a sudden dart of sympathy for Patrice. I can't understand what
he sees in him.

I can see over everyone's heads, needless to say, so I just nod
when Betty whispers that she's going to push through to the front,
and I try to make myself a bit smaller as Petrus' eyes catch mine over
the assembled heads. He's small and slight, dressed in a maroon
pullover, blue open-necked shirt and slacks – not jeans or trousers,
but slacks – in a vague beige colour with a knife-edge crease down
the front. He's standing on two gardening encyclopaedias, a mug in
his hand that says: 'You don't have to be mad to work here, but it
helps'. He's precisely the wrong kind of man to hold a mug like that,
I think, with his raven-black hair, translucent skin and his hands,
clutching the mug, with a bluish tinge to them, as if he isn't quite
human.

His pale-green eyes flick away from mine, like a lizard's, and I feel
my stomach lurch. Then he begins to speak. 'I've asked you to come
in today not for the usual staff meeting. It's rather more serious than
that,' he says, looking solemnly at the contents of his mug. 'I don't
quite know how to put it, so I will just come out with it. Farrell's is
in dire financial straits. Our stock levels are too high, our margins
are too low and our profit margin is nonexistent. If we don't do
something to turn the ship around, well ...' He shrugs, as if this
unfortunate turn of events has nothing whatsoever to do with him.

There's a deafening silence, before Patrice mutters, '*Quelle surprise.*'
He's right. Stock levels are too high because our half-human, half-
alien leader seems to order every single book that takes his fancy

whether it has any chance of selling or not, and the place is overstaffed, considering the number of customers – not that I'm about to mention that, as I have no wish to add looking for another job to my list of things to do. There's also the small matter that the place is a tip, and anyone looking to buy books has to negotiate an obstacle course that would rival the one at Aintree for the Grand National. It's hardly customer friendly and the man standing on the encyclopaedias doesn't exactly look like an agent of change.

Petrus continues in his barely-there voice, 'The reason I've asked you all here is because I would welcome your ideas about how to make this bookshop work more efficiently and to restore our sadly dwindling profits. It must be a team effort because we at Farrell's are one big happy family and we must fight this fight together.'

There's a long silence, as everyone absorbs the news that they are members of his one big happy family. Petrus rocks on his heels.

'So—' he says.

'How about closing unpopular departments?' Nolan shouts out.

'You would say that,' Audrey, the mousy buyer from Anglo-German Relations, says acidly, 'seeing as your department wouldn't be under threat.'

'Well, it's hardly my fault that there's been a boom in dirty realist American novels,' Nolan says smugly.

He looks meaningfully at Patrice and Patrice pipes up, '*Exactement*. We all know which departments are busy and which are not. It is time to cut them loose,' he says dramatically, making a guillotining motion with his hand.

'Traitor,' Audrey mutters. 'You're only agreeing with him because you're sleeping with him.'

There's a collective intake of breath. Patrice's face reddens and

I feel desperately sorry for him, in spite of his craven support for Nolan. So, I was right about them being more than just friends.

I put my hand up to say something, to dig my poor, horrible little French friend out of this hole, when Betty pipes up, 'For God's sake, can we have some sensible suggestions? Our livelihoods are on the line here and this is not the time for personal spats.'

There's another long silence, while the assembled throng tries to think of ideas to save the business. 'I think we need to be more customer friendly,' Michael, from New Fiction, says eventually. 'You know, take for the books at the till and not send people all over the place to buy a book.'

'Yes, but why change the habits of a lifetime?' Damian, from Adult Fiction, says acidly. Damian's department, otherwise known as Soft Porn, is the most profitable in the shop, with a steady stream of men in raincoats heading up the stairs to the second floor, every single one of them pretending he's heading to Agriculture, before making a sudden dart to the left at the top of the stairs. Damian is a heavy-set man with a mane of black hair and a huge beard, who wears Deep Purple and Led Zeppelin T-shirts and whose favoured reading material seems to be science-fiction novels, and he is totally unperturbed by titles like *A Plumber's Adventures*, with its cover portrait of a wrench and a bit of U-bend superimposed over a pair of giant breasts. The Soft Porn department does not do subtlety.

There are various wary glances at Petrus to see how he's taking this attempt to undo his life's work by actually appealing to customers, but he doesn't seem to be listening, rocking on his heels again, a small smile on his lips. 'Well,' he eventually says, as if he'd simply been waiting for the opportunity, 'I wondered about suggesting a voluntary contribution to help with the upkeep of an essential and much-valued part of this neighbourhood. Somewhere in the region of 50p per customer per visit.' He looks pleased with himself, then slightly less sure, as his remarks are met with complete silence.

'Petrus,' Betty says gently, 'we're hardly the V&A.'

'Well, it was just an idea,' Petrus grumbles, for the first time not looking even slightly pleased with himself.

'I know, how about live events?' Nolan shouts. 'Lunches, readings, that kind of thing. They do a great job of them in Waterstone's.'

There's a collective gasp at the mention of the Enemy – the shiny, modern, friendly bookshop on the green down the road, with its radical books-on-shelves policy and staff who show you where things are, big, wide smiles on their friendly faces. I have bought several poetry books there because it's a hell of a lot easier than trying to negotiate the poetry section here, with no book in alphabetical order and many with tatty covers and yellowing pages. It's depressing for a poet to see so many other poets' works clearly left to moulder, not a chance of a sale. Waterstone's does a brisk trade in modern poets and reading them makes me feel happy that at least I'm connecting with the work, even if I'm not writing much. Inspiration these days seems to come in little bursts, gone before I have time to even write my idea down, as if they are fighting for space in my crowded head, full of Misty and Daisy and Amanda and everything else. There's just not enough room for them, I think sadly, not at the moment anyway.

'That's a great idea,' Betty says. 'I know, Emmett can do the poetry. He's actually a poet himself. We can have a Spoken Word night.' She claps her hands together, as everyone turns to look at me.

Being six foot six, I can hardly hide, and instead I smile with fake enthusiasm, unhappy at the idea that my comfy, boring existence in Japanese History is about to end. It was the one and only part of my life where nothing at all was happening and I liked it like that. It was kind of nice.

'Oh, yes,' Audrey adds. 'Do you know, I saw him offering poetry therapy at the community fundraiser? He had a big, long queue of people waiting at his table.'

Petrus' lizard eyes flick over me again. 'Poetry therapy …' he says in a small voice.

'Yes, you come to him with your problems and he solves them. And he reads you out a poem as well,' Audrey says enthusiastically.

'Hang on, I don't solve people's problems,' I begin weakly, but am drowned out by a sudden wave of chatter. 'Poetry therapy, what a good idea.'

'I have this really annoying relative …'

'I wonder if you know anything about wills. My aunty Joan left everything to my sister and forgot me …'

'Will there be any modern American poets?' That's Nolan, smug little git.

Betty claps her hands. 'Quiet, everyone. It's a good idea, but poetry therapy is not going to save Farrell's. We need something bigger than that.'

There's general nodding and murmuring, followed by further silence.

'So,' Petrus says, 'the sum total of our collective efforts amounts to poetry therapy.'

'Well, we can start that anyway, but how about author brunches? We can invite local authors to talk about their books and answer questions and throw in a bit of food. Bob's your uncle,' says Betty. 'We can have a proper programme for spring, with scheduled events in it – or how about a literary festival? Waterstone's doesn't have one.' Betty should really be in charge of this place, I think. She's got the right go-for-it attitude and, it seems, a lot more common sense than her leader.

'Do we have to feed them? It'll cost more money,' Nolan says.

'Quite right,' Damian agrees. 'Let's just get them drunk on cheap wine, the way all the other bookshops do. I mean, if Waterstone's can do it, so can we. Right?'

As if in answer, a plastic sign suddenly falls from its rusty chain, dropping onto the floor with a sad whisper. We all look at Mid-Twentieth-Century African Art, then back at Petrus, as if the answer is entirely obvious. 'Well, the place will need a bit of tidying first,' he murmurs.

The plan is to lure the great and good of literary north London to this dismal independent bookshop, with the promise of cheap wine and soft porn as seating, and to have me administer psychotherapy to the locals, even though I am completely unfit to do so. I can't fix my own life, never mind theirs, I think. But then, if we don't do something, we'll all be out of a job. I look over the heads of the assembled staff and I feel a sudden sense of sadness. In spite of everything, I don't want Farrell's to close because, believe it or not, I actually like the place. Not as it is, of course, but the people who work here, and the little nooks and crannies, and the customers who rely on the place as the one spot in the area where they can lurk more or less undisturbed. I'll bet Waterstone's doesn't let people sit in the French literature section all afternoon, pretending to read Baudrillard but really drying out in front of the gas fire in the corner.

There would be no place for the washed-up, the lonely and the sad of north London were it not for Farrell's.

There would be no place for people like me.

'I think we should do more for the community,' I hear myself saying.

Petrus has jumped off his encyclopaedias at this stage, but at the sound of my voice, he climbs back up again, his lizard eyes flicking over me.

'I mean, look at Waterstone's,' I explain, ignoring another sharp intake of collective breath. 'They cater to the young mums with the bicycle carriers and the office workers and the like …' I don't add 'the normal people' because that would be overstating it. 'But Farrell's has always been a home for real Londoners, for everyone, and we should celebrate that.'

'How exactly do you propose we do that?' Nolan says boredly.

I have no idea, I think. 'Erm … we should have local events. Fundraisers, community open mikes, children's storytelling, that kind of thing …' I say vaguely, my voice tailing off.

'We're not a charity,' Nolan drawls disdainfully.

'Hang on, Emmett has a point,' Betty chips in. 'Who and what is Farrell's for? It's always been at the heart of the community here, so rather than punishing people for it, why not reward them by making the bookshop for everyone in the area?' She looks impassioned, cheeks aflame, chest heaving, and her eye catches mine. I give her a mental thumbs-up.

Petrus rocks on his heels for a while, examining the contents of his coffee cup. 'Put your heads together and bring me some ideas and I'll consider them.'

'Who. Me?' I say.

'Yes. You and Muriel. Consider yourselves a steering committee,' he says, climbing down off his encyclopaedias, going into his office and shutting the door behind him.

'Meeting dismissed,' Audrey mutters.

The crowd disperses and Betty catches up with me. 'Well done,' she says, putting her arm through mine and giving it a little squeeze.

'Thanks for backing me up.'

'No problem. We'll make a good team,' she says, giving my arm another squeeze, smiling up at me.

'I think we will,' I say, squeezing her back. 'I suppose we'd better have a meeting. Bit of a brainstorm.'

'Great idea!' she says. 'Let's get out, though. We'll never come up with good ideas in here. I know!' she says. 'There's a lovely community bookshop in Highgate. Why don't we have a recce there? I've got jive classes on Sunday afternoon, but I'm around next Sunday morning if that suits? Maybe you could bring your daughter along? Get a child's-eye perspective.'

'Great,' I say. 'That's good.'

'What is it?' Betty asks.

She has a cute little line that appears between her eyes when she's frowning, but I tell myself that Betty's cuteness is neither here nor there right now.

'Nothing. Next Sunday would be fantastic,' I say firmly, banishing the idea that was taking shape in my mind. A picture of me and Daisy and Brian walking hand in hand down the canal, watching the brightly coloured barges pass, stopping at a little café, maybe taking in an early show at the Screen on Islington Green ... Stop it, Emmett, I think. You are getting ahead of yourself.

'Well, it's a date!' She winks at me and sashays off to her office.

I reward myself with a look at her retreating bottom as she sways down the stairs, wondering if that's how we men are: that we can think of two women at the same time – can admire one's rear end while thinking romantic thoughts of the other. It's pretty shallow, but then maybe I'm more of a chip off the old block than I thought I was. What is it Mum used to say? 'Men are victims of their impulses, Emmett, so you have to learn to keep them in check.'

Trying to keep my impulses in check, I head for Queenie's to pick up the kids. I can't leave them there for much longer: they'll probably be smoking Pall Malls and drinking Beefeater G and Ts by the time I get there.

I'm speeding down the road when I see Daisy coming towards me in her pea-green granny coat, Brian in his usual spot, attached like a little limpet to her front. He's such a big baby that he's pulling her neck forward and she has to counter that by leaning backwards, taking small steps, as she can't see the ground. She really needs to put him in a buggy, I think, before adding to myself, 'Will you stop? You're not her mother. You're her – What, exactly?' I say to myself. 'What exactly are you?'

'Are you all right?'

'What?'

'It's just, you're talking to yourself.' She looks up at me with an amused smile.

'Oh, God, it's nothing, really. I'm just a bit stressed. I had a meeting,' I say. 'In Farrell's. Petrus always holds them when the shop's closed – it saves money, even if we all hate it. Mind you, this was the first time I'd set eyes on Petrus after four months in Farrell's. He's kind of weedy and a bit strange …' I stop as I realise that I'm chattering stupidly. 'Oh, never mind. How's Brian?' I peer around her at Brian, who is asleep, cheek pressed to her chest. It looks as if my eyes are fixed on her left breast and I'm mortified. This is not like my furtive thoughts about Betty. Absolutely not. Thankfully, she simply sees this as an opportunity to show him off and tilts to one side so that I can see his giant rosy cheek squashed into her, his nose at a strange angle, his woolly hat squeezing his eyes down into narrow slits.

'Oh, he's asleep. For now,' she says faintly. 'Anyway, I was hoping to bump into you.'

'You were?'

'Yes, I wanted to thank you for looking after Brian the other day at the community centre. He slept for hours when we went home.' She gives a small smile that implies this was the first time he had done so in quite a while. 'And, well …' And then, to my astonishment, she bursts into tears.

I stand there, like a fool, as the tears pour down her face and she rummages in her granny coat, pulling out what looks like a Christmas decoration, a soother and a set of keys. 'No,' she says. 'Now, where did I put my … oh, thanks.' She accepts my offered tissue and blows her nose, then folds the tissue and pats at her eyes. 'I'm sorry,' she says eventually. 'It's just, Brian never sleeps, and because he never sleeps, neither do I, and I feel as if my brain has completely melted and my bloody mother – who I invited over to help me, believe it or not, because I just have another two months of maternity leave left – is as useless as I expected her to be, even though I hoped she wouldn't be. I hoped that, just for once, she might drop the Ray Bans, whip off the stupid turban and actually do something! But no, she just sits in front of *Neighbours* and asks me what I think about Lou and what he's going to do about Madge, and as for Brian's dad …' She gives a snort of disgust.

Oh, Daisy.

I'm rooted to the spot, hands jammed into my pockets, wishing that I could disappear, thinking that I should ask her about Brian's dad, but that I also don't want to know. Thankfully, she doesn't seem to notice. Instead, she looks at me and says, in a very small voice. 'Do you think you could help?'

I'm silent for a long time, standing there on the windswept, chilly street, hands in my back pockets, scarf flying loose around my neck. I'm trying to find a nice way of saying 'no', because I know that this is a very bad idea. Eventually, I find the words, 'Help how?'

'Help me with Brian.'

'Oh, I don't think I'd have the time,' I begin. 'You see, I have work four days a week and Misty to take care of the rest of the time …'

'Oh, I didn't mean babysit him.' She gives a short laugh. 'There's no way. He won't even stay with my mother for ten minutes without crying. At least, that's what she tells me …'

'Oh?'

'No, I mean show me how it's done. You seem to have a real knack for it. And you have a daughter already.'

If only you knew! I think. 'Oh, I don't think I'd have anything to teach you,' I say. 'I mean, I know a bit about babies, but I can't remember enough to be of any use and I'm kind of busy …' My voice trails off as she starts to sob again, her shoulders heaving, a trail of tears and snot rolling down her face.

'It's not that bad, surely?'

I want to reach out and put a hand on her shoulder in a kind of fatherly way, but I don't trust myself, so instead I do this awful kind of throat-clearing, as if I'm Queenie trying to hawk up the results of fifty years of Pall Mall smoking. 'Daisy, every parent feels like you do sometimes. Children push us to our limits,' I say confidently, having no real clue what I mean. It's another thing I heard at the school gate, from one mum reassuring another while silently judging her at the same time. It's a skill that I've come to admire from my lonely position, waiting for Misty. I find myself saying, 'I'm sure I can help you – at least, I'll try.'

Her head flicks up and she smiles that smile that I remember so well – a big, broad smile that practically reached each ear. This is such a mistake, you stupid pillock, I tell myself, while trying to make my lips form a smile that mirrors hers. You can't let that heartbreak happen again. OK, it was nobody's fault but your stupid parents' and you were only eight, but you've carried that wound around with you for your entire life. Do you really think opening it up again is such a good idea?

As if in answer, another voice in my head says, But I'm a grown-up now, I can control my feelings, and, besides, it was such a long time ago. We were children, and the world was a different place. Now we're adults. And besides, she has no idea who I am.

Daisy gives me a funny look then and I realise that I must be muttering to myself, the way I sometimes do if I'm trying to work something out.

'Thanks,' she says, a little less enthusiastically.

'You're welcome.'

'So, do you want to come over to mine to start?'

'God, no, I mean … no thanks. It's easier if you come to me because of Misty.' Not to mention that I can't risk setting eyes on your mother again. 'I have a day off tomorrow, so come over to mine and we'll start. Don't forget Brian!'

'Hah …' She gives a little chuckle. 'It's tempting to leave him with my mother and come to yours for a little lie-down. I mean—' She looks flustered.

'I know what you mean. Well, you can do that if you like – on the sofa, that is.'

She blushes bright red. 'Well, see you then.'

'Yep.' I find that if I say, 'yep' it gives the impression that I'm a cheerful, businesslike soul, and I now add a jaunty, 'Well, must be going. Have to pick Misty up from the neighbour's. See you tomorrow – I'm number 65.'

'I know.'

'Oh, well, good then.'

'So …'

'So,' I say. 'Well … I suppose I'd better …'

'Of course.'

I'm about to turn around when I see Queenie, Clive and Misty heading towards me. Oh, no. I can't get lost, because Daisy will think I'm rude and the kids and Queenie will wonder what I'm doing, running off on them. So I'm forced to stand there while they come towards me, very, very slowly, Queenie on her walking stick, the kids dancing around her. And then Misty spots me. Please don't call me Emmett, I think, as I give her a little wave.

She waves back and comes running towards me. 'Look what we got with Queenie,' she says, opening a paper bag to reveal a little pile of lurid blue sweets. Uh-oh. I'll have to have a word with Queenie later. 'And we made jam tarts!'

'They burned our tongues, but they were delicious,' adds Clive, who has caught up with Misty. The two of them proceed to stick their tongues out to see whose is the brightest colour. Misty wins hands down with her sky blue, compared to Clive's jammy red.

'Say hello to Daisy,' I say, and they look at her as if they've only just noticed that she's there. I remember Daisy and I used to be the same as children whenever the adults asked us what we were up to: we could hardly bear to be polite, so eager were we to get back to what we were doing. I look over to Daisy now and she's looking at Misty and Clive intently.

'Hello, Daisy,' they parrot politely.

'This is Misty, and this is Clive,' I say.

'The famous Misty,' Daisy exclaims. 'I've been dying to meet you in person.'

'Why?' Misty asks.

Daisy looks disconcerted for a moment. 'Well, because your dad's told me all about you.' I haven't, actually, but Daisy obviously thinks this is the polite thing to say and Misty nods. Then she looks puzzled for a moment, before saying, 'Are you the same Daisy ...'

I cut across her, 'Misty, love, will you run home and check on Bran for me – here are the keys.' At the sound of Bran's name, Misty runs off with Clive. I have to get out of here, I think, before Queenie finally arrives, but it's too late. For some reason, she's picked up speed all of a sudden and, before I know it, she's standing beside me, looking hopeful.

'Queenie, this is Daisy,' I say eventually, adding 'from number 34a. Daisy, Queenie's our neighbour.'

Queenie peers at Daisy from narrowed eyes. 'Pretty thing, ain't you?'

'Thanks,' Daisy says, blushing.

'You'd never know you were 'is mother. He's a big fellow,' Queenie says, chucking Brian under the chin. Then she peers at me. 'You look good together, the two of you.' And she gives a short nod.

'Oh, we're not together,' I say hastily. 'Daisy and I were just discussing me giving her, erm … parentcraft classes.'

'*You?*' Queenie gives a small chuckle.

'Yes, as it happens.' I find myself using my pompous-ass voice.

'He's very good with babies,' Daisy adds helpfully.

'Is 'e now?' Queenie says. 'Well, I won't tell Mandy, love, you can rely on me.'

'Erm, thanks, I think,' Daisy says, pulling her coat around her. 'Anyway, I'd better be going. Good to meet you, Queenie,' she says, holding out her hand, which Queenie takes in hers.

'Likewise, duck. Don't be a stranger, now.'

'I won't,' Daisy says. 'Bye, John. See you tomorrow.'

'Look forward to it,' I say briskly, waving Daisy down the road and ushering Queenie ahead of me until we're safely at the front door. I can hear Misty and Clive inside. They're probably in their Berber tent, Bran curled up on a cushion at the entrance 'guarding' it.

'John?' she says, taking a big pull on the ciggy she lights up as soon as she's inside, eyes narrowing.

'Don't ask,' I say, waving the smoke away.

'I won't, love, but don't blame me if it all goes Pete Tong,' she says, walking ahead of me down the stairs to the kitchen, where she examines the tomato plants, nodding as she pinches the tops out.

'Pete Tong?'

'Yes, you know, love, wrong. It's the new lingo. I like to keep up with things. To keep modern, you know?'

'Right,' I say wearily and, when she eyes the kettle, 'fancy a cuppa?'

'Now you're talking my language, love. Don't mind if I do.' And she sits down on one of the chairs and puts her feet up on another, pulling her fags out of her pinny pocket and placing them carefully on the table. She sits there for a while, looking out of the kitchen window, accepting her cup of tea silently, before turning to me and saying, 'Nothing good will come of it, you know.'

'Of what?'

'Of lying, son. Nothing good ever comes of lying. Take it from one who knows.'

I'm about to protest that I can't think what she could possibly be talking about, but I catch her eye and she gives me the same look as Mum. 'I'm in big trouble, Queenie.'

'You don't say,' she says, lighting up another fag. 'Tell Queenie all about it.' And she leans back in her chair and waits.

9.

Queenie says that now that I've lied I have two choices – either to tell Daisy the truth about who I am and risk losing her before I've really even found her or to keep on lying. The words 'keep on lyin'' go round and round in my head like a country and western song. What would be wrong with just confessing and hoping that we'll both be friends after all? Would that really be so bad? The thing is, I'm in too deep. I've cast myself as Capable Dad, a jeans-clad superhero, who has flown in, baby bouncer in hand, to Daisy's rescue and I can't let the pretence drop.

She's calling round this morning, so I've dropped Misty to school then raced around to the charity shop where I'd spotted a door bouncer the other week. I'm praying it's still there. Door bouncers are brilliant for fractious babies.

When I get there, I sigh with relief when I see it folded neatly on top of a baby walker, checking it carefully when Doreen behind the counter lifts it out to me. Misty and I have become good friends with Doreen because we spend every Tuesday afternoon combing her selection of old books and comics. Misty is surprisingly keen on *2000 AD*, which I think is a bit violent for her, but she reads every story carefully while I peruse *The Victor*, with its wartime derring-do. I used to love *The Victor*, but Tom was more of a *Roy of the Rovers* man, acting out episodes in the back garden every Friday after he'd gone down to Mrs O'Flaherty in the newsagent's with his 5p.

As I hand Doreen the money for the bouncer, I remember that *Roy* was the one comic Daisy wouldn't let me read when I was with her. She said that it was just men being silly, chasing after a bit of inflated leather. Why did men always have to carry on like that? As if sport and drink were the only things that mattered. Even then, I had a fair idea that Daisy wasn't speaking her own words. That someone else had wondered why men had to carry on like that.

I tuck the bouncer under my arm and sprint back along the main road to the house, pulling the vacuum cleaner, which I haven't actually used until now, out of its designated cabinet in the kitchen and lugging it into the living room, where I hoover bits of old cracker and the remains of one of Misty's post-ballet pizza suppers from the sofa, a bribe to get her to continue visiting Madame Dostoevsky. I'm a bit more practical than Amanda – not above a bit of persuasion every now and again. I suspect that I'm taking the easy way out, but Amanda's not around to tell me, so I have to make it up as I go along.

Bran has followed me into the living room, transfixed by the large, loud machine I'm suddenly pushing in front of me, and decides to attack it, dancing back and forth and growling. I toss a bit of crust in his direction and am rewarded with five minutes' silent chewing. I throw the hoover back into the cupboard and wonder if I can tidy the kitchen in the fifteen minutes I have left before Daisy arrives. I survey the mess of congealing cacao porridge, dirty coffee cups and a copybook that Misty forgot to bring to school. There'll be no parentcraft in here, that's for sure. It doesn't fit with my image. Instead, I put a few spoons of Roland's very expensive Ethiopian coffee into the posh coffee maker and turn it on. There'll be a nice smell of coffee when Daisy gets here and it'll disguise the other not-very-nice smells, like the dog and Misty's trainers.

I run back to the living room and unfurl the door bouncer, clamping the grippers on either side of the door frame, then letting the little seat hang from the ties. The bouncer is red and shaped like an aeroplane, with a little propeller at the front. Without a baby in it, it looks kind of forlorn. Tom used to love his door bouncer, I think suddenly. His was pink because Mrs O'Brien down the road had lent it to us after her daughter, Audrey, had finished with it, and even though he'd bounce all day in it, Mum used to make sure it disappeared before Dad came home from work. Dad had very traditional ideas about what was right for boys and they didn't include the colour pink, which he thought was for 'nancy boys'.

What an idiot, I think to myself as I look at the empty bouncer. As if being a man has anything to do with colour choice – if only it was that bloody simple.

I think I'll test it out before Daisy comes. 'Bran, here, boy,' I say, and, pizza now eaten, he comes trotting along, ever hopeful of a walk. I lift him gently into the bouncer, placing two legs on either side of the seat. I push down and let him go. He looks a bit mystified but allows the chair to carry him, bouncing slowly up and down, before resting his chin on the edge of the seat and giving a little sigh. 'Nice?' I say. In response, he closes his eyes and nods off. I look at him for a few moments, wondering if even six months ago I could have pictured myself in a house in London, a father, bouncing a Chihuahua in a baby bouncer. That wasn't in my stars, I'd have to say. And nor was meeting Daisy.

Then the doorbell rings – a polite single 'bing' – and Bran leaps to attention, scrabbling to get out of the bouncer and assume his normal position beside the front door, tilting his head from side to side and giving a warning growl. 'Come on then,' I say gently, lifting him out but holding him tightly. I don't want him to frighten Daisy or Brian.

I open the front door, holding Bran in front of me like a shield. Daisy is standing there, in her green granny coat, her hair flying around her head with the wind, which is whipping bits of paper along the street, and she puts a hand out to tame it. Her fingernails are short, painted a dark red, and she's wearing a pretty dress ring on her wedding finger. She's put lipstick on and I can't help thinking that it doesn't really suit her. Her lips are just fine as they are.

'Hi.' She gives a little wave.

'Hi.'

We both stand there for a few moments before I remember my manners. 'Sorry, come on in.' I hold the door open and she walks past me, the scent of vanilla filling my nostrils. I take a big sniff, letting it fill my head. Lovely.

She hesitates in the hall, looking around her awkwardly, until I say, 'Just in to the left. Mind the bouncer,' I add, lifting it to one side to let her pass.

'Wow, this is so impressive,' she says as she stands in the living room, taking in the modernist lighting, the modular sofa in green and the expensive carpet.

'Thanks. Erm. We bought it at the bottom of the market,' I explain. 'A complete doer-upper. Took us years, but we're nearly there.' Amazing how one lie can follow another, I think as I invent a new story for myself. When you start, it seems that you can't stop.

'Well, it's amazing. You must have a real eye for design,' Daisy says appreciatively. 'You'd be amazed how many people don't. Who did you use?'

'I'm sorry?'

'As your architect. That's what I do, so I'm interested.' She looks around the living room again, taking in the fireplace, with its marble surround, which Amanda told me once came all the way from Carrara – 'in Italy,' she'd added helpfully, when she'd seen the mystified look on my face.

So, you're an architect, I think, as Daisy looks around in admiration, I always knew you'd be something interesting like that. You always did love drawing and building things out of the Lego Mike bought for me as a present, which didn't interest me one bit.

Then I realise that Daisy's waiting for my answer.

'Oh, Amanda took care of all of that,' I said. 'She's Misty's mum.' I don't know how to introduce her into the conversation without implying that we're together, so I try, 'It's a long story, but we're not together. I'm here to look after Misty while Amanda's away working with her partner, Roland.'

Is that a bit unsubtle, I wonder?

Daisy looks at me with her large grey eyes and says, 'Lucky Amanda. I wish Daisy's father would help out a bit more. We're not together either as you know,' she gives a small smile, 'but that's not the problem, really. He does come to see Brian and I suppose I should be grateful and, when he does, he's fine and everything, but he's not exactly a new man ... He has grown-up kids of his own and he says he's done with dirty nappies.' She gives a rueful smile. 'Maybe if I'd chosen somebody a bit, well, somebody who lived in the twentieth century for a start!'

Somebody like me. The thought pops into my head and I try to push it away, ushering Daisy onto the sofa, the words 'we're not together either', ringing in my ears. Bran jumps up beside her and gives her his best squinty-eyed look, craning his neck to get a look at Brian as Daisy hauls him out of his sling, giving the baby's head a little lick as she lies him down on her knee.

'God, Bran, that's disgusting,' I say. 'Get off!'

'It's fine.' Daisy laughs. 'I like dogs and he – or she? – is so cute. Aren't you?' she says, smoothing Bran's quiff down on his head. He practically purrs with pleasure.

'He's a he. And don't be fooled by the cute routine. He's a killer,' I joke.

'I'm sure you're not, are you?' she says, as Bran snuggles down beside her, giving a little sigh of pleasure at sitting beside his new best friend.

I clap my hands together in what I think is an avuncular manner, but the sound is like a gunshot in the silence. 'Right, so, coffee?'

She shakes her head and wrinkles her nose. 'No, thanks. I can't with Brian. Tea, please.'

'Tea it is,' I say. 'I'll just go down to the kitchen. Back in a sec!' I walk into the door bouncer on the way out and feel her eyes on me as I disentangle myself, my cheeks flushing with fresh embarrassment.

The coffee pot is hissing away on the cooker when I go downstairs to the kitchen and I busy myself putting on the kettle, before remembering that I used up the last of the tea bags on Queenie. They were Earl Grey, which she described as 'proper posh'.

I open the larder and look in, past the neatly tied packages of pulses that I haven't used since my arrival, to a row of tins at the back. I pull one out, take off the lid and give an experimental sniff. Smells like tea anyway. I put a few spoons into a little pot I find under the sink, my hands shaking as I empty the hot water onto the leaves and put the lid on with a clatter. I bring it and the coffee pot upstairs on a tray, pushing past the bloody door bouncer and placing the tray on the coffee table. 'Now,' I say, lifting the lid of the pot to survey a mass of green leaves floating in the water. It smells pretty pungent. 'I think this is herbal tea. Amanda's a big fan of whole foods.'

'That's good. I should be avoiding caffeine anyway at the moment,' Daisy says, nudging forward on the sofa to accept the cup I'm holding out for her. Brian wakes then and gives a little squeak of displeasure. She sighs heavily and gives a sad smile. 'I thought I might get five minutes.'

'Well, that's what the bouncer's for,' I say. 'Let's give it a try.'

She looks at it dubiously. 'He doesn't really like being apart from me.'

'Let's just give it a shot, OK? If he's not happy, we'll take him out.'

She nods while I take Brian gently from her and put him in, a leg in each hole. He hangs there for a few moments, swinging gently, looking a bit puzzled.

'Do you think we should show him how to do it?' Daisy asks.

'He'll work it out,' I assure her. We both stand there staring at Brian, whose face begins to screw up in distaste, a little wail coming from his mouth.

'Oh, no!' Daisy says, going to take him out, but I put a hand on her arm. 'Hang on, just give him a minute.' Her arm feels warm under my hand and solid, not like Amanda's collection of birdlike bones. It's an arm I can really get a grip on, I think, as I hold it for a minute too long then reluctantly take my hand away. I give the bouncer a little push and Brian begins to bounce, and as he bounces, a big smile breaks across his chubby face. He pushes his feet into the floor and bounces higher and the smile becomes a giggle, and before long, he is bouncing and twirling with enthusiasm, laughing away to himself.

'It's amazing,' Daisy says admiringly. 'You really are the Baby Whisperer!'

'Well,' I say modestly, 'it's just experience, you know?'

'Of course, you've done it all before.'

'Sure have!'

I am such a liar, I think, and what's worse, I am actually pretty good at it. It's a depressing yet liberating thought – that I can be anyone I like. That I can simply ditch the 'Emmett, nice guy, but bit of an eejit' tag and replace it with 'John, capable Superdad'. Mum would kill me, but it doesn't actually feel that bad. Maybe I'll be much, much better as John than I was as Emmett.

Daisy takes a sip of the tea and makes a little face.

'What is it?' I say.

'I don't know …' She sniffs it, then takes another sip. She winces. 'What kind of tea is this?'

'I think it's chamomile. Why?' I ask.

She passes the cup over to me and I inhale. It smells like old grass, I think, taking a cautious sip. 'Ew, that's rank. Sorry,' I say, putting the cup down. 'It tastes like mouldy hay. What?' I say, when she lets out a snort, followed by a soft giggle.

'I think it's weed,' she says.

'It is?' I lift the cup and inhale. 'Wow, it does smell a bit like it, I suppose.' I sit back. 'Erm, well,' I say. 'I have no idea … let me get you another cup, I suppose.'

She giggles. 'I think that's probably wise, much as I'd like to partake.'

I catch her eye then and the two of us find ourselves laughing. 'Honestly, I didn't know it was there—' I begin.

She puts a hand on my arm. 'Relax. I won't call the police. And besides,' she says, 'maybe it might come in handy.'

'Not at half-past ten in the morning, though.'

'Probably not.' She shrugs. 'Although …' and we exchange a sheepish laugh again. 'Some other time would be great.'

'Yeah,' I agree, torn between mortification and delight. Is she suggesting that we might see each other again? What's to stop us, if neither of us is attached? And if we do, how will I ever live down the weed-tea incident?

'So …' I say.

'So …' she agrees, and we both laugh again. This is not going at all as I'd planned. I'm like a nervous, tongue-tied teenager. Maybe I should just come clean right now and be done with it.

'Daisy?'

'Yes?'

She looks at me with those lovely eyes, and her face is soft and innocent and hopeful. 'I need to tell you ...'

At that moment, Brian begins to grizzle and Daisy jumps up as if she's been prodded.

'Just give him a minute,' I say.

'But he needs me,' Daisy says, knotting her hands in distress.

'He's fine,' I say. 'He probably just needs another little bounce, don't you?' I say, getting up to go over to him and bouncing him ever so gently. He rewards me with a gummy grin and he's off again, twirling and pirouetting like a ballerina.

Daisy sighs. 'I wish I had whatever it is you have. Can you bottle it?'

'I could put it in a tea, if you like,' I say.

She giggles again, and we spend the next hour talking about controlled crying and timing of feeds and scheduling of walks. I raid my memories of Tom's babyhood and cast myself as the ultimate Good Enough parent, laid back and warmly humorous about the travails of parenting, and it feels good. I find that I like being admired, being looked up to, instead of being considered a complete eejit. It's a bit of a boost to the ego, not to mention that if I focus really hard on being John the Superdad, I can forget, in a tiny way, that it's me and Daisy. Focus, Emmett, I think, when I see her push a curl out of her eye, tucking it behind her ear, or doing that cute thing with her tongue, the tip poking out from between her lips when she's changing Brian's nappy. Focus. You don't want to forget who you are, now, do you?

And then she looks at her watch and says, 'Oh, my God, it's twelve o'clock. I told Mum I'd meet her for lunch in fifteen minutes!' And there's a flurry as she puts everything into the giant nappy bag she carries around with her and puts the sling on. Brian does not want to stop bouncing, giving a wail and waving his arm in the direction of the door bouncer. 'You can come any time you like,' I say merrily, lifting him up and sliding him into the sling. He twists his head around for a better look at the object of his affections and gives another cry of outrage. I know, son, I think, welcome to the rest of your life: the minute you start to enjoy something, it's over.

'So,' Daisy says, when she's ready, letting me help her into the granny coat, then standing there, looking wistfully around her. 'I don't want to leave.' She smiles. 'It's so lovely here. You should see my place.'

'Stay then.'

She gives me that steady look of hers again, then shakes her head. 'Sorry. It's a nice idea, but I have to go. But some other time would be great.'

'Yeah. Some other time,' I agree.

'Tomorrow?' She looks at me hopefully.

Yes! I think. 'Erm, sorry, no. I have work. I'm not free until Monday next, at least, not with Misty's after-school stuff as well …'

'That's OK,' she says sadly.

'But we'll make a date for next Monday, OK? We can do something outdoors if you like – maybe go to Victoria Park. I think they have a band in the bandstand.'

'Sounds good. Maybe we could bring some of that lovely tea you have – put it in a big flask.' She giggles.

'Don't tempt me! Anyway, this was fun.'

'Yeah, it was, wasn't it?' Daisy says. 'It's nice to be on the same wavelength as someone.' She blushes. 'I mean, with Mum it's a bit difficult.'

'I know,' I say, wondering how difficult it might be with Brian's dad, but deciding that I'm not sure I want to know.

'I wish I'd met you months ago,' she says, as we both stand on the front doorstep. It's the end of March and yet it's still freezing, the bare branches of the trees swaying, a thin mist of drizzle falling. 'None of my friends are having babies yet, so it's all been a bit lonely …'

'Better late than never!' I say jauntily, cringing inside.

'Yes,' she laughs, 'Let's look at the bright side. Anyway … thanks, John.'

It takes me a moment, but thankfully I recover. 'You're welcome.'

'Right, then.' Daisy laughs at her reluctance. 'I really must go.'

'Yes, you really must.' I smile.

'Bye.'

'Bye.'

She walks carefully down the steps and onto the street, not looking behind her as she walks. I watch her until she goes around the corner and out of sight.

I spend the rest of the morning in a daze, wandering around the house picking things up, then putting them back down again in the same place. I should be cleaning the kitchen or something, or making some more of those hessian-weave granola bars that Amanda thinks are good for Misty, but nothing seems to interest me. I just can't focus. Eventually, I sit down in front of a medical drama on the telly, letting someone with Legionnaire's disease distract me from my thoughts.

I can still smell Daisy in the room, that vanilla scent mixed with the pungent odour of boiled weed. 'What are you doing, Emmett?' I say out loud. Bran, who is sitting beside me on the sofa, pricks up his ears, then goes back to sleep again. 'What do you want?' Bran opens an eye, wondering whether or not to get excited, then closes it again. 'You meet this girl, the love of your childhood, and you pretend to be someone else. All well and good, but what next? How long can you keep the John routine up and what happens if she finds out?' I say over a new medical incident involving a young child and a diabetic coma. 'She won't find out,' I say firmly. She mustn't find out that the boy she knew twenty years ago, the boy who let her down by keeping his mouth shut when he should have spoken up, is me. I want to begin again with Daisy. Even though I want to know everything about her, what her life has been like, how she came to be living here, just yards away, who she is, I also want to pretend the past never happened, to create a whole new future for both of us. 'That's what I want,' I say out loud. And then I think that maybe I want to be John because if I'm Emmett, I might end up like him. Like Dad.

Not going there, I think firmly to myself. 'C'mon, Bran,' I say, switching off the telly. 'Let's go walkies before we collect Misty from school.' Excited at the prospect of another little walk, Bran leaps up from the sofa and runs to the hall, jumping up at his lead, which is hanging from the antler coat-hanger in the hall. 'All right, all right,' I say. 'You'd swear you'd never been walked.'

I make sure not to go past Daisy's flat, taking the longer route by the park to the main road. I can't help thinking about the very subject I'm trying to avoid. I pass the charity shop, giving Doreen a little wave, past the Greek delicatessen with its huge jars of feta cheese and peppers, past the library where Misty and I go every

Wednesday afternoon to pick up a new book. I turn right at the top of the street and walk past the lovely posh shops and restaurants, then take another turn into the council housing estate, a huge post-war maze of red brick. Many of the flats have Arsenal flags hanging in the window, and through an open door I can hear Radio London, the squawk of cockney blasting out onto the pavement. I'm in the middle of a completely new world, and yet, in my head, I'm back at home, remembering the day Dad came back from his trip to look at the roads in Birmingham, as it were.

It was about two months after that last holiday in Wexford, I think, because Tom was born the following March. Dad opened the hall door and I heard the thump of his suitcase being placed on the hall floor. Mum was working away at the range, putting the kettle onto the hotplate to boil for the tea that would accompany the warm bread that was baking in the oven. When she heard the noise, she froze. I could hear the rattle of keys in the little dish on the hall table and the throat-clearing thing Dad always did to announce his presence. Apart from that one time, Dad didn't go in for drama, which made his aberration all the more unlikely.

I was sitting at the table, waiting for Mum to take a loaf out of the oven, knife poised to dip straight away into the butter dish to spread over the hot, spongy bread, watching it melt before I applied a thin layer of jam. I could see Mum as alert as a sheepdog, but she didn't turn around.

He came into the kitchen, hands in the pockets of his sheepskin jacket. He looked at me in a way that did not invite me to get up and go to him for the handshake that was our usual greeting, so I just sat there, waiting.

'Any chance of a cup of tea, love?' he said. Without turning around, Mum simply moved the kettle further onto the warming plate, placed a tea towel on the counter and, taking the bread out of the oven, tipped it out onto the tea towel, the way she always did, tapping the base of the loaf to see if it sounded hollow, which meant that the bread was done. She did this without even acknowledging Dad's presence, reaching to the knife block and taking out a bread knife, then cutting the loaf into quarters and then slicing one quarter into thick slices, steam rising from the warm bread as she cut. Then she slid the knife under a slice and turned around to hold it out to me, the way she always did.

'Thanks, Mum,' I mumbled.

'Francis?' she said then.

He nodded, and she turned around and slid the knife under another slice and held it out to him. He took it and put it down on the table and she tutted. 'Will you ever use a plate? What kind of manners did they teach you over there?'

Dad's response was to smile briefly, then obediently lift the bread up when she slid a plate underneath it. And then, as if he'd never been gone, he said, 'So, son, how was school today? Did you give Brother Iggy a piece of your mind?'

I smiled at him. Dad had gone to school with Brother Iggy and he always said that Iggy was as damp as an oul' washcloth. 'I did, Dad. I told him to get up the yard with his fractions.' Dad smiled back at me then. 'Good enough for him,' he said, before tucking into his bread and butter and jam. Mum was silent, sipping from her tea and looking thoughtful, and I remember looking from one to the other wondering who might speak first.

Eventually, Dad wiped his mouth with the napkin Mum had handed him and said, 'So, Mary, have you been practising?'

Mum gave him a sharp look. 'Sure, how would I be practising with you gone? I'd take out half the neighbourhood if I drove on my own. There wouldn't be a soul left at nine o'clock mass because they'd all have been mown down by me in my motor car.' She winked at me then and gave Dad the smallest of smiles.

'Well,' Dad said, getting up from his seat. 'No time like the present.'

'Ah, no, Francis,' Mum protested. 'I can't get into one of those blessed death machines.'

'You can,' Dad said. 'And you will. Come on, son. You can sit in the back and give your mother some encouragement.'

And so, like so many times before, Mum and Dad went out to the car, Mum blessing herself before she opened the driver's door, Dad sitting in the passenger seat beside her. 'Right, remember, mirror, signal, manoeuvre.'

'Mirror, signal, manoeuvre,' Mum repeated, turning the key in the ignition. 'May the Lord preserve me,' she said as she put the car into first gear with a loud crunch.

'Clutch,' Dad said.

'I know, I remember, Francis,' Mum said irritably. She pressed the accelerator down and the car began to move slowly forward, Dad helping by lifting the handbrake. The car inched down the driveway to the front gate.

'Take it handy here,' Dad murmured as Mum drove through the front gate onto the road, pressing sharply on the brakes as a tractor came very slowly along the road. 'This fellow will be all day and all night, so you can pull out.'

'I'll wait,' Mum barked. Wisely, Dad said nothing and we all waited for the tractor, which seemed to be doing about five miles an hour, to pass us, Gay Hennessey sitting up in the seat, his dog beside him, lifting his arm in a wave.

'That eejit,' Mum muttered.

'One and the same,' Dad replied.

Mum pulled out very slowly, leaning forward over the steering wheel, clutching it tightly and peering into the windscreen.

'Sit back, Mary, you're restricting your vision there.'

Mum tutted but leaned slightly back into her seat, the car picking up speed as she negotiated the change to second, then third.

'Right, now, into fourth. You have enough road,' Dad said.

'I will not,' Mum bit back. 'Third is quite enough for me, thank you.'

Dad didn't reply and we proceeded at the same stately pace, the ditches and hedgerows with their thick green foliage passing slowly as we drove along. 'We'll take the cemetery road,' Dad announced after a while.

'It's a right turn,' Mum said. 'I don't do right turns.'

'You do now. Or you will if you ever want to go anywhere other than mass,' Dad said firmly. 'So, begin to slow as we get to the junction,' he said.

Mum lifted her foot off the clutch and slammed on the brake, so the car cut out.

'Oh, Sacred Heart,' Mum said, beginning to panic. 'Francis, we'll be rear-ended.'

'Stay calm, Mary, please,' Dad ordered. 'Son,' he said to me. 'Keep an eye out of the back window while we get the show on the road, will you?'

Obediently, I turned to watch the road, the long stretch of black tarmac empty. 'It's fine,' I said, turning back.

'So, keep watching,' Dad said. 'Make sure it stays fine.'

I turned back again while Dad said. 'Right, Mary, put her into neutral.'

'I can't remember where neutral is!' Mum shrieked.

'You can,' Dad said, and when I snuck a look, his hand was on hers on the gear stick and he was guiding it into neutral. 'Now, turn the key in the ignition.'

'Right,' Mum said obediently.

'Dad,' I said.

'Find the biting point ...' Dad was saying to Mum.

'Dad.'

'That's it, now, ease her along ... What is it, son?'

'There's a car coming.'

'Tell me when it's close,' Dad said calmly. 'Now, Mary, press a bit harder on the accelerator, go on, just a bit harder, that's it, easy does it.'

The car, which had seemed a long way away just a few seconds ago was suddenly looming towards us. I had a sudden vision of it not stopping, hitting us, sending our car catapulting into the air. 'Dad!'

'Understood,' Dad said to me. 'Mary, press down and change into second ... good, now, third, that's it. Well done.'

As our car picked up speed, the other car faded away into the distance and I saw that it had actually been driving pretty slowly. We wouldn't have been mown down at all. I allowed myself to let out the breath I'd been holding and turned around to settle back down in my seat. We trundled towards the junction and Mum managed to put her indicator on and turn right and, ten minutes later, we had pulled up outside the graveyard.

Mum turned off the car and leaned forward on the steering wheel. 'I made it,' she murmured, then lifted her head up. 'I made it!' She gave a little cheer, then she leaned over and gave Dad a peck on the cheek. 'Thank you, love.'

'Yes, well,' Dad said, accepting the kiss. 'You can thank your son for acting as lookout.'

Mum turned around to me and a bright beam split her face. 'Thanks, son. We make a good team, the three of us, don't we?'

We did, I think now, as I turn the corner onto the Holloway Road. And when, nine months after Dad came back, Tom was born, we became a team of four. I understood, as I sat in that car, what Dad was for, the steadying presence, the bulwark against what life might throw at us, the man who took charge, who kept us safe. That's some responsibility, I think, as Bran stops to sniff an empty takeaway carton. I suppose that's why he 'strayed', as Mum put it – maybe he wanted to not be that kind of man for a bit, the man who spent every day on the roads of Galway, checking camber and moving ground crews around, then came home to teach his wife how to drive and to do his son's maths homework with him. Maybe that's not the life he'd planned for himself – I have no idea, because I never asked him. But as we pass the Fantasy Emporium, where I'd bought that book on parenting, I understand that this isn't the life I'd planned for me either. That maybe none of us gets the life we've planned.

'That'd make a man think, eh, Bran?' I say, as I realise that we've come as far as the Odeon. Maybe I'll call in to Tom, I think, but then if I do, I'll have to tell him about Daisy, and I can't do that because then I'll have to explain the whole John thing and he won't understand. Tom's pretty literal like that – straight as a die. Tom does not do lies.

I'm hovering in front of the Odeon, looking at the posters to see if there's any film that might be suitable for Misty, when I see him at the other side of the road. Tom. Fancy that, I think as I lift my hand and wave. 'Tom!' I call out.

He doesn't hear me because he's talking to someone – a slight, dark-haired man in a blue denim jacket. Their heads are close together and they're walking quickly, then Tom leans over and gives the man's shoulder a squeeze. The man tilts his head towards Tom and there's a brief peck on the lips, before they part. I stand there, hand in the air, then I lower it. 'What's that about, Bran?' I say. He doesn't look very interested because he's discovered the remains of a chicken box and he's pushing it around the pavement. I debate whether to call out his name again, louder this time, but decide not to. I'm not sure what I'd say to him. Maybe I misread the scene, I think. Maybe they're just friends.

'Come on, you eejit,' I say, tugging at Bran's lead. 'Let's go back and collect Misty from school.' At the sound of Misty's name, the one person Bran loves most in the whole world, he gives a little yelp and turns around, marching swiftly back in the direction he came. You too, I think, wondering why I suddenly feel so alone.

Normally, Misty throws her arms around Bran when she sees him at the gate, but now it's all she can do to acknowledge his presence. 'Hello!' I say brightly, but in response, she just mutters something about being tired.

'What is it?' I ask her.

'Nothing,' she says miserably.

'C'mon, it must be something,' I say. 'You can tell me. Is it Mum?

Do you want to give her a ring later?' We've taken to ringing Amanda every couple of days because of the time Misty called and Amanda told her that she was really lonely in Jamaica. 'I miss you such a lot, Misty-boo,' she'd said, as Misty had stood there, listening, unsure of what to say, of how to address her mother's loneliness. 'I even miss you, Emmett!' she'd added with fake cheer. I'd laughed along but didn't probe because I told myself it was none of my business. Instead, Misty and I made a habit of calling Amanda regularly, even though there's only so much you can say in a phone call. She and I both know that.

Misty looks at the ground. 'No, thank you, Emmett.'

'Well then, what is it?'

'I don't want to talk about it, Emmett, because I'm very sad,' Misty says firmly, clenching her little fists, eyes downcast.

'If you're sad, tell me. Then you won't be so sad.'

She gives a deep sigh. 'When was the Battle of Hastings?'

'Erm, 1066,' I say, baffled.

'I told Clive that, but he said that any idiot knows that and that I needn't think I'm cleverer than him because I'm not. In fact, he said he didn't think that I was very clever at all,' she says sadly.

'You've had a row about the Battle of Hastings?' I say.

She nods sadly.

'Misty?'

'Yes,' she says, stretching out her foot to avoid stepping on a line on the pavement.

'Are you upset about the facts or is it something else?'

She shakes her head. 'No.'

'No, to the fact or, no, it's something else.'

In response to my prodding, she throws her arms around my

legs. 'Oh, Emmett. Clive doesn't like me any more. He's gone off with Sophie and she's really horrible, but she's got a Gameboy.'

'What's a Gameboy?' I ask, imagining Sophie, with her blonde curls, luring Clive away, the little madam.

'It's like a computer and you play games on it. It's really small.'

'Do you want one – is that it?'

'No, I think they're silly – who wants to chase a stupid little man around a screen? – but maybe Clive would like me if I had one.'

'Oh, Misty. I'm sure Clive likes you. Sometimes, people get … distracted, that's all. They don't realise that the other person feels upset.' Boys are really stupid sometimes, I wanted to add but didn't. 'Have you told him how you feel?'

'I told him that he wasn't as clever as he thinks he is because Miss Grace is sending Gordon Stephens to the Science Fair and not him, and he told me that if he wasn't clever, I wasn't either because I got second in the spelling bee.'

Oh, I think, that's probably not telling him how you feel, but we won't go into that now, as Misty dissolves into tears, and I have to pick her up and carry her home and sit her on the sofa while I heat up warm milk and stir in some cacao nibs and a good teaspoon of sugar, praying Amanda doesn't have some kind of CCTV in the house to alert the sugar police.

'Right,' I say, when I bring the drink into the living room and sit down beside her. She allows me to put an arm around her and even to give her a little squeeze, while she sips and sucks her thumb.

'I'm sorry about Clive, Daisy. I'm sure—' I begin, before realising that platitudes are not what's required. 'You must be feeling very sad.'

She nods quietly and her thumb sucking becomes louder. 'Emmett?'

'Yes, Misty?'

'Did you ever have a row with your friend Daisy?'

'Oh, yeah, lots of times. We were always fighting.'

'What kinds of fights?'

'Oh, just silly things, like when we had to share sweets. We'd have to count them out, you know, "one for you, one for me", and I'd count too many for me. Or I'd want to read the *Beano* before she'd finished, that kind of thing.' I'm lying, kind of. We never did row that final day – there was no need. Our parents did all of the rowing for us, but that wasn't the point. By not sticking up for Daisy, by letting her down, I'd sealed our fate.

'I have an idea,' I say. 'Roland has this games thingy in his study. Why don't I see if I can get it to work and we can invite Clive around to play on it? It's Pacman or something. He'll like that.'

Misty looks at me for a long time, then shakes her head. 'I don't want to pretend to be Sophie so that Clive likes me. I want to be myself.'

'You're right. Of course,' I say, marvelling at having been put straight by a seven-year-old. 'Give it time, Misty. It'll be OK. I promise. You and Clive are special friends – he'll remember that before too long.'

Mollified, she nods and tucks herself into me, one hand on my leg and the other on Bran's furry head, and we watch silly cartoons. I nod off for a bit and, when I wake up, it's almost dark outside. Misty has fallen asleep, her head tilted backwards, a little snore coming from her half-open mouth. Poor thing, I think, getting up and stretching, wondering if there's anything left of the lentil lasagne we had last night.

I go into the hall and turn on the light, throwing Misty's trainers into the shoe tidy and hanging Bran's lead on the antlers, and I see a rolled-up piece of paper sticking in through the letter box. I pull it gently out and unfold it.

The handwriting is bold and angular, tilting to the left, and as I read I wonder idly what the handwriting says about the writer. I read somewhere that you can tell a lot about a person from their handwriting – that mass murderers have been rumbled by the slope of their ts.

Hi, Emmett.

Thank you so much for everything. I haven't felt as comfortable "being Mum" ever! You are a great teacher. Thanks again! Daisy x

I look at the x for ages, wondering if I can decode it – if it's a casual x or a romantic x. Is she trying to tell me something, I think, as I scan the cheery sentences for any sign of a subtext. Then I see the PS at the bottom of the note, as if she was half-hoping I wouldn't see it.

Is there any chance you could mind Brian for me on Sunday morning? I'm sorry to ask, but I promised Mum I'd take her to a concert in town and I can't bring Brian. Would you mind terribly? Let me know!'

'Mind terribly?' Of course I wouldn't, I think, sucking in a deep breath. I'd be thrilled.

10.

Oh, crap, I think, when I open my eyes. I completely forgot about Betty. I'd promised to go with her to that bookshop in Highgate, but I can't if I'm minding Brian. Well, I can, but I can hardly lug a friend's baby along, can I? That'd be a bad idea. I mean, he probably won't make much noise, but still. I'll have to nip up to Farrell's and tell Betty, I think. She said she'd meet us outside. She won't mind.

It's early – the dial on my electric alarm clock tells me 7.30 a.m., but Daisy said she'd drop Brian over at 8.30, so that she could get ready for the concert. I'd better get myself together, I think, swinging my legs from the bed.

I take a long shower and use some of Roland's expensive-smelling shower gel. I haven't dared to touch it before now, but the occasion seems to demand it. I shave carefully, brush my teeth and examine my nostrils for any stray hairs, then select my least-creased Levi's from the armchair, pairing them with a shirt that has a small floral pattern that I think is Tom's. Tough, I think, admiring myself in the mirror. It's mine now. An image flits into my mind of Tom and the small man in Holloway, but I let it flit right back out again. I'm a busy man today. No time to waste.

Washed and dressed, I go downstairs to the kitchen, putting on the coffee and tidying away cups and bowls from the dishwasher into the cupboards. I put some porridge on for Misty – she likes porridge because I cook it the way Mum did, with lots of milk and a tiny pinch of salt – then I put a tin of expensive dog food out for Bran, having first let him out to the garden for a wee.

As I work, I hum a little bit, Modern Dad in his kitchen, doing his thing, at one with himself and the universe. Surely, I think, if Daisy didn't like me, she wouldn't ask me to mind Brian. That must be a sign, I think, that she trusts me, at least. And trust is as good a place to start as any.

When the doorbell rings, my John persona is fully in place. I'm laid-back, barefoot but smartly dressed, emanating a whiff of expense thanks to Roland and some designer aftershave I found in the chest of drawers in the bedroom. I'm showing just the right amount of carefree-but-responsible vibes, a bit of casual charm mixed with seriousness. If Mum could see me now, she'd tell me that I was getting notions, but Mum can't see me, I think. Which is a good thing.

'Hey,' I say easily. 'You look lovely.'

When I've said that to Betty before, I didn't mean anything by it, but this time I do. I wonder if Daisy can tell.

She's not wearing the granny coat, but instead a deep blue dress, the colour of cornflowers. The colour reflects in her eyes and she's done that thing again with her hair, twisting it into a knot at the back of her head, pulled together with a pretty clip.

'Thanks,' she says shyly. 'It's only a concert with Mum, but I thought it'd be nice to dress up for once.' She smiles. 'Pretend I'm normal for a change!'

'Well, you should do it more often,' I say smoothly. There's a moment's hesitation while she and I wonder what I mean by this, then I say, 'Let me take Brian.' I pull him gently from his sling and he rewards me with a look of mistrust, anxiously glancing at his mother as she puts a bag the size of a small suitcase down on the hall floor.

'I've left a couple of changes of clothes in it and a bottle in case he gets hungry. If he finishes it, some cooled boiled water would be good, but make sure it isn't warm – he hates that,' she says, as he begins to cry.

'Why don't you get going while Brian and I get reacquainted?' I say, fixing Brian with a big smile. He responds by wailing loudly, holding his arms out to Daisy, who goes to take him back. 'Leave him,' I say, firmly but calmly. 'He'll be fine. Promise.'

'Are you sure?'

'Of course,' I say. 'Sure haven't I done this a million times before?'

'Of course you have,' she says. 'Well, thanks a million, John. I really appreciate it.' And before I can react, she leans across and pecks me on the cheek. Actually, it's more my neck because I'm a foot and a half taller than her. I can feel the imprint of her lips on my skin and I put a hand up to the spot, inhaling that scent again. Vanilla, but this time mixed with something else more sophisticated. Then I remember that Bridget liked Chanel No. 5. That's what it is, I think, the cloying smell now mingling with that of vanilla and with the coffee brewing in the kitchen. It's heady and it's making me feel a bit sick.

'Of course! No problem!' I say merrily, urging Daisy to make a run for it while Brian is distracted laughing at Bran's squeaky chicken, which he's brought to us to show off.

'Bye!' she mouths. 'I'll be back after lunch.'

'Take your time!' I say. 'No rush at all!'

'Oh, my God, the sling,' she says, laughing, lifting it over her head and handing it to me.

And then she's gone in her cloud of perfume and Brian and I are standing in the hall, looking at each other. 'So,' I say. 'How are you, my friend?'

His response is to emit a wail, leaning back and turning his head as far as it will go in search of his mother. 'It's OK,' I say softly. 'She'll be back soon. C'mon, let's go to the kitchen and have a cup of coffee. I mean, me, that is. You are not going to have coffee.'

He looks at me for a long time, but this time the look is quizzical, rather than downright terrified, and I carry him into the kitchen, holding him on my hip as I move around, pouring coffee and putting bread into the toaster. He's solid and heavy and my arm begins to hurt, but I realise I like it. I never got the chance to do this with Misty. By the time I came into her life, there was no more carrying or pushing in buggies, no pointing out bird life and interesting bits of machinery, the way I used to with Tom. He was a great fan of muck-spreaders, as I recall.

I give Brian a little squeeze, feeling the soft rolls of fat around his waist. I missed this, I think, as I pop a little kiss on his bald head.

When Misty comes down to the kitchen, she doesn't say

anything, stepping carefully around Brian, who I've propped up on some cushions on a blanket, and going to the microwave to warm up her porridge. She gives a little yawn and pushes her hair out of her eyes.

'Emmett?'

'Yes, Misty,' I say.

'Why is there a baby here?'

'Oh, we're minding him for Daisy. You remember her?'

Misty nods. 'Emmett?'

'Yes?'

'Isn't it funny that Daisy has the same name as your friend?'

I freeze, then manage, 'It's just a coincidence, Misty – lots of people are called Daisy. Lots of girls, I mean. It'd be silly for boys to be called Daisy.'

I'm joking, but Misty doesn't respond, chewing her porridge in silence. She's not a morning person, so I thank God that she seems to have accepted my story and leave her in peace to eat and twirl the spoon in her bowl, staring vacantly out to the garden. Brian has found that a wooden spoon banged repeatedly against a pot makes a brilliant noise and the noise is making my ears ring, but Misty seems unperturbed.

'May I be excused?' she says when she's finished.

'Yes, you may,' I say, pleased that Misty has remembered the good manners I taught her. I couldn't believe that Amanda, with all her edicts about hand-rolled muesli and essential food groups, didn't teach Misty some table manners. I wonder if we'd have made a good team as parents to Misty. I suppose we already do, in a strange kind of way.

'I'll put on my nice jeans,' Misty is saying, raising her voice just slightly over the din, 'because we are going to the bookshop today,' and she gives a little skip. Misty loves bookshops more than anything, and she's intrigued at the idea of visiting one with me and with Betty, my 'boss from the bookshop'. Misty has never even met her. I think she has romantic notions of the two of us, which is way wide of the mark.

Shit. I forgot to tell Betty, I think, looking at my watch. It's nearly ten o'clock now. I can't cancel at this stage. I'll just have to take Brian along. Something feels not quite right about that, as if I'm mixing one person up with another – John and Emmett – but then, I reason, Betty won't know that. And besides, Misty could do with cheering up. She's still upset about Clive.

'Good idea,' I tell Misty now. 'And something warm. You don't want to catch a cold,' I call after her as she runs out of the kitchen. Misty returns in her jeans, to which she's added a black-and-white spotted top, which I'm sure comes from her Dalmatian pyjamas, a paisley scarf that's Amanda's and a bright pink bobble hat. It's an interesting look and I'm about to suggest that she try another one, but then I think, so what? Who cares if Misty wears the top of her bloody pyjamas? I sure as hell don't.

The next fifteen minutes are spent changing Brian's nappy, which he's soiled with something green and unpleasant – 'Ooh, Emmett, it's slime!' Misty says gleefully – then putting him into his sleepsuit, before trying to put the sling on, pulling at the toggles and belts until it could fit a man of my size, rather than a tiny woman. I'm beginning to understand why Daisy never leaves the house – I'm exhausted just getting ready.

I've turned Brian around to face the front, because I read somewhere that older babies prefer it, and I'm rewarded by Brian kicking me in the crotch every few seconds as he wriggles around. Too late to rearrange myself again, though, so I lift the changing bag onto my shoulder and, finally, looking like a Sherpa ascending Everest, I leave the house, Misty running ahead of me around the corner and up the road to Farrell's.

Betty is waiting outside in a neat dark-grey coat and cute little black suede boots, her hair tied to one side in a kind of bunch.

'Hi!' she says brightly when she sees the two of us. Misty stops about four feet in front of Betty and hops from foot to foot.

'Well, who have we here?' Betty says gaily. 'I like your style.'

'Thank you,' Misty says politely. 'You have very red lips.'

Betty smacks her bright-red lips together and giggles. 'Oh, yes. I thought I'd make a bit of an effort.'

'Why?'

'Erm, because it makes me feel better, I suppose,' Betty says easily, unaffected by Misty's direct manner. 'What's your name? I'm Muriel, by the way,' and she extends a hand.

'Misty,' Misty says, accepting it and giving it a cautious shake.

'Wow, what an amazing name,' Betty says. 'It tells me that you are someone very special, like a princess or a queen. Queen Misty the First. It has a ring to it, doesn't it?'

Misty's little face breaks into a smile and she reaches out and takes Betty's hand, all ready to go. They look completely at ease with each other, as if they've known each other for ages, and a little voice in my head wonders whether Misty would hold Daisy's hand in the same way. Of course she would.

Betty's eyes widen as I come closer, and she sees that there's a baby attached to me.

'Favour for a friend,' I explain.

'Oh,' she says. 'Well … that's nice. We're a little family,' she adds, smiling in that open way she always does, as if the world just makes her happy. It's a bit annoying, to be honest. A bit girl-scout-y.

Misty insists on holding Betty's hand all the way to the bookshop, the two of them chattering away like old friends. In the space of a fifteen-minute bus journey, Misty learns that Betty has two brothers, she has a pet guinea pig, who is seven years old and lives in a shoebox in her kitchen, and that she's really good at Monopoly.

'My mum used to play Monopoly with me,' Misty says sadly. Betty looks at me over Misty's head and I smile blandly.

'Oh, really. Was she as good as me? I get Mayfair every time and I build lots of hotels on it and charge people a fortune.' Betty giggles.

'Oh, yes! I try to get all the train stations,' Misty says. 'Because if you have all of them, you can charge people four times the rent.'

'Thats it!' Betty exclaims. 'We'd make a great team.'

Then Misty launches into her life story, going into unnecessary detail, in my opinion. 'Mummy and Daddy live in Jamaica at the moment and Mummy says that I can go in the Easter holidays if she's still there, but I hope she won't be. Mummy says she's coming home before then, isn't she, Emmett?'

'She is, Misty.'

'She promised,' Misty says sadly.

When Betty looks puzzled at this exchange, I add, 'Roland is, erm, partner to Misty's mum, Amanda. They're away on business at the moment.'

'Oh,' Betty says, surprised that I hadn't told her this before.

'It's complicated,' I say.

'It always is,' she says dryly, giving me a knowing look. I have no idea what she means.

We get off the bus and find the bookshop on a little tree-lined street in Highgate. It stands out on the street because it's been painted a pretty pistachio colour and because it has tables and chairs outside, with people sitting around in the spring sunshine, reading. Well-heeled people who look as if they can afford to buy a book or two. Betty looks at me, full of excitement – to think, her look says, that Farrell's could look like this!

It's also immaculately tidy, with a full, tempting window display and a sign that proclaims 'All welcome – mums, dads, non-mums and non-dads, children, grannies, grandads, even dogs! Come on in, we have just the book for you!'

Could this place be any more cheerful? I think as I manoeuvre Brian and myself through the door. When the girl behind the counter sees me, she runs to hold the door open for me, a welcoming smile on her face. 'Hello,' she says to Brian. 'Aren't you so cute?' In response, he drums his feet on my crotch, sending electric shocks of pain up my groin. I attempt a weak smile in response.

There's an umbrella stand made out of a carved elephant and an immaculate carpet leads us to the fiction section, which is full of staff selections and recommendations and neat little collections grouped in interesting ways.

'It's heaven,' Betty exclaims, walking across the sweet-smelling carpet to a stand full of children's books, their shiny covers gleaming in the sun streaming in through the window. 'Now, this is what a bookshop should be,' she says, wandering off behind a stack of books, then yelling, 'Emmett, come and see this!'

I walk over to where I hear the voice.

'Ta-dah! What do you think of this?' She's standing in the poetry section, which I can see has been lovingly assembled, a pretty table with gorgeous hardback editions in the middle. Hardbacks, I think, picking one up – imagine.

'It's bloody amazing,' I say, taking a large and handsome collection of the poems of Elizabeth Bishop down and examining it. It's lovely – a smart dust jacket with gorgeous creamy pages. I want it. In fact, I want everything in the shop, this lovely place that makes you want to buy books, which, after all, is the purpose of a bookshop. I scan the shop for signs of any homeless people or shoplifters, both hourly occurrences in Farrell's, but there are none. There's an elderly couple perusing a guidebook on the Matterhorn, a family sitting together examining a children's picture book – normal, ordinary people out for a Sunday-morning browse. I shoot Betty a look over the top of Paul Muldoon's *The Annals of Chile* and we're both seized with a fit of the giggles.

'Can you imagine Petrus owning a shop like this?' Betty laughs. 'What we could achieve if we were left to our own devices,' she adds quietly.

'Imagine,' I echo faintly, as we both contemplate the idea.

'You know, I think we could do it,' Betty says. 'The bookshop is on the line, so I'd say he'd be a bit more open to persuasion.'

'Do you think so?' I say doubtfully, wondering if, deep down, I'd really like Farrell's to change all that much.

'Of course! We just need a positive attitude and we can overcome anything!'

Oh, God. 'Yay!' I hear myself saying. I'm not a 'yay' kind of guy. It must be being with Betty – it brings out my sunny side.

Betty looks at me shyly from under her mascaraed lashes. 'Will you help me, Emmett?'

'Erm, sure. Yeah,' I say. 'At least … I'll try.'

Betty looks a bit disappointed with me, so I try a more John response. 'We'll make it happen!' I say.

Betty claps her hands. 'We will!' OK, I think, I can't keep this up for much longer. 'Come on, let's find Misty. I'm sure she's in the children's section.'

Misty is indeed in the children's section, sharing a squashy pouffe with another girl. She's reading *Charlotte's Web* and she has that look of complete concentration on her face, as if nothing in the world can permeate her cocoon.

Charlotte's Web, I think when I see the familiar cover with the little girl with the unruly hair and red dress, her pig friend tucked under her arm, the way Misty tucks Bran under hers. I can still remember sitting on the front step in Wexford beside Daisy while she read that. She cried at the end, when Wilbur the pig was saved by his friend, Charlotte, writing messages in her web, and I had to hug her and tell her that it was a good thing, wasn't it? Wilbur didn't become a pack of rashers but lived to fight another day.

'Are you all right?' Betty says. 'You look a bit off.'

I suddenly feel the ground shifting under me. 'I think I need to go outside for a minute.' I feel the sudden urge to run, even though it's hard with Brian attached to my front. I turn and blunder out of the shop, pushing the door open and stumbling onto the pavement, where I try to suck in deep breaths of cool air. My heart is racing and my mouth feels dry. Maybe I'm having a heart attack, I think. That must be it. Oh, God. Maybe I need an ambulance. I have a vision of being placed onto a stretcher, Brian still attached to me, and being wheeled into the waiting ambulance, Betty and Misty looking anxiously on. My heartbeat races faster and a film of sweat breaks out on my face.

Then Betty is beside me. 'Emmett, it's OK. Take this and breathe into it.' She hands me a paper bag with the logo of the shop on it. 'Go on,' she insists when I look at it uncomprehendingly.

Obediently, I take the bag from her and place it over my mouth, breathing in and out slowly as instructed, until I feel my heartbeat slow, the pounding in my ears lessens. Eventually, I return to myself. I can feel the ground under my feet, I can hear a car horn blow down the street, someone swear in loud cockney.

'What just happened?'

'I think you had a panic attack,' Betty says softly.

'How? Why would I have a panic attack? There's nothing to panic about!' I'm aware that I sound very panicked.

'I don't know, Emmett,' Betty says, as if she's addressing a very small child.

I'm suddenly mortified. 'I'm really sorry. It wasn't you … it's just …'

'For goodness' sake,' Betty says. 'Don't apologise. It's not your fault.'

It is my fault, I think grimly. It absolutely is.

I can hardly wait to get rid of Betty, I'm so embarrassed by my strange outburst, if that's what you can call it. I'm silent all the way home, in spite of Betty's efforts to make cheery conversation. She gives up after a while and she and Misty play 'dogs who look like their owners' the rest of the way. That's my game, I think angrily. Mine and Misty's. When we get to our stop, I practically run off the bus with Brian and Misty, throwing a hasty wave over my shoulder, insisting that I'll be OK and, no, I don't need a cup of tea. I'm perfectly capable of making myself a cup, I think, as I take Misty's hand and stride in what I hope is a purposeful manner up the street.

When we get in, I don't even take off my coat. I just go and sit on the sofa, Brian on my knee. He's fallen asleep, in that miraculous way that babies do in the middle of chaos, and his little cheek is squashed against me. I close my eyes for a second. I'll just rest for a moment, I think – I still feel a bit queasy after earlier.

I don't realise that Misty is calling my name from the kitchen. 'Emmett?'

'Yes, Misty,' I say wearily.

'I'm coming,' she says loudly, then stomps up the stairs into the hall. There's rustling and shuffling and then the door slowly opens. Bran comes in first, then Misty, who is holding a tray out in front of her with a plate of biscuits on it and a glass of water. 'Here you go,' she says, placing it on the sofa beside me. The water slops out of the glass as she puts it down and she tuts gently to herself.

'Drink this,' she says firmly, handing me the glass. I take a sip. It's warm and it makes me gag, but I cough instead and say, 'Thank you, Misty. I really appreciate it.' I look at the plate. 'Where did you get the biscuits?'

'Queenie,' she says. 'She has lots of packets, but she let me pick a special one because I told her they're for you.'

'Oh, thanks, Misty. That's really nice.' I reach out and give her a little squeeze, which she ignores because her eyes are fixed on the plate.

'Can I have one?'

'Sure. Don't tell your mum.'

'I won't.' She takes one and sits on the sofa beside me, breaking off a tiny piece and giving it to Bran, who scoffs it and gives her his best squinty-eyed look.

'Emmett, do you think it would cheer you up to watch *The Fresh Prince of Bel-Air*?'

'I think that would really cheer me up,' I say, handing her the remote control, deciding to take Brian off me while he's asleep and put him on the sofa, so Misty can settle into the crook of my arm, the way she always does when we watch TV. She presses 'play' and the video slides into the slot, and when the familiar theme tune starts, we settle down to watch. Misty makes me drink all of the water, watching me carefully as I sip and try not to be sick, and we both laugh at Will Smith's antics when his aunt and uncle are out of town, until the doorbell rings.

'That must be Daisy,' I say, my heartbeat quickening. 'I'll get it.' As I walk to the front door, my heartbeat is getting faster again and I press my hand to my chest as if trying to slow it down. When I open the door, she's standing on the doorstep, still in the cornflower-blue dress, but with a short black jacket over it. It's nice, but I wonder where the granny coat is.

She doesn't look at me, but instead peers around my shoulder. 'Is he ...?'

'He's asleep,' I say, feeling a bit miffed that she hasn't even said hello. ' 'I managed to get him to nod off earlier,' I add casually.

'What magic did you use?' She smiles.

'It's easy, when you know how,' I say smugly. 'Come on in.'

She hesitates for a second, then says, 'Well, I suppose I'd better take Brian off your hands,' and she gives a soft laugh. 'Did he behave himself?'

'He's no bother at all,' I say smoothly. 'Come down to the kitchen. Misty's watching something on TV.'

Daisy follows me down the hall, walking under the chandelier, and as we do, Daisy looks up at it. 'Wow ... that's interesting.'

'It's awful,' I say, adding hastily, 'It was Roland's choice – Amanda's new partner.'

'Oh, I wouldn't say "awful",' Daisy says, as we both examine it, the long steel tuning forks, the ugly shadows it casts on the wall. She catches my eye and we both laugh awkwardly. 'It's very ... architectural,' she says diplomatically.

I sigh. I'm getting a bit fed up with these stilted conversations, I think. I want something else. I want things to be the way they used to, when I could read Daisy's mind and she could read mine. When we practised telepathy under our tarpaulin. How can I get back there, I wonder? How can I be the person I used to be?

'Daisy ...'

'Yes?' She's looking at me, waiting, but when I don't say anything else, she says, 'Are you all right?' She's looking at me steadily with those huge grey eyes.

No, I'm not. I'm really not, I think. 'I'm fine.' I smile at her broadly, John now firmly back in control. 'Let's have some tea.'

She hesitates for a second, but it's long enough. 'You're busy,' I help her.

'Yes, well, you see, I have a lot on at the moment, and Mum ...'

'Of course.'

'Well ...' she begins. 'I really must—'

She doesn't get the rest of the sentence out because I lunge at her. All I can think of is kissing her. Her lips are soft and her breath tastes of something sweet and her mouth opens to mine and I put my hands in those lovely curls and I give a tiny groan of pleasure as I feel the tip of her tongue with mine. Oh, God. Parts of me that I thought were completely dead are now beginning to stir and I open my mouth wider to kiss her more deeply.

Suddenly, she pulls away from me, leaving me open-mouthed, like a fish. 'Sorry, I … I don't know what came over me. I really must …' She's flustered now, her cheeks flushed, and she's looking around as if she's lost something.

'It's OK,' I say softly. 'It really is', and I lean in again for another kiss. I want more of that, I think.

'No!' Her voice is loud in the silence of the hall. 'I'm sorry, John. I really can't. Things are just too complicated.' She gives me a look then, an I-hope-you-understand look, and I find that I want to scream. I don't understand, Daisy. I really don't. But of course, I'm John, so I have to paste that veneer on again. 'Of course,' I say contritely. 'I understand. I'm sorry.'

'It's OK, really. Erm, I'll just get Brian … Oh!' She turns around then, a look of shock on her face. 'I didn't see you there, Misty.' Daisy pats down her hair. 'I was just coming to get Brian.'

Misty looks at Daisy for a long time, her thumb in her mouth. 'Say hello to Daisy, Misty,' I say.

Misty doesn't react.

'Take your thumb out of your mouth, please.'

'She's fine,' Daisy says. 'Really. How are you, Misty?'

Misty dislodges her thumb from her mouth with a popping sound. 'Fine,' she says quietly.

'Good. That's good. Well, I must be going!' With a flurry, Daisy goes into the living room, scoops Brian into her arms, sling and all, then runs out into the hall, a slightly crazed look on her face, spots the giant changing bag on the antler coatstand and whips it off, lifting it onto her shoulder. The top of the bag has opened and, as she lifts it, a bib and a spare nappy fall out onto the ground. She looks at them, as if begging them to just hop back into her bag. Silently, Misty picks them up and hands them to her.

'Thanks, Misty.'

Misty says nothing, just turns and goes back into the living room.

'She's a bit tired,' I explain.

'Poor little thing,' Daisy says sadly. 'Well, I must be off!' she says and practically runs out of the door, closing it behind her with a big bang.

I stand there for a few minutes before going inside to Misty. I wonder if she saw anything, I think as I sit down beside her and ask her a question about the *Fresh Prince*, which she answers politely. 'Misty …' I venture.

'Yes, Emmett?' Misty says quietly.

'I was just saying goodbye to Daisy. That's all it was.'

She gives me a sceptical look. I know, I think – I should have behaved like a grown-up, and it occurs to me how little adults really think about their children when it comes to that kind of thing. How little they consider the feelings of those they say are most important to them when it comes to love or what passes for it, I think gloomily. I wonder if, twenty years ago, Dad had asked himself the very same question.

Something about that thought makes me get up and go to the phone in the hall and dial the number. I need to talk to her, I think. I need to talk to Mum. I won't tell her about Daisy, but I just need to hear her voice. I wish to God Mum was here, I think, as the phone rings and rings, but just hearing her voice will be the next best thing.

After what seems like ages, there's no answer. Probably just as well, I think morosely, as I go to replace the handset – I'd probably only blab anyway.

I hear it then, a long clearing of a throat followed by a muffled, 'Hello?'

'Dad?' I lift the receiver to my ear.

There's more throat-clearing and rustling, and I hear the click of his lighter, the sucking in of air as he pulls on the cigarette he's just lit. 'Urgh,' he replies, which I take to mean yes.

'Erm, how are you?' I say, for the want of anything better. I want to get the exchange over with so that I can talk to Mum. Dad knows the drill anyway. When he answers, we exchange greetings and one or two rudimentary questions, then he says, 'So, I'll put your mother on', and we both breathe a sigh of relief.

'Grand,' he says now.

'Good … that's great.' And how are you, Emmett? I think, not that he's likely to ask. He leaves all of that to Mum. The emotional heavy lifting.

'How's the girleen?'

'Misty? She's very well, thanks,' I reply to the only question I've been asked on the subject by my father since I found out.

'That's good,' he says.

'So … any news?' I try hopefully.

'Not a bit,' he replies.

Oh, Lord. 'Right, well, where's Mum? Is she out at mass? I can ring back later—' I begin, before he interrupts me.

'Your mother is not at home.' He says each word really clearly, as if he's reading it off a card.

'Will you ask her to call me when she gets back, Dad?'

His voice is muffled at first, as if he's moved away from the phone, but the last bit is clear: '… moved out.'

'She's moved out?' I can't believe what I'm hearing.

'You heard me.'

'Dad, is everything all right. Are you ill?'

'I'm not sick,' he says impatiently. 'I told you. Your mother has left me.'

'Where's she gone?' I'm guessing on a pilgrimage to Lough Derg – she gives out about black tea and praying in her bare feet, but I can tell she loves it. That must be what Dad means.

'Ask your brother,' he says abruptly, then puts down the phone with a bang.

I hold the receiver up in mid-air, even though all I can hear is the long 'brrr' of the dial tone. I look at it for a long time, as if it will tell me what on earth is happening, then I put it slowly down in the cradle.

11.

Bran and I have walked all the way up Albion Road, past the garage, then past the lovely Victorian houses where wealthy business people and politicians live – houses not unlike my own, now that I come to think of it, even though I'm only a temporary resident.

I pass the pet shop where I tried to offload my dog, the fantasy emporium where I bought that book on parenting that I no longer need. I pass the grotty shopping centre and, finally, the Holloway Odeon, where a crowd is gathering to watch *Twister*, which seems appropriate enough – a film about a giant, destructive force of nature. And then I'm back where I started, outside Tom's flat, with the rattle of the Tube in the distance and the smell of grilling lamb from the kebab shop. I told Misty that I had an errand to run while I steered her down the front steps to Queenie's flat. She didn't question me, which is hardly surprising given the day's events. What difference does another surprise arrival or departure really make? I left Misty sitting beside Queenie on the sofa, the two of them watching *The Two Ronnies* special, Misty cuddling into Queenie and inhaling some passive smoke in the process. Queenie's become a second mum to Misty now. Funny how life turns out, I think, as I climb the stairs and knock on the door.

There seems to be a lot of noise coming from inside. Maybe Dympna's hosting some of her camogie cronies again. I'd called Tom the previous week and he'd told me that they hog the sofa there every Sunday night to watch videos of the previous camogie match and to plan strategy. The idea of a roomful of Dympnas makes me feel slightly queasy. I think again of the man in the denim jacket and question what I saw. I must have been imagining it, I conclude.

Then the door is flung open and Tom is standing in front of me. 'Brother!' he shouts, enveloping me in a huge hug. There is man-clapping and a good squeeze, and I have to say, it feels great. I need a hug. 'How did you get here so quickly? You didn't answer the phone – must be that bloody second sight of yours.'

'What do you mean?' I say, stepping in to the tiny hall, feeling instantly at home in the cramped dingy space, with Tom's work boots and hard hat in a heap inside the door. Misty's right, it does smell awful, but, somehow, it's home in a way that Amanda's just isn't.

'I mean that I called you fifteen minutes ago to tell you to come up. Mum's here.'

'What? So Dad was right. I thought he was having me on.'

'What do you mean?'

'I've just spoken to him – he told me Mum had left him.'

'Ah, well.' His face falls for a moment. 'I'll let her tell you herself.'

'He's right. I have left him.' Mum's voice wafts through the open kitchen door.

'What?' I say, following Tom into the living room, which is mercifully clean, *Coronation Street* blasting away on the black-and-white TV set. Mum is sitting right in the middle in her dressing gown, a tray on the sofa beside her with tea and toast on it. She has her big slippers on and her hair is in a net. She has always insisted that a net keeps her hair tidy overnight, so she doesn't need to wash it every day. She completes the look with a thick paperback, balancing on her knees. Mum. I suddenly realise just how much I've missed her.

'Come here to me, son,' she says, pushing down on the sofa with her hands to lever herself up.

'Don't get up,' I say, bending down to hug her. This hug feels great, too. It's softer than Tom's, naturally, and Mum still smells of talc and baking, her hair, inside its net, still that dyed russet that she loves. I let myself be held and squeezed, and it feels just as good as it did when I was ten and I'd fallen off my bike or got a clip on the ear from Brother Ignatius. Now I'm a grown-up, with grown-up problems, but I still need my mum.

'Why didn't you say you were coming?' I say, 'You could have stayed with me. There's more room there.' I look around at the room and I wonder just how quickly Tom managed to pull it all together – how many pairs of underpants are lurking behind that pile of magazines, what might be hiding under the plumped-up cushions.

'In that lovely house that Tom says you're in?' Mum says. 'Ah, no, I couldn't. I want to feel at home. Tom says your place is like some kind of interiors magazine and he says that you don't watch ITV.'

'True, I suppose. *Corrie* isn't Amanda's thing.' I smile. 'Anyway,' I say, sitting down, looking at Tom, who makes a face at me. A 'you ask her' face. 'Mum, what's happened?'

'I told you. I've left him.'

'I know, Mum – he told me.'

She looks at me sadly. 'Is he doing all right? I left a month's meals in the freezer and I labelled them with the days of the week, but the oul' eejit will probably just go to the chipper or half-starve rather than make his own bloody dinner.'

'He'll survive. What about you, though?'

'Me?' Her eyes water. 'Oh, Emmett, pet, I just finally had enough of him. I've had enough of him for years, but now there's no need for me to stay with him. You're both gone and it doesn't seem worth pretending that everything is just great any more. It's not just great. And anyway, everyone's getting separated nowadays. Dolores up the road – you know, the woman with the two Jack Russells and the husband with a limp – she's getting separated. And Tom Mangan in town, he's got a divorce – can you believe it? Mind you, Mary was always a weapon. He's got a new girlfriend now – she's called Magda and she's Polish. She has legs up to her ears and she's only twenty-five. The lads can always get a new model, not like the ladies. We're just on the scrap heap.' At this, she folds her arms across her chest and then dashes a tear out of her eye.

'Ah, Mum,' I say, putting my arm around her. 'I know what Dad can be like' – here, Mum and I exchange a look – 'but separation? Do you really want to after all this time? I thought you'd worked it all out.'

'I know,' Mum says sadly. 'Wouldn't you think it would have happened twenty years ago if it was going to happen at all? But I didn't want it then – I wanted to give our marriage another go. It didn't seem right to end it over … well, you know,' she says, shooting Tom a look over my shoulder. 'I thought we were both stronger than that, and we were, to be fair. It even jizzed our marriage up for a while, as you know. I'm sure you remember us going to London,' Mum says with a sly smile, referring to the first time she'd left the country, when Tom was a year old, leaving us with Auntie Maeve and her inferior apple tarts.

'I do. You were set upon by punks and you had to hide in a phone box.'

She offers me a small smile. 'Oh, you think I'm just a country bumpkin, son, but just you wait. This time, I'm going to take London by storm!'

Uh-oh. Mum gets upset if she has to go the thirty miles to Ballinasloe for the day, so to think that she's going to make a new life for herself in London … 'Mum—' I begin, but I'm interrupted by Tom.

'Sorry, will somebody please tell me what's going on?'

Mum gives me another look. 'It's nothing, son. Your father and I had a … falling out years ago, but we made up then.' She shoots me a look. 'This time, though, it's for real. I want to live my life on my own terms, not with that old moan hanging off me.'

'Hark at Shirley Valentine,' Tom mutters.

'Tom, I'm parched – will you put the kettle on?' I say, making a face at him and nodding in the direction of the kitchen.

Tom sighs. 'All bloody right.' He looks down at Bran then, who is looking at him significantly. 'Come on, you. There's a cold sausage in the fridge.'

'Don't give him the whole thing,' I say. 'It gives him diarrhoea.'

'Great,' Tom says grimly, as Bran, hearing his favourite word – 'sausage' – follows him eagerly into the kitchen.

'So,' I say, when Tom is out of earshot. 'Mum. Is that what really happened? You'd just had enough?'

Mum frowns, looking at the TV as if she suddenly finds Ken Barlow fascinating. Then she says, 'Why wouldn't it be? You know, it's time I had an affair, too. I've been loyal to that man for thirty years and to think that I'll never experience another man's touch ...' Her voice trails off when she realises that she's oversharing. 'I'm bored, Emmett. Bored and lonely and sad, and I need something in my life. Something or someone who makes it worth living.'

'And you think you'll find it here? London takes a bit of getting used to, Mum. It's not home, you know. It's a really big place, full of strangers and it's hard to fit in—'

'And you love it.'

'Yes, I do,' I say. Because as I say the words I realise that they are true.

'Well, if you can do it, so can I,' Mum says, putting up her hands when I go to object. 'Emmett, please don't start. I'll be dead in my grave and I won't even have begun the business of living. Let me at it.'

In response, I give her a tight squeeze, kissing her on the cheek. 'You always could reach those long arms of yours all the way around me.' She smiles, nudging me in the ribs. Then she looks serious. 'Do you think Tom suspects anything?'

'What, about Dad?' That's all I need to say. Mum's eyes close then open again. 'Yes,' she whispers.

'Well, maybe the time has come to tell him, Mum. He knows

that there's something and he's not a child any more – you can't hide it from him.'

'Not that there's that much to hide,' Mum says sadly.

Not that much to hide. How true. I feel the sudden urge to tell Mum about Daisy, but I push it down inside me because I know that it would be cruel, no matter how much I want to confide in her. There's no point in raking that up again after all this time – for me or for her.

We don't talk again about the elephant in the room. Instead, when Tom carries a new tray in from the kitchen, with the first of what seems like a hundred pots of tea, a plate of Nice biscuits beside them, we are filled in on the lives of everyone in the parish, from Mrs O'Neill whose husband wears women's clothes – 'He's even been into Dunnes Stores with her, marching up and down the aisles, as proud as you please, in a lovely skirt suit from Monica's in Castlebar. And he's a vegetarian.' I'm not sure which intrigues Mum more, the vegetarianism or the transvestitism – to Sé Óg, the manic hurler from the village, who is now on the county team. 'That fellow hadn't a brain in his head, but he could puck a sliotar like nobody's business,' Mum says. 'Your father always said …' and her voice trails off.

'So how's Father O'Sullivan?' I say, prompting her to speculate about his closeness to his housekeeper, Miss McFadden, as Tom and I nod and pretend to be interested in the world we have left far behind. And when Mum says that she's tired and needs her bed, we wish her goodnight and watch her retreat into Tom's bedroom in her candlewick dressing gown, with a hot-water bottle under her arm and her paperback, which turns out to be *A Suitable Boy*, under her arm.

'Right, time for a proper drink,' Tom says, going into the kitchen, followed by Bran. 'Nothing for you, mate,' he says, as he returns with a bottle of whiskey and two glasses. He pours a more-than-generous measure into each glass, and we both raise them and clink them together. I take a sip and enjoy the sensation of warmth spreading across my chest.

'So,' Tom begins.

'So,' I reply.

'What do you make of that?'

'No idea.' I do have an idea, but I don't really want to get into it with Tom. It's not fair.

'I'm surprised she didn't leave him years ago,' Tom says, taking a sip.

'What do you mean?' I try to look unmoved – maybe Tom knows, I think, but then he couldn't possibly. It all happened before he was born.

'Ah, he just wants to prune his dahlias and potter around that greenhouse of his. I'd say Mum is bored to death. And he never wants to do anything with Mum and she's hurt about that. She thinks it means that he's not interested in her any more. Not that you could tell if he was – Dad's a bit of an enigma.'

'Dad? He's hardly 007.' In fact, I think ruefully, if he had been a bit more intelligent about the whole thing, none of us would have been any the wiser. 'Clandestine' was hardly a word you could apply to him.

Tom turns his whiskey glass round in his hands, examining the brown liquid. 'Oh, you'd be surprised, Em. You have your head in the clouds – you just don't notice what's going on under your nose.'

'What do you mean?'

He takes a big sip of whiskey and winces as he swallows. 'Ah, nothing,' he says eventually.

I think of the man in the denim jacket. 'How's Dympna?'

Tom takes another sip of his whiskey. 'Dympna's fine,' he says tonelessly. 'How's Misty?'

I shrug. 'She's OK.' Why the sudden change of subject? 'Well, she's a bit down at the moment. Her best friend isn't talking to her – you know what it's like at that age.'

'God, yeah. I had this friend in second class – Mark O'Dwyer, do you remember him?'

'Mark O'Dwyer,' I repeat. 'Oh, yeah,' I say, as I remember a slight boy with those pink-framed spectacles beloved of the public health system, one side covered with a big bit of plaster. 'Little fellow – big bike.'

'That's him. Well, Mark O'Dwyer was my best friend in the whole world when I was eight. He'd moved from Castlebar and we all thought he was terribly sophisticated because he had a Steve McQueen doll.'

I remember, I think, the two of them, heads bent over a big basin of water. They were trying to make Steve McQueen do deep-sea diving, as I recall. I was doing my Leaving and I had to keep telling them to keep the noise down.

'Well, one day Tony Convery – remember him?'

'The little shit.'

'The little shit – one and the same,' Tom says. 'He came over after break in school one day and he called Mark a poofter or a willy-waver or something moronic like that, and do you know what I did?'

'No,' I say, taking a sip of whiskey.

There's a muscle working in Tom's cheek. 'I did nothing. I just stood there while the others all laughed at him, and I didn't say a thing. Not one thing to defend him – my best friend. Then Iggy came in and we all went back to our desks.'

'What happened then?'

'He didn't come into school the next day or the day after that, and when I asked, Mrs Flaherty said he'd gone back to school in Castlebar.'

'Oh. Right. So what are you saying exactly?'

He looks at me and his face has no expression. 'I'm saying that things can seem like a big deal when you're that age, but then you move on and forget all about them.'

'You don't sound as if you've forgotten Mark O'Dwyer,' I say quietly.

'Yeah, well.' He shrugs and the silence in the kitchen stretches.

So, it's not just me, I think.

'Tom, is something bothering you?' I say. 'I mean, more than Mum and all that.'

He examines his whiskey for a long time, then says, 'Nah. It's nothing important.'

'OK,' I say doubtfully. I take a sip, then I say, 'If I tell you something, will you promise not to tell Mum?'

'Depends on what it is.' Tom smiles.

'I've met someone,' I say.

He leans back in his seat, a big grin on his face. 'So you're finally getting some action? Thank Christ. I thought you'd turned into a monk.'

'I am not "getting some action", as you put it. It's not like that,' I say primly.

'Right, sorry,' he says. 'What is it like?'

I sigh. 'Well … it's complicated. She's someone I used to know … a long time ago. I've just bumped into her again recently and, well …'

'What's the problem?'

'I don't think Mum would approve,' I say quietly.

'Why?'

'It's a long story, but you have to promise you won't tell Mum anything.'

He tuts impatiently. 'I won't tell her anything – so who is this girl?'

'Daisy.'

'Daisy. Daisy who?'

'Just Daisy.'

'And is she a KGB agent or something? Is that why you're all cloak-and-dagger?'

I suddenly feel utterly foolish. 'No, it's just … I don't really know how she feels about me.'

'So ask her.'

I think of my lunge, of the look on Daisy's face when I kissed her. But she kissed me back – I know that she did. She said it was complicated, but I don't believe her. I think that if I could just find a way through to her …

'Write her one of your poems if you don't have the nerve to ask her in person. Do a Byron on it.'

'I don't think that'd be a good idea.' I laugh. Tom takes a swig of his whiskey and proclaims, '"I loved you first: but afterwards your love / Outsoaring mine, sang such a loftier song / As drowned the friendly cooings of my dove." Can't remember the rest.'

'Christina Rosetti,' I offer.

'Whatever – the point is, what are you going to do about Daisy?' His voice rings out in the silence and I shush him.

'For God's sake, will you keep your voice down.'

'Fine,' Tom says, 'I'll keep my voice down. But if you like her, and she likes you, do something about it. Take it from me, brother – if you don't, you'll regret it.'

'How do you know?'

'I just know,' Tom says, helping himself to another splash from the bottle. 'I know what it's like to have feelings for someone and not do anything about it. So don't let life pass you by, brother. Go for it. Write a poem, express your love, whatever you have to do, just do it.'

'Just do it,' I repeat.

'That's the spirit!'

We both look at each other and smile ruefully.

'Hang on in there, Em,' Tom says suddenly.

'You too,' I say quietly, raising my glass to his. 'Cheers.'

12.

'Just do it.' Tom's words are ringing in my head as I sit at Roland's huge desk in his study, two weeks after Tuning Fork Gate as I have come to call it, or TFG for short. Bran is curled up at my feet on a cushion, his squirrel tail wrapped around his little rust-coloured body. He doesn't need walkies or feeding. Misty is at school, so I have no parental duties to perform, and I don't have work for another couple of days. For the first time in months, time is stretching ahead of me, and I have no idea what to do with it. Well, I do have some idea, but it's the doing that's the problem.

The Manila folder is in front of me, unopened, and I'm staring at it. Then, in one movement, I lift the flap of the folder and pull out the sheets of paper and torn-off bits of notebook and lay the poems out in front of me. I stare at them for a while, looking at the random thoughts on the sheets of A4. It's my handwriting all right, but the poems are completely unfamiliar to me, the product of a different person. There's something about swans in St James's Park and another about a market seller in the East End. They read like the products of a fourteen-year-old's imagination, gauche and banal. I reach out to shove them back into the folder, but then I stop. I stare into space for a minute, then grab the one about the bloody swans, draw a big line through the lines of stupid verse and write a title at the top. 'Brown Hair.'

I suck my pencil for a moment and look out the window, and then I find myself writing a poem about the different types of hair and the different colours of brown, and when I've finished, I sit back and look at the four lines that I've written. Well, at least it's not about bloody swans. I suck my pencil a bit more and look out the window again. There's a tree at the end of the garden that's in blossom. It's some kind of pear tree, I think, and as I look at it, I grow annoyed at the way one of the branches droops into the neighbour's garden. I wonder if it annoys them too? Maybe I should go down and prune it right now. Yes, that's what I'll do …

But instead, I turn back to my page and begin to write again. This time, I'm in Wexford and the tarpaulin is stretched over us like the Milky Way and the marram grass is rustling and the sea is a faint roar in the distance. We can hear Mike on the sun deck, the long cord of the phone a coil of plastic stretching from the door to the picnic table where he's perched, the red plastic telephone, so trendy, with its white dial and long, narrow receiver, which looks tiny as he roars into the phone. Behind him, Bridget is in the kitchen. There's a song on the radio and she's dancing to it and Dad is dancing with her, his chin on her head, her hand on his shoulder …

I stop dead. What's that got to do with anything? I set out to write a poem about hair, and this is what I write instead. I scan the lines for any sign that I actually wrote them, but the words aren't mine any more: they belong to the page and to whoever will read them. I sit in my chair for a while longer, wondering what exactly I'm going to do with this poem. I can hardly show it to Daisy ... can I? I haven't spoken to her since TFG and I don't want her to get the wrong idea, but then I remember Tom's words. I couldn't completely have misread the situation – could I?

Then I have an idea: I go back over the poem again and the phone cord becomes a coiled serpent, the house and the deck a river bank and the flowing water. And Mike becomes someone else, and when I look at it again, it means exactly the same thing, but the poem is entirely different. I suddenly have the urge to show it to Daisy, and even though it's dangerous, even though she might find out the truth, I want to see her read it and tell me what she thinks. It's important.

Before I can talk myself out of it, I take the sheet of paper, holding it between my thumb and finger as if it will burn me. I run so quickly down the stairs that I nearly trip over Bran, who is speeding along beside me, sensing that some excitement might be afoot, and I have to slow down, take my jacket, put it on, close the door behind me, walk around the corner to Daisy's and lurk behind the bins to see if Bridget is there. I can't risk her seeing me. I wait a while to see if there's any glimpse of a turban through the window, and when the door opens, I shrink back behind the bins. I'm nearly bent double to avoid detection and Bran nudges me curiously. 'Don't make a sound,' I mouth.

'I'll give you a hand with it,' Daisy's voice is coming from the open door as Bridget appears in her pink turban and fur coat, and walks backwards up the steps, pulling something along. The blue buggy bounces up to the pavement and Bridget stands there, waiting, as Daisy appears with Brian, dressed in his snowsuit, even though it's a warm day. 'The child will roast,' I can hear Bridget saying.

'There's still a bit of a chill around,' Daisy says, placing Brian gently into the buggy, then leaning in to kiss him. 'Bye bye, Mummy loves you!'

'For goodness' sake, we're walking up to the village and back, we're not going to Timbuktu!' her mother says.

'Well, you got lost the last time,' Daisy says.

'I did not get lost. I just got delayed because the bus broke down,' Bridget replies. 'Can a grandmother not take her grandchild for a walk?'

'Well, make sure you only take the main road there and back,' Daisy says, unable to hide the note of anxiety in her voice. She stands there and watches her mother and the buggy disappear around the corner.

Just then, Bran gives an impatient squeak. Oh, shit, I think, as Daisy looks surprised for a moment, then walks towards the bins. 'Hello?'

I try to get to my feet, but my back hurts and I have to hold it as I slowly unfold myself to a standing position. 'Sorry, I was just … I just … I thought there was something wrong with your bin.'

'With my bin?' She's smiling at me.

'Yes. It looked … wrong.'

'I see.'

'Yes, I was just on my way to work,' I say, 'and I noticed that your rubbish bin didn't have a lid and … well … anyway, I've written a poem.'

'A poem.' She gives me that wry smile again and I reflect that it's a bit irritating. Is there something basically terribly amusing about me?

'Yes, I'm a poet. It's what I do,' I say, a little more irritably than I'd intended, 'but if you're not interested—'

'Oh, no, I am,' she says suddenly. 'I really am.' And she holds out her hand.

I place the precious bit of lined A4 into it. Don't laugh at me, I think. Please don't laugh at me. I'm standing there in front of her and she's holding the piece of paper in her hand, and she looks as if she's not sure what to do next. Eventually she says, 'I won't read it now. I'll save it for later.'

'Of course you will. Sorry,' I say, bumping into the rubbish bin.

'Thanks for calling,' she says and turns and goes back into the house, leaving me bereft on the pavement. 'Come on, then,' I say wearily to Bran. 'Walkies.' He rewards me with a little squeak.

I try not to make it too obvious that I'm waiting. I come home from work at 5.30, to find Misty and Monica painting each other's nails at the kitchen table, and even though I'm supposed to take her to Madame Dostoevsky, I think, bugger that. Misty hates Madame Dostoevsky, with her fake Russian accent, and she hates ballet and it's costing me a fortune because Amanda's money has just run out after two months and I haven't had the nerve to ask her for more. I don't want to be a kept man anyway. Of course, I don't really admit the real reason I want to stay at home this afternoon – that Daisy might call around to tell me that I'm the new W.B. Yeats and why did she not see it before now. And that she's madly attracted to me into the bargain.

'Do you know, I don't think ballet's on today,' I say after Monica has put on her coat and said goodbye.

Misty is pulling out her Maths homework, but stops suddenly and looks at me hopefully.

'No, I think Madame Dostoevsky has taken to her bed with a bizarre and unpleasant case of shinglymyeletis.'

Misty gives a little giggle.

'And it's contagious,' I add. 'Probably lethal if anyone else is exposed to it.'

Misty laughs louder this time.

'So …' I say gently. 'I think we'll have to think of Plan B.'

'What's Plan B, Emmett?'

'It's an alternative to Plan A,' I say. 'C'mon, let's go for a walk before tea, Bran wants to see someone he hasn't said hello to in a while.' I help her into her coat and we walk around the corner to Albion Road, but instead of turning left to our house, we turn right, towards Clive's. Misty slows down, dragging out of my hand until I have to stop. 'Misty, you're very sad without Clive,' I say. 'Why don't you just make up and then you can be friends again?'

Misty folds her arms and her mouth forms into a little straight line. She looks faintly comical, but I know it's not funny to her. It wasn't funny to me either at her age and it went on not being funny for twenty years, so I'll spare her that, I think. 'Listen, sometimes little things can grow into big things and before you know it … well, you don't always have to be right or wrong about things to be friends. Sometimes, you have to agree to disagree.'

She nods sadly. 'I really miss him, Emmett,' she says softly.

'Well, do you think that if I talk to Maurice for a bit, you might be able to talk to Clive – even just for two minutes?'

She nods again and takes my hand in hers.

'I'll be here with you, OK? I'm not going anywhere.'

We both walk up the path to Maurice's front door and I ring the doorbell. I can see Maurice's shadow shuffling slowly up the hall, and the door opens. When he sees Misty, he beams. 'Young lady – where have you been hiding yourself? Clive has missed you, I can tell you', and he reaches out and pulls her into a hug, pressing her to his fawn-slacked hip. 'And he's not the only one. I missed you too, little lady.' As Misty presses herself to him, he looks over her head at me and smiles. Clive appears from behind him then, clutching his other leg, and he puts a hand on his grandson's shoulder and gives a squeeze. 'What'll I do with the two of you, eh? What'll I do? Oh, me, oh, my,' he says softly, as the two cling to him.

'I'll be back in half an hour,' I say.

'Make that an hour,' Maurice says, patting Misty on the shoulder.

I walk slowly home, wondering at how quickly something can change when you're that age. That impossible closeness that can turn into utter desolation in the blink of an eye and all over something utterly trivial. Sometimes, you just need a bit of help to see that, I think, as Bran sniffs at a little bush on the corner and lifts his leg. Except it isn't trivial, is it? I conclude. Tom's failure to stand up for his friend, that wasn't trivial – and mine to stand up for Daisy, that wasn't trivial either. I had my chance and I didn't take it and I've never quite forgiven myself.

I sit on the wall outside the community hall, the sound of an aerobics class wafting out through the side door, because I don't want to go home just yet. I try not to look up the road towards Daisy's house. Maybe she thinks my poem is so terrible that she doesn't want to say it to my face. Yes, that's it, I decide miserably. It has to be. It's rubbish, I think. That's why there's silence from number 34a. I sigh heavily for the hundredth time and Bran, who has taken up position beside me, lifts his head and gives me a weary look. 'Come on, Bran,' I say. 'Time for a cuppa.' Bran has learned that the word 'cuppa' means 'biscuit' in dog, so he starts to wag his tail and get very excited, shimmying all the way home.

The doorbell rings at seven o'clock and I jump up from my dinner-making station in the kitchen and bound for the front door like a greyhound. 'I'll get it,' I yell, bolting out of the kitchen, taking the stairs in twos, then running across the hall, pushing Bran out of the way with my foot. He loves the doorbell, and when it rings, he positions himself two inches away from the door. He begins his little squeaky bark and I yell, 'Shut up, will you?' just as I open the door.

Daisy is on the doorstep, looking alarmed.

'Sorry, I didn't mean you,' I say. 'I meant the dog.'

'That's OK.' She smiles shyly, tucking a strand of her lovely hair behind her ear. I sigh inwardly.

'Would you like to come in?'

She turns to look down the street, then back at me. She bites her lip.

'I promise not to do anything,' I add. I'm trying to make a joke out of it, but it comes out a bit wrong – like I'm a bit of a creep.

'Better not. Mum's minding Brian and she told me to hurry

up because *EastEnders* was on at half seven. She's become a soap addict. Oh, hello!' she says brightly, tilting her head to one side.

I turn around to see Misty and Clive hovering behind me, curious looks on their faces. They've been playing at Berber tradespeople for the past half an hour, since they came back from Maurice's, so Misty is wearing a tea towel wrapped around her head and Clive has a plastic sword tucked into his belt. 'Hello!' they say in unison, then wait to see what will transpire. 'It's telly time,' I say hopefully, whereupon they both scarper into the living room.

'They're really cute,' Daisy says.

'They are,' I agree. There's a pause that goes on for a bit too long, before Daisy says, 'Anyway, I read the poem ...'

'And? Is it a pile of poop? A turd, an excrement?' I pretend I'm joking, but I'm really not. I desperately want to know what she thinks of it.

'No,' she says softly. 'It's quite good.'

'Quite good.' I don't like 'quite good'. I want 'amazing', 'breath-taking'. I want to hear that I'm a rare find who deserves a bigger audience. Or any audience at all. I don't want to be told that I'm 'quite good'. It's like 'middling' or, worse, 'satisfactory'.

'Oh.'

'Yes, the beginning's great. I like the phone cord that's "like the coiled serpent ready to strike a blow to the mouth"'. Hearing her speak my words changes them, makes it suddenly clear to me how the reader might understand them, and I find myself nodding as she adds, 'But that line in the middle, about the flowing river, I thought that was a bit of a cliché, to be honest.'

'You're right, it is a bit. I thought that something less obvious would be good, like a cataract or something flowing ...' I put my hand to my head. 'I can't think of it right now, but it'll come to me.'

'Cataract. I like that. It makes me think of old ladies,' Daisy says, giggling.

'I mean it in the waterfall sense,' I say pompously.

'I know what you meant,' she says, with what looks to me like a patronising smile. 'It's good, though. Really. I liked the couple that can be seen dancing in the window. That's a nice image.'

I can't think what to say about that. Can you not see? I think. Isn't it obvious? But when I look at her face, it's completely open, so I settle for a 'thanks' and a shrug, as if I couldn't care less.

'Have you done any readings?'

'Oh, God, no, I don't like reading my work out loud.'

'You just need a bit of confidence,' Daisy says. 'There's an open-mike night in Victoria's pub on Wednesday. I think you should read your poem there. Test it out.'

At the sound of the words 'open mike', my stomach gives an involuntary heave.

'You do?'

She nods.

'Why?'

'Because it'll be good for you.'

'Oh, I don't think I could do that,' I say. 'I suffer terribly with nerves. I throw up.' For some reason, I mime the act of vomiting, like an idiot.

'Right.' She gives a small smile. 'Well, why don't I come along for moral support? I'll be your fan club. Consider it repayment for the baby-care lessons.' When I look doubtful, she says, 'C'mon. What have you got to lose?'

'My dignity, self-respect and my artistic spirit, which will be crushed by an uncaring audience.'

'Good. I'll be here at eight. Bye, Misty!' And without another word, she turns and walks back down the street.

Heart thumping, I close the door and walk slowly back through the house. I've just agreed to read my poem out loud – to actual people. Oh, fuck.

As I pass the living room, I hear giggling.

Clive says, in a high voice, 'Oh, Daisy, promise you'll be mine.'

Misty replies in a deep bass, 'I promise, Emmett,' and then there's an explosion of giggles.

It's not funny, I think. Not at all.

My stomach spends the rest of the evening churning like a washing machine, even while I try to maintain a calm exterior. I finish dinner, wash up and, after Clive goes, Misty and I take Bran out for a walk, just like we do every day, and it all seems perfectly normal, except that my mind is running at a mile a minute. I think about Misty and Clive and about Mum, sitting in Tom's flat in Holloway, trying to 'learn the *A–Z*', as she puts it, so that she can pluck up the courage to take a bus down the road to see her granddaughter. Thank God she hasn't mastered it yet, I think, because if she caught sight of Brigid Delaney all hell would break loose. I know that I should feel happy with Daisy back in my life, but instead I feel splintered, as if there are bits of me all over north London.

Later, I read 'The Owl and the Pussycat' to Misty, the familiar words about pea-green boats and runcible spoons failing to soothe me as they would normally, and then it's time for lights out and it feels as if I've reached the end of an obstacle course, hurdling and climbing and running through the ordinary tasks of the day. I can finally be alone with my thoughts, I think, as I close the book.

'Dada?'

'Yes?' I wonder if I heard her right. That she called me 'Dada'. Roland is 'Daddy', but I'm Dada. Clever Misty.

'Do you like Daisy?'

'Oh, Misty,' I say, 'I think I do, but we're just friends – promise.' After Tuning Fork Gate, I don't want to upset Misty by letting her think anything else. It's not fair – not when she's missing her mum and when her world has been turned upside-down. I'll just have to keep my feelings to myself from now on.

Misty looks thoughtful for a few minutes. 'I like Clive.'

'I know you do.'

'He's my best friend ever.'

'I know he is. I'm glad you've made it up with him. It's good to have a best friend ever, isn't it?'

She nods and settles down in the bed, then sits bolt upright. 'I forgot my prayers!' She begins to get out of bed, but I say, 'Just join your hands and say a quick prayer. God will know that you need to go to sleep.'

She closes her eyes and says, 'Please bless Mummy and Daddy and Dada and Bran and Clive and Clive's grandad Maurice and Daisy. Amen.'

Daisy? Surely it's a bit previous to be including her in the night-time prayers? Best not to pass any comment, I think, or I'll be fuelling the fire. 'Good. Night night.'

'Night, Dada. Dada?'

'What? It's late, go to sleep.'

'Could I love Clive the way you loved Daisy your friend a long time ago?'

'I'd say you could.' But maybe a tiny part of me hopes you don't because then you won't get hurt when it all falls apart.

There's a long pause, and I think she's gone to sleep, but then she says, 'That's good. I don't want him to go away, though.'

'I know you don't.' I can't say that he won't because everything changes. Things happen all the time and people move on and others are left behind. That's life. But I don't want to tell Misty that yet. She's too young for such existentialist gloom.

'Now, no more talking. You need your beauty sleep.'

'Night, Dada.'

'Night.'

The night of the open-mike event doesn't begin well, when I spend the best part of the afternoon throwing up in the bathroom, Misty standing outside with a glass of water. I always did throw up when I had to appear on stage. Mum never lets me forget the time I played the back end of a donkey for the school nativity play and I threw up all over Declan O'Riordan's backside. In fairness to him, he continued to play the front end of the donkey, even though I was nearly passing out behind him from illness as well as from the fumes.

'I don't feel well,' I groan, when I eventually emerge.

'I'd say you just have butterflies in your tummy,' Misty says wisely, handing me the glass.

I take a sip and try not to throw up again because the water is warm, as usual. 'I think I need to go to bed,' I say hopefully.

'But then what will Daisy do when she calls over?' Misty says. 'And you have to go and read your poem out loud, Dada,' she says severely. 'Miss Grace says that we all have to overcome our fears.' Misty has appointed herself my very own Susan Jeffers, my feel-the-fear-and-do-it-anyway life coach, and even though I know she's right, I don't want to 'do it anyway'. I want to not do it.

'I don't think I can overcome my fears,' I say miserably.

Misty shrugs, as if such semantics are of no interest to her. 'Come on, Dada, it's time to put on some clothes,' and she looks disparagingly at my worn black Levi's and blue shirt.

'What's wrong with these?'

'They are not nice,' she says firmly, leading me up the stairs to the bedroom, where she pulls open a drawer and removes my thick-knit black jumper, then opens another and pulls out a pair of dark-grey trousers that look quite nice. 'Are they Dad's?' I say.

'They are your trousers, Dada, because they are very long,' she says firmly, putting them on the bed, along with a pair of bright-red socks. 'I will see you downstairs.' And she and Bran leave the room, the door closing firmly behind them. Message received, I think glumly, as I survey the outfit. But there is no way I can go out tonight. I've been sick three times and my stomach is churning. I must be coming down with something. It's the flu, I'm sure. I'd better call it off because I'd hate to infect anyone.

Perhaps I should have a little lie-down, I think, as I perch on the edge of the bed. My eyelids feel heavy and my eyes gritty and I suddenly feel the unbearable urge to sleep. I lie down on the bed and close my eyes. That's better, I think. I'll just have a moment's rest to refresh myself so that, if I do decide to go, I'm fully alert for the open mike and can give my best. Just a very small rest, I think, as I feel sleep overcome me, the words of my poem, which I've practised so often that they are now imprinted on my brain, streaming in front of my closed eyelids.

When I wake up, I'm in a different room, one that smells of fresh paint and new carpet. The window is open and I can hear the sea outside. Daisy is standing by the door, her hand on the door handle, and she seems to be listening. I can hear shouting in the kitchen and the smash of crockery. I want to ask her what's going on, but it seems that I can't speak. I can hear, though, and I know that Bridget is the one yelling, 'That little bitch, wait till I get my hands on her. What do those nuns teach her in that expensive private school we send her to? How to lie? Because she's bloody good at it. I've never heard such rubbish coming out of the mouth of an eight-year-old.'

I want to defend Daisy, but somehow I can't seem to get out of bed. I hear a male voice then, deep and gravelly, and I recognise it as Mike's. 'That's enough, Bridget. You must take me for a bloody fool. Do you not think I have eyes in my head? The two of you ... you are disgusting. Now fuck off out of my sight.'

Then I hear the sound of footsteps coming down the hall and I know that it's Bridget.

'Daisy, where are you? You'd better not be hiding because when I've finished with you ... You've gone too far this time, do you hear me?' The doorknob is rattling and I wonder why Daisy won't get out of the way and she turns to look at me and she mouths, 'Help,' but my body feels like lead in the bed, my limbs so heavy I can barely lift my head off the pillow. And then the door opens ...

My eyes flick open. My heartbeat is thumping in my ears and saliva is dribbling from the corner of my mouth. I shake my head to rid myself of the cotton-wool feeling and get to my feet. I go into the bathroom and splash my face with water, then shuffle back into the bedroom. I'm not sure whether I'm awake or asleep as I sit on the bed and try to remember the dream – or was it a memory? I can't be sure. I feel awful. I just need to climb into bed for the evening, I think, and I'll be right as rain. It's the flu, definitely, I tell myself, because I don't want to admit that it might be something else. It might be the past punching me on the side of the head, that dizzy feeling I'd had the very first time I knew that the woman in the green coat was Daisy. I don't want that, I think now. I just want it to be me and Daisy now: John, not Emmett.

But then Misty appears, seemingly from nowhere, and she's suddenly hovering beside me as I lie in bed, hands on her hips. 'Get up, Dada. Daisy's downstairs!'

'I'm sick,' I say feebly.

'Dada, you are really very silly. Miss Grace says that sometimes our brain tells us that we're sick even when we're not. I think that's what's happened to you.'

'Oh. Right,' I say, closing my eyes and pulling the duvet up under my chin. 'In that case, I'd better let my brain rest.' But Misty's pulling the duvet off me with surprising force. 'Now, Dada. And hurry up.'

There is something humiliating about being given a pep talk by a seven-year-old, I think, getting wearily out of bed and putting on the clothes Misty left out for me. It's time to pull myself together. It was just a bad dream, not some kind of omen. Honestly.

I go back into the bathroom, this time to brush my teeth and splash myself with Roland's expensive cologne, dabbing a tuft of hair that's sticking up back down with a splash of water. There, it'll have to do, I think.

As I walk downstairs, I try to complete my transformation from coward, hiding in an upstairs bedroom, to Capable Dad. I don't think Daisy's ready for the alternative and neither am I. My stomach lurches as I approach the living-room door, from where I can hear Will Smith followed by canned laughter but nothing else. I stick my head around the door and see Daisy sitting at one end of the sofa and Misty at the other. Misty is stroking Bran's fur, thumb in her mouth, eyes fixed on the *Fresh Prince*, and Daisy is laughing, curls bouncing as she throws her head back. She always did have a big laugh.

'Hi.'

'Oh, hi, John. For a moment, I thought you were standing me up,' she says, getting up off the sofa.

'No. I was just getting ready,' I explain, praying that Misty didn't hear her call me John. I have no idea how I'd explain that. 'I'm high maintenance.'

'I can see that,' she says, taking in my jumper and trouser combo.

'Misty picked it for me,' I say, looking down at the trousers, which I'm sure aren't mine. They're too short at the ankle and too large at the waist, but it's too late to change now. That's when I notice that she's not wearing her green coat, and my heart sinks a bit. That coat might bring me luck. But then I see that she's wearing a cute tartan slip dress and cream T-shirt, and decide that that makes up for it. She's put on just a bit of make-up – some mascara and some nice lipstick thing that makes her lips look kind of luscious – and she's tied her hair back. I always like it when she does that because I can see her neck.

As if she knows I'm staring, Daisy brushes her hand against the back of her neck. 'Well, I think she did a very good job,' she says and Misty smiles, jumping up off the sofa, ready for her night watching God knows what with Queenie. The last time she went, they watched *Death Wish II*: Charles Bronson and multiple knife fights and explosions weren't exactly on Amanda's preferred viewing list, but I could hardly dictate the terms on Queenie's turf and Misty didn't seem to be any the worse for it. Besides, I find that I'm so desperate to go out with Daisy that Genghis Khan would seem a reasonable option as a babysitter.

'C'mon, pipsqueak, into Queenie you go,' I say, ushering Misty and Bran out the door and down the steps to Queenie's. Queenie sticks her head out and says, 'Break a leg, my love.'

'Thanks, Queenie,' I say sheepishly, blushing as she winks at me and mouths the name 'John' with glee. I make a face at her and say, 'We'd better hurry up', to Daisy, giving her a slightly ungentlemanly shove out the gate.

We walk up to the main road in silence. I'm conscious of the space between the two of us, humming with a tension that I have no idea how to break. I rack my brains for something to say, but can't think of anything. Maybe this was a bad idea, I think. Maybe we will have absolutely nothing in common as adults. Why would we, just because we were so close twenty years ago? People change, after all.

Eventually, she breaks the ice. 'This is only the second time that I've been out without Brian. It kind of feels strange!'

I nod sagely. 'I'm sure.'

'I've made a lot of progress, thanks to you.'

'That's good.'

'Are you going to do that all night?' She smiles.

'Do what?'

'Answer in two-word sentences.'

'I might.'

'Very funny.'

'It's catching.'

'It is. Stop!' She giggles giving me a gentle push.

I wonder what that push means – that she likes me or that she just sees me as a jokey friend, someone to share a laugh with and a moan about parenting. But I don't want to be that kind of friend, I think suddenly. I don't want to be a mate. I used to be more than that and I want to be more than that again – Tuning Fork Gate notwithstanding.

'So, are you looking forward to tonight?' Her tone is light.

'God, no. I've actually been sick three times today just thinking about it.'

She puts a hand on my arm and gives it a squeeze. 'Oh, you poor thing. You have stage fright.'

'I know, it's really embarrassing,' I say, hoping that she won't take her hand away. 'It's hardly the Albert Hall, and yet here I am, throwing up. I've always had a phobia about speaking in public.'

'It doesn't have to be the Albert Hall, John,' she says, giving my arm another squeeze, this time leaving her hand there. Could she like me? Maybe when she said it was 'complicated' she really meant that – not that she wasn't interested. I'm confused.

We lapse into silence as we duck into a little laneway off the main road, a narrow tunnel of which there are many in London, sudden turnings that give way to a courtyard or a lovely square. I love that about the place, all the layers of history jumbled together in a heap. This tiny laneway comes out at a kind of burned, rubbish-strewn patch of grass that passes for a park in these parts, around which a man is walking a pit bull terrier on a long piece of rope, a cigarette clamped between his lips. 'Here we are!' Daisy says, as we stand in front of the Queen Victoria, with its brown-tiled front and sign of a disapproving queen, outside which has been placed a sandwich board announcing the north London Open-Mike Night – 'Get things off your chest!'

The pub is heaving with the usual assortment of Londoners, bike couriers standing in the corner, leaning over their bikes, pints in hand, office workers in loosened ties guffawing and a group of old hippies clustered at the bar in droopy knitwear and straggly hair. All these tribes, I think, in the one place.

'What would you like to drink?' I ask Daisy.

'Oh, I don't really drink a lot, because I'm still feeding Brian … but, what the hell, I'm out for the night. I'll have a glass of white wine. Booze and snooze as my health visitor says!'

'Which part are you going to do here?' I joke.

'Very funny. "Booze", of course. I wouldn't dream of snoozing through your first stage appearance.'

'Don't remind me,' I say. 'I'd better stick to mineral water. I don't fancy reciting poetry half-cut. Or maybe that's the only way to read it,' I add sadly.

'Oh, you'll be fine,' Daisy says happily. 'Think of how proud you'll be of yourself when you get up on stage and read.'

'Well, I suppose there has to be some incentive,' I say, elbowing my way past one of the couriers, who is holding forth on the traffic around Holborn, and ushering Daisy up to the bar. I'm about to order when I notice something out of the corner of my eye. Patrice's bright-red paisley scarf. Oh no, I think. Don't tell me

Patrice is here. I'll never hear the end of it when I go into work tomorrow.

I look to my right and it's worse than I thought. At a table in the corner, under a painting of gloomy Victorians crammed into a carriage, is a group from Farrell's: Patrice, Nolan, Audrey and, God help me, Betty. Please God may they not have seen me, I think, as I make my order.

I try not to look at the Farrell's lot on my way back through the crowd, but when you're six foot six it's hard to avoid detection. Sure enough, Betty sees me and gives a huge 'Yoohoo!' getting up from her seat and coming towards me. 'Erm, this way,' I say, nudging Daisy in the opposite direction. I need to cut Betty off at the pass, I think, as Daisy finds a seat in a corner. 'I'll be just a sec,' I say, turning around and racing back to the crowd, where Betty is bearing down on me.

'Emmett, there you are! I thought you'd run off on me for a minute,' she says brightly. She's wearing a black polka-dot skirt and a scoop-neck black T-shirt with a jaunty red neckerchief – she looks cute, I think, distracted for a moment.

'It's John,' I blurt out.

'What's John?' She looks at me, surprised.

'I am.'

'I don't follow.'

'Look, do you see that woman behind me?' I say, adding, 'Don't turn around!' when Betty goes to turn around.

'You're being very cloak-and-dagger, Emmett,' she says, her smile slightly less bright.

'I know, sorry. I'm here to read a poem for the open-mike night and that woman is … an old friend. She knows me as John.'

Betty looks disconcerted. 'Is that your real name?'

'Eh, you could say that.'

'Emmett, are you involved in something?' Betty says carefully. 'Is it to do with ... being Irish?'

'God no, I'm not in the IRA, if that's what you think,' I say, a little too loudly because one of the cycle couriers turns around and looks a bit alarmed. 'Look, I can assure you it's nothing sinister, but John's my original name. I changed it to Emmett in secondary school, only now I'm John again for stage purposes.'

I'm not used to lying and I can see I'm doing a really bad job of it because Betty's looking at me as if I'm deranged.

'Fine,' she says eventually. 'John it is.' By her tone, I know that she's not impressed. She thinks less of me now that she knows I'm a liar of some kind, but there's not a lot I can do about that. I've got to finish what I started.

'So, the gang's all here, eh?' I nod towards the Farrell's group.

'Yes, why don't you join us? I'm sure I can explain away the John thing,' she says politely.

'Ah, no, it's OK. I kind of promised Daisy ... anyway, maybe see you later,' I blurt.

'See you,' I can hear Betty say faintly behind me. 'Good luck with the reading.' I close my eyes for a second. How did I get to be such a prick? John indeed.

Daisy is examining the label on her bottle of wine when I get back. When she sees me, she smiles and lifts her coat from the seat beside her. 'I've had two people try to sit down here,' she says. 'One man was nearly ninety and the other was wearing Lycra and cycling shoes. He also smelled.'

'Tough choice,' I say. 'I'd go for the ninety-year-old. At least he won't have BO.'

'Yes, but he didn't have any teeth either.'

'Ah, well, you can't have everything,' I say, sitting down and taking a sip of my water, which tastes like ... water. I long for a real drink, but I don't trust myself. Best to stay sober so that I can lie more effectively. The thought is a depressing one and I think of Betty's obvious disappointment in me. She thought I was one of the good guys, I know. She was wrong.

'So ....' Daisy says.

'So,' I repeat.

'You know, before I came here, I wondered if we'd have something to say to each other outside of the parenting context,' Daisy says, looking at me shyly from underneath her lashes. 'I mean, we've spent so long poring over Brian's bottom and discussing baby rice and teething that I have no idea if we have anything else to say to each other.'

'Hmm,' I say noncommittally. 'I'm sure we can think of something.'

'I'm sure we can,' she says faintly.

There's a long pause and I begin to panic. What if she's right? What if we really do have nothing to say to each other? I think of our conversations when we were children, a long stream of chat that could go on for an entire day, and I wonder if there's any way to reach back and grab hold of it or if it's too late: if we've just changed too much.

'So when did you start writing?' she asks eventually.

'Oh, I've always written,' I begin, before wondering if this will be some kind of clue to her: my early efforts at poetry which I'd read to her in our spot under the bed, silly rhymes that sometimes made us snort with laughter. 'At least … I started more seriously in college and then when I started work.'

'Did you always work in bookshops?'

'Oh, no. I actually worked at the Department of Fisheries. My speciality was processing fishing licences, I'll have you know.'

'Sounds very onerous.' Daisy giggles.

'I know, it wasn't. I just did it because I could get time off to write and flexitime, that kind of thing.' I make a face. 'Not that I've done as much as I should have. I did have a poem published in the *Indo*, and I had a few accepted for literary magazines …' My voice trails off as I realise how little I've achieved in the world to which I'd told myself I was devoting my time and energy. 'What about you? Don't you want to design some iconic building or something like that?'

Daisy wrinkles her nose and takes a sip of her wine.

'I'm sorry. Have I said something—' I begin.

She shakes her head. 'No, it's just … Brian's father is all about the big buildings and the iconic stuff – the willy-waving, if you like.' She smiles. 'I just want to create spaces that people can live in. Normal people, that is.'

'Is Brian's father … someone you knew at work?'

Daisy takes a sip of wine. 'You could say that.' She blushes. 'Actually, he's married.'

'Oh.'

'Yeah, "oh". But it isn't like that, really. He's practically divorced,' she adds.

'Right,' I say. Oh, Daisy, I can't believe you of all people fell for that old chestnut.

'You think I'm naïve and deluded,' Daisy says softly. 'If it's any consolation to you, so does everyone else. I just wanted a baby and I'm happy with that. I don't want him to marry me.' She smiles.

'Oh, really? Why not?'

'Because I don't want to get married. Ever. Marriage is a complete sham, a farce. You stand up in front of a whole lot of people and you vow to love each other for ever and ever, and you dance around and cut a cake and make stupid speeches, and it's all bullshit,' she says fervently. 'Within a year or two, it's all falling apart and yet you continue living a lie just for the sake of respectability.'

'Why don't you say what you really mean?' I try to make it a joke, but I know exactly why Daisy is against marriage, and it has nothing to do with Brian's father.

'Oh, God, will you listen to me,' she says, taking a gulp of wine. 'I'm sorry, John, it's a bit of a hobby horse of mine. I blame my mother.' She laughs.

'Mums are to blame for everything,' I agree. 'And dads,' I add as an afterthought, thinking of my own dad and our monosyllabic relationship.

'Do you ever wonder if you'll end up just like your parents?' Daisy asks.

'What do you mean?'

'I mean, if you'll go through life repeating their patterns, doing the things they did, because you've no idea how to be any different. It's as if the patterns run so deep, they're automatic – you just find yourself doing things without realising.'

'In some ways,' I say, thinking of Dad, 'But in other ways, I kind of hope I will be, actually,' I say. 'I am already in a way. I do the kind of things my parents did, like night-time prayers, and I'm very strict about homework and routines and that kind of thing. I can't believe I'm so old-fashioned about it.' I smile. 'I thought I'd be a really laid-back dad, but I'm not at all.'

'Well, you're lucky then. I sometimes wonder if I'll end up like Mum,' Daisy says sadly, 'too busy looking after myself to bother with anyone else.'

God, no, I think. 'You won't.'

'How do you know?'

'Because you're asking yourself that question, which means that you'll try not to,' I improvise. 'And because I see what you're like with Brian.'

'You have no idea what my mother's like,' Daisy says sadly.

'I don't,' I lie, 'but I'm beginning to develop a picture from what you're saying.'

'She's awful – vain, conceited, self-centred—'

'And yet you love her.'

Daisy blushes and looks fixedly at her wine before muttering, 'Yes, I do. Besides, she's all I've got now. My dad died last year. What?' she says when she sees the expression on my face.

Mike. Mike, with the hands like hams and the bad language and the cheroot smoking. Mike with the cowboy boots and the car coat, who used to bring the two of us down to the shop to get ice-cream every time we asked, which was sometimes three times a day. Mike is dead. I used to dream that one day I'd bump into him somewhere, propping the bar up at some little pub, and I'd be able to say sorry to him. Sorry that we messed his life up so badly when all he ever did was be a nice man. He'd even hugged me that last day when Mum had gone running out of the house to the car, refusing to get out of it until Dad came to drive her home to Galway, never to return. She'd shouted that she'd bloody drive herself only she didn't know how, which was comical in a terrible kind of way. He'd given me a brief squeeze and said, 'Take it easy, cowboy.' He'd pressed something into my hand – something that I didn't look at until I was almost home because I was too busy looking at the backs of my parents' heads, wondering if they'd ever speak to each other again. When I opened my hand, the note was damp and sweaty, a rolled-up fiver with a note inside it. 'I love you, Emmett. Don't forget me. You promised! Daisy xxx'

'What's wrong, John? You look as if you've seen a ghost.'

'Oh, it's just ... nothing.' I shake my head, wishing fervently that my fizzy water wasn't fizzy water. 'It makes you realise how short life is, doesn't it?'

'It sure does,' Daisy says sadly.

'Do you miss him?'

She nods. 'He got married again the year before he died. His new wife, Rita, breeds West Highland terriers. She's really bossy,' she says sadly. 'He loved Rita.'

I could say something trite along the lines of, 'Oh, well, at least he had a year's happiness before he died', but I stop myself. 'Do you keep in touch with her?'

'Not really. I wasn't very nice to Rita, I'm ashamed to say. I'd been Daddy's girl for so long at that stage, because he and Mum separated when I was ten, that I gave her a really hard time. Poor woman.'

So, Mike and Bridget separated, while my mum and dad stayed together. Maybe it was just luck or maybe Mum and Dad had a bond that Dad's stupid thing with Bridget didn't break. Or maybe Mum and Dad had just worked harder to reconcile – but then, Bridget and Mike never did look like a match made in heaven. Bridget was too snooty, too posh for Mike, no matter how much money he made – or at least that's what she always implied: that she was far too good for him.

Daisy gives a little shrug. 'I'm sorry. I didn't mean to put such a downer on things.'

'You're hardly putting a downer on things, Daisy. Your dad died. That's not a trivial thing.'

She nods sadly. 'Thanks.'

'Listen, why don't you write to Rita? Tell her about Brian? I'd say she'd like that,' I suggest. 'Maybe she'd enjoy being a step-grandmother. She's family, after all – and maybe she'd be a bit more … objective than your own mum.'

'Maybe,' Daisy says, shrugging her shoulders. 'Actually, that's quite a good idea.' And she gives the smallest of smiles. 'You always give such good advice.'

'Thanks.' Pity I can't take any, I think sadly. 'Let me get you another drink. "Booze and snooze", as they say.'

Daisy's smile is larger and my heart takes a leap in my chest.

I look straight ahead when I go up to the bar, not daring to even glance at the crowd from Farrell's, and return swiftly with a white wine for Daisy and a single measure of whiskey for myself. I need to quell my nerves, I think, before I have to take to the stage and recite my poem. The poem with Mike in it, sitting on the deck outside the house, phone in his hand, swearing down the line. I can't recite that now knowing that the poor man is dead. Maybe I can think of something else. I wonder if I brought my notebook with me? I think as I sit down, smiling nervously at Daisy.

The open mike has begun and there's a man on stage reading

out a very long short story about pigeon fanciers. The initial respectful silence that greeted him is gradually being replaced by louder chatter as the audience loses interest. I feel my stomach flip. What happens if people heckle me? Or worse, simply ignore me? Then I chide myself: that's hardly the point, is it, when I'm reading what I'm reading. The more I think of it, the more obvious the symbolism becomes. I swallow, but my mouth is tinder dry and my palms begin to sweat. I take a quick swig of the whiskey, feeling it burn my stomach, a warm fire spreading through my chest. That's better, I think.

Daisy takes a big gulp, as if she is dying of thirst. 'That's better,' she says, putting it back. 'I'd forgotten how lovely wine was. Come to think of it, I'd forgotten how nice going out was, and talking to adults who make sense, who don't forget everything or have a fixation on the soaps.' With this, she takes another swig.

'I'm glad to hear that I make sense,' I say. I've polished off the whiskey in two gulps, and can feel it working its magic. I lean back against the velvet banquette, resting my head against the softness. I turn to my right to see that Daisy's head is inches away from mine. She's looking straight ahead, and she blows the wisp of hair hanging down over her forehead away. It bounces back, so she blows it away again.

'Here, let me do that,' I say, leaning over and lifting the lock of hair, then tucking it behind her ear. 'There, that's better.' I feel that I'm outside myself, as I look into her eyes. I can see the rims of grey around her pupils, the dark fringes of her lashes. Her lips are slightly parted and … No, I tell myself, no, Emmett. Resist. Daisy has made it very clear that she doesn't want this.

'I'm sorry,' I begin, about to move away, but she shifts her head closer and kisses me on the lips. Her mouth is soft and warm, and I find myself kissing her back, pressing her gently into the banquette. God, this is good, I think, as she puts her arm around the back of my neck and begins to stroke my hair. This is really good. I reach a hand into her hair, feeling the curls under my fingers, and her kiss becomes more passionate, lips pressed to mine, and we're suddenly necking like teenagers at the back of the cinema on a Saturday night. Oh, God, I think, this is too much, as she presses her mouth to my ear and blows softly. I need to pull myself together. I can't read a poem in this state, I think, as I find her mouth again and kiss it. If I do, she'll surely … She gives a little moan … 'Oh, Daisy,' I say.

'Oh, John,' she says, her voice soft in my ear.

'This isn't a good idea,' I say, as I kiss her again.

'No, it isn't,' she agrees, opening her mouth to mine.

Then I hear a loud voice through a microphone calling John O'Donoghue to the stage. I'm busy, I think, as I continue my work of kissing Daisy. 'Is John O'Donoghue in the house?' the voice roars. 'He'd better be interesting,' it continues, through a screech of feedback, to a roar of laughter.

'Go on,' Daisy says, releasing me, giving me a little shove. Her cheeks have a lovely pink tinge to them and her mouth … Oh, God.

'I'll still be here when you get back.'

'Promise?'

'Promise. Now, break a leg,' she adds, giving a small, flustered smile. A smile that tells me we're not finished yet.

I get up from my seat and walk towards the little stage that's been set up in a corner, a small black dais with a microphone stand. I stand behind it, not sure whether I should grab it, like Jon Bon Jovi, and start swinging it in the air. I'm kind of feeling like a rock star, so maybe I should just go for it. Or maybe it would be more professional to just stand behind it, as if I'm going to make a speech. I opt for speech making, holding out my piece of paper and clearing my throat.

'*Allez, dépêche-toi, mon brave!*' Patrice yells from the Farrell's table. Then I can hear a muttered, '*C'est qui,* John O'Donoghue?'

'It's his stage name,' Betty whispers loudly in reply.

'Erm, hi everyone,' I begin, before I'm nearly blown off the stage by a shriek of feedback. 'Sorry,' I say, standing farther back. 'Right. Well, I'm going to read a poem. It's, erm, it's for Daisy.' I peer at the back of the room, giving her a little wave. There's a sprinkling of applause and a lone wolf whistle, which is followed by silence. I clear my throat and say the first line of the poem. It sounds all right, I think. Normal anyway. Then I read the next line, and the next, taking a second's glance up to see Patrice looking at me, and he doesn't have a sneer on his face. So that's good, I think, my voice gaining in power as I read on and think of Mike on the deck, the coiled serpent of the phone flex in his hand, and as I read aloud, it becomes so obvious to me what the poem is about. Daisy can't possibly miss the meaning, I think – not when I'm reading it to the hushed room and every line is for her.

When I get to the last line, I look up, and I see her staring at me from her seat at the back of the room. Her face seems pale in the gloomy half-light, ghostly, and I can't see what her expression is like from this distance. Maybe she's OK with it, I think. Maybe she hasn't guessed and we can just go on as we were. But then, in a flurry of movement, she gets up from her seat, pulls her coat on, takes her bag and flies out of the pub by the side door.

'Daisy!' I yell, so loudly there's a whine of feedback again.

'Sorry,' I say hurriedly as I hop down off the stage to the ripple of respectable applause, mixed with whooping and cheering from the Farrell's table. 'Well done, Emmett!' Audrey says, coming towards me and giving me a hug.

'It's John,' Betty says drily.

'Well, whatever you're called, you were fantastic.'

'Thanks,' I say. 'Erm, I just need to find my date.'

I know that I'm being rude, but I have to find Daisy now. I walk briskly to the side door, breaking into a sprint as I push it open and run out into the square. It's empty apart from a man letting his boxer dog wee on a lamppost. I run through the little alleyway out onto the main road and then right, picking up speed as I head past the chipper and the kebab shop, the post office and the newsagent's, towards Albion Road. I'm sure she must have gone home, I think as I huff and puff up the main road, weaving past people on their way home from the pub and from work, ignoring the odd cry of 'What's the hurry, mate? Where's the fire?'

Where else would she go? She wouldn't run off on Brian, I think, because she's such a good mum. Then I think I see her, walking around the corner to the little row of shops at the top of the road. 'Daisy!' I yell. If it is her, she doesn't stop, and after I bend over for a second to catch my breath, resting my hands on my knees, I begin to run again. I guess I'll just have to brave Bridget, I think. I'll just have to sit there, with that woman, and tell Daisy who I am and that I'm sorry and that I love her …

I stop for a moment. I love her, I think. I love Daisy.

Then I start to run again, only faster this time. I'm about to pass my house and Queenie's when I notice a black cab parked at the front gate. I hope Queenie hasn't had any of her cronies over, I think, as I run. I don't want Misty exposed to all of that stuff. The door of the cab opens and a woman gets out in a light spring coat, thin legs bare, in slip-on heels. She seems to shiver, shoving her hands into her coat, then looking up at the house. Our house.

I stop when I'm six feet away, breaths coming in short, ragged puffs. 'Amanda?'

The woman turns and my heart sinks to my boots.

'Emmett,' she says, giving a small smile. 'Oh, Emmett,' and she runs into my arms.

13.

'Aren't you glad to see me?' she says, as we hover by the front door. She's spent the past ten minutes sobbing wordlessly in my arms and it's all I can do not to shove her out of the way and keep running to Daisy's. I have to speak to her. I *need* to speak to her, I think, as Amanda softly wails and soaks the front of my jumper and I absently pat her on the shoulder.

'Of course I am,' I say distractedly, rummaging in my pocket for my keys. 'It's just a bit of a shock, that's all.'

'You sound disappointed,' she says sulkily.

I have never been more disappointed to see anyone in my whole life.

'No, I'm not, honestly. I'm delighted, I really am,' I lie. 'It's great to have you home. We really missed you.' I thought that would sound better than 'Misty really missed you', somehow – as if it might soften the blow of my less-than-fulsome welcome.

Amanda brightens slightly. 'That's good.'

'Yes, it is.'

'Emmett, are you all right?' Amanda says.

'Of course I am. Now, let's get you inside,' I say. 'Misty will be beside herself.'

I decide that there's no way I can just dash off to Daisy's, no matter how much I want to. Even though I keep seeing her ghostly face in front of me, the expression as she finally understood, and even though I want to bolt out the door this minute, I have to keep control of myself. Amanda needs it. Misty needs it.

'I can't wait to see her,' Amanda says, hanging her coat up on the antler coat rack in the hall and putting her shoes in the cabinet provided, which has been unused since her departure. 'Let me just run upstairs—'

'She's not here, actually. I was out tonight at an … event and she's in Queenie's.'

'In *Queenie's*?' Amanda looks horrified. 'Emmett, that woman is a degenerate. She drinks in the middle of the day.' She mouths this final bit as if she's afraid someone will overhear us.

'She's not,' I say firmly. 'The G and Ts are for a friend who calls every afternoon, not for Queenie, and she's been very good to Misty. They're great friends.'

'God, I can see a lot's changed around here,' Amanda says, rolling her eyes to heaven.

'Yes, it has,' I snap back.

For a moment, Amanda looks disconcerted, but then she says,

'I'll go and collect her. I need to see her.' She opens the cabinet to take out her shoes, but I interrupt.

'Stop!' My voice is louder than I'd intended and Amanda jumps, her face rigid with shock. 'Sorry, I mean, wait a minute,' I say softly. 'Why don't you tell me why you're home first? And where's Roland?'

'Oh, Emmett,' Amanda says, dropping her hands to her sides in despair, eyes filling with tears again.

I should go to her, I know, and put my arms around her, but instead, I just stand there, waiting, looking at her while she sobs. I didn't want you back, I think, but here you are anyway while the woman I love has run away and I'm powerless to do anything except wait for you to stop crying, and I don't really want to know why you're crying because I'm too angry with you for spoiling everything. The fact that it was me who caused Daisy to run away is neither here nor there – it's easier to blame Amanda.

Eventually, she stops sniffling and lifts her head, her blue eyes red rimmed. 'I think I need a cigarette,' she says softly, walking ahead of me to the kitchen, then out of the French doors, where she pulls out a chair and sits down on it, taking a packet of cigarettes from her coat pocket and putting it on the table, extracting a cigarette and lighting it, closing her eyes and tilting her head to the night sky. She looks tiny, like a little bird, her slender wrists poking out of the arms of her coat like a scarecrow's. She's lost weight, I think, while I busy myself in the kitchen making tea, and it suddenly strikes me how much she's carried on her narrow shoulders all of these years, caring for Misty alone, working to get her law degree ... she deserved to find Roland, I think. She deserved to find Mr Right. But why the hell did she have to turn up now?

'So …' I say, putting a pot of tea down on the table, along with a carton of milk, and pulling up a chair. 'What happened?'

Amanda takes a deep pull on her cigarette. 'Did you not put it in a jug?' Her nose wrinkles as she catches sight of the carton.

'Amanda. What happened?' I sound gentle this time, and her expression softens.

'There was a hurricane.'

'A hurricane? Jesus, are you OK? Is Roland—?'

'He's not dead, if that's what you mean,' Amanda says dryly, reaching down and jabbing her cigarette on the ground. 'Does it sound terrible to say that I wish he was?' she added shakily.

'It depends on what he's done,' I say, taking a sip of my tea.

'Well … where will I even begin?'

'At the beginning.' I take another sip. 'I'm all ears,' I say with fake enthusiasm.

It turned out that the luxury beach huts and the one big deal that would make Roland and Amanda rich was all an illusion. 'The beach wasn't even a beach,' Amanda says miserably. 'It was a kind of mudslide at the far end of the island, where nobody goes. And the financing turned out to be bogus. Some Russian company that was exploiting tax loopholes. The minute I looked at the contracts I knew – it might as well have been written in letters ten feet tall, instead of in subsection B, point 1a,' she adds bitterly.

'And you spotted it in the small print.'

'I did.' She gives a small smile. 'I'm good, you know.'

'I know.'

'Not that it mattered, as there was no beach for the bloody beach huts. The hurricane was the final straw – it all got washed away. Can you believe it?'

'Oh, no,' I say. 'That's terrible.'

There is a long silence, while I struggle to think of something helpful to say. C'mon Emmett, this kind of stuff has always come naturally to you, I chide myself. Then I notice that Amanda's shoulders are shaking. 'Amanda, don't cry,' I say, pulling my chair up beside her and putting an arm around her tiny frame. 'C'mon, it'll be all right. It always is.'

Amanda's shoulders continue to shake and then she throws her head back and guffaws, tears of mirth pouring down her face. 'The ... beach got ... washed away – I mean, can you believe it? You can't have luxury beach huts without a fucking beach, can you?' And she roars with laughter again.

'I wouldn't think so,' I say carefully, not sure if she wants me to laugh along with her. It doesn't seem very funny to me.

'You wouldn't think so!' she cackles, clutching her stomach. 'Oh, God, I've a pain in my tummy from laughing. My mum used to call it hysterical laughter,' she adds, her giggles subsiding. 'She'll be thrilled to hear that Roland's out of the picture, the old bat. I'm sorry, Emmett,' she says, seeing the expression on my face. 'The only way to deal with it is to laugh – it was just so hideous, the whole thing. I had to dress up like a tart and go to all of these awful dinners with fat Russians who kept staring at my boobs, and then hang on Roland's shoulder at the casino while he blew another five thousand of our money. Honestly, I felt like a gangster's moll.'

'Five *thousand*?' I haven't had more than a hundred quid to my name for the past few months, so five thousand seems like a huge amount.

'A night,' Amanda adds helpfully. 'In the end, he blew through a hundred grand. My savings and his, and all for nothing. For another one of his stupid schemes. Honestly, Emmett, I'm not stupid, you know that, but I bloody fell for it – again. After the last time, he promised me never again – but this was supposed to be a sure-fire winner. There was no way we could lose, he said. He knew a guy in the Interior Ministry who would get the wheels in motion and so on … another load of bullshit,' Amanda says fiercely.

So, Queenie was right, I think. Roland led Amanda a merry dance and now she's back where she started. 'C'mon,' I say, pulling her closer and letting her rest her head on my shoulder and sob her heart out. 'There, there,' I soothe, as my mother had soothed me when I was a child. 'It'll be OK.' Just twenty minutes ago, Daisy was in my arms and she felt entirely different. Softer, warmer, more robust, as if there was a life force flowing through her – not like brittle Amanda, taut with tension.

'It won't be OK, but thanks for saying it,' Amanda says. 'I'll have to sell the house,' she adds sadly. 'I can't afford it, and anyway, it just reminds me of everything we built together. Bastard.'

'Well, let's think about that tomorrow,' I say softly. 'Tomorrow is another day, isn't it?'

'Oh, God, tomorrow,' Amanda groans. 'I can't face it.'

'Let's just go and get Misty and go to bed – I mean, in our separate beds, that is – and we'll face whatever has to be faced.'

She nods and gets up, tilting her head to the stars. 'I really missed this,' she says.

'Were there no stars in Jamaica?'

'No, I mean this. This house, this garden. God, I missed Misty. I can't believe that I abandoned her like that.' She crosses her arms over her chest and stifles another sob. 'All for that shit—'

'Stop. Beating yourself up won't solve anything. Let's go and get our daughter, OK?'

'Thanks, Emmett.'

'You're welcome.'

'You're actually pretty special, do you know that?' She gives a small smile.

'I'm not, but thanks for saying it all the same.' I give a little shrug. Actually, I think, I'm bloody heroic after everything that's happened tonight. 'Have you eaten? You go and get Misty and I'll put something on.'

'You mean you can cook now?'

'I'm pretty good, even if I say so myself. I think there's homemade soup in the fridge. Let me heat it up for you.' And before she can say anything further, I retreat into the kitchen and start bashing pans and opening the fridge, pouring the plastic container full of pumpkin soup into a pot and putting it on the stove. I look busy and preoccupied, which is just the way I want it, because when Amanda goes out of the front door and clatters down the steps to Queenie's, I can finally let out the sob I've been holding in for the past hour. And once I start, I can't stop.

I lost Daisy once, I think, as I wipe my nose and stir the soup. I lost her once and now I've lost her again.

Misty was ecstatic to see her mother, of course, sitting on her knee and twisting a lock of Amanda's golden hair round and round while she sucked her thumb – something she hadn't done since she was three, according to Amanda, which made me feel guilty because she's been doing quite a lot of it lately. When she asked where Roland was, Amanda told her that he was just having a little holiday in Jamaica with his mum, looking at me carefully over Misty's shoulder. She didn't add that it would be permanent. How do you tell a child that the man she's always thought of as Dad will no longer be in her life? Amanda says she doesn't want him around, which is unfair, but I have no intention of broaching that subject with her right now. She's too angry.

'Are you OK?' Amanda asks me now, as we both stand on the landing, me with Misty's toothbrush and she with Misty's favourite Dalmatian pyjamas. 'You look as if you've been crying.'

'No, just a bit of hay fever,' I say. 'I always get it in April. All the trees.'

'Right,' she says, hovering in front of Misty's bedroom. 'Emmett, is there something you're not telling me?'

'What do you mean?'

'Oh, just … nothing,' Amanda says, giving a little smile.

I want to scream. Is there something about me that makes women smile in that way? It's so bloody patronising.

'Right then, it's a schoolnight so …'

'Oh, God, of course. Bedtime!' So … do I put Misty to bed or do you?' she says shyly.

'Why don't we both do it?'

'Great!' She goes into Misty's room, where Misty is bouncing around, even though it's nearly eleven o'clock at night, and she shows her mother her book collection, which Amanda pronounces most impressive, and her Barbie dolls, which she's now hidden in a box under the bed because they're 'stupid'.

'I like books more than anything, Mummy,' she says, standing on her bed and twirling around.

'Well, that's lovely, but you need to get down off the bed and put on your pyjamas, Misty,' Amanda says. 'Here you go … oh, my God!' She suddenly gives a shriek as Bran, who has been lying happily curled up in a ball at the end of Misty's bed, gets up and has a little stretch and a yawn. 'What. Is. That. Doing. Here?' Amanda points to Bran.

'Silly Mummy.' Misty giggles. 'He's my best friend after Clive and he always lies on my bed at night. Sometimes, he even gets under the duvet with me and snuggles up.'

Amanda looks as if she'll be sick. 'We'll have to talk about this,' she mutters to me.

'Later,' I say quietly, thinking that it'll be a very difficult conversation. And wait until we get to prayers.

'Into bed, poppet,' Amanda says, pointedly ignoring Bran as she lifts the corner of the duvet up for Misty to climb in.

'I have to say my prayers first, Mummy!' Misty says. 'Let me show you.' And she climbs out of bed and kneels down, resting her elbows on the bed and closing her eyes. 'Dear God, thank you for bringing my mummy home because I really, really missed her. Please bless Roland in Jamaica and I hope he has a nice holiday with *his* mummy and that he comes home soon. And God bless Dada and Clive and Daisy – oh, and Queenie, because she let me eat two Mars bars while we watched *Lethal Weapon*. Amen.'

Amanda looks as if she will pass out, and I mouth to her over Misty's bowed head, 'I'll explain.'

Amanda mouths back, 'You'd better.' But when Misty looks at her for approval, she strokes her hair and says, 'Well, that was just lovely, Misty. Well done. Now, into bed.'

Misty climbs happily into bed and Amanda plumps up her pillows before hugging her tightly. 'I missed you, Misty-boo.'

'I know, Mummy. I missed you too. Are you going away again?'

'Never, ever again,' Amanda says, kissing Misty's hair as Misty wraps her arms around her mother and I stand there, looking on. 'Now, lights out,' Amanda says gently. 'It's very late and you have school in the morning.'

'Oh, no, Mummy, we're not finished yet. Now we have a bedtime story.'

'Do we?' Amanda says, looking at me.

'Yes, we do, Mummy, you sit this side of me so that you can listen to the story and look at the pictures.' Misty pats the bed beside her.

'OK,' Amanda says carefully, sitting down.

'So, what'll it be?' I say, praying for something neutral, like *Horrid Henry*, but oh, no, Misty's pointing at the book of Irish myths and legends.

'Well … why don't we try something else tonight?' I say hopefully. After the dog and the prayers, this will really finish Amanda off, I think.

'No!' Misty says firmly. 'I want Neeve and Osheen. Wait till you hear it, Mummy, it's a very interesting story.'

'I can't wait,' Amanda says faintly.

I take the book and open its glossy colour pages, and I begin the story with Niamh turning up on her white horse, with her long golden hair and her cloak full of stars, and telling Oisín of the place where she and he could be together and never grow old – Tír na nÓg, the land of eternal youth – and I'm trying to concentrate and not to let my mind wander, feeling Amanda's presence, the weight of her judgement of Misty's night-time rituals. I read about how much Oisín missed his father, Fionn Mac Cumhaill, and his family, and how he'd wanted to go home and see them, and how utterly everything had changed – what had seemed to pass in the blink of an eye had, in fact, been three hundred years in the real world. I know how he feels, I think, as I read the words and we digest the knowledge of Oisín's tragedy – falling off his horse and ageing three hundred years in a second. Time is a funny thing: it seems to pass slowly and quickly at the same time. The past few weeks have been the longest of my life and yet they have passed in a heartbeat and I've emerged, like Oisín, changed completely. I can't go back now, I know that, and when I look at Amanda over Misty's head, I know that she feels the same way.

We examine the picture of three-hundred-year-old Oisín, his beard trailing to the ground, his bony legs like a bird's, his wrinkled hands grasping a blackthorn stick, then Misty says, 'Dada?'

'Yes?'

'Would you like to go to Teer na Nohg?'

'Hmmm … maybe? I suppose it would be nice never to grow old, but I wonder what it would be like to just live in the present all the time. I'd say it'd be a bit strange.'

'What do you think, Mummy? Could we all go and live there?'

'Well, I'd like to,' Amanda says. 'Living in the present might be nice, but only if it's a good present, if you see what I mean.' She's not talking to Misty, of course, who looks a bit baffled.

'Yes, but we haven't any choice about what kind of present we get,' I say meaningfully. 'The past is gone and the future isn't here yet, so the present is all we have.'

Amanda thinks that I'm talking about her, of course, or us, but I know that I'm really talking about Daisy. The past we shared is gone, no matter how strong the memories, and all we have left is who we are now. I've been living in the past, I realise, and the Daisy I know now is a stranger, which makes me wonder if I love her now because I loved her then, or whether I love her because, well, I do. I try to imagine us in five years' time. Misty will be twelve and Brian nearly six, and maybe there might be one or two more – but the image just won't come into focus and I realise that I can't imagine that far ahead. The future just seems like a big blur.

'I just want things to stay the same,' Misty says sadly. 'I just want you and Mummy to sit on my bed for ever. We can all pretend we live in Teer na Nohg.'

'I know, pipsqueak,' I say. 'But real life isn't like that: things change all the time and we change with them. Maybe we'd all wake up in three hundred years and find that we were all wrinkly with long, scraggy hair and even longer fingernails.' I make a joke of it, giving Misty a tickle, but Amanda knows that I'm serious. In the real world, things have changed for ever.

'I'll just go and get ready for bed,' Amanda mutters, popping a quick kiss onto Misty's head and leaving the room without giving me another glance.

I sigh heavily.

'Dada, have I made Mummy really sad?' Misty says.

'No, pipsqueak. Mummy's just worked really hard in Jamaica and she needs a rest. Now, if you go to sleep really quickly, you can have a lie-in in the morning and then we can all have breakfast. I'll give you a note for Miss Grace.'

'Thanks, Dada!' Misty says happily, snuggling down under her pink duvet while Bran curls up at her feet. 'I'm so happy,' she sighs.

'I know, love. That's good,' I say soothingly. It's good that one of us is anyway, I think.

I can hear Amanda in the kitchen as I go wearily back downstairs to find the book I've been reading. I know that I should go in to her, to discuss the prayer/dog/bedtime-story issues, but instead, I walk quietly down the hall, open the front door and close it softly behind me.

The street is completely quiet, apart from the low murmur of Queenie's TV set – she stays up late watching true-crime documentaries, the better to terrify herself – and the low growl of two fighting cats. I walk slowly past the silent houses, past the cars and the fox that always rummages in the communal bins of the flats at the corner, my mind filling with all the things I need to say to Daisy – all the questions I need to ask her about whether what we have is over before it has even begun or if she thinks there might be the tiniest chance for us. About whether what we have is real or is simply the echo of long-ago times, now best forgotten. Christ, I think, that sounds like a line from a bad poem.

I take up my usual position behind the bins outside her flat. I know that this makes me look like a deviant of some kind, but I want to suss out the scene before I go barging in. But the door of her flat remains resolutely closed. I wonder if she's inside, putting Brian to bed, watching late-night TV – if she's thinking about me at all. Then I lose patience with myself. For God's sake, will you look at yourself, hiding behind a dustbin? Get on with it, for God's sake, or else, what is this all about?

With one smooth movement, I get up and walk down the steep steps to Daisy's front door. I knock as quietly as I can so that I don't wake the neighbours and wait, fighting the urge to run away. Eventually, just as I'm about to give up, I see a shadow behind the door. My throat tightens and I feel my blood pounding in my ears.

The door slowly opens and Bridget Delaney is standing in front of me.

In the dim light from the hall, she looks as if she's shrunk by a few inches, and her once-black hair is now clearly dyed, now that she's not wearing her signature turban, but her eyes are still the same, big and grey, fringed by dark lashes, just like Daisy's. The only difference is that Bridget has a tiny nose, elegant and thin.

'Bridget,' I begin. 'It's been a long time.'

She looks at me curiously and I wait for her expression to tighten, to close at the realisation that it's her daughter's childhood friend, but instead she just says, 'Who are you?'

I'm disconcerted. 'I'm Emmett.'

She looks puzzled for a minute. 'Emmett? Are you Peter's boy?'

'Eh, no. My father is Francis ...' I don't want to mention my father's name, but it seems as if I have no choice. I wait for her to recoil, but instead she says, 'Oh, Francis. He plays such a good hand of bridge. Always great to play against – I like a bit of a challenge!'

Oh. 'Erm, I'm sure you do. Anyway, is Daisy there?'

'Daisy ...' Bridget says vaguely. 'Daisy's ... out!' she says triumphantly. 'She's brought Brian to the playground.'

'But it's midnight,' I say quietly. 'Are you sure she's not here, Bridget?'

She looks confused. 'How do you know my name? Are you from around here?'

'No, Bridget, I'm from Galway.'

'Galway? And you've come all the way here to see me? That must be two hundred miles,' she says.

There seems no point in telling her that she's in north London, because the fact seems to have escaped her. I think it would only confuse and upset her more. But where the hell is Daisy? I try to look around Bridget into the gloom of the flat, but all I can hear is the radio, the bip-bip of the pips that come before the news.

'You're very tall,' she says looking at me appraisingly.

'Yes, I am.'

'Do you like being tall?'

'Erm, sometimes. It has its advantages.'

She nods vaguely, as if she doesn't really know why she's asked the question, before saying, '*EastEnders* is on. Would you like to come in?'

I can't imagine that *EastEnders* is on in the middle of the night, and I realise that I don't want to go inside with Bridget, to stand with her in the half-darkness of the flat like a stranger who let himself in, who took advantage of a vulnerable woman. There'll be another time to talk to Daisy.

'No, I won't,' I say firmly. 'Will you tell Daisy that Emmett called?' There's no harm in reminding Bridget of my real name, I think, because the chances are she won't remember it and, if she does, it'll only be something Daisy knows already, now that I've stupidly blown my cover.

'Yes. That's a good idea,' she says, turning around and walking back into the darkness of the flat.

'Bridget?'

'Yes?' She turns to look at me, eyes wide with innocence.

'Close the front door. Otherwise someone could break in.'

'Yes, of course. Thank you!' she says, shuffling out into the light again and closing the door in my face.

Time to go home, Emmett, I think miserably, walking back down the road.

14.

Amanda is the mother of my child, and after what she's been through, I can't abandon her, I keep telling myself. So I concentrate on the present, on focusing on what I'm doing at this specific moment in time, getting through the days by being a dutiful other half to Amanda – at least, on the outside – and a father to Misty, going to work and going through the motions, ignoring Patrice's little digs and trying to avoid bumping into Betty.

I've been neglecting Mum: Tom rang me the other day to tell me to get my ass up to Holloway because he was going out of his mind with her, as she's refusing to go any further than the bakery on Holloway Road. 'I might have known,' he said darkly. 'She won't move outside the door at home, so why should London be any different?' I nodded and said I'd be up this week, but I can't handle Mum right now. She'll know immediately that there's something wrong and I can't risk it.

Now I'm downstairs in the English Poetry department, looking up poems for the inaugural Farrell's Literary Lunch – or, rather, for my part in it: the bloody poetry therapy, which I just couldn't get Betty to forget. She's doing it for revenge, I think, as I flick through a collection of Ted Hughes. She keeps calling me John, then going 'whoops', putting one of those dainty hands over her mouth. 'Silly me. I mean Emmett, of course.'

I feel like telling Betty that I couldn't care less. You can call me John all you like or give me disapproving looks – they won't make any difference to how I feel inside, which is miserable. I haven't seen Daisy for three weeks now, since that night when Bridget answered the door. I just didn't have the nerve and, besides, if she really cared, she'd have called into me, wouldn't she? I've taken to going the long way around to Farrell's, turning right instead of left outside the house, then up to the main road, where there's a little coffee shop. There, I sit for ten minutes and drink an espresso, feeling the hot coffee warm my bones, and sometimes I eat the croissant that the owner, Stefano, offers me every time, telling me that I'm too 'theen', and then I trudge down to Farrell's for another day at the coalface. I don't feel motivated to keep my little corner of this dump clean any more: there doesn't seem to be any point to it, even though Betty has got everyone else to do a bit of a spring clean, so that it looks like an investment worth making to the literary lunchers. There doesn't seem to be much point in anything. Whoever said that living in an eternal present could be great – to me, it's agony. I want the days to speed forward to a point when I'll wake up and the first thought in my head won't be Daisy, wondering where she is or what she's doing.

Still, I can't dodge the bloody literary lunch, I think miserably, or the poetry therapy that I'm scheduled to administer after dessert. I suppose giving people advice that they don't want or need can be a form of therapy in itself – distracting me from the thoughts that keep churning in my head.

I scan the shelves for anything by Elizabeth Bishop because her poems are all about the real world. She doesn't have any time for angst or wittering on about her inner pain, I think, so she'll be perfect for my mood, if not my audience. Then I look at my watch: 12.30. A whole three hours gone and another five to go. The thought fills me with a certain heaviness as I go into the loo to check my appearance before the lunch. I bare my teeth to check there are no stray bits of croissant in them, flick the tuft of brown hair that always hangs over my right eye out of the way and straighten the tie Amanda made me wear. 'You have to wear a tie to a luncheon, Emmett. It looks more professional.'

I don't want to look professional, I protest inwardly. I want to look like an artist, with my hollowed-out cheeks and the trousers that hang off my hips. I must have lost weight, I think. Either that or these are Roland's. But then, they can't be: Amanda went through his side of the huge walk-in wardrobe in her bedroom the day after she came back, the clang of hangers and the rustling of plastic making me realise that she was getting rid of any trace of him from her life. The act hadn't been lost on Misty, who had seen Amanda loading up Roland's BMW – which is going back to the dealer next week – with bags.

'Is Daddy coming home soon, Emmett?' she asked me.

'I'm sure he is, pipsqueak. I think Mummy has a lot of dry cleaning to do, that's all.' It wasn't for me to tell her the truth, I thought. She doesn't need to find out about Roland yet. I've tried to speak to Amanda about him, to encourage her to at least let Misty see him when he comes back. 'He's the only father she's ever known,' I told her.

'No, he's not,' she responded sharply. 'Misty has a father.' And, she added softly, 'A very good one.'

I am a good dad, I think, as I pat down my hair with a bit of water. Look at the dismal specimen that I was when I arrived here just a few months ago. Where on earth would I be without Misty? Probably still in a corner in the Department of Fisheries, mouldering away, thinking about the great life I'd have instead of living it. The thing is, when you really live life, you get hurt, and that's hard.

Then the door opens and Betty appears, walking to the mirror and examining herself in it, tidying her hair and opening her handbag, producing a lipstick with which she carefully outlines her lips. She's not wearing her usual rockabilly-princess uniform, but a drab grey suit that makes her look drawn and a bit depressed.

'It's the gents,' I say.

'I know,' she replies. 'But I wanted to talk to you and you've been avoiding me.'

'I've been avoiding *you*? I thought you were avoiding me.'

She twists the lipstick back in its case and puts it into her handbag. Then she gives me a long, hard stare. 'Do you know how important this lunch is? Do you understand that our jobs are on the line here?'

'I know that,' I say defensively.

'Well then, cop the hell on and do something,' she barks. 'Stop moping like a lovelorn teenager while the ship sinks and bloody well help me.'

'I will,' I say sulkily.

'You promised,' she says more softly.

'Sorry, I know I did.'

There's a long pause. 'What's wrong with you, Emmett? Or, sorry, should that be John? I find it hard to remember these days,' she says sarcastically.

'Ouch.'

She shrugs. 'I'm not the one lying about myself, Emmett.'

'No? What about the costume change every time there's a new man in your life?'

There's a long silence while Betty rummages in her handbag, pulling the zip back and tossing a collection of old tissues, a powder compact and a Tube ticket onto the counter.

'Muriel, I'm sorry, that was uncalled for,' I say.

She says nothing for a while, picking up the powder compact, opening it then closing it again. 'At least I never lied about myself to someone else,' she says eventually.

'There was a reason for that, but I suppose you don't want to hear it.'

'Try me,' she says, more kindly than I deserve.

'I did it to impress someone I used to know a long time ago. I didn't want her to know that it was me because I thought she might give me another chance if she didn't know, and now she does know and that's why she's gone and Amanda's back and my mother into the bargain and I'm surrounded by all of these women and I think Amanda wants me to stay with her and I just can't play happy families like that. It's just wrong and …' I run out of steam, then I add, uselessly, 'Sorry.'

'Do you know what?'

'What?' I reply.

'I will kill you if you keep saying sorry.'

'Sorry.' I laugh.

'So you lied.'

'Yes. Yes, I did,' I say shamefacedly. 'I pretended to be John, this really grown-up, together person to impress her – I even gave her baby-care lessons.'

'Why?'

'Because she has a baby and she asked me.'

'I don't mean that. I mean, why did you pretend you were someone else? What were you afraid of?'

'I was afraid I wouldn't be good enough. Because I let her down years ago. I made her a promise and I broke it.'

Betty tuts, arms folded. 'You broke it when you were how old?'

'Ten.'

'Ten years old.' Betty looks at me sternly. 'For God's sake.'

'What? I've never forgotten it.'

'I'll bet you haven't,' she says, rolling her eyes to heaven.

'What do you mean?' I say indignantly.

'Oh, Jesus,' Betty says. 'You are so in love with all of that Byronic stuff, all the gloom and the broken-hearted routine, wearing your pain on your sleeve. Well, this might surprise you, but you're a grown-up now and it's time to ditch that stuff and start behaving like one. I think you know what to do. You know what's right, so you just have to do it.'

There's a long silence while I contemplate Betty's complete lack of pity for me, her bracing remarks in the face of my sulky 'carry-on', as Mum would put it. She's right. I do know what to do – all I have to do is simply do it. That's it. It really is as straightforward as that. 'Sorry I've been a bit of a tit,' I say.

'You have, but you can stop being one now. You said you'd help me and I'm counting on you.'

'I know. I won't let you down.'

'Good,' she says. 'Now, I am going to go upstairs to Petrus' office and I am going to pin a smile on my face and charm the pants off all of the old farts to get them to part with their money and you are going to do exactly the same. When you've finished, you can slink off to your dungeon and wring your hands, but for the next two hours, I need you to at least pretend to be a grown-up – would that be too much to ask?'

'No,' I whisper, shaking my head.

'Well, that's decided then,' Betty says, turning on her heel and marching out the door, which swings back and forth after her, like a saloon door after the cowboy has left.

Jesus, Betty, I think to myself, why don't you say what you really mean? The fact that you're right is neither here nor there.

The lunch is as tinder dry as I'd expected, a mixture of genteel older artists and people who are clearly loaded, but I give it the full-on charm offensive, listening attentively to Timothy Falstaff, a travel writer who specialises in jaunts around historic parts of the Middle East, and a small woman to his left with a bird's nest of hair on her head, whose name badge proclaims her to be

Tatiana Tolstoy, who, rumour has it, is descended from the last tsar of Russia. I proclaim this to be the most fascinating thing I've ever heard and beg her to tell me all about it, ignoring Betty's widened-eye expression, which tells me that I'm overdoing it. Tough, I think. You did ask.

I listen to Timothy Falstaff's interminable anecdote about his trip to the Khyber Pass, which makes me think of the *Carry On* movie, which used to make Dad roar with laughter, which doesn't help me as it induces a strange fit of repressed laughter every time Timothy parts with another nugget of information, and I nod and spoon the very peculiar milky dessert into my mouth, and then someone says. 'Reminds me of the *Carry On* movie.'

I look to my left and Tatiana Tolstoy has moved to sit beside Petrus, the better to part with her cash, leaving a man in a tweed waistcoat and rumpled white shirt sitting beside me. He's sturdy, with a head of reddish curls, and he reminds me of a character from a Thomas Hardy novel. He extends a hand. 'Jago Galsworthy.'

'Emmett O'Donoghue,' I reply, taking his hand and giving it a good shake. Dad said that you could tell the character of a man from the strength of his handshake and I make sure that mine is always firm and sincere, but not knuckle-breaking. I say, '*The* Jago Galsworthy, publisher of the Poetry Press?'

'None other than,' he says. 'I'm surprised you've heard of me. Only about three people have.' He smiles.

'Well, I'm a poet,' I say shyly.

'Right,' he says, looking totally disinterested.

'I'm sure people say that to you all the time before pressing their collection into your hands.'

'Hah,' he says shortly. 'They most certainly do.'

'Well, I promise that I won't.'

'Thank you,' he says, then, as if unable to help himself. 'What kind of stuff do you write?'

'Bad stuff,' I say honestly. 'But it's getting better.'

His smile this time is warm. 'Good. I assume you'll inflict some of it on us after lunch?'

'Well, I'm giving poetry therapy,' I say. He looks alarmed, so I add, 'I ask people to tell me some problem they're having and then I read an appropriate poem. I had thought of Elizabeth Bishop for starters.'

'Well, that would be much better, obviously.' He smiles, spooning some of the vanilla panna cotta into his mouth. 'But I'd say a bit of a missed opportunity, wouldn't you?'

'Quite possibly,' I acknowledge.

'Well then,' he says. 'I see that Muriel has some very impressive ideas about this place – I hope she gets the chance to do something with it.'

He's changing the subject and we both grab it like a life raft, discussing floor sizes and subjects that should really be stocked in a decent neighbourhood bookshop, and then it's my turn to be the 'postprandial entertainment', as Petrus puts it, after he's given a long and boring speech about how devoted he is to Farrell's and to the idea of a bookshop for the community. I read out the same poem that I read at the poetry evening at the Queen Victoria, figuring that it may be cursed in some terrible way but at least it's mine.

When I finish, the applause is polite, but Jago Galsworthy looks thoughtful. And as Petrus leads Tatiana Tolstoy into his office, quite obviously to write a cheque, he comes up to me and hands me his card. 'It's good, you know. At least, it's not terrible anyway.'

'Thanks,' I respond.

'But something tells me you can do better,' Jago says.

'Something does?' I echo.

'Something does,' he agrees.

'Like what?'

'Oh, I don't know,' he says. 'Something more … meaningful. Something worthwhile.'

Oh, sure, I think bitterly. Something meaningful coming right up. I smile and thank Jago Bloody Galsworthy, with his semi-ironic manner and red corduroy trousers, and promise him that I'll be in touch, gritting my teeth and seething inwardly. I make my exit as quickly as possible, avoiding Betty's eye, and I trudge home, going straight up to Roland's study and pushing Bran out of his expensive chair, the better to sit in it and sulk. Honestly, I think, who the hell does Betty think she is, lecturing me like that. And that Jago guy … honestly.

I rummage in my satchel for my house keys, but just as I do, the first line of a poem comes into my head. A love poem. About Daisy. I open the door, run upstairs before anyone can intercept me, into Roland's study, where I sit down and begin to write.

I keep on writing until I have six kind-of poems in front of me. That's a lot more than I've ever done before, when I've toiled over a single poem for hours. Now, it feels as if they are flowing out of me, a river of words about my actual life – about Daisy and Misty and Amanda, about Queenie – about all of the women in my life. I'm sure that five of them aren't very good, but it doesn't matter. My heart feels a little bit lighter now that I've written them.

I lean back in my chair and I listen to the noises of dinner-making and TV downstairs and I wonder if the poems have helped me to make any sense of what's happening in my life – if they've made it simpler somehow, made the chaos recede. I don't really know but at least it's a start – and I can work on them anyway. That's what they're for – to be worked on until they half-resemble something decent.

I hear a soft knocking on the door then and a little voice calls out, 'Dada?'

'Come in.' Misty's ready for bed and she's wearing her Dalmatian pyjamas. Her lovely brown hair has been washed and brushed by her mother – a hundred times, like the princess – and she's brushed her teeth, using the timer that Amanda has installed in the bathroom. Order has been restored.

'I came to say goodnight, Dada,' she says shyly, sliding onto my knee.

'Goodnight, pipsqueak, nincompoop, scallywag,' I say as I pop a kiss on her head, putting my arms around her. Her little body feels warm and solid in my arms, and I ask myself how I could possibly not have wanted this way back at the beginning, when I was an idiot. But then, I reason, I was just scared, and I'm not scared any more. I know that I'm a good dad to Misty, whether anyone else sees it or not. When this last thought occurs to me, a brief image of Daisy sitting on my sofa while I played peekaboo with Brian flits into my mind. Why did I find it so important to be the big man with her, to be Superdad? What did I have to prove. It doesn't matter a jot – what matters is the doing, not the being seen to be doing.

'Dada?'

'Yes?' I pop a kiss on her lovely head, which smells of strawberry shampoo.

'Are you and Mummy going to get married instead of Mummy and Roland?'

'Why do you say that?'

'Because Roland's not here any more and Mummy told me not to call him Daddy and you're here instead. With Mummy.'

She's playing with her toes, clutching them with her fingers and pushing her leg out, then pulling it back in again, and the other hand is around my neck, playing with the chain of my Miraculous Medal. I know that kind of fidgeting – it's not good.

'Ah. Well,' I begin, thinking of what white lie I can tell her, but then I decide that the truth is what's needed now, of all times. 'Mummy and Dada are great friends, Misty, but we're not getting married.'

As I say the words, I think of Betty in the loos in Farrell's, telling me that I'd know to do the right thing, that I was a grown-up, but I push the idea out of my mind.

'Why not? You're my dada and she's my mummy.'

'Yes, but we don't have to be married to each other to look after you really, really well or to be good friends who look after each other – the way you and Clive do.' I think if I mention Clive that will give her a frame of reference.

'Is Roland ever coming home from his mummy's in Jamaica?'

'Well, he's got a lot of work to do there at the moment,' I say diplomatically, 'but I'll talk to Mummy about it and see what she can tell you, is that OK?'

Misty nods sadly. 'I miss Daddy.'

'I know you do, Misty. I'm sorry. It's just … he's having to work really hard on his beach huts' – that's an understatement – 'but I'm sure that he's thinking of you every single day.'

There's silence while Misty digests this. She's probably wondering whether or not to believe me. Eventually, she says in a small voice, 'I think he's forgotten all about me.'

I give her a tight squeeze. 'He hasn't, Misty. I can promise you that.' Whatever you want to say about Roland, he was always a good dad to Misty. I'll have to talk to Amanda about this, I think, which I'm not looking forward to – Misty needs her dad.

Then she sits up a bit. 'Are you writing a poem, Dada?'

'I am.'

'What is it about?' Then she looks at me slyly. 'Is it about Daisy?'

'Oh, you're too clever for your own good,' I say, tickling her feet, where I know she's very ticklish, and being rewarded by a giggle. Then I say, 'Actually, it's not just about Daisy. It's about you and Mummy and Queenie, too, and it's about friendship and keeping your promises and about the past and the future, I suppose.' That makes my poems sound all-encompassing, which they're not, but I'm trying. Perhaps I'm trying to do too much, but at least I'm making the effort and that feels different somehow.

Misty sits up on my knee and says eagerly, 'Like I promised Clive that he could stay the night when we break up for the summer holidays. That's in the future, isn't it?'

'It is, and that's a promise that you must keep,' I say.

Her eyebrows crease with worry. 'But what happens if I can't keep it? How will I know if something has changed if I don't know yet?'

It's a bit mangled, but I know what she means. 'Oh, love,' I say, giving her a tight squeeze. 'None of us can see into the future. Not yet anyway.'

'Some people can. There was a lady with a crystal ball at the school fair and she told me that I'd travel all over the world.'

'Well, we'll have to see if that happens, won't we? We'll just have to see what comes.'

'Hmm.' Misty's silent for a few moments. 'Will Clive never speak to me again if the future changes?'

I'm not sure what she's getting at for a moment, then I understand. For Misty, the future is something that will happen, not that might happen. She's just waiting for time to jump forward a month or two, to that point where she and Clive will be in their Berber tent, reading and telling each other silly jokes. She doesn't know that that future might never happen, at least, not in that way. And then it dawns on me: neither did I when I made that promise to Daisy. I couldn't have known how the future would change us both: that I would find myself a father, that she would lose her father and, now, her mother – at least, a part of her. We made each other a promise based on a future that we had mapped out before us – all we had to do was wait. Meanwhile, time had its way.

'You know, Misty, I made my friend Daisy a promise about the future – did you know that?'

'What did you say, Dada?'

'I told her that we'd be together some day, and that all we had to do was wait.'

Misty turns eagerly to me. 'And you were right, Dada. See?'

I shake my head. 'I got it all wrong, pet, but that's life. If I hadn't, I'd never have had you or met Mum or come here or anything.' I ruffle Misty's hair. 'So you make Clive a promise and you try to stick to it, but don't worry too much about the future. All we have is now – do you understand what I'm saying?' I shift a bit in my seat, Misty's weight beginning to tell on me. 'And now, it's time for bed!' I try to lighten the tone, but Misty is as thoughtful as ever.

'I won't need to break my promise,' Misty says, 'because I just won't. Not like Mummy and Daddy did.' Before I can respond, she jumps down from my knee. 'Dada, will you read another legend to me? I think I like the one about the queen of the banshees – can I have that one?'

'You know what? I think Mummy would really like to read a story to you tonight,' I say. 'Let's see if she's around – maybe she'll read *The BFG* or *James and the Giant Peach* – you like them.'

Misty looks sulky for a moment, but I'm firm. 'Mummy would love that, Misty – and, besides, I won't ever be a famous poet if I don't do any more work, now, will I?'

I lift Misty up and throw her over my shoulder, the way Dad used to do to me when I was the same age, and she roars with laughter as I walk her gently in to her bedroom and pop her down on the bed with a little bounce. Her mother is arranging her clothes for school the next day, laying out her uniform, socks, pants and vest, her little polished black shoes, her immaculately ironed shirt, and I reflect on how it used to be, when I would spend twenty minutes on a Monday morning frantically trying to locate the other one of her grey socks or ironing the skirt that I'd forgotten to wash after school on Friday. With Amanda's return, there's an air of order about the house, of calm, now that everything has been restored to its rightful place, and Misty has once again been subjected to discipline and hard work, as well as fatherly indulgence. We make a good team, Amanda and I.

'Hello, angel,' Amanda says. 'Ready for bed?'

'Yes, Dada says you're to read to me,' Misty says happily, hopping into bed. Bran has been banned from sleeping on the duvet, much to Misty's disgust, but instead, in what was a big concession from Amanda, he has been given a tiny little bed to sleep in, and he curls up now beside Misty's bedside table, giving a little sigh.

'He does, does he?' Amanda looks at me, smiling. 'Well, if he insists.'

'I do. I have work to do,' I say politely, heading off to my lair, where I look at my poems again for a bit, tinkering with a word here, a phrase there. They're better, I think after a while. But not good enough. They need something …

I can hear Amanda reading *The BFG* to Misty, and she's not doing a bad job of it. She doesn't do the accents or the funny voices, so I'm sure Misty isn't that impressed, but still – it's a start. Before, Amanda thought that stories and poems were frivolous somehow, a waste of valuable time and energy that could have been spent folding, ironing or looking over Roland's spreadsheets, but she can see how much they do for Misty, so she's trying. We're both trying – at what, neither of us is entirely sure.

I need to get out of here, I suddenly think. All at once, the air in Roland's study seems thicker and more oppressive, and when I look out the window, the air seems clearer, brighter. It's nearly May now and the nights are longer. There's a general air of excitement about the place. The scut across the road is readying himself for the European Cup, putting out his England flag and marching up and down to the pub in his white shirt with the three lions on it. Whenever he sees me, he roars, 'Eng-el-and' in my face. It's not hard to ignore him, as he barely comes up to the top of my leg, but I resist the temptation to roar back at him and give him further ammunition. 'Fucking Paddy,' he mutters as he strides off down the road.

I put my work away in the Manila folder and get up to go downstairs. Bran, hearing me and thinking that a walk might be on the horizon, comes scuttling out of Misty's bedroom and follows me down to the hall, where he does a little dance, turning round and round and squeaking until I say, 'All right then, go and get your lead.'

He runs off to the cupboard where Amanda neatly hangs all of our coats, instead of on the antlers in the hall, and rummages about, giving little barks, until he emerges with the lead in his mouth.

'Good boy,' I say, clipping the lead to his collar. I pick him up and give him a little hug and he licks my chin and I wonder how I could ever have wanted to get rid of him. He might look like a hairy rat, but he's part of the family now.

We step outside into the cool spring evening. I stand on the steps for a few moments, deciding where to go and then I have an idea. 'C'mon,' I say to him. 'Let's go and visit Mum and Uncle Tom.'

I walk up Albion Road and around the corner before I can remind myself not to go that way – but it's too late, because I can see the bins in front of me and I remember the times I lurked there, like a deviant. Then there's her door at the bottom of the steps, only it's not yellow any more, it's bright red, and there's a bicycle outside it. While I'm standing there, the door opens and a man comes out, taking the bike and lugging it to the top of the steps, where he turns and says, 'Bye, love.' A girl with the blonde hair who has appeared at the door says, 'Yeah, see you,' and gives a little wave.

I don't bother to duck behind the bins because I don't need to any more. The man has no idea who I am. A stranger is now living in Daisy's flat, which must mean that she's gone. 'Well, Bran, I wasn't expecting that,' I say softly. He's nosing around the bin, lifting a leg to wee on it. I give the lead a gentle tug.

'C'mon, buster, maybe Uncle Tom will want a drink.'

Uncle Tom does indeed want a drink, so we leave Bran with Mum, after giving her reassurances that I will bring Misty to see her the very next day, because she's still 'finding her feet' in Holloway. She says this as Tom rolls his eyes to heaven behind her.

The two of us head to the Dog and Duck, the only non-Irish pub in Holloway, thankfully, so we're not likely to be hailed by every Galway exile as we drink. The pub is more or less empty, the only sound the 'ting' of the pinball machine in the corner, the hum of the traffic outside. Tom and I perch on red-leather barstools at the counter. 'What'll you have?' Tom says, lifting a finger to summon the barman.

'A double whiskey, as you're buying.'

'Cheeky sod,' Tom says. 'Two doubles please,' he nods to the barman.

When our whiskies arrive, Tom stares into his, as if he's trying to see to the bottom of the sea. What's up with you? I wonder.

'How's Mum?' I ask.

'Jesus, Mary and Joseph, she's worse than she is at home. I tried to get her to go to mass at St Bartholomew's last Sunday, but she point-blank refused. Said something about being an atheist.' He takes a big swig of his drink and gives me a half-smile.

'Sorry I haven't been around,' I say. 'Things have been a bit hectic.'

'Yeah? How's that girl you were seeing – Daisy, was that her name?'

It's my turn to take a big swig of my drink. 'It's over,' I say. 'It never began, really.'

'Do you want to talk about it?' It's nice of him to ask, but I can tell he doesn't mean it.

'God, no,' I say. 'I just want to get drunk and forget about everything.'

'Ditto,' he says, clinking his glass against mine. Then he gives a small smile. 'Got any good poems for a man in my state?'

'Depends on what state you're in,' I say.

He's silent again, his big hands, with their coating of cement dust, cradling the glass. He has an intense look on his face, which is unlike him – Tom cultivates this easy-as-you-like expression that I know is a shield, but this— 'Is it Dympna?' I nudge him.

He makes a face. 'You could say that.' Then he shrugs. 'Ah, sure, now is not the time anyway.'

'What do you mean "now is not the time"? I'm your brother, of course it's the time. And besides, it'll take my mind off my own stuff.'

He gives a long sigh. 'Have you ever thought that you've been trying to hide something about yourself, something that you think others will judge you for?'

'No,' I lie.

He looks hurt. 'Oh, well,' he says and crosses his arms.

'Actually, yes,' I say, taking a sip of the whiskey, then, noticing that my glass is almost empty, I nod towards the barman, 'Any chance of another?'

Two more doubles are placed on the counter in front of us.

'Cheers,' I say, lifting the glass to my lips. 'So, I'm listening.'

There's a long silence. 'There's someone else. In my life.'

I know, I think. 'Does Dympna know?'

He shakes his head. 'She'd fucking kill me with her bare hands.'

'I'd say those hands are capable of killing.'

He gives me a rueful smile.

'So, what's his name?'

His head shoots up. 'How the fuck did you know?'

'Call it intuition,' I reply.

'Fuck off,' Tom reples in mock anger, but I can tell he's relieved that he doesn't have to make a big, dramatic revelation.

'So ... how long have you known?'

'Oh, always,' he says. 'It's the kind of thing you know about yourself, inside, you know? It just takes years to stop feeling that it's wrong. That you're wrong – that you don't fit in with all of the other lads. All that towel-flicking in the changing rooms after football, all that standing around stark bollock naked in the showers after work – I used to dread it, because I had something to hide and I'd be scared shitless that someone would find out and kick the crap out of me.' His face creases now with pain.

I reach out and squeeze his hand and he squeezes back, his big, meaty fingers over my long, weedy ones. 'Why did you not say anything to me?'

'Because I was too busy hiding it from myself,' he says, taking a big swig of whiskey. 'How could I tell you when I couldn't even admit it to myself?'

'And this guy changed that?'

'He did,' His face flushes. 'I think I love him, Em.' He looks at me like a teenager, all gooey eyes and forlorn looks – like Byron. He's in love all right.

'Well, good,' I say, for the want of anything else and because I'm trying to take it in. All of that swagger, that belching and farting and overdone masculinity – that's what it was all about. Poor Tom, having to push that down inside of him for all of those years.

'Good?' He laughs. 'Not good, brother. Dympna will kill me when I tell her and then I won't be any use to anyone.'

'She won't. It's not like a personality trait, Tom – a tendency to bad temper or meanness – that you can change. It's who you are. And you have to be who you are. Otherwise …' My voice trails off, because I'm really talking to myself. 'Look, the point is that you're doing something about it.'

He blushes. 'I am.'

'Oh, God, spare me the details.'

'It's good, brother. It really is.' The tension in his face melts away and I see now that he's a different Tom, now that he's not holding it all inside. He looks younger, lighter, that muscle no longer twitching in his jaw.

'Well, I'm happy for you, you idiot,' I say, standing up and swaying slightly, the two doubles having done their job. 'Give your brother a hug.' He leans into my arms and rests his head on my shoulder, the way he used to when he was six years old and I stroke his head and pat his shoulder and remind myself again how much I love him.

'Em?' he says eventually.

'Yeah?'

'How the fuck am I going to tell Dympna?'

At this, we both explode into raucous laughter.

Well, well, I think to myself as I womble home, Bran trotting ahead of me. It's a chilly night and stars are visible in the navy sky. Good for Tom, finally coming clean and having the nerve to be himself. I wonder if Mum knows, I think, before understanding that she probably does. That's where I got my 'sixth sense' from, for all the good it's done me.

It must have taken a lot for Tom to be truthful with himself, I think drunkenly, to stop hiding from himself. I could probably do with a lesson or two in that department, I decide, as I cross the road and head towards home.

When I get there, Amanda is in the kitchen, tidying the already immaculate cupboards. The radio is on and 'Wonderwall' is playing and she's humming along as she puts labels onto pasta jars and lines the spaghetti up so that it's completely vertical in the jar. She's wearing a pretty floral T-shirt thing and neat jeans, and her hair is pulled into a messy bun. She looks good, I think – fresh and lovely, like when we first met.

When she sees me, she gives a little start. 'Em – I didn't hear you come in.'

'Em' – I like it when she calls me that, I think. It feels … intimate. I walk towards her and she says, 'What are you doing – are you a bit tiddly?'

I take her left hand in mine, put my right hand on her waist and begin to dance. She giggles. 'You're being silly.'

But as I waltz her around the kitchen, she grows silent and, after a while, she leans her head against my chest and gives a small sigh, and when the music stops, she doesn't push me away and say that she's got some more labelling to do. She remains where she is, leaning against me. Then the music changes and it's George Michael and 'I'm Your Man'. That should change the tempo, I think, but Amanda doesn't move. Instead, she snakes an arm around my waist and pulls me closer.

'Amanda?' I say softly.

'Mm?' she replies dreamily.

'Will you marry me?'

15.

'Dada!' Misty is yelling at me from five centimetres away, standing over my bed with her school uniform on, her hair in two neat braids with red ribbons at the end. My head is throbbing and my throat feels like it's been rubbed raw. Amanda and I drank two bottles of champagne last night, on top of my double whiskies, while I'd persuaded her to do the right thing and let me marry her. It felt a bit more like a business presentation than a proposal, but then, I figured, Amanda likes that kind of thing. So I gave her the PowerPoint on me as potential husband: reliable, supportive, a father to Misty – and lonely. Very, very lonely.

'I'm lonely, too,' Amanda had confessed as we'd huddled under the cashmere blanket she'd produced to keep us warm as we sat outside in the garden.

'So, let's be lonely together,' I insisted.

She hesitated for a humiliatingly long time before tilting her head back and saying, 'Will you just look at those stars? Isn't it amazing to think that we're so small? It kind of puts it in perspective.'

'Amanda?'

She sighed then, a long, weary sigh, before leaning her head on my shoulder. 'I'm tired, Em. Tired and afraid.'

'I know,' I said. 'Let me do the right thing, Amanda. Please?'

Her answer had been a brief nod and a big swig from the bottle of champagne, which she'd then handed to me. As marriage proposals go, it might not have been the most romantic, but that doesn't make it less real. I know that I'm doing the right thing. How I feel is neither here nor there.

'Oh, God, Misty, do you have to shout?' I groan.

'Yes, I do!' she yells. 'There's a lady on the phone for you. She sounds like you do.'

'She does?' I sit up very slowly, the room spinning around me.

'She said, "Am I speaking to my granddaughter?" but I said I don't know. Who is she, Dada?'

'She's my mum,' I say. 'Your granny from Ireland.'

'The lady who makes the apple tarts?' Misty says carefully.

'That's her,' I say. 'Will you tell her I'll be there in a second, love? I need to splash water on my face.'

'OK,' she says happily, bouncing out of the room and down the stairs, where she picks up the phone. 'Granny? Dada will be down in a second.' There's silence, followed by, 'Yes. Yes, Granny ... No, Granny ... I think so ... I'm only nearly eight', and then a little giggle.

Mum must be giving her the third degree, I think as I experiment with standing up, deciding that it's unwise and sitting back down on the bed again. Oh, God. Did last night really happen? Did I really propose to Amanda and did she really say yes? I'm not sure, I think, as I pick my jeans up from the floor and shove on a T-shirt. 'Thanks, love,' I say to Misty when she hands me the phone.

'Hello, Mum?'

'Son!' she roars. 'Listen, I've got the hang of the *A–Z* now. I've been to the Nag's Head shopping centre and to the bakery that does those lovely macaroons, so I think I can manage a bus trip to see this fancy house of yours. I want to meet my first grandchild face to face.'

'Well done, Mum. That's great progress. Let me just see what Amanda says. Hang on,' I say, putting the phone down.

'Amanda?' I shout, wishing I hadn't as the sound ricochets around my head.

'In the kitchen.'

I walk slowly down the hall. 'Hi,' I say, hovering at the top of the steps.

'Hi!' she says. She's wearing a slightly too small bathrobe and her legs are long and tanned. 'I'm just making pancakes. Maple syrup or lemon and sugar?'

'Erm, I don't really mind,' I say. 'Mum's on the phone. She wants to visit – is that OK?'

'Of course it's OK, Em. It's your house, too, you know,' she says, waving a spatula and flipping over a pancake, which she does perfectly, of course.

'Right, well, great then.'

'Ask her to dinner. I'll pick something up on the way back from my yoga class. Does your mum eat lamb?'

'Yeah,' I say, 'but she doesn't need anything fancy, Amanda. Mum's has simple enough tastes when it comes to food.'

'But we have to celebrate!' Amanda says. 'It's a big deal,' and she flashes me a shy smile.

'It is,' I agree. 'It's a really big deal.' A film of sweat breaks out on my forehead and I begin to feel a bit queasy. Must be the champagne. 'I'll just tell her.'

'So, it's a date then,' she says when I come back, flipping a pancake onto a plate and putting it on the table beside the cafetière, which has been filled with rich, dark coffee. I could get used to this, I think, as I sit down in front of my breakfast, even if it is a bit … staged.

'Thanks, Amanda,' I say, tucking in.

'You're welcome!' she sings, leaning over and popping a kiss on my cheek. I blush bright red and she laughs. 'See you later!'

I follow her to the door and watch as she leaves for yoga, hopping down the front steps in a bright-red leotard and grey sweatpants, a mat rolled up under her arm. I try to imagine what it will be like to see her do this twice a week for the next forty years and my chest tightens. I practise saying the words 'my wife' out loud to see how they'll sound, but they keep getting stuck on my tongue.

I wanted to order Mum a taxi, but she insisted on taking the bus. 'It'll get me out and about,' she said breezily, 'so I can feel like a real Londoner.' When I hesitated, she said, 'Do you think your mother isn't capable of taking public transport?'

I told her that of course she was, even if I have my doubts. It's a family joke that Mum would get lost between mass and home, a distance of half a mile, so I gave her detailed instructions on which bus to take from which stop and when to get off. 'Now, do you have your *A–Z*?'

'Of course I have my *A–Z*. I'm a Londoner!' she said gleefully.

'Right,' I replied faintly, reminding her to avoid the shortcut beside the shops because it's a bit dodgy.

'Sure wouldn't I be well able for it!' she countered.

'If you like getting mugged, Mum,' I said.

'Don't you be smart with your mother. You might think that I'm not capable of getting around on my own, love, but wait till you see. There's life in the old bird yet.'

This new Mum is exhausting, I think, as I sit hunched over my poems later that morning, Bran curled up on Roland's expensive chair in the corner. The poem with Misty in it is OK, but the one with Daisy, it's just … unfinished. I look at it for a long time, at the opening line about Brian like a hermit crab in Daisy's shell … it's nice, but there's something missing. I stare at it for a while longer and then I realise that it doesn't feel like a love poem because it's written to a stranger, or an almost stranger. I no longer know Daisy. I used to, like the back of my hand, but the grown-up Daisy is a stranger to me.

I sit there for a long time, looking out into the garden, before picking up my pen and deleting all of the 'Daisy' references, replacing them with 'Amanda'. I read the poem out loud, but it doesn't feel quite right either. I add in a line about champagne, but it looks silly – you can't write a love poem to one person and then simply substitute another. Can you?

I sigh heavily, putting the work back into the Manila folder and getting up. 'I'm stuck, Bran,' I say. 'Completely stuck.' He lifts his head and looks at me disinterestedly, before resting his chin on his paws with a sigh. 'Fine then. Be like that,' I say. 'How about a little walk?' He leaps off the chair and runs downstairs to the hall.

I make sure to walk past Daisy's when I'm out, as if I expect her to have returned somehow, but when I see the bicycle at the bottom of the steps, I know that she hasn't. I wonder where she is now and what she's doing. I wonder how Brian is. I even wonder about Bridget. She shouldn't be here on her own, I think. She needs help – and so does Daisy if Bridget is in that kind of state. Maybe I should call social services, I think – but then, what would I tell them? That a woman who used to live at number 34a Albion Road may have dementia? 'Don't be stupid,' I say out loud. 'Daisy's gone and you have to accept that and get on with your life. You are getting on with your life – that's why you're marrying Amanda.' I'm talking to myself and two boys kicking a football to each other on the street, clad in their England jerseys, look at me curiously. I give an 'I'm perfectly normal!' wave, but they look doubtful.

When I get back, Amanda has the lamb in the oven and she's making a salad. I watch her calm movements as she chops and lifts handfuls of veg into the large salad bowl. It's the same scene as last night. She's wearing a pretty dress this time, but her hair is still in a loose bun and the radio is playing, and all I have to do is sneak up behind her and put my arms around her and ask her to dance because I love her – I know that now. I love her as the mother of my child and I love her because she's strong and resilient and I love her because she's tidy. I know it sounds ridiculous, but it's so calming, so soothing – it makes me feel safe, that someone is in control. I wonder if love might grow for the two of us if we simply will it to happen. Isn't that good enough?

'Oh, you're back!' Amanda exclaims, turning around, chopping knife in her hand.

I peer into the oven. 'Looks good.'

'Thanks,' she says happily, slicing into sun-dried tomatoes. 'Jim at the organic butcher's jointed it for me. And then I bought this lovely mint dressing to go with it. Does your mum like asparagus? I thought I'd put some in the salad. It's nice just griddled with a bit of olive oil. Oh, and I got a gorgeous lemon tart for dessert.'

'Great!' I say. 'How do you make it all happen?'

'It's magic.' She laughs.

'Thanks, Amanda,' I say sincerely. I wonder if she expects me to kiss her – surely we should be doing more of that kind of thing, I wonder. Mind you, she doesn't look terribly interested, chopping away serenely.

'Did you do any potatoes?'

'No,' Amanda says, surprised. 'Why?

'Mum has to have potatoes with meat,' I say apologetically. 'She thinks it's not dinner if it doesn't have potatoes in it.'

'Oh.' Amanda looks hurt. 'Well, erm, I suppose I could peel some—'

'It's OK,' I say, giving her shoulder a squeeze. 'I have just the thing – there are some cooked baby new potatoes in the fridge. I'll just make some potato salad with them. It'll be a spring dinner!'

'Right,' Amanda says quietly.

'She's lovely,' I say. 'Honest. She's impossible to dislike and I say that as her first born, even though I am, of course, biased.'

Amanda is mollified. 'I'm sorry. It's just that my mother is such a horrible old bat. I assume everyone else's is.'

'Nope. Potatoes are the only thing that she gets excited about,'

I joke. 'Now, why don't you let me finish here and you go upstairs and have a lie-down or something.'

'Are you trying to get rid of me?' Amanda smiles.

'I sure am. I will check every item for its Irishness, and when it is passed fit, I'll put it on the table.'

'Cheeky,' Amanda says, pointing her knife at me. 'Let me just finish these tomatoes then,' and she continues chopping for a few minutes, before saying, 'Emmett?'

'Yeah?'

'Did you mean what you said last night?'

I don't answer straight away. I take out a chopping board so that I can chop parsley for the potatoes. 'Of course,' I say finally.

'Well,' she says. 'You see, I – oh, what the hell is it?' she says as there is a loud and persistent ringing on the doorbell. 'It's only half-seven. When did you say your mum was coming?'

'Eight,' I reply, wiping my hands on the tea towel, omitting to mention that Mum is early for everything. 'It's probably Queenie anyway.'

'Oh, God, I can't open another bottle for her. You got her into some very bad habits when you were on your own here,' Amanda says, retreating into the hall.

As if there is something wrong with opening lids for an old woman, I think.

I hear my mother's voice, like a foghorn, coming from the hall. 'I made it! Oh, it was such an adventure. I didn't even need the map in the end because this nice man in a turban told me where Albion Road is. Everyone's so friendly here!' As I come up the stairs, Mum puts the two gigantic carrier bags she's carrying down on the floor with a thud and runs towards Misty, who has been watching the whirlwind, puts a hand to each of Misty's cheeks and gives them a little pinch. 'Well, well, Misty, *a stoirín*, aren't you the prettiest girl in the world? Emmett, you never told me your daughter was so gorgeous,' and she takes Misty into her warm, granny embrace. Misty looks faintly terrified yet pleased at the same time.

'You're very welcome, Mrs O'Donoghue,' Amanda says, offering her hand, but Mum ignores it and just barrels towards Amanda, arms open, giving her a huge hug. 'Call me Nuala, for God's sake,' she says. When she stands back, she has tears in her eyes. 'Oh, Emmett, you have two beautiful girls like this in your life. Do you know what a lucky man you are?'

I nod and agree that my family are lovely. I give my mother a penetrating look to indicate that she's overdoing it, but she blithely ignores me, taking off her coat and exclaiming in delight at the coat hook made out of a dead animal. 'Isn't that genius,' she chuckles, as Amanda hangs her coat on one of the antlers.

'Come on in Mrs ... Nuala.' Amanda pronounces it 'Noo-*ahl*-a', which Mum finds highly amusing.

'Thank you, love. My goodness, this house is just spectacular,' and she lets herself be guided through the rooms by Amanda, who shows her the expensive leather sofa, the shutters which she had imported from France, the modern dining table and chairs made out of clear plastic. Mum oohs and aahs and exclaims over the house's beauty, then announces that she simply has to see the princess' palace, letting Misty take her by the hand and lead her upstairs to her room.

'Your mother is just lovely,' Amanda says dreamily. 'So ... cuddly and warm. I love her!'

'So do I,' I say, because I do.

My mother keeps the show on the road all the way through dinner, which she proclaims 'delicious', exclaiming that the new-potato salad is 'very modern', which makes Amanda smile, and the lamb is 'so tender'. 'Your father would love it,' she says to me. 'He's a sucker for rare lamb.' And then, as if remembering what she's said, she says, 'Yes, well', and eats in silence for a few minutes.

Amanda shoots me a questioning look and I mouth, 'Tell you later', then pretend to find my lamb fascinating.

Then Mum exclaims, 'So, Misty, I believe you're a great reader. I am too!' And the jolly atmosphere is restored. Misty tells Mum all about Horrid Henry and *Charlotte's Web*, 'which is my favourite book ever.' The mention of *Charlotte's Web* makes my stomach lurch.

'So,' Amanda pipes up, 'Noo-ah-la, are you staying for long?'

'Oh, yes,' Mum replies. 'I'm here for the foreseeable future.'

'How lovely.'

Amanda is clearly at a loss, so I chip in. 'Mum's decided to take an extended trip … She has family in Coventry.' I give Mum a look and she smiles obediently.

'Oh, that's nice,' Amanda says. 'Have you seen the cathedral? It's amazing. It was built after the war—'

'Oh, well, I'll have to see it then,' Mum says, a puzzled expression on her face.

'So …' Amanda says brightly, looking at me and then at my mother.

'What?' I mouth.

'Aren't you going to tell her?' Amanda mouths back, pointing at her ring finger.

'Oh,' I say out loud. 'Of course. Misty, love, would you go and get the ice-cream out of the freezer. We'll let it defrost a bit.' When Misty trots off, I mutter, 'We need to give her time.'

Amanda nods.

I clear my throat. 'Mum, Amanda and I have some news. We haven't told Misty yet because we want to … prepare her, but, well—'

'We're getting married!' Amanda breaks in.

Mum has been cutting into a bit of lamb, but she stops dead now, placing her knife and fork carefully down on the plate. Her face pales. 'Well,' she says quietly. 'Well.'

'Aren't you going to say anything else?' I say. 'It's good news, isn't it?'

Mum clears her throat as if there's something stuck there, then her face suddenly brightens, as if she's putting on a mask. 'It is, of course. Where on earth are my manners? Congratulations!' she says, getting up out of her seat and pulling Amanda to her in a big hug, then pulling me to her cushiony bosom. 'Many happy returns to you both,' she says, going to her place and lifting her wine glass into the air. 'To Mr and Mrs O'Donoghue!'

She's doing all the right things, I think, as I lift my glass and Amanda squeezes my hand, but her eyes are glittering with tears. Oh, Mum.

The two of them spend the next twenty minutes in wedding chat, having dispatched Misty to the living room to watch TV, their voices low and conspiratorial, punctuated by the occasional giggle. There's something about the chat that feels artificial, as if they are both playing a game, I think as I stand in the kitchen making tea. I swirl hot water around in the tea pot, which is made of clear glass with a kind of tube in the middle to hold the tea leaves. Why isn't Mum happy for me? I think, as I fill the tube up with tea leaves.

'Can I help you, love?' I turn around and Mum is stepping carefully down the steps into the kitchen, hand resting on the wall for balance. When she gets to the bottom, she looks around in wonder. Even though it's not at its minimalist best, the kitchen still looks spectacular with its vast white cupboards and shiny work surfaces. Mum glares at Bran because she thinks that dogs should only live outside, then decides to pick him up, gingerly holding him and patting his head. Her reward is the faraway gaze and the little lick. 'Ah, you're a wee pet, aren't you?' she coos. She puts him gently down on the floor and says, 'Emmett, love, can I ask you a question?'

'Sure,' I say.

'Why are you marrying Amanda?'

'Jesus, Mum!' I clatter cups and saucers down onto a tray, hands shaking.

'Well, when you want a straight answer, you ask a straight question.'

'What do you mean?'

She gives me 'the look', the one that tells me that I've been rumbled, but I press on. 'Because I love her.'

'Because you love her.'

'Yes, Mum, because I love her. That's the normal reason for getting married, isn't it?'

She sighs heavily. 'It is, son. You're right, of course.'

'But?'

'But what?' she says, opening the fridge and taking out the carton of milk that's in the door. 'Do you have a jug for the milk or will this do? If I don't get tea into me, I'll pass out. I'm parched.'

I'm silent, teapot in hand.

Mum takes it from me, helps herself to tea, pouring it out of the pot, adding milk and closing her eyes after the first sip. 'Thank God,' she says. She opens her eyes again. 'Make sure you're doing it for the right reasons, will you, pet?'

'I am doing it for the right reasons, for God's sake. Can you not just be happy for me?' I say, feeling a bubble of anger rise inside me. 'How do you know who I love? And what business is it of yours anyway?'

Mum's mouth is set in a thin line as she puts her teacup down on the tray. 'If you'll excuse me, as the woman who wiped your bottom when you were a baby, fed and watered you, read to you and helped you with your sums, I feel that your happiness is my business.' She lifts the tray and moves to bring it into the dining room, but I stop her.

'Mum, I'm sorry. I didn't mean it. I am happy, honest. I love my job – well, sort of – I have an amazing home and an amazing daughter and Amanda and I ... well, we're a good team. I know we are.'

Mum's face softens. 'I know all of that, son, and yet, I can see you're not happy. What's wrong?'

'Oh, Mum,' I say, and my shoulders drop, and when she puts the tray down and comes over to hug me, I find myself weeping into her russet hair as she pats my shoulder and shushes me softly.

When I've calmed down a bit, she says, 'See – you're never too old for a bit of mother's love.'

I wipe my nose with a tissue that I find in my pocket. 'I'm sorry.

I don't know what came over me. This should be the happiest day of my life.'

'I do. You've moved country, changed job and inherited a little girl, as well as finding yourself in charge on your own for the first time, and that's a lot, son, for a few months. I think you've probably surprised yourself by how much you're capable of, but that doesn't mean it's easy. And finding yourself living with Amanda …'

'I know.' I sigh softly. 'I just want to do the right thing, you know?'

'Of course you do, son, but sometimes doing the "right thing" is the wrong thing.' Mum gives me another squeeze. 'If you catch my drift.'

I nod slowly. 'I do, Mum, but I know that I'm doing the right thing. Honest.'

'I know you are – you always did do the right thing, even when it wasn't easy.' A pause. 'So, who is she?'

'What do you mean?'

'Oh, you could never fool your mother,' she says, taking another sip of tea.

'You wouldn't believe me if I told you,' I say softly.

Mum looks puzzled for a moment, before brightening. 'Is it that girl you were seeing from the department – with the sharp tongue and the bright red hair?'

'Who? Oh, Eimear, no, it's not her.'

'Well, Lord save us, Emmett, who is it?'

'It's Daisy, Mum.'

There's a silence that drags on for so long that I would do anything to break it, but I just can't. Eventually, Mum lifts the cup to her lips again, but her hands are shaking, so the rim of the cup clatters against her teeth. She puts the cup down with a bang on the counter. 'It's too bloody hot!'

'I'm sorry, Mum, I didn't mean for it to happen. It was just that I bumped into her in the bookshop and she has a baby and she asked me for some advice and then … well. Look, nothing happened, if that's any help. And she's gone, anyway.'

'Oh, son,' Mum says sadly. 'You always did love little Daisy.'

'I did, didn't I?'

She shakes her head. 'You did.'

'I'm not going to do anything about it, Mum,' I say softly.

Her head shoots up. 'Why not?'

'Well, apart from the fact that I don't know where she lives now, I just don't want to rake it all up again, especially now that you and Dad—'

'And you think that has something to do with that madam, Bridget Delaney?' Mum's eyes flash.

'Well, I did wonder …'

'Well, you must be an awful eejit if you think that, Emmett O'Donoghue. Bridget Delaney is a bitch, God forgive me for saying so, and my husband was a stupid, weak man who couldn't say no, but that isn't why I left him. I left him because I realised that I need to live life on my own terms, son, not hide away in the arse end of nowhere, as your brother calls it, being afraid of my own shadow. It has nothing to do with your father. I don't even have my faith to fall back on any more. One day, I went up to mass and Father O'Sullivan was giving his sermon and it suddenly seemed like such nonsense to me – a load of gobbledygook. Sure, all it is is words to keep us from being scared of dying. And we all die, whether we believe in God or not.'

'But Mum, are you sure about that?' I ask, wondering if Mum is having some kind of breakdown.

Mum gives me a withering look. 'Am I sure we're all going to die? Yes, love.'

'I didn't mean that,' I say softly. 'I mean that your faith has always been so important to you and you passed it on to me. I might not go to mass, but I have Misty saying her prayers every night.'

'I know, son – she told me all about it, but it's not about "religion", God help me, it's about doing what's right in the last few years that I have left. Life is short, son, and you don't want to wake up in ten or twenty years' time and realise that you've wasted so much of it. So, if you want to be with Amanda, Emmett, be with Amanda, but if you don't … don't make a fool out of her. She deserves better than that.'

'I know,' I whisper.

'And if you want to be with Daisy, be with Daisy, but for the right reasons – not because you want to make your peace with the past and with any guilt you might be feeling – but because you want Daisy as she is now. Take her down off the pedestal.'

'I would if I knew where she lives.' I smile, before adding, 'How come you were always so wise, Mum?'

'I am not wise at all, Emmett, but I'm beginning to understand that wisdom is overrated.' Mum smiles. 'Now, let's take our tea into the dining room to Amanda – she'll be wondering where we are.' With that, she picks up the tray and carries it out of the room. She turns on the top step and says to me, 'Do the right thing, love, will you?' And then she's gone, her footsteps clattering on the wooden hall floor.

'Here we are. Amanda, you must be parched. Let me put down

this tray. I don't know if you'd like a biscuit, but I brought a packet in my bag. Let me get them.'

'Oh, biscuits, what a treat,' I can hear Amanda say gamely. Amanda regards biscuits as the devil's food, and, once again, I'm grateful to her for playing along, even though it's not for the reasons I thought. Amanda is being nice to Mum because she's a good person, and so is my mother, and they like each other, not unreasonably, which is good, as they'll get to know each other pretty well over the next few years.

I try to imagine the wedding, the christening, maybe the Holy Communion, the sound of children running through the house, Mum and Amanda poring over wedding magazines or christening presents, and I feel a wave of panic wash over me. I repeat 'I am doing the right thing', over and over again, until my breathing steadies. I stay in the kitchen for a while, the hum of their conversation in the living room in the background, the tick of the fridge in the corner, the slow hiss of the kettle. I let the silence settle around me and I wonder why Mum is able to let go of it all, to let go of the past and its hold over her, while I am not. Part of me is still there, on the sand in Wexford with Daisy, digging holes and creating entire worlds around us. I thought that I was leaving that part of me behind on that beach by asking Amanda to marry me. I could move forward with the life I now have, having dug a dark, deep hole in the sand to bury that old part of me. But I know now that I can't. Not yet.

'Why is that?' I say into the silence. 'What's keeping me there?'

I owe it to Amanda, I tell myself, to see if what I have with Daisy is real. And if it is? I have no idea what I'll do then, but I also know that I have to find out.

16.

The train to Brighton is crowded, but I manage to get a seat beside a young mother and her two children, who spend the whole journey playing Snap, the younger of the two, a little boy with white-blond hair, roaring with outrage when his sister wins a round, to which his mother says calmly, 'Well, don't play it then if you don't like losing', catching my eye as she speaks and giving me a smile.

I watch them and wonder if, in time, Misty will be fighting with a younger brother or sister over a game of cards and what that picture might look like.

Tom and I never really fought because he was so much younger than me; instead, I was the patient older brother, an almost father figure to him, burping him and changing nappies when he was a baby, bringing him to school on his first day, when I was almost a grown-up in Sixth Class, forging notes to Brother Andrew in secondary school when Tom had thrown up all night after raiding his friend's parents' cocktail cabinet, promising not to breathe a word to Mum and Dad.

The little girl's hand is hovering over her pile of cards, waiting for the chance to slap it down on a matching pair. 'You're cheating,' her brother wails. 'Mummy, that's not fair!'

Their mum looks up from her magazine and says, 'Come on, you two, play nicely.' She catches my eye again and we exchange the meaningful glance of the parent. When the children are silent again, absorbed in dealing the cards into equal piles, she says, 'You look as if all of this is familiar.'

'Oh, it is. I have a seven-year-old,' I say, thinking that just nine months ago I had no idea my seven-year-old even existed. If this woman had met me then, she would have seen a young man who lived in a strange kind of bubble, insulated from reality in a sleepy office where no one was going anywhere, protected from the world by the shield of the poetry he proclaimed to write. Now she's meeting a worker, a father, a partner – all labels, I suppose, but ones which I've grown into, I realise now, almost without even being aware of it. 'She's my only child, but I've had to stop playing cards with her because she gets so upset when she loses.'

While I'm talking, the boy has developed a new strategy of sticking his face two inches above the cards, the better to intercept any matches, and his sister is pushing firmly under his chin to move him out of the way. 'Dominic, you are not playing fair,' she announces. 'And everyone has to play fair.'

'If only she knew,' her mother says to me.

'I know, but she doesn't need to learn that just yet,' I say, smiling.

'So, are you on a day trip?' she asks.

'Erm, yeah, you could say that. I've never been to Brighton so I thought I'd visit.' It's true, in part, but I'm not about to share the real reason for my visit.

'Make sure you see the pavilion – it's really something,' she says. 'And the pier – it's got a great fish and chip shop if you like that sort of thing.'

'And we love the rides,' the girl says, looking up from her station at the cards. 'Mummy, do you remember we went on the roller coaster and Dom got sick and all of the vomit blew back on us.' She gives an explosive giggle, while her brother, unperturbed, deals another hand.

'Yes, well, I don't think the nice man needs to know that,' the woman says, rolling her eyes to heaven.

'Well, that could be very useful information,' I say. 'I'll make sure not to eat before I go on.'

They laugh and I wonder how I can be outwardly so cheerful when inside my stomach is flopping like a fish and my thoughts are spinning around in my head. Maybe it's the distraction, I think, as I catch a glimpse of the sea through the window, a bright June blue against the creamy brown of the pebble beach, and people begin to ready themselves as the train nears Brighton. The kids tidy up their cards and put them away and their mum begins to gather juice boxes and leftover sandwich crusts into a bag. 'Have a lovely time,' she says as I stand up to let them out.

'I will!' I say cheerfully, pulling my satchel down from the overhead rack, opening it and checking carefully to see that the poems are still inside. I wondered about making them into a little book but thought that might look completely amateurish, like a child trying to please the teacher. Best just to leave them as they are, I think, looking at the typewritten pages of A4. They feel more authentic like that, more immediate.

I've spent the past couple of weeks working on them, taking away words and adding in hopefully better ones, chopping out anything mawkish or sentimental, and, finally, I've concluded that they are the best they can be for the moment. Before I can do anything more with them, I have to show them to the person to whom I wrote them.

In the end, it didn't take me long to track Daisy down. All I had to do was call into her flat and, when the man with the bike answered, explain that I was a neighbour who had a parcel for her and could I have her address to forward it to her. 'Sure,' the guy said, 'it's here somewhere,' and he'd disappeared into the gloom before returning with a piece of torn-off envelope, the address written on it in sloping black pen.

She's gone, was my first thought when I'd seen the Brighton address. I mean, gone gone. To another city. And then my second thought: all because of me. Then another thought: will you get over yourself? Who knows why she's moved – she could have all kinds of reasons – maybe it's because her mother likes the sea air or because it's cheaper than London. I suppose all I have to do is ask her.

I stand outside the station and inhale the tang of salt air, hear the screeches of the seagulls circling overhead. For a moment, I hesitate, then I take the map I've brought out of my satchel. I'd marked the route in green highlighter: down to the seafront, then right, past the Grand Hotel, which has been rebuilt since those grainy TV pictures we'd all watched on the news twelve years before, and all of those lovely white Regency houses I've seen on postcards. Daisy lives two streets back from the seafront, according to my map.

I walk down the narrow, twisting lanes with their little shops, selling antiques and bright handmade jewellery, colourful bunting strung over my head. It's pretty in that twee English way and I can see Daisy, in her green granny coat, fitting in, walking the tiny streets with Brian in his sling. Eventually, I come out at a street with a long terrace of tall houses in ice-cream colours, walking along it until I get to number thirteen. I almost think that I should crouch behind the bins, but there are no bins in sight, nor any rubbish blowing in the breeze, none of the grime and grit of a London street. It's pretty but kind of dull, I think, as I stand in front of the pink house halfway down and look up to the first-floor flat. I wonder if Daisy is looking down at me now, standing here behind the gatepost. Well, if she is, I think, what does it matter, as I stride purposefully towards the front door and ring the bell. That's why I've come, after all.

Still, as I wait, my feet seem to take on a life of their own, almost turning of their own accord and running down the street. It's all I can do to will them to stay put as I peer through the frosted glass window. Nobody there, I think, with a mixture of sadness and relief. I'm about to turn around when I see a shadow behind the glass. Oh, no, I think, as the door slowly opens.

The woman is tiny and wearing a sari. 'Yes?' she says cautiously, looking at me with her dark-brown eyes.

'I'm looking for Daisy,' I say.

'Oh, she lives on the second floor,' the woman says. 'Her bell is broken, so she probably doesn't hear you.' A pause, then, 'Is she expecting you?'

'I hope so,' I say brightly. 'I'm a friend from Ireland.'

The woman gives a polite smile then walks up the stairs, before turning to me. 'Come along then.'

I follow her to the second floor and to the left of the two doors on the landing. The woman gives a short knock, then opens the letter box, calling in, 'Daisy. It's Daljit. You have a visitor.'

I hear Daisy's voice then, from far away. 'Coming!' Then the door opens and she's standing there in front of me, Brian on her hip. 'Oh!'

'Erm, hi.'

'Hi,' Daisy says, transferring Brian to the other hip. Her expression doesn't give anything away, but there are two spots of pink on her cheeks. Brian seems to recognise me, leaning away from Daisy and stretching an arm out to me, babbling something.

'Hi, Brian,' I say, giving him a little wave.

Daljit stands there, unmoving, obviously thinking that something interesting is afoot, until Daisy says, 'Thanks, Daljit. You're very good to have opened the door. I must get the bell fixed!'

'You're very good' – Irish shorthand for 'why on earth did you do that?' Daljit takes this as her cue to disappear, which she does elegantly, wafting down the stairs in her lovely pink sari, long black plait trailing down her back. And then it's just the two of us, standing there looking at each other.

Finally, Daisy says, 'Sorry, where are my manners, come in!'

At the same time, I blurt, 'I'm sorry, I should have called first or written …'

We're talking over each other until she stops abruptly. 'You first.'

'I've written some poems and I wanted you to read them.'

The statement is bald and I wonder if I should qualify it with my usual wittering, but there seems to be no need. She simply nods and says, 'Well, come in then and I'll read them.' As if I'd simply popped around from my bit of Albion Road to hers.

The flat is bright and airy, the large bay window open to let in a breeze that lifts the pile of papers on the coffee table. It's a pretty shade of seashell pink and the mantelpiece is full of framed photos of Brian. Brian in the park at the bottom of Albion Road, in the little baby swing, his feet encased in his giant blue snowsuit, Brian holding out a bit of bread for the ducks, and another one of Daisy looking pale, big circles under her eyes as she holds Brian in her arms, his little newborn face scrunched up. As I look at it, I wonder who took it and what it might have been like for me to have been there – but then, I think, that would have been a bit strange because I'm not Brian's father.

'Tea?' Daisy's voice sounds unnaturally bright as she walks through a beaded curtain into a tiny kitchen. 'Sorry, you'll have to excuse the mess,' she shouts. 'I've just moved in.'

'That's fine,' I shout back. 'I see you still have the door bouncer.' It's hanging in the doorway that leads into a bedroom, the sheets crumpled on an unmade bed, a slant of sunlight on the pale cream duvet. I find myself blushing as I wonder what it would be like to lie on it with Daisy and I'm still blushing when she reappears with a pot in one hand and two mugs in another. A wail comes from the kitchen and she says, 'I'm coming!'

'I'll get him,' I say and, before she can argue, I walk into the little kitchen and take Brian out of the high chair where Daisy had put him while she made the tea. He feels solid in my arms, twisting slightly to get a better view of me, head tilted backwards, a worried frown on his face. 'It's all right, mate,' I say softly. 'Mummy's in the living room. Don't you remember me?'

Brian's answer is to screw his face up and let out a tentative cry, at which Daisy comes running, hands outstretched. 'C'mere, you silly boy,' she says, taking him into her arms and popping a kiss on his cheek. He calms down instantly, surveying me from the safe distance of his mother's hip.

Daisy pours the tea and asks me if I want milk and if I'd like a biscuit and, finally, all social niceties exhausted, she says, 'Well.'

She sits on the floor opposite the sofa and when I ask her if she would like to sit next to me she shakes her head. 'Thanks, I'm comfy enough here.'

Here. At a safe distance.

'So,' she says, clapping her hands together like a junior infants teacher. 'You brought me your poems. Let's see them!'

I take them out of my satchel and hand them to her, six sheets of typed A4, and she puts Brian down on the rug, handing him a cuddly toy, which he flings a surprising distance to the corner of the room. She tuts slightly and hands him another toy, which he also hurls into the distance, and eventually she gives up, taking the first of the sheets of paper into her hands and reading it. I can see her eyes scanning the words, her lips moving, the way they always did when she was a child, reading the *Beano* under the bed. Her cheeks begin to colour, but she says nothing, putting the poem carefully down beside her and taking up the next. She does the same thing another four times, in complete silence, until she's read all six of them, then she puts them down with a small sigh.

'Well, they're very good. So ... powerful, so emotional.'

'Thanks.'

She looks startled at my sarcasm. 'I'm not sure what you expect me to say—'

'You might start with why you moved all of the way to Brighton to avoid me.' I'm well aware of how childish I sound – as if I've returned to my eight-year-old self – but I feel powerless to stop myself. I feel as if my emotions are all on the surface, no longer tightly packed inside of me. I feel vulnerable and foolish, but I can't help it.

She sighs. 'It isn't like that. Look, Brian's father is here and … well, he wants to be closer to Brian. I wasn't expecting it – I thought he'd gone back to his wife' – she spits out the word 'wife' – 'but he really is getting a divorce. As it turns out, he'd really like to be a father to Brian and, well, he asked me if I'd consider moving. And so I did.' She turns up her palms in a what-am-I-supposed-to-do-about-it gesture. 'It was having Mum to stay that made me realise I couldn't do it on my own. A baby on one hand and amother with dementia on the other.' She gives a rueful smile.

'I'm sorry to hear that.' I feign surprise. 'Where's your mum now?' In spite of myself, I feel a flash of concern for her, remembering her at the door that night, innocent face turned to mine, inviting me in to watch *EastEnders*.

'She has a sister in Donegal,' Daisy said softly. 'There's a nice facility near her and she got Mum into it. We were lucky. And we can visit!' She says this as if the trip from Brighton to Donegal is going to be a regular occurrence, which we both know it's not.

'Are you relieved?'

She shrugs. 'Sort of,' she says softly.

'Well, are you and Brian's dad … together?'

'God, no!' she says. 'He's great and he's learning to be a dad to

Brian, but that's as far as it goes. He wants to marry me, but I've said absolutely no. Like you and Amanda!' she finishes cheerfully.

'Like me and Amanda,' I say bleakly.

There's a long silence, while I debate whether to tell her that I've asked Amanda to marry me, that I'm betraying my future wife by even being here. Maybe I should grab my poems and run, I think, because I feel foolish enough as it is. I have no desire to endure further humiliation.

'Daisy?'

'Yes?'

'Why did you run out on me that night? At the reading.'

She sighs and gives me a look that tells me I already know the answer. 'Well, you're not a very good liar.'

'I know,' I say sadly. 'When did you work it out?'

'At the Open Mike. It was the poem that gave you away – but once I knew, I realised that I''d probably always known, deep down.'

You did – how? I want to ask, even though it doesn't really matter any more.

'I'm sorry. I just wanted to impress you by pretending to be someone a lot cooler than I actually am,' I say ruefully.

'There was no need,' Daisy says softly. 'Besides, you haven't changed much, you know,' she says with a small smile.

'Well, I'm about three feet taller,' I say, wondering if she's telling me the truth – but what does that matter now anyway?

'Apart from that, you're exactly the same,' she says. 'Your hands are the same and your feet and you still have that bit of hair that flicks up at the front. And you still have that earnestness about you.' She blushes and looks over at Brian, who is silent for once, playing with his toes. 'Do you still like the *Beano*?'

'I've moved on,' I say, which I know to be a lie. 'I like *The Guardian* now and the *TLS*. They're more earnest,' I say dryly. 'Do you still like practical jokes and Black Jacks?'

'I'm more of a Fruit Salad girl now.' She laughs. 'But I still like a practical joke.'

'Are you still afraid of spiders?'

'Ha! Yes, as it happens. Every time I see one I have to call Daljit to get rid of it. I won't let her kill them, though. She has to put them in a jar and carry them out to the garden. She's a Hindu, so she believes in reincarnation. She thinks I'll be blessed because I won't kill them.' Daisy reaches out and takes Brian's foot gently in her hand, swinging it gently from side to side. 'The poems really are very good, Emmett. Have you tried to get them published?'

I don't know why at this moment that I lose it – maybe because I feel that she's patronising me – but I do. 'All that time that I spent waiting and hoping and then, finally, you were there, and that's all you can think of – they're very good and I should get them published?' I blurt. Well, actually, I shout, because Brian suddenly looks up from his toes, a startled expression on his face, which turns to a little cry. 'I'm sorry,' I say, squeezing his other foot. 'It's OK, Brian, I didn't mean to shout.'

'Emmett, I'm not sure what you expected.'

'They're for you.' I nod towards the poems, which she has neatly stacked beside her on the floor.

'I know … but I didn't ask for them. I didn't ask you to write them or to feel about me the way that you did.'

'Do.'

'Fine. Do.' She gives a small sigh of impatience. 'Emmett, what do you want from me?'

'I want you to love me the way that I love you.'

Her expression softens. 'Oh, Em,' she says sadly. 'Oh, dear.'

Her face crumples then and tears slide down her cheeks, but when I get up to go to her, she holds up her hands in defence. 'Please don't.'

'I don't understand,' I say. 'You told me to wait for you. You asked me if we'd always be together and it was only a matter of time.' My voice breaks on the word 'time' and I feel a sudden rush of shame, humiliating myself like this in front of Daisy, who doesn't feel the way that I do. That's obvious. 'What happened to everything that we shared? What about lying under the tarpaulin? What about looking at the stars and secrets and those summers on the beach? Didn't they mean anything?'

'We were ten years old, Emmett. It was a lifetime ago, like a dream. And you have to wake up from dreams,' she says sadly, 'and get on with reality. I'm sorry, Em, I'm sorry if I led you to believe that we had … something in London.'

Em. Amanda calls me Em, I think, as I try frantically to compose myself.

'We did. Don't lie to me, you know that we did!' My voice is high now, almost girlish, and I can feel the lump in my throat that I'm trying to push down. What a fool I am, I think. A bloody fool.

'Maybe, Emmett. Maybe I just wanted to believe it because you were so … persuasive and I was all alone with Brian. And you were so good – you *are* so good with babies. You're a natural, Emmett, and you'll make someone a brilliant dad. I mean, someone besides Misty. And you're an amazing poet and you … just have your whole future in front of you. You don't need me.'

'Christ, you sound like a careers teacher,' I say bitterly.

She gets up then and comes to sit beside me on the sofa, and her hair is falling around her face and her skin has a lovely brown sheen to it. It must be the sea air, I think idly, as she takes my hands in hers. 'Emmett, I'm very sorry. We shared so much as children and I'll always remember those days on the beach, but there's nothing whatsoever to be gained by a trip down memory lane. The past is the strangest thing because we all remember it differently. You might remember Mum and your dad and think it was the most awful thing but, to be honest, if it hadn't been Francis, it would have been someone else. That's the truth. Mum loved Dad, believe it or not, but she never thought he was good enough for her, so she decided to show him that she was better than him.'

'I know.'

'And your mum and dad had something. A bond that wouldn't break. And it didn't – did it?'

I won't tell her about Mum because there's no point and, besides, I'm not sure that her break for freedom is real and that she's serious about leaving Dad. I think something else is bothering Mum, but that's for another time. I shake my head. 'No, it didn't. That's where my little brother Tom comes from.'

She gives a smile and squeezes my hands tightly, but when I lean closer to kiss her, she leans back. 'No.'

'Please.' I find myself begging. It's demeaning, I know. Humiliating, but I can't help it. I want Daisy now, more than I've ever wanted her. She is more beautiful and mysterious to me than she ever was, and I can't bear to be without her.

'Emmett,' she says softly. 'The truth is …'

'Yes?' I say hopefully.

'The truth is that I don't love you. I'm sorry. I like you and I admire you and I'm in awe of your talent. But I don't love you. There's no other way to say it that won't lead to more misunderstanding and disappointment.'

I pull my hands away and put them on my knees, examining them. They are the most awful, terrible hands, I think. If I could cut them off now, I would.

'Do you know what Flaubert says?' I ask.

Daisy looks startled. 'No. What does he say?'

'He says that only three things are infinite: "The sky in its stars, the sea in its drops of water, the heart in its tears."'

I get up then and pick the sheets of paper, and my heart, back up off the floor. I lean over and squeeze Brian's little foot and he rewards me with a gummy smile. I put the poems in my satchel and I turn at the door and say, 'Goodbye, Daisy.'

'Hang on, Emmett, I'll show you out.'

'There's no need,' I say stiffly, trying to summon my most dignified look. It's killing me, but I will do it, I think, as I walk through the doorway into the hall. I want Daisy's last glimpse of me to be of a man in full control of his feelings, salvaging something out of this awful encounter.

As I do, I don't notice that the lintel is too low and I hit my head with a crack. The pain is agonising and I clutch my head in my hands. 'Owww. Jesus Christ!'

'Oh, God, Emmett!' Daisy shrieks, jumping up and running over to me. Brian begins to wail and I press my hands against my throbbing head, going 'Aargh' repeatedly. My forehead feels as if it's on fire and I think I'm going to be sick.

'Sit down,' Daisy says gently, holding my arm.

'No,' I wail, clutching my forehead. 'It's only a bump, it'll be fine.'

'Sit down, for God's sake,' she says, ushering me to the sofa, where she makes me take my hand away and examines the swelling lump. 'Hmm, you've got a bit of a gash here. I think you'll need to go to Casualty with that.'

Oh, God, I think sadly, my Byronic departure foiled. I sit heavily down on the sofa and lean my head back, while Daisy puts a frozen bag of peas wrapped in a tea towel on it. I lie there silently for a few moments, before saying, 'I hope you understand that I have never felt more foolish in my entire life,' I say.

'There's no need to feel foolish,' Daisy says softly. 'I'm honoured that you feel about me the way that you do. Truly.' And she places a soft kiss on my cheek. I sigh as I feel my eyelids close. 'I really need to take a nap', are the last words that I hear.

The doctor wanted me to say the night for observation because he was afraid I had a concussion, but my only thought was of leaving. I couldn't stay in Brighton another minute. It was all I could do to sit in Casualty on a red plastic seat, a makeshift bandage of a pink paisley-patterned scarf wrapped around my head. Daisy insisted on waiting with me, jiggling Brian around when he got restless, taking him for little walks in the car park, while a junior house doctor stitched up the cut on my forehead and asked me if I felt sick or sleepy. I feel both, I thought, but I'm not about to tell you that because I need to get home. In the end, with a promise of visiting Casualty nearer home if I felt any further symptoms, I was released with a more fitting gauze dressing and a prescription for a painkiller.

When I left the hospital, six hours after I'd arrived, it was dark and there was a stiff breeze blowing up from the sea, which had turned from a lovely blue to a churning grey. The pretty lanes were deserted and chip wrappers were being whipped up by the wind.

'I'll walk you to the station,' Daisy said. 'I wouldn't like you to fall into the sea!' She's trying for a cheery tone, but I'm morose beside her, like a sulky teenager, and even though I know it's wrong and I want to be mature about this, my feelings betray me, and I walk up the deserted seafront with her in a gloomy mood. I wish she'd just go away. She's said what she had to say, so why hang around, rubbing salt in the wound? Why not just get lost? Go back to that guy of hers and her new life and leave me to my self-pity.

The wait on the platform for the 10.30 train is only ten minutes, but each one feels like an hour. Daisy has stopped trying to chat now, and she's just standing there, Brian on his usual perch. Finally, as the train appears in the distance, she turns to me. 'Emmett, I don't want things to end like this. Can't we be friends?'

'Can't we be friends?' The single worst thing a woman can say to a man. I shake my head. 'No. No, Daisy. We can't be friends.'

'Oh,' she says sadly. 'Why not?'

Where will I start? I think bleakly. 'Because I don't want to be your friend, Daisy. I want to be something else, and I have to accept that you don't feel the same way. So we can't be friends, but we can be grown-ups,' I say. 'Or, at least, I can try to be anyway. I think you're a bit ahead of me there,' I say ruefully. 'I love you, Daisy. I always have and I always will, and I'll think of you and Brian all the time, but I want to go home now.'

'But I don't want to leave things like this,' she says. 'Can't we just talk about it, at least?' I shake my head, give her a peck on the cheek and, when the train pulls up to the platform, I step carefully into the carriage, dipping down so I don't bang my head and ruin my second attempt at dignity in defeat. Then, as the doors close, I turn and wave. Brian waves back gaily as he and Daisy fade into the distance.

I don't know how I'll ever get over her, I think bleakly as I walk up the main road home. My head is throbbing and I have a funny darting pain in my left eye. I also look a fright, as I realise when I catch a glimpse of myself in the mirror in the bathroom shop. My hair is sticking up, encrusted with blood, and the bandage over my eye is bright red. How am I going to explain this to Amanda? I think. She thinks I've gone to a bookseller's conference. 'Lying already, Emmett,' I say to myself. 'That's not a good sign.'

When I turn the key in the door, I pray that Amanda's gone to bed, and I slip into the hall as quietly as I can – but she's coming up the stairs from the kitchen and when she sees me, her eyes widen. 'What on earth happened?' she asks.

'I hit my head,' I say shortly, hanging up my coat on the antler coat rack.

'I can see that. Come downstairs to the kitchen and I'll put some ice on it,' Amanda says quietly.

'I've already had it seen to, thanks. Listen, Amanda, I'm really tired. I'm just going to go to bed,' I say, but she interrupts me.

'Emmett, stop!'

I've never heard Amanda yell like that and so I do. I stop dead, one foot hovering over the bottom step of the stairs.

'I need to talk to you,' she says.

'Can't it wait until tomorrow?' I say hopefully.

She shakes her head. 'No, Em. It can't.' She takes in a deep breath, then says to herself, 'Amanda, you can do this.'

Oh, God, I think – what now?

'Emmett, I don't want to marry you. I know, I thought we were doing the best thing for Misty, but if we don't love each other, it'd just be a sham and, in the end, we'd make things worse than they are and maybe Misty would lose another dad in the process. I'm sorry, I know this isn't what you want to hear but, you see, I've met someone else.' She lets out a gush of breath. 'There, I've said it. What?' she says, when she catches sight of me, a frown creasing her lovely forehead, 'What on earth is so funny, Emmett?'

I find that when I start laughing, I just can't stop. I'm holding my stomach and the laughter just keeps bubbling up, wave after wave of it, tears filling my eyes.

'Well, if that's the way you see it,' Amanda says angrily, 'that our engagement is just a big joke to you, maybe it's just as well.'

'I'm sorry, Amanda,' I say eventually, when I've managed to get myself half under control. 'It's just … two rejections in one day. It must be some kind of a record,' and I begin to laugh again.

'Emmett, are you feeling OK? Maybe you got concussion when you hit your head.'

'I'm not confused, Amanda,' I say. 'In fact, I have never been less confused in my whole life. About half an hour ago, I realised that I'm not ready to marry anyone because I'm … well, I'm not mature enough,' I say diplomatically. 'But I also realised that I love you and Misty more than anything and I'll always be there for you both.' Because, I add silently to myself, that's what being a grown-up means. 'I'm glad you've met someone, I really am.'

'Oh, Em,' Amanda says sadly, tears filling her eyes.

I reach into my pocket for a hankie and I dab her eyes with it and then I give her a big hug, feeling her fragile, tiny body leaning into mine, and I promise her that we'll always respect each other and do the right thing for Misty, and she tells me that she promises me too. And then I say, 'Amanda, will you do one thing for me?'

'Anything, Em.'

'Let Roland see Misty. She misses him and he's as much her dad as I am.'

She's silent for a long while, but I can see that her mind is working, and eventually she nods. 'OK.'

'Good,' I say. 'If you want, I'll handle it.'

'It's fine,' she says, smiling bravely. 'I know that you're right, Em, but I was just too hurt to see it until now. I'll call him in the morning.'

'Thanks.' Then I tell her that I really, really need to lie down, so I climb the stairs and I stick my head around the door to Misty's bedroom. She's a tiny little mound in the bed and Bran has somehow vacated his basket on the floor and is curled up beside her. 'Shove over,' I say, lifting him up and putting him in his basket, from where he looks at me reproachfully, before settling down with a sigh. I climb in beside Misty, putting an arm gently around her and I let her steady breathing lull me to sleep.

The next day, I'm in the kitchen in Farrell's stirring a cup of tea with a biro. I know that I'll never tell Amanda about Daisy. It feels too raw and too private and I don't want her to think of me in that way – as Emmett, the lovelorn fool, when she's got used to seeing me as Emmett the responsible adult. Maybe the adult thing is an act,

I think, as I take the biro out and tap the inky tea splashes into the sink – but that's not fair. It was an act at the start because I didn't know any better, but now – now it's real.

Nobody tells you when you reach eighteen or twenty-one that, along with the keys to the Volkswagen Golf, you will be handed more pain, more confusion and more doubt than you'll ever have experienced before. Being a grown-up means … what exactly? I wonder as I take my first sip of tea, wincing slightly at the plasticky taste of melted biro. My dad knew exactly what was expected of him: to get a job, find a nice girlfriend, buy a car and settle down. This he duly did, until he fell spectacularly off the adult wagon, only managing to clamber on again with Mum's forbearance. And look at Mum – like a mad teenager, careering around London. She rang me this morning to tell me that she'd gone clubbing with Tom last night.

On the other hand, I don't really know what's expected of me. I love Misty and I love Amanda – for different reasons, but I love them, I know that. Does that make me a grown-up, loving other people no matter what? Does saying goodbye to Daisy count? Putting away these childish things, as St Paul put it, these fantasies that we cling on to about the life we'd like to have, not the one that is actually happening all around us.

'Time for a biccy,' I say to myself, opening the cupboard and examining the half-eaten packet of digestives, removing one and nibbling it, making a face when I realise that it's stale.

'They're Patrice's – he leaves them open deliberately so you'll eat the stale one and then leave them alone.' Betty comes into the kitchen and stands behind me, and when I turn around, she starts in surprise. 'What happened to you?'

'Hit my head off a door lintel,' I say.

'Oh. I'm surprised that doesn't happen all the time,' she says, flicking the switch on the kettle and taking a mug out of the cupboard.

'It does, but normally I'm careful. I got a bit distracted this time and *wham*.' I mime the act of my head hitting the frame.

'Ouch.'

I shrug. 'It's OK. I've learned my lesson anyway.' You have no idea how, I think.

'So,' she says. 'There's a poetry reading in that lovely bookshop in Highgate on Sunday. Do you have any plans?'

'Erm, I don't think so,' I say vaguely. Truthfully, I don't want to go to the bookshop with Betty. I'm too sad right now and am afraid I'll be miserable and that's not fair. But then, I think, why not? It's not as if I have anything else planned in my fantastic life, is it, and Misty will like it. 'Sure,' I say. 'That'd be fun.'

'Great! Let's meet here at eleven. I think the reading's on at twelve so we should make it if the bus comes. There's this really cool Antiguan poet I've been dying to see.'

'Sounds good,' I say, feigning delight. I even give a little skip of joy for good measure. Betty looks at me quizzically. Don't mind me, I feel like saying. I'm just half-mad with grief and shame. To distract from my dishevelled state, I say, 'I like your outfit.'

Betty makes a face, looking down at her simple white T-shirt and blue jeans. 'Yes. I broke up with Dave – he's the rockabilly guy – and I threw out all of those clothes. God, I hated those plaid shirts and too-tight dresses. Now I'm dressing for myself,' she says proudly, helping herself to a biscuit. 'Listen, have you seen the new collection from Alice Oswald? She's just amazing. Such brilliant rural imagery. You have to read it.'

'I will, but you're changing the subject.' I smile.

'I know,' she says sadly. 'I'm too unhappy to talk about it right now. It's just too … raw, too new.'

'Me too,' I agree.

She looks at me and gives a small, wan smile. 'Well, we'll be company for each other in our misery, won't we?'

'We will,' I agree. 'As long as you promise not to ask me about it.'

'Oh, I won't,' she says. 'Promise you won't ask me either.'

'Promise.'

'It'll be as if the past never happened,' she says.

'As if the past never happened,' I agree, as I accompany her up the stairs to begin the day's work.

17.

One month later

The doorbell rings, but there's so much noise in the living room that I barely hear it until it rings again, more insistently.

'For the love of God, will someone answer that?' Mum says from her perch on the sofa. She's wearing a three lions soccer jersey – Dad would faint if he caught sight of her in it – and she has a giant bowl of crisps on her knees. Clive is perched behind Amanda, wearing an Ireland shirt, which makes me feel proud, and he's waiting with Bran for Misty, who is out with Roland for the afternoon. The irony of the role reversal is not lost on me, I think, as I look at Amanda sitting happily beside Django, her new boyfriend, who has come along to meet the family. I feel faintly sorry for him.

'Jesus, what a name', was my mother's only reaction when I told her that she was about to meet her kind-of son-in-law for the first time. At least he's wearing a top. He doesn't believe in clothing, only wearing trousers to business meetings, while being otherwise bare chested, Iggy Pop style, but he's agreed to wear an England shirt for the match, and now he's squatting beside Amanda, legs crossed, clutching a bottle of beer. He's very handsome, lithe and supple and he's also breathtakingly rich. Which is why Amanda and I have been able to agree to leave Misty where she is in this house, while Amanda and I orbit around her. Me from my grotty flat in Holloway – now all mine since Tom moved out – and Amanda from Django's gigantic house in Highgate. I'm glad for Amanda – Django's faint air of bogus mysticism balances out her practicality and even though she's working hard to get back on her feet, I can see that she's relieved not to have to worry about money. Amanda could never be a Buddhist monk, but she has many other qualities.

I don't mind living in Holloway for part of the week. It's grown on me, in the same way a wart might: it's ugly and often chaotic, but it's home – and I have plenty of time to write in the evenings when I come home from Farrell's, Bran snuffling around for any bits of food, asking constantly to be let out for a wee. Bloody nuisance, I think fondly, as I look at him, chin resting on Clive's leg.

I have to finish my poems anyway because they're going to be published – or at least, I hope they will if Jago Galsworthy is still interested. He pronounced the first six poems, 'Some of the most powerful about love that I've ever read.' They should be, I thought when I read his letter: my heart and soul went into them. But maybe these later ones will be different, now that the pain has faded just a bit. Now I only think about Daisy two or three times a day – which is progress. Maybe they won't have the same intensity, but I know that I need to write them, to finish what I started and to put that part of my life into another place.

We've had to give Queenie the chair closest to the telly, 'on account of my eyesight, duck'. I know this to be a lie because she can see a packet of her favourite cheese and onion crisps at five hundred yards' but, at her age, she's entitled to the best seat in the house and to a bottle of beer, which I open for her, making sure that she's comfy, before I go to answer the door. It must be the lads, I think – Nev and Tom said that they'd bring an Irish flag for good measure, but I told them we were going to be English just for one day. 'Just pretend,' I emphasised. Nev is the man in the denim jacket and he's nice – quiet and self-contained, which suits Tom's bluster. I can still remember him telling me, and how it came as absolutely no surprise. 'What does it matter?' I said. 'All that matters is that you be who you truly are.' Which is rich coming from me, but still, I think as I open the door to them.

'What your father would have to say about that,' Mum said when I told her that we'd be pretend English for the duration of the soccer match which we have all gathered to watch. 'Well, I suppose it doesn't matter.' She shook her head. 'He's not here to spout all of that Republican nonsense he goes on with. The Struggle, my backside.' I think she's missing him more than she lets on, but she's enjoying her new life in London, and even though I've offered to act as a go-between between her and Dad, who rings once a week after mass on Sunday and enquires about her health, she has remained firm. 'I'm not ready to go home yet, son. When I am, I'll go of my own accord.' Fair enough – she's a grown-up and in charge of her own life.

I thought that the city would terrify her but, after a shaky start, she's adapted to it. 'It's the most anonymous place on earth and that's why I like it,' she says.

She's right, it is anonymous, but we're all in the same boat here. We're *all* anonymous, and we're all lonely and so we have to create our families, our tribe, where we can. I'm not watching England play in the semi-final of the European Championship because I feel English – God, no – it's because this city has welcomed me and become my home. And besides, Ireland aren't in it, so I have to cheer for someone.

The doorbell rings again. 'Coming!' I say. I open the door to find Misty jumping up and down on the doorstep, wearing an outsize England shirt. 'Dada, I thought we'd have to wait here all day. I need to see the match,' she says, pushing past me into the house. Roland stands there awkwardly, looking past my shoulder to the hall and to the tuning-fork chandelier, in the home that was once his. I can't help wondering how he feels about this role reversal. 'Will you come in?' I say politely.

'Nah, it's OK, mate. A few of us are going to the Lamb and Flag to watch, you know …'

'Sure. Well, any time.'

He gives a rueful smile. 'Thanks, mate. Take it easy.'

'I will,' I say, closing the door behind him, thinking about how quickly life can change. Once upon a time, I was the weekend dad, the guy who sat across from his little girl in McDonald's or at the zoo and now Roland is. It's the loneliest place in the world, I think, and I don't envy Roland – still, at least the permafrost with Amanda has thawed a little and Misty has her dad and her dada in her life. It's as it should be, I think – a bit complicated, but we're all trying to do our best.

I'm just walking back into the living room when the doorbell rings again. 'For the love of God!' Mum yells from the living room, as if she has the slightest intention of actually answering it, I think, turning on my heel and opening it once more.

I find Betty standing there, in full English strip, a six pack in her hand. 'You cut a dash,' I say. 'You resemble Paul Gascoigne – maybe it's the hair.'

She laughs and hands me the beer. 'I think it's my best outfit yet,' as she comes into the hall, to a deafening roar from the living room. 'They must have scored,' I say, taking her hand to usher her into the room.

'Ah, there she is,' Mum says, giving her a little wave. 'Amanda, budge up there till we make room for Muriel. Muriel, pet, will you have a cup of tea? I'm just going to put the kettle on. What, for God's sake?' she says, at the chorus of booing that comes from the crowd in the living room as she disrupts their viewing. 'Can a woman not have a cup of tea? Anyone would think we weren't civilised.'

Mum is very fond of Muriel and I catch her looking at me significantly every time she calls to the door for another one of our literary outings, but I'm not ready. I like Betty, I think: I admire the guts that have allowed her to take Farrell's by the scruff of the neck and begin to transform it into something resembling a nice place to buy books, and I like her sense of humour and the way that her nose wrinkles when she laughs ... but I have to get over Daisy first – at least, that's what I tell myself.

'I'll have one, duck,' Queenie says from her chair. 'Got any biccies, Mandy, or those 'orrible grey porridgey things you eat?'

'They're hand-rolled oatcakes, Queenie, and, yes, they're behind the pasta jars in the cupboard.'

'Well, I don't want them,' Queenie says, 'they wreak havoc with my back passage. Misty, be a love and go into mine and get that packet of Custard Creams, will you? Clive, duck, you run along with her.'

'Custard creams!' Misty exclaims delightedly, taking Clive's hand and jumping down off the sofa.

'Just one,' Amanda says anxiously. She still has that fear of processed food of any description.

'OK, Mummy,' Misty says, making a face. 'Clive can have two, though. Maurice says he can,' and she gives a sly smile. She's still as thick as thieves with Clive, and when I look at them both, I'm glad that they have each other because who knows what the years will bring. A lot can change, I know, in a very short space of time.

'Budge up,' I say to Amanda, who nudges closer to the lovely Django, leaving room for Betty and me to sit down. We spend the next ninety minutes cheering and booing, listening to the roars of our neighbours as they watch England edge closer to a penalty shootout.

'Oh, Sacred Heart,' Mum says as Gareth Southgate lines up to take his shot. 'I can't take another minute of it.' She puts a hand over her eyes as we wait, ready to jump up and cheer when he hits the back of the net. He misses. 'The bloody eejit,' Mum roars. 'After what he put me through – sure *I* could score from that distance.'

'Ah, Mum, give the lad a break,' Tom says, from his perch on the edge of Queenie's seat, the only spot available when he and Nev turned up at half-time, singing 'Olé Olé' and wearing green jerseys. 'The whole world is watching him – he'll never live it down, poor sod.' He gives Nev's hand a quick squeeze as they sit on either side of Queenie, delighted with herself, of course, to have two fine men sitting with her.

Mum's delighted about Nev too, as it happens. Tom worked himself up into a tizz to tell her, only to be told, 'I know, pet. The dogs on the street know.'

I think he was a bit offended by that, but he'll get over it as quickly as Dympna seems to, her initial embarrassment having been replaced by a determination to locate Mr Right once more. Her new man is an accountant from Tuam, Tom tells me, which sounds perfect.

After all the excitement, the atmosphere is now muted, as we watch Southgate's teammates console him. Queenie blows loudly into her hankie and announces that she needs a wee, and slowly, people wander off around the house, Django and Amanda into the garden, where I'm sure Django will light a gigantic spliff. He's very fond of the weed, is Django, in spite of the yoga.

Finally, the only two people left are me and Betty, watching the sobbing and wretched players on the field. I turn to her to make some silly remark about how the British are terrible losers, but see that there are tears in her eyes. I put an arm around her shoulder and give her a brotherly squeeze. 'It's only a game,' I say.

She shakes her head. 'Are you joking? You have no idea – it's a complete disaster! I'll be upset about this for weeks. I can't believe that it's all over.' And then she begins to cry in earnest. Oh, Lord, I think as I pat my pockets to see if I have any tissues. I had no idea she was such a die-hard fan. I look at the TV and see that she and Paul Gascoigne are crying in unison, which has a certain poetry to it.

'You know, I don't think I could go out with an England

supporter,' I find myself saying. 'They're too emotional. Too … unpredictable.'

'Get lost,' she says, giving me a jab to the ribs, wiping away her tears and sitting up a little straighter. 'Who said anything about going out with me anyway?'

I feel my face redden.

'I don't think I could go out with an Ireland supporter,' she says, breaking the awkward silence. 'All that "Olé Olé" – they're just too … enthusiastic. It's just embarrassing.'

'Well, then, it's fortunate that you won't have to any time soon,' I joke. I give her shoulder another brotherly squeeze and I contemplate a little peck on the cheek, but decide against it. Too soon.

'Right,' she says, 'that's enough. Time to move on. Let's go and have our hundredth cup of tea.'

'Good idea.'

'I can't get up.'

'Why not?'

'Because you're holding my hand.'

'So I am,' I reply, looking at our two hands intertwined. 'I think I've been holding it for a while.'

'You have. Are you going to let go of it?'

'No.'

'Well, we'll just have to sit here all night then.'

'Guess we will,' I reply, squeezing it as tightly as I can.

Acknowledgements

To my family, as always: to Colm, of course, and also to Eoin, now spreading his wings, to Niamh and to Cian. To my sister, Caitriona, for the usual laughs and sisterly support, and to my niece, Sadhbh and nephew, Danann, whose company and chat are so welcome. To the wider O'Gaora clan, my thanks for a fund of stories – no, I am not making notes.

Thanks to my agent, Marianne Gunn O'Connor, for her steadfast support and to Patrick Lynch for shared reading burdens. Thanks also to all at Hachette Ireland, in particular my editor, Ciara Doorley, who has the knack of hitting the nail on the head every time, and to Joanna Smyth, Breda Purdue, Jim Binchy, Ciara Considine, Bernard Hoban, Siobhan Tierney and Ruth Shern. Thanks again to Emma Dunne for excellent suggestions at the copy-editing stage.

To my friends Nerea Lerchundi and Eleanor Kennedy, thanks for the sustaining chat and to David Silke and Sara Morris for helpful suggestions.

Thanks to Enda Wyley for inspiration and advice on all things poetic.

Alison Walsh
October 2017

Also by Alison Walsh

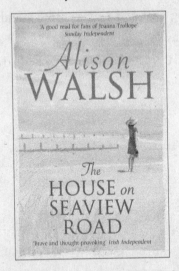

'A good read for fans of Joanna Trollope'
Sunday Independent

Alison
WALSH

The
**HOUSE on
SEAVIEW
ROAD**

'Brave and thought-provoking' *Irish Independent*

THE HOUSE ON SEAVIEW ROAD

Marie Stephenson has decided that it's her last summer in Seaview – just a few months left before she can break free of her suburban home, go out into the world and make her mark. If only it weren't for the promise she made to her dying mother. This promise – to look after her younger sister – is one she has always kept, even though Marie sometimes feels that the cosseted Grainne doesn't deserve it.

But then the sudden appearance of intense, rebellious Con on Seaview Beach one afternoon changes everything.

As her innocence comes to a sudden and shocking end, Marie must make some choices about her future.

But will she find the courage to become the woman she was meant to be?

Also available as an ebook

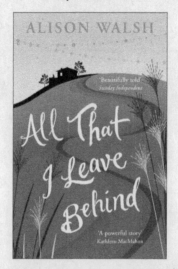